CRASH
INTO
PIECES

The Haylie Black Series: Book Two

CHRISTOPHER KERNS

CRASH INTO PIECES

CHRISTOPHER KERNS

OLD BALLARD PRESS, LLC

All hacks and exploits in this book
are based on real technology.

ONE

Yale University Art Gallery
New Haven, CT
August 2nd, 9:56PM

The man inside the coffin lay stiff as a board, his hands fanned out at his sides, fighting to remain still. Strings of wax fell in clumsy, sloppy clumps as candles swayed around him, like shooting stars leaving trails of white through the darkness. He trembled as the chanting rose up again—Latin phrases tumbling over one another, bellowed deep from the throats of robed figures standing in a semicircle. The coffin rocked, suspended by cloaked arms.

"Doesn't look like a lot of fun down there," Caesar Black whispered, sneaking a glance past the edge of the roof at the building below. He clutched his phone and watched the scene play out on a flickering video stream in the palm of his hand. His breath pushed clouds of steam across the screen as he lifted the device higher, searching for a better Wi-Fi signal. The Yale Art Museum had a strong network signal inside its walls, but out on the far edge of the second-floor roof, it wasn't quite as reliable.

1

"You think they have any idea we're watching?" Charlotte asked, her jaw shivering from the cold as she spoke. "That we hacked their network in, like, five seconds? And could you pick a colder place for us to watch next time?"

Caesar shook his head, pulling his black wool hat down, feeling his fingers beginning to go numb. Bobbing up and down in an awkward squat, he blew on his hands for warmth. It didn't help. The rooftop was cold, and having to stay below the roof's short wall to remain out of sight wasn't helping one bit.

"Just wait," Caesar said. "This will be worth it. This is going to be epic."

Caesar switched his phone over to the infrared camera and zoomed in on the Tomb, the headquarters for Yale University's most famous—and secretive—society, Skull and Bones. The infrared showed blobs of red, yellow, green, and blue moving through the otherwise dark building. The bright yellow heat signatures of candles formed a halo around the coffin, leaving smeared traces across his phone's screen.

"I don't know about *epic*," Charlotte muttered back. "This whole operation—the hack, these clowns in their robes, us being up here exposed—seems complicated. Too complicated if you ask me."

"A complicated thing is just a bunch of easy things, all put together," Caesar said, switching between apps on his phone, making sure everything was perfect.

"Yeah, you've said that like a hundred times," Charlotte whispered as her teeth chattered. "Doesn't change the fact that we're stuck here in private-school central while plenty of real criminals are running around the world. Criminals we could be busting. We're wasting our time up here—got any words of wisdom for that, old man?" She peered over the other side of their rooftop perch and then quickly recoiled, curling herself up into a ball next to the door.

"No words of wisdom," Caesar chuckled. "Maybe just suck it up?"

"Uh huh," Charlotte shot back, leaning into her corner with a huff. "Just wake me up when it's time to start breaking into stuff."

Switching back to the video feed, Caesar notched the volume up a few bars in his earpiece. He could make out the chanting chorus of voices repeating the same word, over and over, in unison. They'd dispensed with the Latin and now spoke in English.

"*Reborn. Reborn. Reborn. Reborn.*"

"When we left the Project, I bet you never thought we'd end up doing anything like this," Charlotte said. "Seems like forever ago."

"Yeah, but it's only been six months or close to that," Caesar whispered, pulling his binoculars up from his neck and scanning the street, checking for visitors. He saw a few students floating into the Starbucks on the opposite corner, laptops in hand ready for a late-night study session, but nothing else. Crouching back down onto the crunch of rooftop gravel, he looked over at Charlotte—the Australian wonder kid who could break into anything you pointed her at—and flashed a quick smile. She had really grown on him over the past few months and even reminded him of his sister Haylie from time to time.

"Being on the run from the government sure sounded a lot sexier when we were drawing it up," Charlotte said. "I was picturing private planes and being handcuffed to briefcases. That sort of thing."

"This isn't like the movies," Caesar said. "With the code we have now, we can get into any system in the world. We could buy you a plane tomorrow if we wanted to, but that's not the smart way to go. You know that."

"I know, I know," Charlotte muttered. "I'm just saying—a plane would be pretty sweet. The least we could do is hack secret societies someplace warm. Why is it so cold here? It's August."

"A freak cold front came in, I guess," Caesar said. "Besides, Brazil was warm. And what about that OilCorp operation in India a few

3

months back? We've seen plenty of warm. The cold is good for you, keeps you alert."

Caesar leaned over the side of the rail to get a visual of the Tomb's perimeter. He thought through the history of the building sitting below them—about the men who had entered its doors and left to head out into the world with a new sense of privilege—and nodded to himself.

Tonight's going to be a bad night for you guys.

"Skull and Bones," Charlotte said. "I don't get the big deal. A bunch of man-boys running around in smoking jackets, using secret phrases and congratulating themselves. Chanting and all that. Who cares? Let them have their little secret club."

"This little club has produced some of the most powerful people in the world. Privilege, influence—all behind closed doors. Aren't you a bit curious about what goes on in there?" Caesar sneered as he looked down at the building below.

Snobby little kids, that's all they are. Snobby kids who turn into titans, just by the luck of the draw. I'd like to punch every one of them right in the throat.

Charlotte rose to a crouched position and snuck her eyes past the top edge of the wall. "Seems harmless enough."

"I'm sure it started off as harmless," Caesar said. "Most things do. But now it's grown into a machine that generates a separate class. Skull and Bones doesn't stop at Yale, it's everywhere. Anytime these guys need a favor, they've got one. Anytime they need a job, boom, it's right there waiting for them. And not just any job—*elite* positions. Stuff regular people would kill for. It's not right."

"Sometimes I think you care more about what's right than what's a good idea." Charlotte looked at Caesar with a raised eyebrow as the fog of her breath shot out in small spurts. "You sound like a crazy person."

"Crazy, yeah," Caesar said. "*Crazy* is their best defense. The things they're doing—no one would ever believe it, right? You'd have to be crazy to think any of this stuff is true."

"That's exactly what a crazy person would say, I don't know—maybe they're just rich guys who are kind of bored."

Caesar shook his head. "The membership roster for this place is nuts. Presidents, senators, congressmen, Supreme Court justices. Even Senator Hancock was a member back when he was in school."

Charlotte smirked. "Hancock—what a piece of work. You see his press conference last night?"

Caesar nodded. "He's getting more desperate as the election gets closer. Grasping at straws, trying to find any message that will stick. You want to talk about crazy—he's your guy."

"Nothing scares me more than a man with nothing left to lose," Charlotte said. "He'll say whatever it takes to be president."

"I hate politics," Caesar said. "Big waste of time. Like I said," he pointed down at the Skull and Bones headquarters below, "it's all rigged."

"Well, I think the real question is: why would anyone be dumb enough to put cameras in their secret meeting place? Kind of defeats the purpose, doesn't it?"

"I know," Caesar whispered. "Luckily for us, their new sergeant-at-arms is an internet-of-things geek. Has a blog about it and every-thing. But, as it turns out, he's terrible with passwords."

Caesar scrolled through the mobile interface to the collection of documents he had taken from the Skull and Bones archives the day before. Meeting notes, membership rosters, chapter secrets. The documents went back for decades, piles of scanned paperwork. Even after reading for almost an hour earlier in the day, he hadn't scratched the surface of what lay inside.

"Can we get moving?" Charlotte asked with a huff. "Just post the video and be on our way?"

"Oh, we don't have to post the video anywhere," Caesar said, continuing to read the documents on his phone, opening new folders as he went. "I'm live streaming their little ceremony on the Yale homepage."

"You're *what?*" Charlotte plucked her phone from her pocket and brought the site up. "Are you joking? Dude, we need to get the hell out of here."

"We're fine," Caesar said. "Hold tight. I just want to watch their faces when it happens."

He scrolled down to a subfolder labeled "Reprisal" and his eyes narrowed with curiosity. He tapped the screen to check the contents, reading the first few paragraphs. He froze in his tracks.

"No way," he breathed, continuing to read. "You've got to be kidding me."

"What is it?"

He continued reading. As more details unfolded, his eyes grew wide. He placed a hand over his mouth without even realizing the motion. "There's dirt about everyone in here. Even about Hancock. This is going to make headlines. This is going to change everything."

"How long is changing everything going to take?" Charlotte said, switching her phone over to infrared and scanning the Skull and Bones building. "They don't appear to be going anywhere. All seven are still in there, chanting or whatever."

Caesar, still thinking about the Hancock documents, looked up as the words registered.

Seven?

"Wait a minute," he said. "Didn't there used to be nine?"

Caesar craned his neck to see her camera's view, counting the heat signatures.

One, two, three, four, five, six...

A loud pop came from behind them, steel hitting concrete, then light flooded from the door to the roof and into his eyes. Caesar could see two silhouettes now standing in the doorway, thick legs at shoulder width, standing firm.

"That's them," said a man's voice.

"I knew they'd be up here—drop the camera," another man's voice rang out.

Caesar and Charlotte both froze in place, exchanging glances.

"He said, drop the camera." One of the men took a step forward and let the door close behind them. "You deaf? We know what you've been doing—filming us. My girlfriend saw it on the internet and texted me."

"Yeah," the other man said. "What's your problem?"

Caesar smiled at Charlotte, dropping his phone in his pocket. He faced the men, although it was too dark to make out any of their features. "No problem here. Not for me."

"I'll give you a problem," the man on the left said. "We've already called the cops."

"They called the cops," Charlotte said to Caesar, and then turned back to the men. "You called the cops? Wow, fellas, way to man up. Maybe you could call your moms next time?"

"Funny," one of the voices said. "Just don't move until they get here."

"How about this," Caesar said. "If you guys go back downstairs, collect your little robes, close the front door to the Tomb and throw away the key, then we'll forget this whole thing ever happened."

"Shut up, dude," one of the men growled. "You're the one who's in trouble here, not us. We were just minding our own business and you had to go mess with us." As he spoke, his speech began to slur, showing cracks in his bravado.

"It's a shame you don't realize what you're doing," Caesar continued. "You're hurting our country—our whole society."

"Here he goes," Charlotte muttered. "You went and got him all excited."

7

"I'm serious," Caesar continued. "You're creating an unsustainable system. One of privilege, not right. It was only a matter of time before it crumbled, even you guys had to realize that, right?"

"Dude, what are you even talking about?" one of the voices laughed. "You don't know nothing. We're not doing anything wrong. And it's a private club, we're allowed to do what we want. People like you get jealous, always jealous. You're just mad you weren't chosen, that you're not good enough."

"How about me?" Charlotte said, taking a step forward into the light. "Can I join your little club?"

"No girls ... I mean *women* ... allowed. Everyone knows that."

Even in the darkness, Caesar could see Charlotte's eyebrow raise halfway up her face.

One of the men's phone screens illuminated in the darkness. "I don't know where those stupid cops are. I'm going to call again. For all the money we pay in tuition, you'd think they'd be here already."

"Right," Charlotte said. "The cops—the ones you called. Did the voice on the other end of the line sound anything like this?" She unlocked her phone's screen and raised it into the air, hitting a play button. A recording of the Skull and Bones 911 call played at full volume.

"How'd you get that?" the man asked.

"You weren't really talking to the police," Caesar said. "We intercepted the call and rerouted it to someone else on our team."

"What do you mean, your *team*?"

"Listen—last chance, seriously," Caesar said. "Go shut it down. You can focus on getting better grades. You can make new friends. Your parents will be thrilled."

"How about I just kick your ass?" one of the men suggested, falling back into slurred speech.

Caesar heard the crunch of a footstep and saw one of the silhouettes moving towards him. He felt the tightness in his fist rising, numbing his entire forearm. *Just take one more step. I'll rip your head off, you spoiled little brat.* He took a breath, knowing he had to remain in control, knowing that doing what he wanted to do would put them both at risk.

"You got it ready?" Caesar asked Charlotte, swallowing his heart back in his throat.

"Got it right here," Charlotte chimed, pulling up her phone and displaying an app with a single, giant button.

"What's that?" one of the men asked. "I can't see it."

"One tap of this button releases all of your data from the past fifty years," she said. "Meeting notes. Payments to officials all over the world. Membership rosters and favors handed out. All the Skull and Bones nonsense goes out to six different news outlets. Just. Like. That."

"You're lying," he stammered.

"Nope," Caesar said. "There's so much good stuff in there: back-room deals for Supreme Court positions, campaign finance violations. Members making assault charges disappear from campus records."

Silence hung over the rooftop.

"Don't do it. We ... we can help."

"Yeah, he's right," the other man shouted with growing desperation. "I mean ... we can get you things. Anything you want. You said it yourself—we have connections. We know people. Anything you want, man."

"You want a job? Is that it? Like, Wall Street? We can do that."

"What I want?" Caesar asked, stepping forward. "What *I* want is the same thing *you* want. I want you to be *reborn.*"

"Dude, c'mon," one of the men pleaded.

"What do you think?" Caesar said to Charlotte. "Should we press the button?"

"Oh, *this* button?" Charlotte said in a mocking tone. "I pressed it ten minutes ago. Sorry, I'm not very good with computers, I'm just a girl." She raised her middle finger in front of the illuminated screen, directing it towards the men in the doorway.

The men backtracked, disappearing through the door at full sprint, back into the building. The door closed and the light from the hallway disappeared, shrouding them in darkness.

"Well, I think that went well," Caesar said, rubbing his eyes.

"Warmed me right up," Charlotte beamed. "Now, let's get the hell out of here. For real."

They tossed their bags onto their shoulders and threw the rope ladder over the side of the rooftop. Charlotte stepped down first into the darkness below. Caesar threw his leg over the side of the rooftop, disappearing into the night.

This is going to change everything.

TWO

Littlefield Hall, University of Texas
Austin, TX
October 23rd, 3:39PM

Click.

Haylie sat huddled in her college dorm hallway, knees twisted and body upright, struggling to keep her eyes level with the doorknob. She craned her neck to the left, fighting for a good view inside of the lock's chamber. She pushed down with the hairpin in her right hand, turning gently to the right. With her left hand, she slid the second pin inside, searching for the right rod by touch, testing for the one that would give the most resistance against the chamber.

"A complicated thing is just a bunch of easy things, all put together," Haylie whispered to herself as she inched the tool inward.

She moved her cheek closer to the door, working her way through the mounting pain—her right wrist was burning from the constant torque—and fighting to maintain her concentration.

You're almost there. Don't ... stop ... now.

Checking each of the pins for movement, her tool found one

11

sliding slower than the rest. She smiled, giving the pin a delicate push up as she felt the gritty metallic friction between the two pieces slowly giving way.

She held her breath, feeling the movement, picturing the pin sliding into place and being careful not to push it too far.

Click.

One more to go.

Haylie turned the tension of the lock clockwise with her right hand and again began searching with the bent hairpin in her left. She found the last remaining rod, bringing her tool underneath its base and pushing gently towards—

"Keys work too, you know," a familiar voice rang through the hallway.

Haylie jumped, startled, as the two mangled hairpins in her hands dropped down to the worn carpet. She could hear the staccato of all five of the lock's pins clicking firmly back into place, right back where they had started.

Goddamnit.

Slumping back onto her hands and throwing a nasty look at the lock, she knew the man standing behind her without even looking. Unfortunately, over the past few months, she had grown to know him all too well.

"Well, thanks for that," she said, rubbing her wrists, finally looking up to see Agent Norman Hernandez, FBI, hovering above her. He was wearing his standard-issue charcoal suit, white shirt, no tie, and had an amused smirk plastered across his face.

"I've been working on that lock for fifteen minutes—I almost had it."

"Let me guess," Agent Hernandez said, gesturing at the door. "Your keys are in there?"

"Of course, they are."

"I thought college kids were supposed to be smart. You need some help?"

"No," Haylie shot back. "I like to do things myself."

"Even so, you might want to try learning how to pick locks while keeping your keys in your pocket. Just in case."

Haylie glared at him and crossed her arms. "If I had the keys, why would I need to pick the lock?"

"Sounds like something you'd say. You know you shouldn't be doing this, right? It's probably a violation of your parole. I should probably look that up at some point."

"Don't care," she snapped back.

"I'm just trying to keep you out of trouble," Agent Hernandez said. "It is my job, you know. Until both of our lives get back to the way they were."

Haylie scoffed. *Things will never be the way they were.* She thought back eight short months to a different time. She had spent every possible moment online—chatting with friends, writing code, hacking systems, building things. She was a savant when it came to technology—although she'd never use that word herself—and after her brother, Caesar, had disappeared trying to solve a mysterious online puzzle, Haylie had tracked him down by solving each step herself. But the puzzle wasn't what it had seemed. The truth behind the puzzle, and the group that had created it, ended up dragging her into a worldwide conspiracy: the last thing a seventeen-year-old expects to find on her permanent record.

Having an FBI agent hang over her every move was just one of the wonderful pieces of her plea bargain. Haylie had agreed to a set of terms that would keep her out of a cell, but the prison she found herself in now might have been worse. She was, as of this morning, eight months into a two-year "no-fly zone" for technology, all while starting her first year of college at the University of Texas. If she used a computer, touched a phone, or even clicked a remote control to watch Netflix, that clock would reset. And Agent Hernandez's job was to stay close by—living just a few rooms down in the dorm—and make sure she stuck to the rules.

"It doesn't have to be this hard, you know," Agent Hernandez said. "You can just read books. Make friends. Enjoy your time off from connectivity—college is supposed to be fun. Don't be Crash for a while, just be Haylie."

After the events in London, Haylie's hacker screen name—Crash —had been plastered over every magazine cover across the globe. It wasn't uncommon for students she had never even met to throw her a fist bump with a head-nod, shouting the name at her as she walked right by without a response.

"Oh, don't worry, I'm still connected," Haylie shot back, pointing down to the chunky ankle bracelet strapped around her leg, the small green LED blinking every few seconds, tracking her location.

"None of this is my fault," Hernandez said. "You took the deal; with any deal, you have to give something up. I'm just saying you could try to make the most of it. Everything that happened in London with your brother, that was some serious stuff. Give yourself some slack, and don't force yourself to break into your dorm room every day."

"I like solving puzzles," Haylie grumbled, beginning to work on the lock again. "If I just sit around, I'll never learn anything. I bet you're the kind of guy who just had everything handed to you, aren't you?"

"Not really," Hernandez said, thinking about the question. "My parents came to the States with nothing, had to scrape together text-books from wherever I could get them. Hell, some of them were so old, I wasn't really sure how World War II ended until I was in my twenties. Helped my mom clean hotel rooms while all the other kids my age were playing video games. I still send them money now, you know."

"Okay, fine."

"Top of my class at NYU," Hernandez continued. "Same at the FBI Academy, now that I think about it. That's not easy when you're working two jobs—"

"I said I get it," Haylie said, twisting her arm to find the right position. "I take it back."

"Well, this has been fun, as usual," Hernandez said, checking his watch. "I've got a status call I need to jump on."

"Wait, what time is it?"

"Three fifty," he said.

She threw her bent hairpins at the door and cursed. "There's no way I can pick this lock before class. I'm going to be late again. That'll be four times this month." She leaned back against the hallway door. "I'll get some kind of suspension or whatever they call it around here."

"Why are you late so much?" Agent Hernandez asked. "That doesn't seem like you."

Haylie turned to look up at him. "Because I can't set an alarm on anything, thanks to you. I don't have a phone. Nothing is pinging me on my laptop, telling me it's time for class. I can't even have one of those stupid Casio watches."

"You're a smart girl," Hernandez said. "I'm sure you'll figure it out. If it helps, I have a key to your room." He produced a key ring from his pocket, dangling it in his fingertips. "All you have to do is say the word."

Haylie stared at the shining key ring, swaying back and forth above her head. Her eyes flicked between Hernandez and the door.

Just as she took a breath to speak, she heard the lock mechanism click and the door pull open from the inside. A head popped out, looking over at Agent Hernandez, and then down to Haylie.

It was Vector, her best friend, with perfect timing, as always. *Thank God.*

"Crash, there you are," Vector said. "We need to get going, you know. Class is about to—" Noticing Agent Hernandez around the corner, he stiffened his posture and his British accent took on a more formal tone. "And a good afternoon to you, Officer Hernandez."

"It's *Agent* Hernandez," he said. "But I'm pretty sure you know that. How are you doing today, Liam?"

Vector winced at the sound of his given name. "Just wonderful, cheers," he replied and turned back towards Haylie. "Well, let's get on with it then."

"How did you get in there?" Haylie asked, rising to her feet. "Did you steal my key?"

"Heavens, no," Vector said, keeping an eye on Agent Hernandez. "I'm no common thief. Besides, there's always more than one way in, isn't that right?"

"You'd better not tell me how you did it," Haylie said, sliding into her room and snatching her backpack from her desk chair. "I want to figure it out."

"Yes, of course, you like to do things yourself." Vector looked over to Hernandez as he closed the door firmly behind him. "She likes to do things herself."

"Yeah, I kind of pieced that together," Hernandez said.

Haylie and Vector trotted down the hall, chuckling, as the double doors slammed behind them.

16

THREE

University of Texas, POB Building Room 2.302

Austin, TX

October 23rd, 3:58PM

Haylie stepped inside the auditorium lobby to a welcomed rush of cold air. The weather in Austin normally cooled by October, but this year, all of Texas was still melting under a heat wave, with temperature and humidity levels scaring the pants off the transplants in the new freshman class.

"No way," Haylie said, stopping in her tracks as she read the poster for that afternoon's seminar. The board showed a picture of one of her favorite local technology CEOs, a woman who ran the most advanced artificial intelligence group in the country. "Guest speaker today?"

"Yeah, why did you think I wanted to come?" Vector answered. "I don't usually run across campus for a 4 p.m. class"

The pair moved down the hall, filtering into the crammed seminar room through a mass of students bottlenecked at the top of the stairs. Haylie bobbed up onto her tiptoes, trying to weave her way through the sea of students to get a better view of the stage below.

Vector turned to Haylie and motioned for her to follow. They ducked through the crowd, making their way to the seminar seating area where two other students waved their arms, backpacks covering the two seats next to them.

"Thanks, guys—you're lifesavers," Vector said, exchanging fist bumps with the two classmates from their Data Mining class as he and Haylie plopped down.

"We didn't think you'd make it in time. This CEO brought her own security, and they're not messing around—I don't think they're going to let stragglers in at all," said one of the guys, pointing towards the stage.

Haylie turned to see four men—two in suits, the other two in dress pants and dark pullover sweaters—standing at attention along the front edge of the stage. The men studied the crowd with expressions of dead calm. As the man directly in front of Haylie looked to his left, she could see the transparent plastic earpiece coiled into his left ear. He turned back to look her dead in the eyes, and she quickly flicked her gaze away.

"I'm so excited to see her speak in person, she's such a badass," Haylie said, wringing her hands with excitement. "I can't believe she's actually here today."

"How did you not know about this?" the student next to her asked. "It's been up on the class website for a few weeks..." He stopped speaking as he slowly realized what he had just said. "Oh, right."

Vector jumped in. "Yeah, I've heard she doesn't do a lot of speaking engagements, but she'll come here every now and then."

"Well, I just hope they give us time for questions," Haylie said, eager eyes staring up at the podium sitting empty under a spotlight,

"I'd love to hear more about their machine learning inputs, and how they plan to train—"

Before Haylie could finish her sentence, she felt a tap on her left shoulder. She turned and looked up—way up—to see a stone-faced man in a dark suit standing over her.

"Ma'am. Ms. Black? You'll need to come with me," the man said with a stony expression chiseled onto his face.

"What?" Haylie stared back at him, gears turning in her head. She leaned back in her chair, crossing her arms, and looked him up and down. "What are you talking about?"

"What seems to be the problem here, mate?" Vector asked, leaning in towards the suit.

Haylie pushed her arm out against Vector, signaling for him to back off. "Don't worry, I've got this." She rose from her seat and squared up against the man. "What's your name, handsome?"

The man took half a step back, now in a staggered stance, arms half-cocked at his sides. A university staffer approached, inserting himself between the man and Haylie with a shaking hand.

"Ms. Black, if you could please come with me. We'll talk about this out in the hallway. It's not a big deal," the staffer rattled out in a nervous series of breaths.

"It's a big deal to *me*," Haylie said, raising her voice. "And I don't want to go outside. I want to stay right here."

"That's the thing, Haylie," the staffer said with a forced chuckle, gesturing towards the podium on the stage, still sitting empty under the spotlight. "If you stay here, there's not going to be a seminar."

Haylie's eyes fell to the floor as reality slowly sunk in. She turned to see the entire room—hundreds of students—watching her next move. A wave of silence hit the crowd. She could hear every breath, see every blinking eye. All watching her. Agent Hernandez's words from earlier that afternoon looped through her mind.

You took the deal.

With any deal, you have to give something up.

She reached down to grab her backpack and rose from her seat, her eyes falling to the floor.

"Crash," Vector said, standing and reaching out an arm in her direction. "I'm coming with you."

"No, you stay here," she said, flashing her best fake smile. "I need you to take good notes, ask good questions. I want to hear all about it later, okay? They can't take that away from me."

He descended slowly back into his seat, with eyes that told her that he knew what she really wanted to say.

"Thanks, Vector."

With one last gaze at the empty stage, Haylie threw her backpack over her shoulder. The staffer led her up the stairs, the suit following close behind. She shrugged off his one attempt to take her by the arm, shooting back a look of poison that he wouldn't forget anytime soon. The crowd at the top of the stairs parted as the three made their way through the double doors and back into the empty hallway. The doors shut behind them.

Haylie spun on her heels, pointing her finger in the staffer's face as she felt her temperature rise. "What the hell is going on?" Haylie yelled. "Why'd you have to do that to me in front of everyone?"

"My client is an important woman," the guard replied, straightening his jacket. "We don't need any bad press today. I'd like to ask you to move along."

"What kind of bad press?" Haylie said.

The university staff member jumped in. "Ms. Black ... Being seen in the same room as you with cameras around is ... a risk. You must know this."

"Why don't we ask *her* that?" Haylie said, pointing back into the seminar room. "Bring her out here, I want to talk to her. She'll understand."

"Ms. Black, I'm afraid *you're* the one who doesn't understand," the guard said. "This request came directly from her."

Haylie leaned back against the wall as the last trickle of students filed past her and through the doors. After a few seconds of catching her breath, she heard a chorus of muffled applause and cheering as one of her heroes took the stage on the other side of the wall.

The staffer glanced nervously over his shoulder, fighting for words. "Now, of course, we'll have a recording of the talk available if you'd like to—"

"Don't do me any favors," Haylie muttered, her head hung low as she paced alone down the hallway. She reached the doors, pushed at the weight of the glass door with her shoulder as a wave of heat hit her in the face.

She sat down on a bench, staring down at the intersection of asphalt pathways, littered with dried leaves and dead grass, wondering what to do next.

With any deal, you have to give something up.

———

The barista pounded his filter, knocking out the puck of spent coffee grounds, and quickly refilled it for another shot of espresso. Haylie leaned against the lacquered wooden bar, staring with dull eyes at the menu looming overhead.

The options were scratched into three columns of white, slanted chalk text. She mouthed the words without a sound as she waited.

Espresso. Americano. Macchiato. Cappuccino.

"You must really like the menu," the barista said, catching Haylie's glance out the corner of his eye as he continued working on her drink behind the bar. "Trying to memorize it?"

"Nothing else to look at," Haylie responded. "Nothing else to do at all, really."

"You're that girl, aren't you?" he said, stopping his work for a moment. "The one who saved the world?"

"People say I look like her," Haylie shrugged. "I get that a lot."

Smiling, the barista handed Haylie's drink over the bar in a heavy ceramic mug. "I bet you do."

Haylie pushed her way up the stairs as she balanced her coffee in her left hand, sliding along the worn railing with her right. Her arm swayed, scraping her knuckles against the brick wall that led up to the coffee shop's second floor.

Even the scents of dark roasted beans, crisp sugar and fresh pastries couldn't cheer her up after the humiliation at the seminar. Haylie spotted a dark chocolate leather couch sitting empty against the wall, far away from the small groups of students sitting huddled at tables.

She sank into the cushions, kicking her feet up on the table barely large enough to hold the heft of her boots. She twisted to get a view of the old-fashioned clock hanging over her head.

4:12

"Four twelve," she whispered to herself. "Four twelve. One hour to kill before meeting back up with Vector. I can do that, right?" She surveyed the room, nodding. "Piece of cake."

She took a sip of her Americano, squinting through the afternoon sun that cast long shadows across the floor. A woman sitting three tables away checked her email, her laptop's screen burning white and perfectly within Haylie's view.

Scanning the rest of the crowd, she saw laptops, tablets, phones everywhere; even the people deep in conversation were staring into the dull glow of their screens, sometimes on both sides of the table. Haylie could only rub her hands together, wringing her fingers.

They don't know what they have—they can do anything they want. Build anything they want. Talk to friends across the world with a few clicks.

Without it, they wouldn't know who they are.

Haylie craned her neck to get a better look at the woman's laptop screen. She had begun to browse Rockyrd, a popular message board hosting "the best of the best of the day's internet," an essential list for anyone that wanted to be in-the-know. The site's algorithm refreshed the list every five minutes, making it as addictive as the coffee warming her hands. It was a site that Haylie remembered as a poison to productivity—she'd even installed an app that blocked access to Rockyrd back in high school to help her focus during coding sprints.

The woman jumped from link to link, reading headlines. A new Inca temple discovered by a teenager using only Google Maps. A new electric car being revealed tomorrow. And a video of dogs trying to catch tennis balls, but failing miserably. Haylie cracked a smile as the video looped, the woman at the table giggling uncontrollably.

Click on that other one—the one with the guy from the X-Men movie. What's that one about?

Pictures from NASA. Olympic trials. Presidential election news. Scenes from Comic-Con. The pictures and articles flew through her mind as the woman surfed. As Haylie leaned in closer to get a better look at a punchline, a pair of young men glided into the chairs next to the woman, shutting down Haylie's view.

She threw herself back onto the cushions, crossing her arms with a huff.

Sixteen more months. Maybe it'll fly by. Maybe the worst is over.

She pulled her notebook from her bag, turning the pages, pretending to get lost in something important. *I hate this.* Her eyes darted around the room, fully aware that she was the only person

23

sitting by herself. *They're all looking at me. They're all asking questions.*

Don't let them bother you.

She pivoted, stretching her legs across the cushions and facing the TV affixed to the wall. She watched the talking heads as closed captioning rolled across the bottom of the screen.

WITH LESS THAN FOUR WEEKS LEFT UNTIL THE PRESIDENTIAL ELECTION, THE NATIONAL DEBATE IS HEATING UP...
THE BALANCE BETWEEN NATIONAL SECURITY AND PERSONAL PRIVACY HAS NEVER BEEN A BIGGER TOPIC...
THIS RACE LOOKS TO BE DOWN TO THE WIRE. NO ONE CAN CALL THE WINNER AT THIS POINT.

She tried to sync the mouths with the delayed closed captioned transcriptions below them, but the cameras cut too fast, and with a three-person panel all yelling at the same time, it seemed even the poor staffer typing couldn't tell who was saying what.

After what seemed like an hour, Haylie turned away from the newscast, having learned nothing that she hadn't known before.

It must almost be time.

She looked up at the clock, hoping she wasn't late to meet Vector. The clock stared back at her.

4:12

Her face twisted into a question mark, and she craned her neck to check the hands from a few different directions. A student walked by the couch on his way to the stairs, pointing up at the clock.

"That thing's broken," he said, tossing his coffee cup in the trash bin. "Been broken for months."

She watched the student tread down the stairs as her anger rose. She jumped to her feet, throwing her backpack over her shoulder and walking to the end of the couch. She reached out and, with a single movement, yanked the TV's cord from the wall. The set gave out a fleeting pop as it went dead; the cord fell against the plaster with a thud and was left swinging against the wall in her wake.

FOUR

Xasis Resort & Casino
Las Vegas, NV
October 23rd, 9:43PM

"Hey, kid, get your ass over here," the boy's father said, waving his hand at him without even as much as a look. He sipped on his coffee and gestured towards the largest screen on the wall with a lazy swing of his mug. "Maybe you'll learn something."

The boy stood pressed into the corner—his feet locked close together—as he gazed in wonder, in awe of the scenes flashing across the sixteen LCD screens arranged on the security suite's wall.

His father was a tank of a man—five foot eight and thick as a barrel. As far as the boy could tell, his father had always loved this job more than anything else in the world. At least, he hoped so.

I mean, he must love something, right?

"What is it, Dad?" the boy asked sheepishly, taking a few gentle steps forward. He looked back and forth between his father's eyes and the screens.

"Most people that walk into this casino, they don't even know they're being watched," his father said, eyes scanning from screen to screen. "Or maybe they know, and they just don't really want to think about it, you know?" He smiled and crossed his arms, puffing out his already bulging chest. "I'm watching every one of these bastards. They're in my house now. *My* house. Illusion is the key—provide the appearance of entertainment, but always under constraints and control. With control, we make money every hour, every day. And up here, we're always in control. *Always.*"

The boy had heard tall tales about his father's job but hadn't seen it with his own eyes until tonight—stories told every other weekend about cheats and liars and fights breaking out on the casino floor. How his dad had always seen them coming—every single time—and did so from the best seat in the house. The boy had never actually seen the old man in action, but with his mother out of town, tonight was his night, at least until bedtime.

The room was a high-tech fortress, with screens and flashing lights and important-looking people speaking into headsets with hushed voices. An entire wall of glass lined the far wall, behind it a collection of smart-looking grown-ups sitting at desks in front of racks and racks of flashing lights and computer terminals. The whole thing looked like something that Tony Stark would have in his secret basement lair.

It was *awesome.*

Jabbing a stubby finger at a monitor two down, three from the left, his father's eyes showed a rare sparkle as he inched forward and rested his coffee down on a tabletop.

"Look at his hands—always watch the hands," his father said under his breath. "Sarah, can you zoom in on table 42, please? Position 2."

A woman gave a polite nod and edged her chair towards her keyboard, surrounded by a sea of phones blinking with pale red and white lights. Her eyes locked on the screen as she typed a few commands.

The boy found himself pulled back and forth through the different scenes on every monitor—top-down views of faceless guests drinking and smoking, a mix of black and white video feeds—some grainy, others crisp and clear.

Sarah reached to her right to find a black, kidney-shaped controller pad. After a few taps on the keypad, she grabbed control of the foam joystick. The boy watched as camera #1025 zoomed in on the man sitting one seat from the far right of blackjack table 42.

"Here comes the shuffle," his father said, breathing the words out, almost in a trance. "Notice how his fingers are extended when the cards are in play, but not when the bets are being paid out?" He clapped his hands together with a sudden rush of energy. "Okay— let's survey the surrounding tables. Sarah—start checking the eye-level cameras for anyone else that might be helping him out."

The boy could see that the suspect had amassed a large pile of chips in front of him—small, crumbling towers mixed with blacks and reds and greens, all in a haphazard lump like the base of a sandcastle, being eroded away with the rising tide. As the boy's eyes flicked from screen to screen, he watched the joy of blackjack dealers hitting 21, the wooden stick pulling back tumbling dice, and a spinning roulette wheel with anonymous hands shoving bets onto numbers.

I could watch this all day.

"You should have seen this place when I showed up," his father beamed as he gave the rest of the room a quick once-over. "It was a mess. An absolute mess. I've spent years making the Xasis the most advanced gaming facility in this town—maybe even in the whole world. Guys like this..." he pointed back to the screen, "used to get away every night. Cheats and liars." He stood up straight, tucking in his shirt and looking down at the boy with a smile. "But not anymore. We've busted fifteen people counting cards and stealing chips tonight, just in the hour before you got here. And let me tell you, kid, it's been a slow night."

The boy nodded, walking over to a bay of screens and running his hand along the chrome edge of the rack. He saw camera views of not just the casino floor, but also the parking garage, the dice-and-card destruction room, the warehouse, the kitchen, and a gray-paneled room where men with large guns guarded the stacks of cash being counted by three white-gloved employees.

"Your school tries to teach you about history and current events and all that." His father grabbed a radio from the charging station and held it up by his shoulder, at the ready. He turned to face the boy. "Tries to teach you about the world. Well, let me tell you, son—*this* is where life happens. I see it all, every day. Right here in this room. Life may feel like freedom, but there's always something going on that you don't know about. A hand that's pushing the world. Keeping everything under control."

Just then, a slow, steady beep filled the boy's ears, like the microwave oven at home where he heated up his chicken nuggets. But this noise didn't stop after a few beeps—it kept sounding and sounding, constantly chiming every other second, echoing through the room. The boy looked up over at the glass wall and something caught his eye. He walked over to pull on his father's sleeve, watching the glass as he tugged.

His dad brought his radio down from his ear, his eyes showing a quick blaze of anger as he spun to meet his son's stare. "Don't do that," he snapped. "I'm working,"

"Dad," the boy said. "What is that room back there, behind the glass?"

Jerking his sleeve back out of the boy's grasp, the man shook his head, keeping his eyes locked on the main screen in front of him. "We call that 'the Fishbowl.' It's nothing—that's just where we keep the computer nerds."

"But," the boy stammered, stopping himself before getting permission to continue.

His father let out a loud exhale. "What is it?"

"What," the boy stammered, "what is that man doing?"

There, on the other side of the glass, was a short, thin man. He was standing spread-eagled, waving his arms, as the other people scattered around the room, carving their paths around desks, holding laptops as they ran, yelling at each other from different sides of the room.

His father's face dropped. "What the hell?" He dropped his radio and jogged towards the Fishbowl, breaking into a run just before he reached the door. He quickly typed a seven-digit code into the electronic keypad, triggering a loud metallic click.

He pulled at the handle, releasing a loud chorus of server fans mixed with whoop-whoop-whoop alert tones, a swirl of ringing phones and people yelling, popping in and out of server racks at a fever pitch. A stuffy, hot scent filled the boy's nostrils as he filed in behind his father to prop the weight of the door open, trying his best to help.

"We're losing the system!" yelled the head engineer, bent over his laptop and switching frantically between desktop windows. "Someone's in our network, machines are going down all over the place."

"Talk to me," the boy's father yelled. "What is it?"

"Everything's rebooting, we don't know why," the engineer yelled back, waving off another staff member who was trying to get his attention. "When the machines finally do come back online, each one is dead; all data is wiped clean."

"So cut the pipe," his father said, obviously trying his best to keep a calm tone. "You can do that, right?"

"Of course, I can do that," the engineer spat back. "But as far as I can tell, the attack is coming from *inside* our network."

Frantically searching the room, the boy's father helplessly

checked random screens and stared through the glass at his control room, now with the eyes of his entire staff staring back.

The boy took a few steps away from the chaos, keeping the door propped open but wanting to fade into the wall. To disappear. Engineers brushed against him as they ran by, holding laptops and phones to their ears, yelling words the boy knew he wasn't supposed to repeat. His heart felt like it was beating through his chest as the alarms continued to shout, now coming in from multiple different sources and mixing with the row of ringing, blinking phones on every wall—all combining to create a constant, ear-numbing wall of sound.

"Stop whatever this is," his father yelled. "Lock down the network or whatever it is that you do."

"It doesn't work that way, sir," the head engineer yelled back, typing at his keyboard. "Our local system isn't the only potential source, all of our global systems are connected, it could be coming from an East Coast location, or right here in Vegas. Maybe Europe, I just don't know. This is going to take time."

Sprinting back to the door and standing halfway between the two rooms, frantic, the boy's father raised his hands to his head, his face flush. "And why do the phones keep ringing? Can you just shut those up?"

"That's all our people calling—none of our employees can log in," the engineer yelled. "Their laptops are all dead. Nothing's working, they're calling us for help."

"You," his father pointed at the main engineer with a stiff finger. "I paid good money for you to handle all of this computer crap. Fix it. Now."

The engineer threw his arms up into the air, stepping back a few paces, palms out. "This global internal network is new, even to me. I need a few—"

"FIX IT."

The engineer grabbed both sides of his desk and hunched over.

After a deep breath, he looked up at the rest of his team. "Okay—any of you who can still get in the system, we need to stop the bleeding. Shut down the Active Directory servers before this spreads to Asia. And lock down the customer database. The last thing we need is a privacy breach."

An engineer yelled, "Hold on, hold on!" as he typed. After a few seconds, he shook his head. "I'm seeing new files in here, compressed folders that I don't recognize. They have timestamps from just a few hours ago, and we sure as hell didn't put them there. It looks like someone zipped the customer data and downloaded it. It's sloppy work, but there's a good chance our data has been compromised. How did we not see this happening?"

"What's the source?" the main engineer asked.

"Our Foxchaser location," the other engineer said. "The resort in Pennsylvania. They've been seeing dictionary attacks on their webservers over the—"

The engineer was interrupted by a security guard bounding through the main door to the control room. He was built like a pro wrestler and stuffed into his suit, with beads of sweat running off his massive, shaved head as he huffed heavy breaths.

"The elevators are down ... The front desk is a mad house," the guard said between gasps for air. "Guest keycards have stopped working—all of them. What the hell is going on up here?"

"I don't know—I just don't know," the engineer said, wringing his hands as he spoke, one over the other. "If someone got in the network, they could be anywhere right now. Everything is run off this main system—*everything*."

The boy watched as his father's eyes flew back to the bay of screens. He walked slowly, calmly, over to the view of the money room where the white-gloved employees continued to sort and count the taped, bound stacks of cash under the watchful eye of armed guards.

And then the screen went dead.

The boy heard the room gasp. The boy watched his father's posture freeze, the radio still dangling from his hand. Every camera view—from the eyes in the sky to the hidden table-views—now showed only blank screens. They were blind.

His father ran full speed through the control room door. The boy followed, stepping as quickly down the stairs as his legs would go. The boy passed by men and women leaning back, hugging the wall with shocked expressions as they let them pass.

He lost sight of his father around the first floor turn in the stairwell and ran through the only door he saw. He found himself on the main casino floor, greeted with the sounds of chiming slot machines, passing crowds, and the smell of old cigarettes. The boy recognized his dad, now running towards the center of the closest gambling pit, surrounded by card and dice tables. He ran behind the computer terminal and began pulling cords from the wall with violent jerks, pointing and shouting at other workers to do the same. The boy crept forward, watching as every power plug and every network cable— some snapping off at the base, others being ripped from the machines with circuit boards still attached—were thrown onto the floor.

His father wiped the sweat from his brow as he ran to the next station, shouting frantic, desperate commands at any employee who would listen. Phones rang as security personnel sprinted across the casino floor.

The boy sat on the edge of a stool at a nearby blackjack table as security ran in one direction and guests ran in the other, people swirling all around him. Looking behind the table, he could see a single computer screen at the center of the pit, one of the few that had been missed. It was still plugged in and displaying a "Welcome to the Xasis Casino" desktop background.

Suddenly, the screen blinked and went dead, then the hotel logo was quickly replaced by a new picture—a black and white sketch on a stark white background. The boy stood and walked to the other side of the table, grasping both sides of the monitor as he looked at the image staring back at him.

The sketch showed a bird—a picture of a pigeon, maybe—sitting peacefully on a diagonal wire. The gray and white details highlighted the ripples and valleys of its feathered wing; the single dull, black eye stared off into the distance.

Underneath the picture was a line of text, a phrase that he repeated in his mind, again and again, as he read the words. The boy ran his finger down the screen, tracing each letter.

THEY CALL ME
THE ENDLING.
SOON EVERYONE
WILL KNOW MY NAME.

FIVE

Haylie sat on the windowsill, wiping a single finger across the glass, watching the students passing below on worn dirt paths.

She looked over her desk, unopened envelopes scattered in a pile. Job offers—hundreds of them—had been flowing in through the good old U.S. Postal Service, the only way that hedge funds and startups could reach her. Tacked to the wall over the desk, was a new poster looking down on her—a print of simple graffiti scrawled across a brick wall. Her expression grew heavy as she read the words, over and over.

ONLY TRUST
THE GOVERNMENT
AS MUCH AS
THE GOVERNMENT
TRUSTS YOU.

A knock at the door broke her concentration, sounding out a familiar pattern. She had been the target of a good amount of pranks since school had started—students trying to get a selfie as part of a scavenger hunt, that kind of thing—and she and Vector had worked out a special knock so she could ignore the rest: three rapid knocks, a one second pause, and then two more.

Unlocking the deadbolt, she saw Vector in the hallway with a smile on his face. She turned without a word and retreated back to her window, leaving the door open for him to follow.

He pulled his earbuds out, the black cords dangling in his hand. "So you ready to talk about that seminar yet?" he asked. "Calmed down a bit? Not to worry—you didn't really miss anything."

"Yeah, sure I didn't," Haylie said, slouching back into her window seat. "Lying about it just makes it worse."

"Right," he said. "It was actually pretty cool. Some of the models they are building out are fascinating." Tossing his backpack in the corner, Vector pulled the chair away from the desk and into the center of the room. "But time is ticking away, isn't it? You've only—"

"Four hundred and seventy-nine more days," she said without flinching.

"Well, sure beats jail time," he said to the window and the sunshine filling the courtyard below. "And this isn't such a terrible place to wait it out, you know?"

"I never should've taken this deal," Haylie said. "You don't know what it's like—being offline. It's worse than jail, it's torture. You wouldn't make it through one day. I feel like I just should have gone with Caesar when I had the chance."

"Sure, run away with your brother," Vector said with a chuckle. "Be a fugitive from the law, run around the world with a team of notorious hackers. A bunch of digital Robin Hoods, aren't they? Yeah, that definitely would have passed the 'Vector test.'"

"What the hell are you talking about?"

"The 'Vector Test.' It's the question I ask myself anytime I've got a big decision to make. I simply ask myself, 'What would make the better story?' and go in that direction."

Haylie stared back at him and blinked a few times, processing the idiocy of her best friend. "That's the dumbest thing I've ever heard. You seriously go through life like that?"

"How do you think I ended up here? You think I joined you in trying to take down the most powerful people in the world because it was a well-thought-out, rational idea? Not to worry, we'll get through it." He pulled his phone out and opened a news app. "Want me to read the headlines to you?"

Her face scrunched, eyes following the students filing by underneath the window in ones and twos. "Okay."

Dragging the desk chair from the center of the room to the window, Vector held the screen in front of his face. "Right, here we go. We've got just under three weeks until the presidential election."

"Don't care. Next."

"You *should* care," he said. "I think it's fascinating; I've been reading up on the election recently. The whole thing takes so long. Superdelegates and debates and something called a 'swing state.' And then you've got this Senator Hancock guy."

"What about him?"

"He's turning up the volume on securing the nation," he said. "But he's saying that hackers are the big new threat. Not sure what got him running with that talk track, but it's polling through the roof, so we can expect him to keep doing it. He's neck-and-neck with Ortega at this point. Seems people like you and I aren't that popular with mainstream America."

"Again, don't care about the election. What else you got?"

A sharp knock at the door turned both of their heads. Vector looked back to Haylie, who shrugged.

"Probably another prank," she whispered, jumping off the

window seat. She raised her voice and aimed it at the door. "If I find out there's some idiot behind this door, I'm going to take control of your phone, your laptop, and your bank account." She stopped in front of the door. "You've got two seconds to get the hell away from my door before I destroy your entire life."

Leaning in and pressing her eye against the keyhole, she stood back with a scowl. She turned the doorknob in her hand, peeking through the crack.

"Oh, hi, Agent Hernandez."

"Hello, Haylie," he said. "May I come in? That is if you're not going to threaten a federal agent again?"

She stepped aside, letting Hernandez into her room. "Sorry about that, but you know kids these days," she said, "You have to set them on the right track, teach them a lesson."

Buttoning his jacket, he nodded. "I know your secret knock, you know. I don't use it out of respect, but I'd appreciate it if you didn't find different ways to aggravate me every time I—" He stopped when he noticed Vector on the other side of the room.

"Liam. Good to see you, as always."

"General," Vector said, with a mocking salute.

Agent Hernandez ignored the insult. "Haylie, I need to talk to you." Looking back over to Vector, he continued. "*Alone.*"

"He's fine," Haylie replied, returning to her perch at the window. "He can hear whatever you have to say."

"Fine." Agent Hernandez shrugged and raised his hand, showing a folded stack of paperwork. "Haylie Black, your assistance is being requested by an ongoing government investigation. If you choose to assist, the government is willing to offer—"

"Not interested," she shot back. "I'm just here to serve my time, not to help you do any of your dirty work."

"Yes, I figured you might say that," Hernandez said. "Because that's what you've said the last *five* times I came to you with one of these offers. But I really need you to consider this one."

"I considered it," she said. "And I'm not interested."

"She's not interested," Vector repeated with a smile.

"This could help you reduce your sentence," Hernandez said. "The faster you get out of here, the faster *I* get out of here. Can we just work together on..." His eyes drifted across the room to her desk. "Wait, is that a new poster?" He read the words and his face morphed into a disappointed grimace.

"It was a gift from me," Vector said, proudly.

"Anyway," Hernandez continued. "What I can tell you in mixed company is that thanks to your superior negotiating tactics of just saying 'no' every time, they've upped the offer."

"How'd you get away with that?" Haylie asked.

"Turns out the NSA has a bit more pull than I do, and they requested your help on a small project they are working on that—"

"The NSA?" Haylie asked, a scowl beginning to grow across her face. "You're not NSA, you're FBI. Why are you dealing with those clowns?"

"It seems we've traded your services over to the NSA for this project," Hernandez replied. "This kind of thing happens from time to time..."

"Traded for what?" Vector asked.

"A player to be named later. It doesn't matter—" Hernandez said.

"It matters," Haylie interrupted. "My deal was with you, and that has turned out bad enough. Nobody ever said anything about the NSA. Those guys are bad news—wiretaps, illegal searches. They're everything that's wrong with the government."

"Regardless, I have the details here," Agent Hernandez said, holding out a stack of papers. "This is an internal priority. If you make material progress on this investigation, your remaining house arrest time will be—"

"I'm not interested," Haylie said.

"—will be completely forgiven."

Haylie stopped in her tracks, struggling to take a breath. She held out one hand, balancing herself against the desk, replaying the words in her mind.

Completely? Forgiven?

"You mean she helps with this case, and then she's back online?" Vector said, sitting up at attention. "No more house arrest? No ankle bracelets or anything, just like that?"

Agent Hernandez nodded back.

"This is huge," Vector laughed. "This must be a big one, Crash. They must really be desperate."

"Please, Liam, stop helping," Hernandez said, turning back to Haylie. "Haylie—you want to get back online, right? This is your chance to make that happen a hell of a lot sooner than you thought it would."

Haylie pivoted back to the window, rubbing the bridge of her nose as she thought. She looked over to Vector with question marks in her eyes.

Vector pointed at the documents hanging in Agent Hernandez's hand, silently mouthing the words, "What would make the better story?"

She snatched the papers out of Hernandez's hand with a single motion and pulled them towards her.

She flipped the front page over and began to read.

SIX

NSA Texas Cryptologic Center
San Antonio, TX
October 25th, 7:42AM

Layers of clouds hung low overhead as Agent Hernandez rolled his government-issued Ford Taurus down the road. Haylie angled herself towards the window to see the stark black rectangular security cameras pointed down. She leaned back into her seat, closing her eyes.

It was early—*way* too early. She didn't sleep well anymore: not since the events in London, and not since she had been taken offline. When school had started, she had stacked her course schedule to have nothing before 11 a.m., trying to get some breathing room in the morning—no classes, no people, just her. Just enough time to shake off the haze of fatigue that was growing with each day. But there would be no time to herself today.

Peering through the web of black chain-link topped with razor wire, Haylie could make out a series of non-descript buildings: one in the foreground that stood five or six stories tall, another shorter set of structures tucked in behind. A few sedans and SUVs littered the parking lot, but most of the staff hadn't shown up yet this morning.

Government hours.

"Any details you have about this whole thing would be great," Haylie said, watching through the windshield as they approached the main security checkpoint.

"I gave you the file," Agent Hernandez replied. "Everything you need to know is in the file."

Haylie shook her head, glancing down at the paperwork that held a few useless pieces of government boilerplate.

"So, what you're saying is you don't know anything more than I do," she said. "Super helpful."

Hernandez gave her a sideways glance before rolling down his window, extending his badge to the officer at the roadside checkpoint. The officer took the credentials in his hand, shot a quick glance through the vehicle at Haylie, and retreated back to his security shack.

"They'll tell you everything you need to know inside," Hernandez said, eyes locked on the gate in front of them, both hands on the wheel.

The black gates cracked open. Haylie craned her neck to get a better look at the complex, the main building now coming into full view as they rolled forward. She saw a huge, oval-shaped structure carved into the center; it looked like the Hall of Justice from the old *Super Friends* cartoons she had discovered on YouTube last year.

After parking, they approached the main entrance, walking through a courtyard of newly planted trees and shrubs framing a single American flag at the center of the circular garden.

This feels way too much like a country club.

Agent Hernandez jogged ahead to grab the door. Haylie walked into an atrium filled with white light and glass—a few small tables here and there with muted red and blue chairs alternating in different patterns, planters placed against the wall of glass, slowly curving across the length of the lobby's polished marble floors. A row of pillars lined the far side, drawing Haylie's eyes up to the vaulted ceiling, where a series of glass bridges supported a handful of people walking with hurried steps, beginning their mornings.

"Haylie," Agent Hernandez said, startling her and pulling her from her daze. "This way."

They made their way to a receiving desk with three separate desks side-by-side nestled in neatly behind a wall of glass. *Probably bulletproof.* Two of the three chairs were manned by security guards, their eyes fixed on screens hidden behind the counter. The guard at the center desk leaned towards a microphone.

"Agent Hernandez and Ms. Black," the guard said through the speaker, eyes fixed on the two guests. "The gate called to let me know you were here. I can help you at desk two."

There were ID checks for both Hernandez and Haylie, followed by a series of forms to fill out—pens tied to clipboards. Hernandez took care of most of the signatures and information, while Haylie looked up to note at least four cameras pointed at them from various directions.

"One last thing," the security guard said through the microphone, reviewing the checklist in front of him. "There are no computers, phones, smart watches, or weapons allowed inside. I'm going to need you to place anything you have—"

"The computer part won't be a problem," Haylie said, eyeing Agent Hernandez. She lifted the leg of her jeans to show off her favorite accessory. "But this might."

The guard frowned, standing and sliding the paperwork back through the metal security drawer.

As they worked their way through another security checkpoint—including a hand-held metal detector and fingerprint checks, Haylie saw a woman in a dark blue business suit waiting for them on the other side. She stood without expression, looking professional and cold, her short hair pulled back tight, lips pursed. She had a single thick manila folder tucked under her arm.

As they cleared security, Agent Hernandez took the lead, approaching the woman and extending a hand.

"Head Agent Andrea Wilcox, NSA." Agent Wilcox's southern drawl pushed her words together, like a rolling verse out of an old country song. She turned sharply to face Haylie, extending her hand a second time without expression. "Ms. Black."

Haylie shook her hand, watching for any sign of life beyond the gray government façade, but received nothing.

The agents walked side-by-side, speaking in hushed tones, as Haylie followed closely behind. They made their way down a narrow walkway with walls of glass on both sides, a single door at the end of the long stretch. Haylie read the small, blue sign affixed to the door as Agent Wilcox swiped her keycard.

TAILORED ACCESS OPERATIONS

Inside, Haylie saw another stark white hallway lined with rooms every ten feet or so, each door marked with non-descript numbers. Agent Wilcox led them to a room where they each took a seat around a stark white table.

Haylie sat in silence as Agent Wilcox cracked open her folder and began to read, slowly turning page after page, reading with care. After what seemed like ten minutes, Haylie couldn't take it any longer.

"Are we going to get started?" Haylie asked. "I saw there's a taco place across the road, and I'm starving."

Agent Wilcox crossed her legs, leaned back, and kept her eyes on the file. "I'm going to need a few more minutes to catch up on all your greatest hits," Agent Wilcox responded. "Hacking into the systems at the Super Bowl, the Bohemian Grove, my goodness, pretty much every type of exploit known to man and God above. Not to mention all the business over there in London. And it looks like you have a birthday coming up, isn't that exciting?"

"I wanted a bracelet," Haylie said. "But Hernandez here was nice enough to get me one a few months back. Now I'm a girl who has everything."

"Ms. Black," Agent Wilcox said, staring Haylie in the eyes. "Agent Hernandez was kind enough to bring you here today to offer you a chance at reducing the length of your probation. If you're not interested—"

"She's interested," Agent Hernandez said, motioning for Haylie to agree. Haylie just shrugged with a defiant smirk.

"Well, then," Agent Wilcox said. "That's exactly what I was hoping to hear. Ms. Black, if you're interested in helping me out here today, I'd appreciate it if you'd start acting like it."

Haylie pushed her glasses up the bridge of her nose, trying to get a better look at the papers lying in the open folder on the table. "You work for the TAO team?"

"No," Agent Wilcox said, leaning forward. "I *lead* the TAO team."

Shuffling in his chair, Agent Hernandez managed to get out a few nervous words. "Could someone tell me what—"

"TAO is the intelligence-gathering unit of the NSA," Haylie explained, still staring down Agent Wilcox. "In the past, they've focused on incoming signals from terrorists and other bad guys outside of the U.S., but in the past few years that scope has increased."

Agent Wilcox watched Haylie, not cracking her poker face.

"These days," Haylie continued, "they're also gathering intelligence on U.S. citizens, isn't that right? Saying that the new threat is everywhere? That we must be vigilant in—"

"Our Cyber Investigation unit has increased its scope," Agent Wilcox said. "If we don't evolve with the times, if we don't adjust as new threats emerge, our great country is put at risk. And I don't know about you, Ms. Black, but around here, we don't care much for risk."

Haylie scoffed. "That's dumb. And FYI, nobody says 'cyber' anymore. It was cool when William Gibson used it, but then people like you came in and messed it up."

Clearing her throat, Agent Wilcox continued. "Two days ago, there was an attack on the Xasis Casino in Las Vegas, Nevada. I am leading up that investigation."

"A casino?" Haylie said. "What's the big deal? That kind of stuff happens all the time."

"It does, indeed," Agent Wilcox said. "But not with this profile. This attack was different. If it wasn't, I wouldn't have bothered you and plucked you out of your nice fancy college dorm room."

"You're the NSA," Haylie scoffed. "You know everything about everyone, right? Rules don't matter to you guys. Why don't you just wiretap the whole city of Vegas until something turns up?"

"I don't know what you've been reading in the papers, but we don't work that way. We follow rules—"

"What do you want from me?" Haylie said, cutting the agent off, to her obvious dissatisfaction.

"I want you to help us catch whoever is behind this," Agent Wilcox said. "If our experts are correct, this won't be the last of these we see. A few gentlemen back in Washington are asking me to make sure this one goes away quickly and quietly, and that's exactly what I'm fixin' to do. With your help, I'd like to think we can do exactly that."

Haylie could feel the weight of the ankle bracelet on her leg, scraping at her skin. Looking down at the folder, she saw a thick collection of documents not about the casino, but about her. There must have been hundreds of pages.

What's in that folder? My chats. My phone calls. Everything from my hard drive. The NSA knows anything they want to know.

What's worse—doing another year offline, or turning into something that you hate?

She stood from her chair.

"Hernandez, let's get out of here." She pointed a finger at Agent Wilcox. "I don't want to work for you. I want nothing to do with the government—not now, not ever again. This deal I made was the worst decision of my life. I should have just gone with—"

"Your brother?" Agent Wilcox said, cracking her first smile of the day. "Tell me, have you seen him lately? Sending any postcards?"

The blood rushing through her veins. Haylie's eyes turned to slits as she tried her best to calm her pulse.

"You know what he'd say if he were here? You know what he'd tell me to do with you and your file?" Haylie spat back. "He'd say the same thing as he always did when we were kids and I was about to do something stupid. 'You and I—we're better than this.' You could learn a thing or two from him—if you had any idea of how to catch him."

Haylie stood and bolted for the door, the anger welling up inside of her. She reached for the doorknob with her head hung low and twisted. It didn't budge.

"You have a chance to do something smart here, Haylie," Agent Wilcox said. "You'll have access to technology, and more importantly, if you help my investigation in a substantial manner, you'll be done with this—the FBI, the NSA, all of it. You'll help us catch someone doing some very bad things, and who knows, maybe you'll even like it."

"That's what you think?" Haylie shouted. "You think this is *fun?* Tracking U.S. citizens? Going after people's machines without warrants, just in case you happen to find something interesting? You're not on the right side of the law here, don't kid yourself."

Agent Wilcox stood, walking towards Haylie, the folder in her hand. "Now, I'm not perfect. I know that. And that goes for the agency I work for as well. But you knew all that before you walked in the door. So, let me ask you, what is it that you want? Why did you come all the way down to San Antonio and waste a perfectly good, God-given Texas morning with me?"

Haylie looked down and saw the blinking green light on her ankle bracelet pinging away. She thought back to London, to school, to Vector. She thought about Caesar, somewhere out there, on the run. Haylie released her grip on the doorknob, letting her hand fall to her side.

"I just..." Haylie stammered. "I just want things to go back to the way they were before."

"I don't know much, but I know your world will never be the same as it used to be," Agent Wilcox said. "Things happen, and these things—they change our worlds. Your life is different now. Every day, I see people muck up the rest of their lives trying to get back to the way things were. Lots of people just can't let it go, clawing and fighting their way back to something that's not even there anymore. Now, I can help you to look ahead, to start building your new life. And here, with the *Cyber* Investigation team, you can do exactly that."

Haylie looked back at the table, where Agent Hernandez sat at attention. He nodded, looking Haylie in the eyes.

"Fine," Haylie said with an exhausted breath. "What do you need me to do?"

SEVEN

Wrigleyville Apartments, 4D
Chicago, IL
October 25th, 10:05AM

Pushing one thin, fragile strip of die-cut wood flush against another, Anthony Feist paused for a breath, commanding his hands to be still. He nudged the metal tips of the tweezers gently against the supports —*we can't have any blemishes or dents or scrapes, then we'd have to throw the whole thing out and start over*—and pressed as tight as the wood would allow.

"What will they say, when the news breaks?" he whispered to himself with a half-smile. "I just wonder ... Which words will they choose? *Clever? Dangerous? Rogue?*" He blew a breath of hot air across the model's skeleton frame, watching strands of loose glue wave in the wind.

"*Genius?*"

He tilted his head to the side at a sharp angle, wincing as he kept a steady pressure on the wood. All he could see—and really, all that was there—was a mattress pushed into the corner and a small IKEA lamp, its neck craned over towards the floor-to-ceiling window covered in tin foil and thick curtains. There was nothing else on the dark hardwood floors, which echoed his hollow footsteps anytime he moved. Anytime he walked. As he looked up at the single picture hanging on the wall, he saw a face staring back at him from behind the glass. He flashed a muddy smirk at the image, shaking his head to slide his bushy hair from his eyes.

"Almost done," he said to the picture, reaching back to scratch an itch on his forehead with the butt of his bent wrist.

The scent of balsa wood mixed with wisps of glue hit his nostrils, making his piercing blue eyes squint through the fumes. He grimaced as he fought to keep his focus, clearing his mind, his fingers burning with concentration as he locked into the moment.

I have been here before; I will be here again.

I have been here before; I will be here again.

The mantra, rammed into Anthony's mind long ago by his hack of a therapist, was the only good thing that had come from years of sessions. That, and having his juvenile criminal record wiped clean while he played nice, acting out the part of the bad boy turned good.

"I have been here before; I will be here again," he whispered.

He fought to clear his mind, pushing out the sneaky bits trying to wiggle back in through the corners and floorboards and swinging doors left open somewhere deep inside.

They're all going to love you. They're all going to wonder who you are and talk about you and it's never, ever going to stop because you're never, ever going to stop.

He felt his pulse begin to race, his hands shaking along with each rush of blood through his veins. He dropped the tweezers from his hands, closed his eyes and pictured a state of nothing. He gripped the tabletop with both hands, taking deep breaths and arching his back, his head pointed towards the ceiling, stretching out his neck, his Adam's apple. He began to laugh, feeling his body shake and quiver.

Don't let the fear take over.
No. No. That was the old way. That's the weakness talking.
With the new way, you're the fire. You're the star.
I have been here before; I will be here again.

He released his grip, flexing his fingers in and out and stretching his arms to the sides. His heartbeat fell back to a normal rhythm, the sweat on his forehead began to dry. He opened his eyes, turning to face his laptop, and hit refresh on his News Alerts script.

SEARCH:>
"Xasis"
AND
("hack" OR "exploit" OR "systems" OR "breach")

There were no results—not yet. He had assumed that would be the case before he even hit the "execute" button, but he tried anyway. A secondary script was designed to ping him the moment something popped up on the news wires, but it never hurt to check. Sometimes, code didn't work the way you thought it was going to work.

He wrung his hands together, feeling the foreign grit—small whispers of drying glue peeling from his skin. He rubbed his palms, watching the glue fall like snowflakes onto the wax paper below.

"Out of the shadows," he whispered, "and into the spotlight. Right where you belong."

He reached down to test the strength of the model, pulling gently at the supports to make sure the glue had set. The rest of the structure tugged along with the beam as Anthony nodded. *Good, good.*

He hadn't built a model in years, ever since he was a kid. But with his recent run of activities, with the stress and the pressure building, he found himself running back to the only thing that had ever worked to calm the rising waves, back to days in the therapist's office when the doctor would let him build any wooden model he asked for. With models, the doctor explained, a patient's self-control could be tested. And it still worked—not to eliminate his rage, but to practice pushing it down deep inside.

An opportunity like Xasis didn't come around every day. It wasn't like Anthony hadn't tried before, it was just that he needed a little nudge in the right direction. Just a little nudge.

They'll fear me when the news hits. Experts will shake their heads in awe. Companies all over the world will fear the mention of my name. The press will line up, they'll all want the story of the man behind it all.

The mastermind.

Anthony ran the news alert search again, scowling at the result.

"Why aren't they talking yet?" he spat. "Why are they holding back? They know how big this is. They can't IGNORE this ANY LONGER—"

He braced his hands against the desk, taking a deep breath. "Stop it, Anthony," he whispered, closing his eyes for a few seconds of pause. As his eyelids flicked open, he focused back on the wooden slats of the model.

"I have been here before; I will be here again."

It made no sense. He had read on all the hacking forums that the FBI always took at least a day to investigate a crime before going public with the news, but that mark had passed a few hours ago. They should be going full force now—using the press to help them fish out their suspects. Especially with a hack that was a big deal.

And this was a big deal.

"Stop it," he whispered, his eyes pressed closed. "Focus. Finish what you started, Anthony, always finish what you start."

He reached out for the final piece of the model, flipping it over and sideways through his fingers, inspecting it for flaws. Grasping the crisscrossed handle of his X-Acto knife, he balanced its weight as he carved away a few stray splinters. He placed the knife down carefully on the tabletop, holding the wood with both hands and placing it a few millimeters above the top of the model. He held his breath, keeping the angle steady, and released.

He leaned closer to examine his work. *I have been here before; I will be here again.* The wood formed a perfect seal; the connection held strong and was stable, no residual glue or fibers to be seen. A relieved smile flashed across his face. He removed his glasses with both hands and gently placed them on the table. The biplane model was complete, the bottom pair of wings supporting the uppers with an intricate array of small, toothpick-wide supports that formed a maze of patterns, angles, and shadows. He gently cradled the craft to inspect the undercarriage and placed it back down on the wax paper.

And that's when he heard the ding from his laptop.

He flew over to the keyboard and clicked on the result, reaching back for his glasses to read the full text. The script had returned an article from the *Las Vegas Herald*, from their "Local News" section.

LAS VEGAS – Breaking news from the strip, multiple eyewitness accounts from the Xasis Casino reporting an issue with the power systems last night. According to their spokesman, a power outage caused minutes of confusion for a few lucky visitors.

What authorities are calling a "systems anomaly" took many of their systems offline, while others overloaded. Visitors reported seeing a few banks of slot machines shooting coins out into the halls of the casino.

The Xasis fixed the problem minutes later, but not before handing out free breakfast coupons to everyone affected by the outage. It seems that in Las Vegas, everything can be a moment for marketing.

Anthony's hands shook as he slid his palms down to his sides.

I have been here before; I will be here again.

Wincing with anger, he turned back to the model as the voices rushed into his head. *They'll never know you.* He closed his eyes, praying for silence in his mind. *You've never been good enough.* Sweat ran down his brow and his hands trembled as he tried to fight his way back to the calm.

You'll never be more than you are right now.

Slamming his hands down, Anthony's eyes snapped open as something pierced his flesh, shards and splinters were flying in every direction, the core of the model's corpse mashed into a ball of wood and glue. Pain searing through him. The X-Acto knife had cut clean through his palm, leaving a trail of blood and forming a smeared mix of crimson dots that pooled on the wax paper below.

He lifted his hand to eye-level, inspecting a splinter wedged deep under his fingernail. As his hand throbbed, he stood, brushing the broken remnants of the plane off the desk with one quick sweep, and turned to the framed photo on the opposite wall.

"There she is. That famous, bright shining star."

He walked towards the picture, blood dripping down off onto the floor. He took slow, careful steps, tilting his head to get a better view past the lamp light reflecting off the glass.

"They're going to talk about me," he whispered, "they really are. They're going to talk about me the way they talk about *you.*"

He smiled as the face in the picture became clear through the darkness: Haylie Black, her chestnut hair pulled back in a tight pony-tail, her glasses hiding her hazel eyes. She was surrounded by images of computer code and screens. It was just one of the many magazine covers that had appeared since she had stumbled her way to great-ness. Since she had become the reluctant hero next door.

The headline, printed below her chin, read:

Haylie Black is Crash
The Hacker Who Just Saved the World

He reached out with his hand, trails of blood running down his sleeve, and planted his palm on her face, smearing the glass with red.

He traced his bloody finger on the empty wall next to the frame, chuckling as he spelled out the only word that made the pain go away.

ENDLING

He stepped back and read the word again and again.
It calmed his racing heart.

EIGHT

NSA Texas Cryptologic Center
San Antonio, TX
October 25th, 10:21 AM

"Sign here, here, and here," Agent Wilcox said, pointing to three different lines on the top sheet of the thick stack of paperwork.

Haylie snatched the pen off the tabletop, quickly scrawling her name across each line.

Agent Hernandez tried to move into her view. "You should probably have a lawyer look at the details of—"

"Let's get started," Haylie said. "I want to get this over with."

Pulling the papers in her direction, Agent Wilcox nodded and opened the folder. "All right, now, let's start at the beginning. The Xasis casino is the largest in Las Vegas—matter of fact, their holding company owns twelve of the twenty-eight major casinos on the strip."

"That would give them a huge security budget," Haylie said. "How did these guys get past their defense tech?"

"The Xasis has properties across the country: Tahoe, Reno, upstate New York, Pennsylvania," Agent Wilcox said. "My team identified an attack vector that originated on the web servers of one of the properties on the East Coast. The hacker started by attacking the VPN for a few hours—basic dictionary attacks, that sort of thing—but he didn't have any luck. Not at first."

"Did that trigger a warning for the security team?" Agent Hernandez asked.

"Unfortunately, that class of attack isn't enough to set off alarms," Wilcox replied. "Six days later, it looks like the same hacker found an unsecured test server on the network, a web dev machine. Once inside, he used a cracking tool—something called BeachDogz—to secure credentials from the box."

Haylie nodded. "BeachDogz. It's a package that grabs passwords out of memory. Once you've breached the first level, it's a great tool to get anywhere you want, really cool stuff."

Agent Wilcox did a poor job of hiding her scowl, if she was even trying, and continued. "From there, he used credentials for a Vegas administrator who had been out on a visit to the Pennsylvania location a week earlier. Once he got into the central server, he made his way through every system he could find—he was pretty messy, left a lot of traces behind—and had himself a field day."

Haylie leaned back and stared down at the folder.

He was sloppy—that will help. If I can get into the server logs, I can write a script to create a timeline to retrace his steps, pull the whole picture together. This might actually work.

"Do you have a clue who this guy is?" Haylie asked. "Or if it's even more than one person? Any idea at all?"

"We have a few leads, but nothing I'd call substantial," Wilcox said. "Turns out my team are some of the best in the world when it comes to tracking down known suspects—terrorists, drug lords, those types of people—but we usually know who they are before we start hunting. With the Xasis hack, we don't have a name. At least, we don't have his *real* name."

Real name?

Agent Wilcox reached inside her jacket, retrieving a folded, crisp piece of white paper from her inner pocket. "The hacker left a calling card, something for us to remember him by. Wanted to make our acquaintance."

Wilcox unfolded the paper and slid it across the desk, turning it in Haylie's direction. Haylie caught it on he side of the table. Slowly, she drew her palm back from the paper and studied the image printed on the sheet.

It was a black and white photo of a pigeon, its feet resting gently on a diagonal wire etched across the bottom of the picture. The bird's back was turned, a single black eye gazing out into the gray sky. Underneath the image was printed:

THEY CALL ME
THE ENDLING.
SOON EVERYONE
WILL KNOW MY NAME.

"What's an endling?" Agent Hernandez asked, pulling the paper gently from Haylie's grasp.

"That's exactly what I asked," Agent Wilcox said. "Turns out it's the scientific term for the last member of a species. When an animal is heading for extinction, the last survivor is called an endling. We did a reverse image search on this one here—the bird's name is Martha ... The last passenger pigeon on Earth ... died in 1914."

"If he wants you to know his name, then he's not done," Haylie said, pulling the paper back over to her. "This wasn't a one-time thing. He's going to strike again."

"As it turns out, the Xasis was the second attack," Wilcox said. "That's the reason we've brought in ... additional resources. A hacker calling himself 'the Endling' struck a few weeks ago. The target was a major credit card database."

"The Voyage Card hack?" Haylie said, leaning in. "Vector told me all about that—it was huge."

"Correct," Agent Wilcox replied, her eyes falling down to her notes. "One of the biggest I've seen. Twenty-six million people's personal information exposed through the exploit. Our experts suspected that a foreign government was involved, which is why my team is here."

Shaking her head, Haylie thought through the connections. "Foreign governments wouldn't leave a calling card—they'd just get in and out. They wouldn't want to taunt the FBI or NSA, either."

"Agreed," Agent Wilcox said.

"Well, if these guys are sloppy, that's good for us," Haylie said. "Let's talk logistics. I'll need a MacBook—I can build it myself, just give me something vanilla and out of the box, and I'll add all the packages I need to replicate the Xasis attack. Once I get access I'll—"

Wilcox looked over to Hernandez, and then down to the signed agreement at her fingertips. She closed the folder and leaned back.

"Now, we should be clear about our arrangement, Ms. Black," Agent Wilcox said. "Like I said before, we have one of the best teams in the world working on the exploit side of this case. What we're looking for your help on is more on the observing and consulting side of the equation."

Observing and consulting? What the hell does that mean?

"You said," Haylie said pointing across the table at Wilcox, "you said I could get back online. You said I'd be part of the team."

"And you will be," Agent Wilcox said. "But not on the front lines, Ms. Black. You must understand—you're one of the most dangerous hackers in the world. I'm not going to just give you access to the NSA's network in hopes of some kind of Hail Mary here. I'll get run out of this agency faster than … well, you know. We've brought you in for your counsel, with some technology exposure. To help advise."

"Advise?" Haylie yelled. "Observe and consult? This isn't what I signed up for."

"Actually," Agent Hernandez broke into the conversation, "this is exactly what you signed up for, Haylie. As I said before, you probably should have had a lawyer look at the—"

"Shut up, Hernandez," Haylie snapped. Turning back to Wilcox, she took a long breath, trying to calm herself. "So what kind of access will I have? What are we talking about here?"

"I think you'll actually enjoy it, Ms. Black," Agent Wilcox said. "We're looking for you to monitor the hacker community. You know —message boards, IRC channels—the different online nooks and crannies that you know about. We think that a hacker who leaves a calling card is bound to talk about their exploits somewhere."

Haylie's face dropped as she realized what she had just gotten herself into. *Watch hacker forums? I don't even get to write any code?*

"You'll be in there anonymously, of course," Wilcox continued. "The last thing we want to do is raise your hand as Crash or anyone connected with the NSA. The good news is that our plan allows you to be online, at least in a limited capacity. Now if—"

"A limited capacity?" Haylie said, leaning in close to Agent Wilcox's eye level. "Let me get this straight. You bring me here to ask for my help. You dangle this idea that I can get out of my sentence, get back to my normal life." Haylie began wringing her hands together, the sweat sliding between her palms, as the anger rose in her eyes. "But I'm not allowed to do any of the stuff I'm good at? You want me to just load forums into a web browser and just … hit refresh all day?"

Agent Wilcox replied without flinching. "That's correct. We have an entire team here working forensics on any and all digital signatures hiding in logs and servers. But if someone out there is talking about this, we need to know who they are and what they're looking to do next. That's the plan, and we stick to the plan. We *always* stick to the plan."

"The chance that I'll find something," Haylie said, "that I'll actually be able to find this guy are almost zero this way. This is a waste of time."

There was a quiet knock on the door. The knob turned and an analyst walked in with a laptop under his arm. Nodding to Agent Wilcox, he stepped towards the table and laid the machine down. Haylie looked down to see an ancient gray and black plastic laptop with a large black and white government ID tag glued to the top. It looked like it weighed ten pounds.

"No hacking, just observing," Agent Wilcox said, motioning towards the laptop. "This is the machine you'll be using. Agent Hernandez here will be watching over your shoulder every time you're online, just so you don't get lonely."

Haylie stood, pressing her palms on the table for support. She stared down at the dusty machine, its lid tightly shut.

"Haylie," Agent Hernandez said taking on a helpful, optimistic tone, "if you think about it, there's really no downside to—"

"Shut up, Hernandez," Haylie said. "I'm doing it. Just shut up."

She slunk back into her chair, pulling the laptop in her direction with a grunt and cracking the lid open.

"One last thing before we get started," Haylie said. "How much money did this guy take from the Xasis? And from the credit card company? What levels of theft are we talking about here?"

Agent Wilcox looked over to Hernandez with a cautious glance and closed the folder with a gentle sweep of her hand.

"That's what I can't figure out, Haylie," she said. "He hasn't taken a dime."

NINE

Luna Park
Sydney, Australia
October 26th, 10:17AM

Caesar had a spark in his eye as he was carried by the flow of the crowd towards the audacious entrance to the amusement park. The gate was shaped like a giant mouth, complete with a row of jagged, bright-white teeth hanging above the hordes of excited children underneath. As he passed through, his view met the cartoonish eyes of the thirty-foot-wide face as it welcomed visitors to the park.

That thing is going to give me nightmares.

Caesar strolled past rows of carnival games as the scents of popcorn and wafting sugar mixed with the salted air from Sydney Harbor and blew back the lapels of his jacket.

"Not sure we could have picked a place any creepier than this. Char—this is the last time you get to pick the location." He spoke softly, his chin nestled slightly into his right shoulder to make sure his Bluetooth earpiece picked up his voice.

"No worries, mate," Charlotte said back over the channel. "I came here all the time when I was a little girl. I was always fine with it, not sure what that says about you. Besides, you can consider it payback for the Skull and Bones op."

"Deal. We're even," Caesar said with a smile. "We good with meeting up with our contact today?"

"I know this guy," Charlotte said. "Friend of a friend. Nothing to worry about."

"I'm not worried," Caesar said, tilting his head back to enjoy a ray of sunlight across his forehead, drinking it in. "Feels like the government is peeling off a bit recently. Maybe they have bigger fish to fry. Kind of makes me wonder if we shouldn't get working on some bigger projects, you know?"

"I like this speed just fine," Charlotte chimed back.

"Any change to the meeting spot?" Caesar asked.

"Negative," her voice rang in his ear. "We're all set. The client should be at the meetup point with the code phrase—standard protocol. I'll be in an adjacent building to the right, second floor if you need me."

"Don't do anything stupid," another voice rang over the line.

Oh, hi Sean.

"Sean," Caesar said. "Haven't heard your voice in a week or so."

"The Malta mission is a wrap," Sean replied over the earpiece. "I took an extra day for some beach time. I'm in Sydney—downtown with Phillip and Margo. We'll be on the channel but from a distance."

"So, what you're saying is," Caesar said, "you were going to be here and overslept?"

"I'm not the one heading all the way up to Yale just for some Skull and Bones nonsense," Sean shot back with a chuckle. "We should talk about that."

"Consider it my vacation," Caesar laughed. "Char loved it. Didn't you, Char?"

"Did not," Charlotte said over the line. "Did not love."

Caesar smiled as he traced one hand along the chipping red paint on the railing. The beat of the tide drummed and sloshed under the boardwalk and meshed with the rush of the roller coasters rattling across their tracks. The air filled with the slow grind of organ music, cut into every few seconds by eager screams from above as passengers hit sharp corners. Crowds with floppy hats and sunscreen followed children running with hopeful eyes, never wanting their day to end.

"One more thing," Sean said. "I have an update on the Eagle project: Phase two of five is complete, we're a go for the third."

"Sounds good," Caesar said. "Hopefully we won't even have to go ahead with the final stage, but it's always nice to have an insurance policy. After we get this op kicked off, I'm going to take lead on Eagle. Get me in contact with the guy in the field."

"Are you sure about that?" Sean said. "We don't use outside people all that often, not sure it makes sense to—"

"Quiet on the channel," Caesar said. "I'm almost at the location. All idiots who don't need to talk should go silent."

"I have a higher IQ than you," Sean muttered back. "So you're going to need to turn your radio off first."

Caesar felt a smile creep across his face. *Haylie used to say the same thing. I wonder what she's up to right now. I wonder when I'll get to see her again.* The past six months had been a revolving door of fake passports, aliases, and new projects every few weeks. Buying new clothes at every port of call, paying for dinner bills with discreet stacks of cash. No matter how good he felt about his team's rhythm right now, he always got nervous before a first meeting. Always. That rush of adrenaline, a new spark of energy caused by knowing he could change someone's life.

Let's find out what this guy wants. Let him know we can help. Let's do some good today.

As he continued down the main strip, a giant Ferris wheel came into view. Alternating green and blue and red passenger cars flew through the air, with the Sydney Harbor Bridge serving as a majestic backdrop. The wheel spun, gently rocking the cars, some tipping back and forth, as passengers scurried about, checking different windows for the best angle to take a selfie.

Turning to his right, Caesar saw a carousel in the distance. He walked under a sign reading '100 Years of FUN!' and took a spot on the rail next to a man in a gray jacket.

"The Ghost Train is catching fire," the man next to him said in a thick French accent, checking over his shoulder with a nervous twitch.

"Calm down, friend," Caesar said. "Can you say that again?"

Clearing his throat with a subtle nod, the man repeated, "The Ghost Train is catching fire," this time with a more pronounced tone.

Caesar looked down at the ground and kept his voice low. "So you must be Moreau?"

"You're late," Moreau said in a low voice, turning to face Caesar.

"Sorry about that," Caesar said. "You don't have a phone on you, do you?"

"No phones," Moreau whispered back. "Just like the instructions said."

"Then we're good," Caesar said, raising his voice to be heard over the shouts and screams from the rides above. "It's crazy, I know. But governments have access to the microphone and camera in any phone they want. They can just—*click*—turn them on whenever they feel like it. We can't take that kind of risk."

Moreau looked back with worry weighing down his cheeks, whispering back. "Keep your voice down. Someone will hear us."

Caesar pivoted on his heels, pointing around at the different rides, vendors, and children skipping by. "What, here? It's an *amusement park*. There's no better place to *not* be heard. People aren't paying attention to us, they want to go ride the giant worm or stuff their face or whatever. Did you see that clown on the way in? Was that freaky or what?"

"You're not what I was expecting," Moreau said, staring at Caesar. "Can we get down to—"

"Again," Caesar said, "you need to calm down. You've been watching too many movies." He waited for a smile that Moreau never gave him. "All right, down to business, then. What can I do for you?"

Moreau took a long breath. "It's my brother—the captain of an ocean freighter. *The Blue Queen*. He was hijacked last week, taken hostage by pirates."

"Where?" Caesar asked, leaning back against the rail.

"Off the coast of Somalia," Moreau replied.

Caesar nodded. "And you know he's still alive?"

"I think so," Moreau said. "I hope so. These pirates, they usually just take the ships for ransom. Insurance payoffs, you know? They don't mess with killing people. Not usually."

"Not usually. Famous last words."

"He's a good man," Moreau pleaded. "He has a young son and daughter—twins—and a wife at home. She's scared to death. The families of the captain and crew, we don't have any resources; no one is listening to us. I'm the only one that is even able to function well enough to ask for help, but no one is doing anything."

Gazing out to the water, Caesar watched the ferries and pleasure craft gliding slowly by on the choppy sea.

"Seems like a job for the military," Caesar said.

Moreau shook his head. "We've tried that but the group is French, a few Italians. No Americans—Americans are the only ones with the resources and the balls to go in and take out pirates these days."

"Can you just raise some money?" Caesar asked. "Pay the ransom?"

"We would, but they don't want money this time," Moreau said.

"They want prisoners released from jails across Europe, stuff we can't do."

"I can't release prisoners. You know that."

"I've heard that you—you and your group—you have exactly what I need. You can break into any computer in the world."

Caesar took a breath. "And what makes you think any of that is true?"

"All that business in London last year—Prime Minister Crowne trying to take over the world. You were there—I just know you were. And if you and the rest of your team got out, that means you got their code. From what I've heard, you're the best shot I have."

Caesar looked on without a word.

Moreau continued. "Ocean freighters these days—they are like floating supercomputers. Navigation systems, inventory control—everything is done by machine. With your access, you can get into their system, steer the boat someplace where we can intercept it."

"My team can access the systems, but it will cause mass confusion onboard," Caesar said. "It won't do you any good."

"No, no, that's the thing," Moreau pleaded. "These pirates, it's obvious they're in way over their heads. You could sail this thing to New York City and they wouldn't have a clue unless they ran straight into the Statue of Liberty. I want to redirect the ship to a nearby port at night—they won't know what happened until they wake up the next morning. I'll arrange for a team on the ground to take care of the rest."

Caesar moved away from the railing, turning to face the carousel. Its collection of animals—horses, camels, giant swans, and roosters—zipped by, some with children hanging on to their necks, others bobbing up and down all on their own. Even in the sunlight, the bright lights of the roof above shining down off the mirrored surfaces put him into a trance, making him lose his balance for a moment as he leaned with the flow.

"I have money," Moreau said, "if that's the problem. I can—"

"We don't take money," Caesar replied, gesturing over to a few men in clown outfits, twisting balloons into animal shapes. "I mean, when you're traveling to exotic locations like *this*, that's reward enough." He laughed but, once again, didn't get a laugh in return. "Money isn't the problem. I'm just not sure how I'm going to pull this off. What you need—it's too fast. We'd have to learn the systems in less than twenty-four hours." Caesar spun, looking up to the second-floor windows across from the Ferris wheel, seeing if he could make out any sign of Charlotte looking down from her perch. Nothing from this angle.

"Please," Moreau said, tears welling in his eyes. "You're all I've got."

Feeling the wind of the whirling carousel pushing across his neck, Caesar drew a breath and nodded.

"All right," he muttered. "But no promises."

"Oh, thank you," Moreau exclaimed, reaching out with both hands, fumbling as if he suddenly had no idea what to do with them. He drew back, his face flushed red. "When do we begin?"

"Team, let's get moving on this," Caesar said into his earpiece. "I'm going to share the Dropbox location and give this one a green light."

Hearing nothing back, Caesar tapped the Bluetooth earpiece a few times.

"Anyone on the line?" he asked. "I'm not getting a signal here, might be interference."

The joints of the Ferris wheel squealed above him, the long afternoon shadows now shining through its braces and shooting a fresh, screaming bolt of sun into his eyes with the turn of each car. He squinted and looked back to Moreau.

"Give us all the information you've got on the ship," Caesar said. He fished in his pocket for the instructions he had written by hand a few hours earlier. "Drop it in this location and we'll see what we can do. Like I said—no promises."

Caesar did a quick check up to the second-floor window, seeing nothing, and turned back to face Moreau. "I have to go."

He paused for a moment, waiting for Charlotte's reply.

That's the phrase we agreed on. Your turn to chime in, Char.

Moreau smiled with relief, carefully pulling the paper from Caesar's hand and sliding it back into his pocket.

"I have to go," Caesar repeated, pressing the receiver deeper into his ear. His eyes flicked across the area, checking for any of his team members on the move. He saw only tourists and families, snacking on popcorn and skipping to the organ grinder soundtrack playing in the background.

"Thank you—thank you so much," Moreau said, stepping closer and lowering his voice. "I knew this would work. But if we're in a hurry, let me just write the details down right now. It will only take a minute."

Caesar watched Moreau fish in his pockets for something to write with. Caesar's pulse quickened as the seconds ticked by.

"It's here somewhere," Moreau stammered with an embarrassed grin. "I might have a location, and it can be tricky. The Kenyan coast has a bunch of different hiding places with—"

"What was that?" Caesar said, turning to face Moreau. "What did you say?"

He said Somalia before.

Moreau stared back at Caesar like a deer in headlights. He froze, hands still in his pockets. Before he could say anything, a ring tone chimed through the air. Moreau looked down to his jacket pocket with panic growing in his eyes.

"We said no phones," Caesar said, glaring back at Moreau. "What is this?"

He's a liar. He's not who he says he is.

"I'm sorry, I must have forgotten about the phone," Moreau said. "Just one more second, I've got the information here, I know it. The families—they're just so worried that something is going to happen."

He's going to get you caught. He's one of them.

Caesar stared down Moreau, feeling the rage creep up his spine. He took a step forward, his arms reaching up towards the man's throat. He stopped himself, horrified. *You're losing control. Just get out of here. Just get out.* Caesar winced as the beams of sunlight continued to hit his eyes. He pulled his hand back to block the light, looking up at the Ferris wheel, studying each car. At the top, he saw a man in sunglasses, hanging out of the open window a handheld radio at his lips.

Goddamnit.

"I have to get out of here," Caesar whispered as he backed a few careful steps away. Caesar tapped his Bluetooth earpiece with his palm and whispered. "We're compromised. Char—get moving."

Caesar bolted, sprinting down the boardwalk, sucking in heavy breaths as he darted along the main path. He turned to look over his shoulder between gasps, seeing the man calling himself Moreau about fifty feet behind him.

She went silent minutes ago. They got her first. I was next.

He took a sharp left, darting past a maze of iron railings, painted with alternating yellow and red stripes. He could hear the click-clack beats of the roller coaster making its way around the track as he flew into the darkness of an unmarked door.

He stopped for a moment to get his bearings, letting his eyes adjust as much as they could. He ran straight ahead, turning through a maze of hallways until he pushed his way through a closed door marked 'Water Access.'

Inside, he found a hatch with a ladder wrapping around the side. *You've got to be kidding me.* He flipped the lid open, looking down into the dark abyss of the harbor, and was hit with a gust of saltwater air.

"Char, can you hear me?" He breathed into his earpiece, checking one last time. "Are you there?"

They have her. She's gone. I won't let them take me. I'll never let them take me.

The black waters of Sydney Harbor, splashing off the wooden pylons supporting the pier, lay thirty feet below him. He heard footsteps in the hallway as he shook his head and took a breath.

He jumped.

TEN

Littlefield Hall, University of Texas
Austin, TX
October 26th, 7:20PM

Haylie sat on her window perch, legs curled up to her chest and her arms wrapped tight. The ninety-minute drive back up from San Antonio had felt like days as Agent Hernandez had tried a continuous string of attempts at small talk, none of which found its mark. She looked down to the single piece of paper at her feet: the agreement between her and the NSA and everything that came with it.

Just do your best. What do I have to lose here? Why wouldn't I just—

Haylie was jolted by Vector's signature knock at the door. Grunting as she jumped up, she tucked the NSA paperwork under a notebook on her desk and cracked the door open.

Vector stood in the hallway, holding a pizza in his hands. "Would it kill you to come over to *my* room sometime?" he said. "How come I always have to come over here?"

"A pizza?" Haylie said with a smile. "It's a little early for dinner."

"It's Thursday," he said, walking past her and into the room. "Thursday is pizza night, and I have some stuff we need to talk about. Can I come in?"

She cleared the coffee table, pushing books and a day-old coffee cup aside to make way for their dinner.

"Oh man," Vector started in, "did you miss some good stuff in Data Structures today. Professor Farley came in all ready to talk about loops and arrays—kids' stuff, right?—acting like he had invented them. Then that one guy who always asks questions raises his hand—"

Haylie took a slow bite of pizza and felt her gaze drifting off to the window, her mind replaying what had happened out in San Antonio earlier that morning. If the Endling was really planning more attacks, how could she find him on the forums? Would he really be dumb enough to—

"Hey, are you even listening?" Vector shifted over to the chair across from her, waving a hand in front of her face. "Where the hell were you today? Is everything all right?"

She snapped out of her trance and looked down at the pizza box, studying the angles of each remaining piece. "I'm good. I'm fine. Agent Hernandez just took me on a little field trip this morning, that's all."

"Off saving the world again?" Vector said. "Just like your brother?"

"No, nothing like that," she said meekly, curling up on the couch and looking down at the floor. "I can't talk about it, but it's nothing. I signed some paperwork, I'm trying to help them with something."

"Well, that's a good thing, right?" Vector replied. He grabbed his pizza slice with two hands and took a bite. "As long as it gets you back online. What kind of work is it?"

"I said I can't say," she shot back.

Vector stopped his chewing and dropped the pizza down to his napkin. "I was with you in London, if you remember. We're supposed to be in this together, you and me." He pointed a finger in the direction of Hernandez's room. "Agent Hernandez knows that, and I thought you did, too."

"I'd tell you," Haylie said, searching for the right words, "but there are rules that come along with the deal. I don't know—I'm not even sure I should have signed up for this thing in the first place. I've said too much already. Let's talk about something else." She reached for her pizza slice and took a large bite as the cheese burned the roof of her mouth. "You said you wanted to talk about something. Whatcha got?"

Rubbing his hands together, Vector rested his elbows on his knees as his head fell down for a moment. He took his time, his eyes nervously searching around the room, and then looked up with a clap of his hands. "Okay, here goes nothing."

Haylie stopped breathing altogether as she slowly chewed.

Oh no, don't do this right now.

"Listen," Vector began, looking past Haylie's shoulder, avoiding her line of sight altogether. "I was talking to a few people before class today, and since you weren't there—well, maybe not *because* you weren't there but *probably* because you weren't there—one of them kept asking questions about you and me."

Oh no. No, no, no.

Haylie swallowed as Vector paused for a moment. "Asking questions ... about ... what, exactly?"

"Well that's the thing," Vector said. "I actually hear this all the time from people, but I've never brought it up with you before now. I get a lot of questions—every few days—about if we are, like, *a couple.* You know?"

An air of silence hung over the room as the two friends formed a standoff of sorts, competing to see who could hold out the longest.

Haylie cleared her throat and filled the empty space. "So, you said 'no,' right?"

Not giving up ground, Vector continued. "Well, that's the thing. See—we spend all this time together. Like, every minute of every day. And lately, when people have been asking me, I have started wondering if we should ... maybe ... try something like that out?"

Biting her lip, Haylie searched for words. She tossed the pizza slice down on the oily cardboard box and rubbed the crumbs from her palms. "I ... We should talk about this, but right now really isn't the time. With all the stuff happening at the moment, I just—I just can't put anything else in my head, you know?"

Vector sat still as a stone. He reached into his pocket, retrieving his phone. He flicked across the screen with his thumb as she leaned in across the table.

"Listen, Vector," she said, "it doesn't mean that it can't—"

"No," he interrupted, sliding the phone back in his pocket with a grimace, "I get it. It's fine. Brilliant—you've got a lot going on, I get it."

"I'd love to talk about this, but right now is just a really bad time—"

"Haylie, there's not going to be any better time," Vector said, standing and tossing his pizza back into the box as well. "We're here at school, together. I spend every waking moment making sure that you're up to speed on the latest news and class assignments and the cafeteria menu every day. When will there ever be a better—"

There was a loud knock on the door as Haylie looked Vector in the eyes, trying to figure out the right thing to say. *Why did you have to pick today, you big idiot?*

"You'd better get that," Vector said. "You've got a lot going on right now, would hate for you to miss something important."

She rolled her eyes and walked to the door, pulling it open violently without even bothering to look through the peephole.

"Haylie," Agent Hernandez said, hooking his neck through the door. "Hey, Liam, I'm sorry, I didn't realize you were—"

"It's fine," Vector said back.

"Haylie," Hernandez said in a low tone, "it's time for our block of hours tonight. We need to get started."

Haylie slunk back to her chair and plopped down to face Vector. He was buried in his phone again, avoiding eye contact. He blindly reached for his backpack and without even looking up, slung it over his shoulder.

"Enjoy your dinner," he said as he crept out the door.

ELEVEN

Littlefield Hall, University of Texas
Austin, TX
October 26th, 7:45PM

Okay, Endling. What the hell are you up to?

Haylie took off her glasses and rubbed her eyes with balled fists, trying to snap herself out of the boredom that lay thick over the room. Without access to anything electronic, she wasn't even able to play music to break the silence—no streaming radio, no MP3s, not even an old CD player. And Agent Hernandez humming some song she'd never heard of wasn't helping.

"There's nothing here," she said, dully scrolling through a message board with her chin resting on her free hand. "I'm telling you, if you loosen the leash on me, I could probably find something. It could be our secret, just between you and me."

"Observe and consult will be fine," Hernandez said, keeping one eye on her as he scrolled through email on his phone. "Just stick to the plan."

"Just because there's a plan doesn't mean the plan doesn't suck."

She switched tabs, sorting by new posts as the dated machine pushed its processor, trying to keep up. Searching for keywords: 'Xasis,' 'Endling,' 'casino.' It was useless—there was nothing to find.

No one leaves a calling card without bragging about it the next day. Which one of you is it going to be?

"Let's post a message about Xasis," Haylie said, perking up at the prospect. "Bait them to answer a question, you know?"

"Can't do that," Hernandez said through a mouthful of coffee. "Against the rules. No posting, just listening. Try that other one."

Haylie shook her head and typed in another hacker message board, logging in with her credentials.

"Nice," Hernandez whispered as the site loaded. "We're in."

"We're in?" Haylie shot back. "Did you really just say that? We're in? What do you mean, *we're in?*"

"You know, we're on the inside. With the hackers."

"Where, exactly is *in?*" Haylie asked. "In *where?* Because from where I'm sitting, all we did was log into a stupid message board."

"Alright, fine," Hernandez said. "Have it your way. Just trying to help."

"Stop helping. Just stop."

Haylie could feel Hernandez's stare crawl up the back of her neck as she paged through subject line after subject line. Hackers discussing everything under the sun: zero-day exploits, Wi-Fi router vulnerabilities, government leaks. Everything but the one thing she wanted.

This is worse than just being offline.

"Do you really need to be here?" Haylie asked, trying to muster up the nicest, most helpful tone she could. "Hovering over my shoulder? There's software that can track my activity to make sure I'm not running around messing with nuclear reactors or anything like that. That's pretty common tech."

Nodding, Hernandez crossed his arms and leaned back. "I know,

I think they've got something like that rigged up," he said. "There's a thing. It's ... routing ... something. For the network. But I need to be here, too. Trust me, neither of us is enjoying ourselves right now."

"They're routing my IP through one of their proxies. Is that what you meant to say?"

Hernandez looked like a deer in headlights. "Yes?"

"You don't know what an IP is, do you?" After staring at him for a few moments of disbelief, Haylie leaned in and took on her best teacher's tone. "An IP address is like the address for your house, but on the Internet. It's the only one of its kind, and it lets computers understand who you are and where you are coming from."

Nodding, taking another sip from his mug, Hernandez looked like he was genuinely surprised to hear that technology actually existed.

"How is it that you got this job?" Haylie asked. "Being my shadow? You don't know a thing about this stuff."

"All agents with a heavy technical background are currently assigned to higher priority assignments. And they are at a higher pay grade. Budget cuts."

"So that means *you're* at a lower pay grade?" Haylie said.

"Like I said." Hernandez looked back at her without expression. "Budget cuts."

Haylie turned to her laptop with a loud exhale, tabbing back to the first hacking forum and trying a few new searches that might bring up something, anything, from someone who could be the Endling.

It's only a matter of time, but I get the feeling my time is running out.

That morning, the more Haylie had learned about the Xasis exploit, the more confused she had grown about what the Endling was doing. He had downloaded the personal information for all casino visitors from the past few years including contact information, credit cards, and fingerprints that were required for with high-value loans.

"Any new information you'd like to share with me?" Haylie asked. "Anything that might help?"

Shaking his head and continuing to stare down at his phone, Hernandez muttered, "You're smart, right? You'll figure it out. Just keep looking."

Haylie turned back, narrowing her eyes, the frustration growing. *This is driving me nuts. I know I can find something with just a little bit of code here—watching the public feeds isn't going to help. He'd never notice if I ran a quick script. What's the worst they'll do, just yank this agreement? They'd be doing me a favor.*

There was a loud, shrill, ear-piercing ring from behind her, causing her to jump out of her chair. She turned to see Hernandez scrambling to check his phone. He looked down at the screen and then back up to Haylie with a hint of panic in his eyes.

"Sorry," he said, rising from his chair, "I know it's loud. My wife gets pissed when I miss a call." Hernandez looked back and forth between his phone and Haylie's laptop, frozen in indecision. "It's her … I have to take this."

"Just answer it," she said in her best dismissive tone. "You can check my browser history when you get back if you really want to."

"Don't go anywhere," he said, making his way towards the door. "I'll just be a minute."

She pointed down to the ankle bracelet with a raised eyebrow, but Hernandez had already run out into the hallway, his phone to his ear. The door slid shut behind him, and all Haylie could hear were the muffled remnants of a conversation through the wall.

She brought up a new browser tab, quickly changing the settings over to "private mode," which would keep her browser history nice and clean. Tabbing through the forums, she checked the footer of each website. Eight of the ten hacking message boards were built on the same software platform—a message board product named XZTalk—which happened to power the majority of all forums across the globe.

Turning back to a new tab, she began a search on a new forum, one that she hadn't brought up in front of Hernandez. NetSecAgenda was the private hacking board where she always found her best leads on fresh exploits, and as far as she knew, it was still unknown to the authorities. Keying in her old credentials, she searched and found a recent bug that gave full access to the XZTalk message system through the company's new mobile interface, which was still in beta and full of bugs. News of the hack was still only known by a few people and hadn't been widely reported as of yet.

She took a breath, looking over at the door with nervous eyes. Hernandez must have found refuge in his room down the hall, sitting on his bunk, huddled over the phone. She closed her eyes, feeling her heart pound.

Think, Haylie.

The messages that people are posting are only one part of the equation here. I need to find the data behind the data.

She opened a mobile emulator website and quickly gained administrator access to the eight forums that were running the XZTalk software, paging through analytics dashboards and activity logs. She sorted by each user's last recorded activity—logins, posts, replies, searches. Filtering down to just the search terms, she scrolled until she found the one term that really mattered.

Endling

Two IP addresses came up, both with searches across eight different forums. She quickly cut and pasted the—

"Hey, Haylie," she heard from behind her. She swiveled to see Hernandez's head poking through the door, his ear still to the phone.

Her heart raced, and she fought the urge to slam the laptop lid shut in panic.

"What's the name of that—hold on, honey—what's the name of that thing they put in the breakfast tacos down here? The thing I like?"

She took a deep swallow, breathing slowly and blocking her screen with her shoulders.

"Migas?"

"Migas! Thank you, yes." He turned back into the hallway as the door slowly closed behind him, his voice becoming muffled once more. "So, they're called migas, you have to try them out. It's like eggs with ..."

She turned back to her laptop, wiping the sweat from her forehead. She pasted the first value into a lookup tool and leaned back to take in the results.

Okay—here's everyone across all eight hacker forums searching for 'The Endling' or 'Xasis' right now.

One of these is in Austin, here at UT—that's obviously me.

She shook her head—if her IP was showing up in her current location, it turns out they weren't actually rerouting her network traffic after all. *Budget cuts.*

She cut the second IP address and pasted it into the tool.

The page refreshed with results. She pushed back from her desk and winced as she read the location.

San Antonio, TX

Clicking on the coordinates, she zoomed in, her eyes darting around the map. She could feel the anger rising through her as she stared at the pin, sitting at the center of the familiar-looking outline of a building.

You've got to be kidding me.

Suddenly, four new log entries jumped into Haylie's search results. Then five. Then six. Searches for "Xasis" and "Endling" across multiple message boards. She watched the logs, following the user as he drifted to another thread on the same forum, one listing corporate network backdoors for sale.

Researching backdoors? Is that you, Endling? Where are you heading next?

Out of nowhere, she heard a voice directly over her right shoulder.

"Okay," Agent Hernandez said, bent over and inspecting her screen, "so what is this browser history thing you were talking about?"

Haylie stood, turning to face Hernandez, stepping aside to give him a full view of her screen. She pointed down with one extended finger at the location data.

"Wait a minute," Hernandez said as he read the coordinates. "You're not supposed to be—"

"Don't," she shot back, grabbing her jacket off the back of her chair. "We need to talk to Agent Wilcox. *Now.*"

TWELVE

"You set me up," Haylie said, pointing a finger across the table at Agent Wilcox. "And I don't like getting set up. I never had a chance."

"I'm sure I don't know what you're getting on about," Agent Wilcox said, slightly winded, as the door shut behind her. Haylie had noticed that Wilcox leaned in on the southern drawl in her voice when she was looking to dodge a question, and the drawl was plenty heavy tonight. Wilcox zipped her running jacket over her fitted gym clothes, the traces of sweat still visible on her forehead. "And I'm not happy that you pulled me in here this late."

"I found someone watching every hacker message board that I was assigned to," Haylie said. "All accounts for that user were created within the last week. None of them has posted a single message, zero. This person was just watching. Lurking."

"Well, then," Wilcox said, leaning in. "Sounds like you may have found our guy."

84

"Yeah, that's what I thought. But as it turns out, the IP address was from right here in San Antonio."

Agent Wilcox's face fell. Her eyes darted around the room for a few seconds but then quickly fixed back on Haylie.

"Convenient," Wilcox said. "Quite a coincidence."

"The IP address isn't just from San Antonio," Haylie continued. "It's coming from inside the NSA. From inside *this building*."

"This doesn't change anything," Wilcox said, turning back to her phone, digging in her heels. "I've got a whole team working this case, overtime and everything. And besides, what you're describing is impossible. We re-route all of our traffic. It's untraceable. There's no way you would even know—"

"Exactly," Haylie responded. "That's why this is so strange. This person wasn't blocked. Somebody at the NSA is working around your systems and running the exact same searches as I am."

"I still don't know what this has to do with—"

"The whole point of this is for me to find something. Something big that helps the investigation. But if your team finds that thing first, I get nothing. Isn't that right?"

Agent Wilcox looked over at Agent Hernandez with a cocked eyebrow.

Haylie heard Caesar's voice in her head as she fumed. *You never should have trusted them, little sister. You and I—we're better than this.*

"So if you have someone tailing me, this plan doesn't really work out for me, does it?" Haylie yelled. "You think I don't know what you're up to? You're going to take credit for all my work and leave me right back where I started. You never planned to help me; you just wanted to use me. I don't know why I'm surprised."

"Ms. Black." Agent Wilcox leaned back, forcing a smile. "Right now, I'm focused on finding our guy. I'm going to need to ask you to focus as well. We don't do conspiracies around here—"

"I'm out," Haylie said, sliding her chair back from the table. "I didn't want to do this in the first place, and I should have trusted my gut. Screw you."

"Let's not be so dramatic. If you happened to find..." Agent Wilcox paused, snapping her head back up with an angry snarl across her face. "Now, wait a minute. How did you get that type of data from the forums? That's not something users can see—IP address information, location data."

"I don't know," Haylie said, staring back at her. "I just figured it out."

"You *figured it out?*" Wilcox replied with a laugh. "Well, my goodness, aren't you the little scientist, now? There's a problem with that, Ms. Black. I asked you to read a few online forums and somehow—magically, by some sort of technical miracle—you gained access to admin logs and IP lookup information. That's a violation of your agreement."

Haylie kept her eyes pointed right at Wilcox. "So?"

"Did you write code?" Agent Wilcox asked. "Did you—Hernandez, did you let her actually write *code?*"

"It's not his fault," Haylie said with a smirk. "He had to leave the room to take a call." She silently mouthed the remaining words over to Agent Wilcox. "*His wife.*"

"You left the room?" Wilcox yelled at Hernandez, the anger cresting over. "While she was at the keyboard?"

"I may have," Hernandez said. "I *may* have left the room. We can't be one hundred percent sure exactly what I was doing at the time without—"

Agent Wilcox shook her head at Haylie. "You're done," Agent Wilcox said, bringing her phone up to eye level and tapping at the screen. "No more access. I can't believe I even went for this in the first place."

"Go ahead," Haylie said. "But that doesn't get you any closer to solving this case. You need to catch this guy, and I'm your best shot."

"And I'm supposed to trust you, Ms. Black? You've been on the case for less than twenty-four hours, and you've already broken the rules."

"Give me more access," Haylie said. "You've seen what I can do with just a few minutes online. Take the leash off me, let me run. I'll find your guy."

"More access? I've already got a big mess to clean up here," Agent Wilcox scoffed. "You're dreaming."

"Who knows?" Haylie said. "Maybe I found something already."

Agent Wilcox stared back, looking over to Hernandez. "Did she find something?"

"I really don't know," Hernandez said. "I'll be honest, I'm not as much in the loop here as I should—"

"I saw him," Haylie said. "The Endling. He logged on just as Hernandez came back in the room. I had to shut my script down, but I could find him again, I know I could."

"Here's the deal," Agent Wilcox said with a shake of her head. "You screwed up. The rules were simple. You knew them, and you broke them. I can't trust you anymore, and I don't work with people I can't trust. And yes, I had someone tailing you from inside the NSA. It's standard procedure to double-up on a lead when you don't have anywhere else to go."

"I knew it," Haylie whispered.

"You're going to meet with your double, tell how you found the Endling—if that's really what happened. After that, I never want to see you again."

"And what if I don't want to tell them anything?"

"Then I'll wake up a judge and tack twelve more months onto your probation," Wilcox said, tapping the folder. "Just like our agreement allows."

Haylie looked over at Agent Hernandez who was nodding back in her direction.

"You really should have read the agreement, Haylie," he said.

Haylie slumped back in her chair, arms folded. She was furious—not just at Wilcox, but at herself. For agreeing to anything with the NSA in the first place. For not trusting her gut. And for not taking ten minutes to read that damn paperwork.

"I can't believe I'm not just kicking you out of the building," Agent Wilcox muttered, dialing a number. "Wilcox here. I'm going to need Mary in the interrogation room first thing tomorrow morning."

"Mary?" Haylie looked over at Agent Hernandez. "Who the hell is Mary?"

THIRTEEN

N Wells St.
Chicago, IL
October 27th, 9:06AM

Today's the day. After today, they'll have no choice. People can ignore a raindrop here and there. But nobody can ignore a flood. And that's what I'm about to become.

A flood that will sweep them away.

The echo of wheels on winding tracks—*clack clack clack clack*—shook the sidewalk as Anthony crunched through a bed of leaves. The L train didn't always make so much of a racket, but when it hit a curved piece of track, the tension between the metal struts buckled under the strain. He gazed up at the steel bridge overhead, seeing ripples of rust washing over each beam like an autumn fog.

He walked towards the storefront, recognizing the logo etched on the glass: a golden coffee cup with an old-fashioned pair of spectacles in the middle, the letters underneath reading 'Burby Brothers Roasting Company.' Anthony flexed his hand in and out, feeling the gauze pull his wound slightly apart with each move. The motion felt comforting—each flash and spark of pain filling him with life.

Pulling at the door, Anthony felt a wave of warmth bathe his face as a pair of bells signaled his arrival. The deep, chocolate scents of coffee filled his nostrils. None of the patrons inside bothered to look up to greet him; they all sat, sucked into their various screens, numbed by their headphones.

This place will be perfect.

Years ago, one of the first tips he had read on a hacking message board, on the topic of "how a noob can get started without getting caught," was to never hack from home. As he had tried his best to piece together his skill set, Anthony had built up a long list of coffee shops throughout the Chicago area, never trying his exploits in the same place twice. Today's visit had him across town—taking the Red Line train from Wrigleyville to Fullerton, and then jumping on the Brown Line to the Merchandise Mart stop.

He drifted gingerly over to the counter, looking up at the menu hanging above. A gilded, old-time cash register stood below a fishing net full of tweed and wooden speakers hanging down from the ceiling, each facing a different direction and blaring out some band he had never heard of. *Bunch of hipsters.* He looked down past the tip jar and saw a bowl full of matches adorned with the shop's logo. He pocketed one with a single, sweeping motion.

Craning his neck around the counter, he saw the barista, tied up in a bath of steam, both hands furiously shuffling to craft the last remaining order. The barista caught sight of Anthony with the corner of his eye and threw an 'I'll be right over' head nod his way.

Anthony felt all eyes falling on the back of his head as he stood, waiting. *They're all looking at you. They're all whispering about you—what you look like, your clothes. Laughing because you're alone.* The tension crept up the back of his neck as he shuffled his weight. *They think you don't belong here.*

Anthony shouted out, "I'll just have a large coffee," and slapped a five-dollar bill down on the counter with a shaking hand.

The barista glared, his hands still full. "Just a minute, *sir*," the final word echoing through the shop as he took his time with the orders.

He's doing that on purpose. He's one of them.

Anthony stomped off to the corner window seat he had been eying since he had walked in. A full view of the street, but enough of an angle to keep his screen far, far away from roaming eyes.

He did a quick check of his different social media platforms, taking note of his follower count on each. He had a system of sending out hacking and technology news on a three-posts-per-day basis, making sure to use the appropriate hashtags. His blog was a collection of diatribes on technology and the philosophy of hacking—long ramblings that flowed from his stream of consciousness like a gift to the world—tying the root of what it really meant to be a hacker to core principles of Buddhism, framing it as a type of modern meditation. All under a pseudonym, of course, and certainly not "the Endling." But when the public tied the two together, oh what a day that would be. He would not just be a hacker for the ages: he would be a leader of men. He could create a movement.

A philosopher king.

Anthony made a check of the rest of the crowd in the shop and reached into his pocket, retrieving two scraps of paper. That morning, he had received an email from his source, and the next step on his mission was clear. He brought up a command line window and connected to the target system through an anonymous client with the command:

torific ssh bglenn22@patriarchWellness.com

Patriarch Wellness was the largest health care conglomerate in the United States. Their ads were everywhere—TV commercials, billboards, even a big banner outside of Wrigley Field. Money-hungry doctors fueled by greed, that's all they were.

The Patriarch system pinged, asking for his password. Anthony smiled as he flattened the second piece of paper on the table. He typed the password with single keystrokes and hovered his finger over the "return" key.

"Anthony—is that you?" The voice came from Anthony's left side and his eyes jumped up, staring at the woman standing next to him with a curious smile. "Anthony? From high school? From Payton High?"

His heart raced as his fingers froze on the keys, his eyes did not know where to go. Slowly pulling the top shell of his laptop down, he forced an awkward, confused push of his eyebrow as he leaned his elbow on the top of the computer.

Be cool. Be cool.

"Sorry, I think you must have the wrong person," he replied, his words tumbling over each other. "My name is Dave. Or David."

"Dave or…" The woman looked back at him with a confused smile, stepping forward to get a better view of his face. "It's me—Margaret Chen … We were in a biology class together? You sat in the back row, right?" She flipped her hair behind her shoulder and laughed. "I can't believe I still remember that. It's crazy how the brain works, you know? I mean, I haven't thought about high school in *ages.*"

Anthony gazed back at her with a blank face, hoping he was hiding the growing panic boiling behind his eyes.

Get rid of her.

"I'm sorry," he said, crossing his arms over the laptop. "I really don't know who you are. My name is Dave." Nodding to himself, he repeated the words again, not knowing what else to do. "I'm Dave."

Puzzled, she shifted her weight, tugging at the lapels of her coat.

"All right," she said as she slunk away, mumbling. "If that's the way it's going to be. You were always weird, anyway."

He watched her make her way to the counter, grab her order, and then walk out the door, her last throwaway words burning in his mind. *You were always weird anyway. You were always weird anyway.* Anthony clenched his fingers into balled fists, muttering to himself under his breath.

His eyes flew around the room, jumping from person to person, looking for anything out of the ordinary, anyone looking in his direction. He stretched out his palms flat on the table, feeling the sweat slide across the wood. He closed his eyes to calm himself, but it was no use. His heart was beating like a bass drum—he knew everyone could see it in his throat, in his veins.

I have been here before; I will be here again.

I have been here before; I will be here again.

Locking his vision on the wall directly in front of him, he focused on individual points, one at a time, just like he had been taught. A squeeze bottle of honey, only a third full, sitting on the wooden counter next to the cream.

I have been here before; I will be here again.

His heart raced. The three, bright green shelves holding stir sticks and boxes of teas. The small, red metallic trash can with a white plastic bag wrapped haphazardly across its top, the flip-top lid jacked permanently open.

I have been here before; I will be here again.

He breathed in and out. In and out.

You have a job to do. You're here for a reason.

He cracked his eyes back open as he felt the rush of anger slip and melt away. It had passed, for now. As bad as it was in the moment, he knew the wave always passed, eventually. But he also knew that it would come back. It always came back.

He logged in to his laptop again, controlling his breathing and seeing the blinking cursor still active within the Patriarch network, waiting for his command. He hit the "return" key, watching the login sequence process his credentials and giving him a new prompt.

Last login: Fri Oct 2 19:18:58 from 75.132.267.98
[bglenn22@webAccess11 ~]$

His eyes grew wide as he watched the cursor pulse.
It worked. Of course, it did. Of course, it did.
He leaned in and typed out commands to identify his location in the file system. After a few nervous sips of coffee—holding the giant coffee mug with two shaking hands—he turned back to the command line and found what he was looking for, a folder named "customer_records."
I was always weird, is that right, Margaret Chen?
With a few quick keystrokes, he was downloading the entire customer database of the Patriarch network, separated into zipped files grouped by state and region. He sat and drank his coffee, watching the download progress of each climb from zero to one-hundred percent, then moving on to the next. He watched the other customers, busy with their pathetic lives, sitting within arms-reach of one of the greatest hacks in U.S. history.
Twenty-five minutes later, the downloads were complete. Eighty-two million customer records, complete with names, addresses, social security numbers, medical histories, and, in some cases, fingerprint data. All of the fields were accurate except for one: the "balance due" field for one Margaret Lindsay Chen of 128 Rosemont Avenue, Chicago IL. That number had been raised to $225,567.
Some people don't know when to shut their mouths.

Anthony shoved the slips of paper back into his pocket. He dove back into the Patriarch network, finding the production files for the central web server. He deleted the index.php file and replaced it with a few new lines of code, uploading a file to the /images/ directory, and then terminating the connection. Navigating quickly to check the PatriarchWellness.com home page, the screen refreshed as a blank white digital slate, showing only a single image with a line of text underneath.

The image was a distorted photo of a Pinta Island tortoise—the last one in the world before it died a pitiful death—standing at attention. The animal's head extended from his enormous shell and dull, black, stupid eyes staring straight into the camera as if to say, "There's nothing I can do." The words below the photo read:

The Endling Strikes Again

He packed his laptop and walked out the door, the chiming bells ringing behind him. He knew he'd never again return to Burby Brothers Coffee in his life.

Cutting into the parking lot, Anthony huddled into the warmth of his jacket and walked behind a line of cars parked against a brick wall. He stooped down behind the bumper of a dated American hatchback and pulled the scraps of paper with the Patriarch credentials from one pocket and his new book of matches from the other.

Cupping his hands, he struck a match and touched it to the paper's edge, watching its tint morph from yellow to black, flaking into ash. Remnants fell to the ground and found gusts of wind, blowing into nothing, never to be seen again.

FOURTEEN

Haylie crinkled the sheet of paper in her palm as she walked down the hallway, checking room numbers. She saw a familiar, engraved number on the small plaque to the left of the next door and straightened her jacket.

This is the place.

She tried the handle, but it stuck, not giving an inch. She exhaled, looking up to the security camera nestled in the corner, staring down at her like a bird on a wire. She checked the paper again, making sure she was at the right door.

I guess I'll just knock?

As she brought her hand to the door, she heard a loud, metallic thud from the other side, and the door swung inward. Haylie jumped back, her hands extended out.

"Ms. Black?" a man's voice rang out from inside. "Please follow me."

Inside, the cramped room held a small desk under a row of windows, the metal mesh inside the glass drawing faint rectangle patterns into the next room. The man, dressed in all black with a neck thicker than your average tree trunk, pointed her towards the log book.

"I'll need you to sign the sheet," he said, gesturing at the clipboard. "Then you can go in. She's waiting for you."

Haylie inspected the list and saw her name and the date already printed at the top, with a long list of blank spaces below. She signed and placed the pen back on the table with a click.

The man pressed a keycard up to a plate on the door, pulling at the handle and gesturing for Haylie to enter.

"If you need anything," he said with a dull tone, "just bang on the window."

Just bang on the window? Is he serious?

As the door shut behind her with a firm thud, she surveyed the room. It held only a long, white table with a pair of metal loops screwed onto the top. Through one of the loops was a pair of handcuffs, attached to a woman sitting patiently, her eyes locked on Haylie. The woman had stringy, long white hair pulled down the sides of her face. She was thin and frail, and her aged skin showed a tired, pale complexion that almost matched her gray prison jumpsuit.

"Hello," Haylie said, trying to look like she had done this before. "I'm Haylie."

The woman shifted her weight in her chair, tugging gently at her cuffs as she stared back. She looked down at the empty chair sitting across the table.

Haylie took the hint and slid into the chair, never losing eye contact with the woman.

"So," the woman said. The words rumbled with a droll cadence from her lips. "You're the girl. The one who was in London. The one who calls herself Crash." She wasn't asking questions—she had the look of a woman who already knew the answers.

"Right," Haylie said. "Crash. That's my screen name. I'm Haylie. It's nice to meet you. What's your name?"

The woman's eyes went narrow as she cocked her head with a hint of suspicion, looking over to the door and back to Haylie. "I'm Mary," she said. "Inmate #45099256 from the Lewisburg Penitentiary."

"Lewisburg? Where's that?"

"Someplace you don't want to go," Mary replied slowly, methodically. "But I'll admit I don't have much time to explore the area. Just a ten-by-ten exercise yard for thirty minutes a day. Rain or shine."

"I'm sorry," Haylie said. "I thought I was supposed to be meeting with an NSA analyst?"

"I've been helping the NSA, same as you," Mary said. "I was the one trailing you yesterday. On the forums."

Haylie's eyes narrowed as she inspected Mary. *They had an inmate trailing me? What the hell?*

"Quite a mess you made," Mary said.

"Sorry, what?"

"In London. Quite a mess."

Haylie nodded with a nervous laugh. "Right, yes, London. Someone else made the mess, I was just kind of there to clean it up, you know?"

"Yes, of course," Mary said leaning back. "Of course. I read about it in the papers—the parts they let me read, anyway."

"So," Haylie said, working to change the subject. "They have you working on this Endling project, too?"

"They asked for my help, and here I am."

"If you don't mind me asking," Haylie said. "Why? Why would you help them?"

Tilting her head to the side and taking in a deep breath, Mary's eyes moved off Haylie and up to the ceiling. "Because ... because," she whispered. "Because I got to go on a bus ride. And now I have a window and a gray jumpsuit instead of an orange one. This one matches my eyes." A slow smile crept out of the corners of her mouth.

Haylie smiled back. "It looks very nice."

"I've helped them a good deal over the years," Mary said. "This one is bigger than the others, which I suppose explains all the special treatment, but I'll pitch in here and there when they don't have enough techs on staff. It's kept my coding up to date, and it's just nice to use a computer now and then. But I don't have to tell you that."

"Is that what you're in for?" Haylie asked. "Digital crimes?"

"We didn't call it *digital* back in my day, my dear," Mary said, her eyes locked back on Haylie. "I'm in here because I caused trouble. I was young and stupid at the time, a lot like you."

Haylie's eyes narrowed. "I was smart enough to stay out of jail."

"Well then, look at you. The smartest girl in the room. How's that deal working out for you?"

Haylie frowned, shaking the comment off. She brought her tone down to a whisper, leaning in towards Mary and away from the security camera in the corner. "How'd you get caught? What were you doing?"

"Some system cracking, phone hacks, TV broadcasts—that sort of thing. It was a different time ... Not everything was connected back then. Less things we could mess with."

"Broadcasts?" Haylie asked. "What kind of broadcasts?"

Smiling and looking down at her handcuffs, Mary slowly rotated her wrists, stretching them, testing the metal. She looked up with a grin.

"Broadcast signal intrusion," Mary said. "You ever read about the Chicago TV hack? Twice in the same night, two different channels?"

Haylie's jaw dropped. *No way.* She had read all about the Chicago hacks, or the "Max Headroom hacks," as they were known.

They were two of the great unsolved exploits of the past thirty years, a topic that always got the message boards rolling. Videos of the hack, transferred off of grainy VHS tapes, were available on YouTube and were creepy enough that it took Haylie a few attempts before she could watch them all the way through.

Haylie's eyes opened wide. "The first hack was on WGN. The—"

"The newscast was interrupted by a video feed, a man in a mask and sunglasses," Mary said. "Ribbed metal sheeting behind him, tilting violently to the right and left. Nothing was said, just the man bobbing and nodding to a beat that wasn't there, the audio filled with fuzzy static. After twenty seconds of air time, the transmission cut out and went back to the newscast. The sportscaster looked around the studio nervously and said—"

" 'Well, if you're wondering what just happened, so am I'," Haylie said in amazement.

Mary nodded. "Later that night, another attack on another channel. This time the man in the mask had found his voice, yelling insults, using soda cans as props, mocking marketing slogans and humming theme songs."

"I thought they never caught the guy who did that?" Haylie said as she hung on Mary's every word.

"They didn't catch any guys," Mary replied, her smile now joined by a twinkle in her eye. "They caught *me*."

Laughing, Haylie shook her head. "No way."

"I'm afraid so," Mary whispered back, laughing and leaning across the table.

"But I've seen the videos," Haylie said. "It was a man. The posture, the voice. That was a guy in the mask, right?"

Nodding, Mary looked past Haylie's shoulder at the wall behind her. "He was the star," Mary said with a haze in her eyes. "But I was the brains. The feds found me but never found out how I did it. I still won't tell—and that got me an extra ten years." She turned back to Haylie and her smile returned. "Like I said earlier, I was young and stupid."

I can't believe it—she's a legend. Haylie looked down to the handcuffs and Mary's thin wrists, tied to the table like she was some kind of animal.

"And now, it seems, we'll be working together," Mary said.

"No, I don't think so. It was nice to meet you, but I'm done with all of this. I'm just going to serve out the rest of my sentence and play solitaire or something."

"So young. So stupid. I can see so much of myself in you, Crash."

Haylie leaned back, raising an eyebrow. "I'm sorry, but you don't know me. You don't know anything about me."

"Oh, darling girl," Mary said with a sideways grin. "But I do. I do, I do, I do."

Haylie pushed the chair back and shot to her feet. "I'm just here to tell you what I know, not to make friends. I don't need a pen pal."

"My dear, you have to start trusting *someone*. You owe that to yourself, don't you think? You and me, we're in this together, like it or not. This is the only chance we've got."

"I don't know what you're talking about," Haylie said, standing from the table. "I'm done with all this. You're smart enough to figure out what I've seen. Just do me a favor and make something up to tell Wilcox, will you? Something that convinces the government I've been helpful or whatever it is they want."

Haylie walked towards the door, looking back at her reflection in the glass. She looked tired. She *was* tired. Behind her image, she saw Mary's silhouette—a hood of gray—sitting firm. She extended her arm out towards the glass to knock.

"There's been another hack, Haylie," Mary said. "Patriarch Wellness, the big fancy health insurance company."

Haylie froze. She wanted nothing more than to knock on the

window, to head back to Austin and forget all about this place. But she couldn't. She had to know. It was killing her—she couldn't figure out what the Endling was doing. No money, just data. It was a puzzle she couldn't crack, and another hack—another clue—might do the trick. She had to ask, no matter how much it bruised her up inside to do it. "What did he take this time?"

"Data," Mary said. "Same as the Xasis. Same as the credit card company. Just names and information. No cash transfers, no ransoms —just data."

"And the calling card?" Haylie said, half turning back to Mary. "Did he leave—"

"A tortoise," Mary said. "The last of its kind. Another endling, Crash. Same as before."

Haylie shook her head. "It's none of my business anymore."

"I know it isn't, dear," Mary said. "And I know you have to be going. But one thing; just one favor. Because we'll never meet again, I have to know. How do you think he got into the casino?"

Haylie stopped, dropped her arm to her side and turned to face Mary. "Through the dev server in Pennsylvania. That's what Agent Wilcox told—"

"No, my dear," Mary said. "Think bigger. How did *this guy* get into the Xasis?"

"I'm not sure I—"

"You haven't seen the logs, I have. He left traces everywhere. He's sloppy. He's got raw talent, but no refinement. How does someone like that get into one of the most secure systems in the world?"

Haylie looked back at Mary, thinking. "I don't know, maybe he got lucky, maybe he—"

"Wrong," Mary said. "You know better than that. There's no such thing as luck in our world."

Haylie stared back at her in silence.

"And why isn't he talking?" Mary continued. "He's left a calling card everywhere but my front porch, so why isn't he all over the message boards, bragging about all this nonsense?"

It doesn't make any sense.

"You're the smartest girl in the room, remember?" Mary said. "So tell me how any of this makes sense."

Haylie said the only thing that didn't sound crazy. "Because he can't get in on his own. Someone else got him in. And that same person told him—"

"Told him to keep his mouth shut," Mary nodded. "That's what I think, too. He's not doing this alone. There's someone else. You see, Haylie, I'm not interested in finding the Endling, I'm interested in finding out who's really behind this."

"Why? Why do you give a rat's ass about any of this?"

"Because we're the only people in this building who know how this guy thinks. We just figured out more in five minutes together than that whole team of NSA stooges out there. They need us. This is our ticket out of here. Both of our tickets. And if there's someone else out there pulling the strings, they must have something bigger in mind. This is going to keep going. Tell me, what did you find on the forums?"

"I saw him," Haylie said. "He was researching backdoors."

"He's not done," Mary nodded. "He's going to hit somewhere else. Soon. He's going to continue collecting data—data about people. Why is he doing this, Haylie? Why would someone be collecting *people*?"

"I don't know."

"Things are happening," Mary said. "The Endling is finding his feet, and your world is changing as well. Even if you don't know it yet."

Haylie extended an arm out to the window and leaned heavily on the glass, catching her breath.

"Take it from someone who knows, Crash. Where you go, what you become ... It all gets decided right here."

"I don't want the government to turn on me. I don't want to end up like my brother."

"Neither do I, my dear. But aren't you interested in finding out what's going on? We'll catch the Endling—you and I—but even better, we'll solve the puzzle. The *truth*. The man behind the curtain. And the truth—that's what's going to set us both free. If there's a conspiracy here and we can uncover it, they'll give us whatever we ask for."

Haylie nodded. She took long steps back to the table. Just as she took her seat, there was a knock at the door and the man from the desk poked his head in.

"It's time, Ms. Black," he said.

"I'll talk to Agent Wilcox," Mary leaned across the table with a smile. "I'll tell her that I won't do this without you. We're in this together, you and I."

Haylie nodded, shuffling back towards the door, her head hung low. She turned to face Mary.

"If the Endling's not calling the shots here," Haylie asked, "why is he doing this? Is it money? Fame?"

A smile made its way onto Mary's face as she leaned back in her chair. "Now you're asking the right questions. He's not interested in money; he could have grabbed millions from the Xasis, but he didn't. For him, it's about the calling card. He wants to be someone who can't be ignored. He wants to be in the headlines. He wants his name to be known across the globe."

"He wants—" Haylie stopped short when she realized what she was about to say. A chill went down her spine.

"He wants to be *you*, Crash," Mary said. "He wants to be you."

FIFTEEN

Cape Town, South Africa
October 28th, 11:47AM

The faded signs hung crooked across the sides of each street corner, were the only hint of color that Caesar could see anywhere on the whole damn block. The streets of Cape Town were washed with beige and tan—even under the blanket of afternoon shadows, the city felt like it had been whitewashed. His sandals slid on the ever-present grit of sand under his feet as he crossed over to the next block.

He paced past the African Art Wholesale Market and a cheap hostel to an alley lined with short, black posts keeping traffic off the sidewalk. As he sank deeper into the next city block, the surroundings grew with life and color, and he felt himself drifting into a new world. There, below a bright purple awning, was the sign he had been looking for: A1 ESPRESSO BAR.

The coffee house was an indoor-outdoor type of setup, with tables inside under the cover of the building but wide-open barn doors that let in the ocean breeze. Inside he saw Sean, sipping a small cup of coffee with his laptop open, lined up next to Margo and Phillip. Caesar slid onto the stool directly across from them.

"You're encrypting your traffic, I hope," Caesar said to Sean.

"Don't be an idiot," Sean said. "Of course I am. Do you think I got stupider after Sydney?"

"What are you looking at?" Caesar asked.

"We've been searching for any mentions of Char since last week," Margo said. "But there's nothing. Not in the mainstream press, nothing on the hacking boards or underground channels. It's like she just disappeared into thin air."

Caesar looked up at the waitress as she flashed the half-smile of a woman that would rather be surfing. He ordered a double espresso and checked the row of televisions above the bar, one showing a feed from CNN International. Senator Hancock took up most of the screen, standing at a podium and preaching to his followers, his arms flailing and hair wildly blowing in every direction, even upwards. He had the look of a madman who was given a bullhorn, to the delight of the crowd. The banner behind him read 'A NEW SECURITY FOR A NEW TIME.'

"My guess is," Caesar said with a gesture to the screen, "we'll either hear a lot about Char, or nothing at all. That seems to be the way things are headed these days."

Sean turned to look at the TV. "You shouldn't have picked a fight with Hancock. I don't think that was smart."

"Who, me?" Caesar said, crossing his arms with a smile.

"You really think this is a coincidence?" Phillip said. "That he's decided to make his war on hackers one of the biggest pieces of his campaign right after you released the Skull and Bones files?"

"He didn't get the worst of it," Caesar shot back. "Besides, his followers are so crazy, the stuff I released on him bounced right off him. His people don't care about facts."

"He knows it was you," Margo said, shaking her head. "He must

—that's the only thing that explains what happened in Sydney. You've created a monster, Caesar, one that won't be happy until every hacker in America is behind bars."

"But we're not *in* America," Caesar said. "Besides, that idiot isn't going to win the election. We all know that. In a couple of weeks, he'll just be a loudmouth on the speaking circuit. He'll have no power."

"He still has a few weeks to go," Phillip said. "And he already got Char. We weren't smart enough to see that coming, were we? They could already be on to us, and we wouldn't have a clue."

"His talk track is having an impact," Margo said. "All of these speeches about hackers being the next big threat to security—the public is responding to them. The media has started giving Hancock twice as much coverage as Ortega—this hacker stuff just makes for better television. A few months ago, we didn't have anyone on our tails, we could do whatever we wanted. But ever since you decided to release that goddamned data, we've been running. We can't even stop and take a breath."

"What do you call this?" Caesar said, gesturing around the room. "We're in South Africa. It's beautiful here—sun and sand and surf."

"And where will we be tomorrow?" Margo said. "You have no idea, do you? This is no way to live."

She gestured over to Phillip, who rose from his seat. The two packed up their laptops, threw backpack straps over their shoulders, and disappeared through the front doors.

Caesar watched them walk away, his eyes narrowing to slits. *Just walk away. It's just that easy for you, isn't it?*

"They have a point, you know," Sean said, sipping his coffee as the dust settled.

"They're not right."

"They're not wrong," Sean shot back. "We're in a place where we can't find a rhythm, can't relax. The Skull and Bones operation broke too many eggs."

"Well, maybe we shouldn't have been relaxing in the first place," Caesar said, still glaring at the exit where Margo and Phillip were no longer to be seen. *They don't know how hard this is. They don't understand the pressure. If they did, they wouldn't act like a couple of children. A couple of brats who don't deserve what they have.*

"We have code that will get us into any system in the world; maybe we should be using it. Breaking *more* eggs."

"Maybe we should chill," Sean said. "Back off, just for a bit. Phillip and Margo—they could use a few weeks off."

"We can't." Caesar pointed up at the election coverage on the screen. His mind raced, looping and spiraling, as he tried to push thoughts of his team imploding out of his mind. *Stay positive. Stay positive.* "This isn't the time. If we stop now, we could just get deeper into this mess." He placed his fingers on his temples to try and block out the rush. His breath turned into short huffs, stuttering in and out in rapid pushes of air. He gripped the wooden bar with one hand, just to make sure he wasn't falling.

"You okay, man?" Sean asked. "You've been pretty on edge since Sydney."

Caesar cracked his eyes open as he heard the sound of his coffee arriving. He stirred the spoon, around and around, without pouring in any sugar or milk, to feel the calm liquid swirl at his command. "I need you to stick with me. Just for a few more weeks. We need to see this through, and then, I promise, we'll take a nice long vacation. All of us. We'll hack the systems of the nicest resort on the French Rivera and get us all suites for the week. Massages and drinks and everything. Sound good?"

Sean nodded, watching the television screen as Hancock continued to scream to the crowd. "It feels like it's only going to get harder from here on."

"Doesn't matter," Caesar said. "I'll do whatever it takes."

Pushing back from the bar and keeping a careful eye on Caesar, Sean chose his words carefully. "Easy there, man. I think you need to pump the brakes a bit. I know Char was a tough loss but—"

"She's not lost," Caesar snapped back. "We'll figure out a way to get her back. She's still part of the team." He looked up at the screen, his eyes scrolling left to right to follow the closed captioning display.

Our democracy is at risk. It's at risk, and no one is paying attention, certainly not your current leaders. We don't need warships and tanks like Senator Ortega says. We need a new form of security. The threats from overseas and terrorists all over the world no longer come from bombs but from computer code. This new breed of terrorist—the hacker—is putting not only our national security at risk, but also our bank accounts, our privacy, and the safety of our children. It's time for a change, and I'm the only candidate who understands that the new world of security comes from technology. We need to lock these criminals up and throw away the key.

"He's going to blow a gasket up there," Caesar said. "It doesn't help that he has no idea what he's talking about."

"It doesn't matter," Sean said. "The people believe him. He started as just another crazy politician, but now that he has the nomination, the talking heads are starting to come around to his viewpoint."

"He won't win," Caesar said. "We both know that."

"The polls are close. It's a dead tie," Sean shot back.

The two sat without talking for a minute, staring down at the coffee. Sean finally broke the silence.

"How's your sister doing?" Sean asked. "You check in on her recently?"

"Not today," Caesar said. He opened his laptop and logged into the NSA's central tracking database through a Tor browser, pinging Haylie's ID that he had found a few months back. A smile grew across his face when he saw the geolocation blinking away in her dorm room, safe and sound. The anger left him, drifting away with each blink of the dot. A few seconds later, he felt almost normal.

"How much longer does she have?" Sean asked. "A year?"

"Year and a half, something like that," Caesar said. "She can do the time; she can make it as long as they keep their side of the bargain. I just hope she doesn't trust them too much."

"She's a smart girl," Sean nodded. "Probably smarter than us. She was right to take that deal."

"We need to be more careful," Caesar said. "They got Char— they're not done. They managed to not only find us but work their way into our workflow. Our systems and processes are secure, but we got sloppy somewhere. We need to tighten things up, and we need to get back on track. The team needs another win. Just one win, and we can get some momentum back."

"Stockholm," Sean said. "I have friends up there—there's a safe house and a potential project. It should be off the radar." Sean brought up the details of the project, tilting the screen in Caesar's direction. As Caesar read, Sean lifted his coffee cup up and drained the last few drops.

"Cheer up, we're the good guys," Caesar said, forcing a smile as he reviewed the project details. A human-rights lawyer being black-mailed, his personal emails that contained a few too many secrets being held for ransom. "This one is perfect, we can help this guy. Ping the team. We're heading to Sweden." He slapped Sean on the shoulder. "C'mon, this is going to be fun."

SIXTEEN

NSA Texas Cryptologic Center
San Antonio, TX
October 28th, 10:54AM

Haylie beamed, soaking in the technology from all directions as she slid into the seat next to Mary at the heart of the NSA's command center. Dozens of workstations were arranged in semicircles around the perimeter, all facing the giant wall of screens at the front of the room. Agents turned to take in the spectacle forming behind them—two notorious hackers sitting just feet away—with looks that said: "I didn't expect this when I walked into work today."

Haylie resisted the urge to reach out for the keyboard in front of her and just hover her hands over the keys and feel the slick black plastic under her fingertips. She looked over at Mary, who was angled towards the glow from the row of windows on the other side of the room. The view wasn't anything to write home about—a parking lot, littered with off-white sedans and with a chain-link fence supporting lines of razor wire above—but Mary balanced her chin on her palm, staring at the sky, happy as a clam.

"Let's not be shy, ladies," Agent Wilcox said as she approached. "I just received authorization from my supervisor and the Lord above to grant full access for both of you, heaven help us. I want you to use that machine however you see fit, as long as I'm watching." Wilcox shot a poisonous glance over to Agent Hernandez. "And I *will* be watching."

Mary grinned, turning from the window, the sunlight illuminating the wrinkles branching out from the corners of her mouth. She nodded her head at Haylie and then down to the laptop.

Haylie reached out to the keyboard, extending her fingers. *I can do anything I want. Anything.* She cracked her knuckles, closing her eyes, her heart pounding.

"Where do you want to start?" Mary asked. "What do we have to work with?"

Haylie sat up in her chair, pushing her glasses back into place. "Let's begin with the healthcare hack. I can write a script to index the log files from Patriarch, compare them to the ones from the Xasis hack. With any luck, the Endling left the same pattern behind on both."

"That's good, but I've got another idea," Mary said. "Let's chart our own course. Let's walk through the problem at a high level, not rush into the tech side of the answer. Never spin yourself in circles on work you don't have to do."

"What do you mean?" Haylie asked, sitting back in her chair.

"Let's take ourselves through the Endling's journey so far," Mary said. "Walk me through it."

"The credit card company, that was his first test. He was trying to break through, trying to see if he could actually do it. It was brute force, not elegance."

"Good. What's next?"

"Xasis. Tough security, but he found a hole. Took a back way in.

Went through an unsecured server at a satellite location. Getting better, but still working around the edges."

"And what about Patriarch?" Mary asked.

Haylie could see Agent Wilcox leaning in towards her, giving Hernandez a look as he did the same.

"Patriarch," Haylie repeated. "From what the files say, that one he knew he could get into. He grabbed everything he could. And this time, he went public with the calling card, he didn't just leave it on the internal systems for the FBI to find. It was on the homepage."

"Why?"

"He was pissed off that the press hadn't started talking about him after the Xasis. He didn't want to take the chance of that happening again."

"He's growing bolder, yes?" Mary said.

"He is," Haylie said. "But also better. The Xasis casino took persistence, but the actual exploit was relatively trivial. The Patriarch hack was a backdoor, something you could find on the black market, but you still need to know what you're doing once you're inside. He's getting more comfortable."

"Where do you think he is?"

"Somewhere here, in the U.S., definitely. His use of language, his targets. I'd guess a large city in the U.S."

"Why a large city?"

"He needs to be able to go unnoticed. Disappear. In small towns, people talk. People know your name. If you spend your days and nights cooped up in your room with nothing but machines around you, people will start asking questions."

"So where do we find him?"

Haylie looked around the room, seeing all eyes on her. She flinched when she saw that all the analysts from every corner of the room had stopped what they were doing to listen in.

A mist of sweat formed on the back of her neck. Her throat closed up—she shut her eyes as her heart pounded deep in her chest. *Stop looking at me.*

Stop looking at me.

"We need a starting point, Crash," Mary said. "What do we do? Where do we begin?"

"There's..." Haylie did her best to stammer out her thoughts. "He's got to be out there ... looking for his next hack. That means he'll be using tech to store notes and plans—online storage locations, things like that."

"Too wide of a target," Mary said. "Even if we could get access to every online Dropbox in the world, it would take years to comb through them."

Haylie's eyes darted through the room as the crowd still hung on her every word. Their whispers felt like a weight pushing her down into her chair, causing her shoulders and back to ache. "We send him a payload—a file, something with his name on it. He'd have to click on that, right? To find out what's inside?"

Mary smiled and sat back. "But we don't know who he is, dear. If we knew that, this whole thing would be over in a few hours."

"I don't know," Haylie said. She put her fingers to her temples as she thought, slumping in her chair. "I just don't know."

"Sure you do, dear. Just say whatever's on your mind. It all matters. It all matters."

Haylie swallowed a dry gulp of air. She looked down at the keyboard, trying to push the room out of her mind, trying to focus.

Mary whispered. "Silence sometimes speaks louder than any voice. I can't think with them here, either, Crash. But we must. We have to push through, ignore the others. Let's talk about the silence. We checked those forums. Why wasn't he posting there?"

"I don't know," Haylie said. "For the first time in his life, he feels like he's in the zone. He's getting into systems he never dreamed of before."

"Mmm," Mary said, nodding. "That's what I love about silence. It's relative—it's not absolute. Silence from the Endling doesn't mean he's not speaking. Maybe it just means we're listening in the wrong places."

Haylie turned her head, looking Mary in the eyes. "What do you mean?"

Haylie looked around the room, all eyes still on her, and sat up. Glancing down at the laptop screen, her mind began to race. "The forums," Haylie said. "This isn't a guy with friends. This isn't a guy who goes to meetups or hangs out to talk technology. He needs an outlet; it has to be online, somewhere."

Mary nodded. "A place where people won't judge him. Make fun of him."

"Beginner sites," Haylie said with a spark in her eye. "HackLite, ExploitZone, even Brux—places where people go to learn," Haylie said, putting it all together. "We were mining advanced communities. People on the inside, discussions between some of the top hackers in the world. But that's not *his* world. We were looking in the wrong place."

Mary smiled. "So it seems we'll need to..."

"I'm going to need to write a script," Haylie said, staring off into the distance, a smile cracking through. "Natural language processing. Analyzing text patterns from beginner forum posts that match his behavior. Going back for the past couple of years."

"Just what I was thinking," Mary said, gesturing down at the laptop. "How long have you been waiting to write something like that?"

"Months," Haylie beamed. "But it feels like years."

"Well, don't let me get in your way. Let's get started."

———

University of Texas
Austin, TX

A rare, welcome rain streaked down the other side of the glass as Haylie sat, knees pulled into her chest, walking back through her day. "Think how happy those trees must be right now," Haylie could hear her mom saying, like she did every time a surprise storm rolled in. "They must love the rain."

The room grew dark as the clouds collected overhead, gray swirls rolling through the sky. A lone lamp across her room shone a spotlight down onto her empty desk, clear of any cords or connections, just one neat stack of paper notebooks next to a University of Texas mug full of an assortment of pens.

It was during quiet times like this that she wondered about her brother. *Where is he? Out there, somewhere. Helping people.*

She thought about her afternoon at the NSA. She and Mary had worked for hours, throwing ideas back and forth about how to best track down the Endling from his message board history. That wonderful mix of laughter and accomplishment that just bonded people together, even if they had just met. Haylie had done most of the coding, but Mary was already correcting her syntax as they built out logic. Even though she had left a few hours earlier, Mary's words still echoed through her mind.

"Let's chart our own course."

Haylie pictured Mary sitting politely in her gray prison jumpsuit, white hair pulled down across her temples, staring right into Haylie's eyes, not letting any of it bother her, always staying positive. She thought about everything Mary had told her that day—guiding her, making her think bigger. Not just with technical pieces, but with the entire approach. Mary had a gift for seeing the big picture, something that Haylie knew she needed to learn. And now, she had someone to teach her.

"The truth—that's what's going to set us both free."

She turned back to face the window, watching soaked students, unprepared for the rainstorm, running for cover with textbooks and backpacks held tightly above their heads. Each step sloshed water across the asphalt paths and onto the brown grass, pooling up on either side, the waves and ripples forming short-lived patterns and then smoothing back out to nothing.

Haylie jumped at the sound of a familiar pattern of knocks at the door. "It's open," she yelled back. Vector's face appeared, surrounded by a rush of white light from the hallway. Haylie pivoted from her fetal position to face the door with a wide smile across her face.

"You wouldn't believe the day I've had," she said. "This project— it's so cool. And this ... person ... this person I'm working with. It's just amazing. I can't wait to tell you about it ... at some point, you know? You're going to love it."

"That's great," Vector said, letting his backpack fall to the floor. He took a seat, flicking the water from his hair with a shake of his head. "Sounds like a good day."

"This thing, it's so much better than I thought it was going to be. I mean—I actually have a chance to catch ... whoever it is we're going after. The stuff we're working on, it's just fascinating."

She jumped up from her seat, strolling over towards Vector and sitting on the desk next to him, bobbing her leg up and down with excitement.

"Do you want to read me some headlines?" she asked. "I want to know what's going on out there. Who knows, maybe something from the news will help in the investigation, you know?"

Vector sat silently.

"What is it?" Haylie asked.

"Crash, you were supposed to meet me at Medici. For coffee."

"Oh no ... I'm so sorry." Haylie's face dropped as she realized that she had missed their weekly meet up. "I'm so..."

"I waited for about an hour, maybe more, I don't even know. I shouldn't have stayed that long—I mean, it was obvious that you weren't going to show up after a certain point—but it was raining, you know, and I just wanted to wait it out."

"I got held back," Haylie said, reaching an arm out. "I'm so sorry. I don't have a phone—you know that—and I just—"

"I know, you're busy." Vector's head, cloaked in shadow, barely moved as he spoke. "I get it. But I just wish you wouldn't forget about me in the process."

"Listen," Haylie said, standing. "I'm sorry about the coffee shop, but this is important stuff. If I could tell you, you'd understand all about it."

"About what, the Endling?" Vector asked, raising his head.

Haylie jumped back. *What did I say? How did I already screw this up?* She searched her mind for anything she had said, any clues she had given.

"Don't worry, you didn't say anything," Vector said. "But it's pretty obvious, with you and Hernandez running around like crazy people all the time, mixed with some headlines that are starting to pop up. It wasn't that difficult to put the pieces together."

Relieved, Haylie sunk back into her chair. "I wish you could be part of this. I wish you could help, you'd love it. You're a better hacker than I am by a longshot, and plus, I think you'd get a kick out of it."

"What have you found so far?"

"Unfortunately, not much," she said. "We're just getting started, really. I'm sorry, Vector. I'm sorry that I'm not around as much as usual, but I'll be back. I mean—if you know about the Endling, then you know how important this is."

"Important," Vector said, deadpan. He stood, snatching his backpack off the ground with a quick swipe and walking over to the door. "At least you think something's important in your life. That's good to know."

He turned the knob and slipped through the door, washing the room with a bright rush of light from the hallway. As the door shut behind him, it fell back to black.

Haylie watched the door in silence for minutes, sitting in the dark, hoping—praying—to hear Vector's knock. All she heard were the words in her head, playing back from that morning. Mary's words, swirling in her mind, like the rain pooling on the asphalt below.

SEVENTEEN

Wrigleyville Apartments – 4D
Chicago, IL
October 29th, 1:25PM

I am a beam of light, caked in radiance.

Anthony arranged the windows across his desktop just so, placing the FileDrop location front and center and pushing various hacking forum windows and running scripts onto the screens to his left and right.

I am a method to the madness. I am a path.

The files for the next exploit were late, but he wasn't going to let that bother him, not today. Today, he was on his way to where he had always wanted to be. Besides, he was still running the script for the exploit that he had kicked off last night.

Anthony reached across the desk to pump up the pounding EDM beats as he bobbed his head, keeping careful watch of each window.

Today is the day. I'm ready. Give me the fuel.

The details for last night's hack had arrived early that morning in Anthony's burner email account. It seemed that BridgeLink—the country's largest cable and wireless provider—had a problem with their customer service portal. By simply typing "test" in the lost password "mother's maiden name" field, the site would grant you full access to any account. Some idiot developer had forgotten to remove the test code when putting the site live. All Anthony—or anyone, really—needed was a valid email address in the BridgeLink database.

I am not here by chance. I was placed here. I was created.

The sheep, the chaff, the others: they don't know.

To make that hack substantial, Anthony needed email addresses —lots of them. He had found them in a few different ways: some he had downloaded from forums, collected by hackers for dictionary attacks against major sites; others he had purchased from marketing firms scattered across the internet. Emails are surprisingly easy to buy since so many contests and giveaways were designed to just collect contact information and sell it off to the highest bidder.

How many people have lived—throughout all of time? About one hundred billion? And how many of those do people know about? Even their names, let alone the great feats that they've done? Napoleon. Julius Caesar. Jesus Christ. Maybe three hundred? Four hundred, if you're lucky? Out of all those souls?

It's not just because people forget; it's that most people don't do great things. Not even close. They consume. They waste oxygen. And then they die.

With both the exploit and a list of emails, all he had needed to do was to ping BridgeLink's servers from multiple machines across the globe with random timing patterns. He figured that, with Bridge-Link's monopoly on cable television and internet, within a few days he could collect around thirty to forty percent of the personal information of people in Virginia, Ohio, Florida, Pennsylvania, and Michigan from this hack alone. And that's exactly what his scripts were doing right now—pinging, collecting, and then moving on to the next victim.

But the details of the next hack were still late. Anthony checked the file location again, hitting refresh. Still nothing.

Don't give up on me now. We're doing so well. We're growing into something no one ever saw coming.

The agreement said very plainly that the files would be in the FileDrop location by 1 p.m. Central. Maybe they were running into problems. After all, these men who were paying him, they were mere mortals. They wouldn't know perfection like Anthony did. He couldn't expect them to be as focused as he was, day in and day out.

I follow orders, but it's not the orders that matter. It's me. I'll be here after they're here. I'll be known after they're forgotten.

Anthony tapped the desktop with jittery fingers as his eyes flicked from monitor to monitor. No files in the Dropbox.

Eight minutes late now. Don't cut me off, not now. We're just getting started. We're just getting warmed up.

The money was in his account, that he knew. Half of the money always came before the files. Quick and easy. Anthony looked back to the empty file drop location, sucking in deep breaths as his pulse raced through his veins. He pushed his chair back, stood, paced in front of his desk.

He thought back to the single verbal conversation with the man calling the shots—both sides masking their voices with software. To actually speak to him, to hear him describe the next few steps, even offering a few pieces of encouragement, had been enlightening. Exhilarating.

"It's fine. Everything's fine," he whispered, raising his voice just enough so that he could hear his own words over the pounding music. The scripts continued showing each name and data collection status, then moving on to the next. They wouldn't stop until they were told to stop, but he knew he needed more. He couldn't wait.

"We're doing such wonderful things. We're in this together. We're running in lock step. We're dancing, you and I. Don't cut me off." He ran his hands through his hair as he leaned back, stretching his spine, trying to relieve the tension.

I'm going to be one of those—the remembered. I have to be one of those. Why else would I be here?

He paced heavily, his stomps growing louder, boots hitting hardwood. He walked from one corner of the room to the other, keeping his eyes on the floor.

"We're doing so well together," he said. "We've been out fishing and having such a good day. The fish are biting. We just need more bait. Give me more bait."

I want this one to be big. Please, make this one big. We're building towards that, aren't we? That has to be where we are headed. Hand in hand.

"But I can't do it without the instructions!" Anthony shouted, his face growing red, leaning back over the desktop. "I need to be in on the plan. Let. Me. In. That was the deal ... We had a deal!"

Still perched above his keyboard, arms extended and palms flat on the desk, Anthony turned his head over to face the far wall. There, he saw the framed, broken magazine cover with Haylie Black's face looking back at him. His eyes narrowed as his focus drifted from her face to the smears of blood now dried on the glass and down the edges of the frame.

"This will be my Haylie Black moment," he said, nodding to himself as he ground his teeth, the music continuing to pound in the background, shaking the keyboard under his fingers with each beat. "I see you, Crash. But all you are is vapor. *Vapor.* You weren't meant to be where you are. You were a *mistake.* And I hate mistakes."

A ping came from his laptop's speakers and Anthony twisted back towards his machine. He brought the file drop window to full screen and leaned in close to the monitor, close enough to make out the edges of a few individual pixels around the text label of a single file. It was just sitting there in the Dropbox location, labeled 'four,' waiting for him to click.

One simple, glorious file.

Anthony opened the document as he slid back into his chair. As he studied each word of the instructions, a twisting laugh rolled from his belly and was met with tears that welled in the corners of his eyes.

"Oh my," Anthony said. "You're a big fish, aren't you?"

EIGHTEEN

"Show me what you've got," Agent Wilcox asked, reviewing the report handed to her seconds earlier.

Haylie cleared her throat, pointed up at the screens on the far wall. Agents Wilcox and Hernandez gave her their full attention, along with the few other new government officials—all wearing matching charcoal suits—who had come in for the update. The monitors displayed a collection of data from hacker message boards: single messages, user profiles, and a few open threads.

"We built a script pinging entry-level hacker forums for posting patterns," Haylie explained. "We matched newer posts on subject matter that lines up to the latest string of hacks to a full catalog of older posts."

Agent Hernandez was the first to speak up. "I don't get it."

"Sorry," Haylie said, looking over to Mary. "It's simple, really."

"This had better be legal," Agent Wilcox said, eying the suits standing around her. "My instructions were clear in that area."

"It's fine," Haylie said. "Mary, do you want to tell them?"

"No, dear," Mary said with a smile. "You go ahead. You're the one who ended up finding the language patterns that—"

"Could one of you please just tell us what the hell is going on here?" Agent Wilcox said with a raised voice. "In English?"

Haylie nodded. "Here's the deal. We can tell the Endling is new at this based on what he does once he's inside each system. So we looked for posts on hacker boards that asked about some of his recent exploits. We then used natural language processing—"

"*English*," Hernandez repeated.

"We think we found a bunch of posts from him from over the past few years. And not just a high number, but *long* posts. He goes on and on in these write-ups—he writes four or five paragraphs when others are writing quick one or two sentence blurbs. We matched his communication patterns with older messages on the boards from all different accounts, assuming he created a new one every few months. His newer accounts were pretty well locked down, but with those early accounts—when he was just getting started—we figured he'd be more likely to have let his guard down without even knowing it."

Agent Wilcox nodded. "So, you've got him?"

"Yes and no," Haylie said. "I ran language pattern checks across a majority of the posts for the last eight months, and these six accounts were a match for length, word choice, and punctuation. We've used the script to identify his current account, but we can't get a location from him. He's smarter now, using the Tor network to mask his location."

"I don't see anything here," Agent Wilcox said. "Why did you bring us in here?"

"Well, we *might* have him," Haylie said.

"What are you talking about?" Agent Hernandez jumped in. "Details, please?"

Haylie eyed the collection of NSA brass as she chose her next words carefully. "We can't get a location on him, but we know his user account. If the NSA happened to have a platform—like you're rumored to have—where you can target malicious ad banners at users, then with admin access to these forums, we'll be able to take over his machine."

"Ad banners?" Agent Hernandez asked. "Why would the NSA have anything like that?"

"There was a news story recently," Haylie said. "Vector told me about it—all about a malvertising platform that's out in the wild. People were guessing the NSA was behind it."

"I'm not in the ad business," Agent Wilcox said, doing a quick check of the company around her. "If I were, I'd get paid a lot more. And, besides, that would be—"

"Illegal, I know," Haylie said. She turned back to a confused Agent Hernandez. "Malvertising takes over a website's ad banner network. It serves up viruses to users through those ads, attacking you from a site that you trust. Users don't even see it happening. If the NSA does have one of these platforms, now would be a good time to use it."

"Roar-4." Mary's voice echoed through the room as all heads turned her way. "The NSA's platform is called Roar-4. It downloads a Trojan to the user's machine and uses a known vulnerability called 'drive-by downloading,' where we can trigger his machine to execute files without alerting him with even as much as a pop-up."

Hernandez stared at Mary as the room fell silent. "How do you—"

"This isn't the first time the NSA has asked for my help, isn't that right, Agent Wilcox?"

Agent Wilcox sat back in her chair, her hands folded over her lap.

"What can it access?" Haylie asked.

Mary opened her mouth to answer but was cut off.

"It monitors all keystrokes," Agent Wilcox said, softly. "Gives us access to the webcam, audio, and screencasting capabilities. It has its own API—once it's fully installed, we can just send it commands and ask for data back."

Haylie considered the implications. "Can you install it here?" She pointed up at the screen. "On any of these hacking forums?"

Agent Wilcox stared at Haylie in silence.

"The thing Agent Wilcox doesn't want to say," Mary said, "is that Roar-4 is *already on* those hacking forums. And thousands of other sites across the internet."

"You've got to be kidding me," Haylie said, pushing back from the desk.

But—that's criminal. The people on these sites haven't done anything wrong. There are no warrants, no judge or jury.

Agent Wilcox nodded in agreement. "The Roar-4 project has been active for the past year or so. The number of active installs is classified."

"So if we can get this virus on his machine," Agent Hernandez asked Wilcox. "We should be able to track him down, right?"

"We just need his user ID," Agent Wilcox said.

Mary scribbled on a scrap of paper and handed it over to a waiting analyst. The analyst turned to her machine and, typing in the forum's user identification number with a few keystrokes, brought up a new window on the main screen. She cycled through a few command line instructions as the room waited and watched.

A few seconds later, a video feed went live, rendering slowly, showing the edges and corners of a darkened room. Haylie could discern the outlines of distant light bulbs in the background, all strung down like a grapevine, illuminating part of a wall and a light switch. Grays and blacks filled the remainder of the frame, except for the man at the center. Poorly lit by only his LCD monitor, his pale white skin made him look like a ghost floating in the darkness. He leaned in, eyes flicking left and right across the camera, his wavy, gelled hair combed back. His expression was lifeless as he mouthed words to himself, blinking in bursts.

Haylie stared into his eyes, watching every movement.

Hello, Endling.

She heard the squeal of a chair pulling back as Agent Hernandez stood and took a few steps towards the screen. He pointed up to at the image.

"Can ... Can he see us?" Hernandez stammered. "Does he know we're watching?"

"Don't worry," Mary said. "He has no idea what's going on. Completely clueless."

"Any matches with the facial recognition database?" Agent Wilcox asked the NSA analyst. "Any location data?"

"No matching mug shot in our system," the analyst replied. "Looks like this is his first rodeo."

"We can't get his location via IP address," Mary said. "He's masking that. But we can check his hard drive. Browsing history, documents." She yelled over to the NSA analyst. "Let's grab everything we can."

The analyst nodded, typing away at the keyboard. A progress bar appeared, showing a slow crawl copying every file over to the NSA's local servers. As soon as the job pinged 'complete,' the analyst dove in.

"Here we go," the analyst said, scrolling through a list of documents. "Spreadsheets. Applications. Music files. Lists and notes. Address book. A few—"

"Hold it right there," Haylie yelled, pointing at the screen. "The notes application. Bring that up."

The analyst stopped and double-clicked into the folder, scrolling through a list of to-dos, notes labeled 'random thoughts,' 'blog post ideas,' 'coffee shops.'

"There!" Haylie said. "Coffee shops. That's it."

The list appeared on the screen as the analyst looked back to her.

Ground Trooth
Caffeine Palace
Coffee Nation XL
Boystown Coffee

The list went on and on.

Mary looked up from her keyboard at a search result list. "These are all in the downtown Chicago area. I'm guessing he uses those—"

"For his attacks," Haylie said. "He's using a different location for each new exploit. Never two hacks from the same place. That's what I would do, anyway."

"If I was going to start searching," Mary said. "I'd start here. Work my way down the list."

"Let's get on a plane," Agent Wilcox said. "We're heading to Chicago. Ms. Black—you're coming with us. I want you on the ground."

Haylie stepped back. *What?*

"Mary has been running me through all the help you've been providing," Wilcox said. She pointed up the screen. "Told me how none of this would have been possible without your input."

Haylie's eyes fell down on Mary, who gave her a smile. The motion from the video looming over them showed the Endling scratching his chin and mouthing words they couldn't hear. He leaned in towards them with dead eyes.

"When we find this guy," Agent Wilcox said. "We're going to need someone there to help guide our interrogation. Ask him the right questions."

"Why do we need to go?" Haylie said. "Don't you have agents up there?"

"We see our investigations through," Wilcox shot back. "And it's going to be faster for me to jump on a plane than spend eight hours walking a bunch of Yankees through the details. Trust me, I wish that wasn't the case. Besides—this isn't a sure thing yet; we still have work to do once we land, to actually find him."

"I think Mary should go," Haylie said. "She's—"

"Mary stays here," Wilcox said with authority. She turned to the rest of the room. "We're wasting time. C'mon people, let's go get this guy."

NINETEEN

The mid-afternoon crowd was a mix of young locals and wide-eyed tourists, all beginning to slow down a bit after a day of walking the hills of Stockholm's Old City. Caesar sat in the back of a pitch-black pub—carved out of a wall somewhere at the tail end of a sloped alley, waiting.

He stirred his ice water with his straw, keeping his eyes glued to the door. He flipped his phone over on the table, checking the time.

Fifteen minutes late. No—sixteen. When should I start to get worried?

He snatched the crumpled English-language newspaper off the bench and held it up close to his eyes, trying to make out the headline in the darkness.

HACKER CELLS
RAIDED IN MINNEAPOLIS

"Hacker cells," Caesar whispered under his breath. "That's a new one. What does that even mean?"

He brought up his phone and checked the status of Haylie's ankle bracelet, something that had become his new version of social media over the past few weeks. Just to make sure that light was still blinking. The location honed in on a complex just northwest of downtown San Antonio.

Hmm ... Maybe she's on a day trip?

He laid his phone down and slid the oil from the newsprint between his fingers. The past few days hadn't been any better than the ones before: shaking off suspicious looks at the border when they presented their fake passports, Phillip getting spooked at the hotel by a man sitting in the corner of the lobby for more than an hour. It was the little things that scared him these days. And there were little things everywhere.

Momentum—that's all we need. Once we get that under our belts and Hancock is out of the picture, we can get back to doing what we're good at.

The door cracked open, spilling white light across Caesar's view. Caesar rubbed his eyes and as his vision returned, Sean appeared at the rail in front of him.

"You're late," Caesar said, sliding down the bench to give Sean some room. "Where are the others? I almost ordered for everyone, but wasn't sure if it was too late for coffee."

Sean slid in, not saying a word, and motioned over to the waiter. He ordered a beer and picked up the newspaper, staring through the headlines and tossing it back on the bar.

"I've got a new plan," Caesar said. "After Eagle is all said and done, we head for someplace nice. The Caymans—a place where there's enough civilization to stay online, but far enough away from all of this. Give the team that break we've been talking about, they deserve it."

"They're gone," Sean muttered, staring back at his own reflection in the mirror behind the bar.

Caesar waited for Sean to elaborate, but got nothing. The bartender slid Sean's beer in front of him and glided away to the other side of the bar.

"What do you mean?" Caesar asked, looking down at the newspaper. "This Minneapolis thing? It's nothing—probably just some script kiddies, the feds just want to get some good headlines in before—"

"Not Minneapolis," Sean said, raising his voice and throwing the newspaper back at Caesar. "I don't care about that. I'm talking about Phillip and Margo."

Caesar looked down at the faded wood of the bar and ran his finger across the water beading on the surface. He knew this would happen—just didn't know when. All he could manage was a single word.

"How?"

"How?" Sean spat back. "I'll tell you *how*, they just left. It was that simple. They walked away, said they'd had enough. And I'll tell you the truth: I was tempted to follow them out the door."

Caesar's heart sank. He felt the walls begin to ratchet slowly in towards him, the light fading, the darkness winning. His eyes darted frantically around the room, looking for something to focus on, but seeing only black. If they were gone, Sean could be next. And he knew he couldn't do this alone.

Did he get to them—Hancock? Is he on the inside now? If he got to them then he can get to Sean. He can get to me.

"Where do you think they..." Caesar stuttered, trying to keep the conversation going, but coming up blank with what to say next.

"We need to figure out what we're doing here, man," Sean said. "You picked a fight with a U.S. senator and you're losing. Our team is getting whittled away—that's exactly what he wants. You never should have hacked those records."

"I'm going to take care of it," Caesar shot back. "The whole thing. I'm on it. I told the team that, I told them every time they asked."

"Yeah, well maybe they got tired of asking."

"Nobody said this was going to be easy. We just need to make it through this stretch."

Caesar stared at himself in the mirror. He looked tired—his hair beginning to show flashes of gray. Bags under his eyes. He didn't used to look this tired.

"You're not going to leave, too, are you?" Caesar muttered.

"You think I'd be sitting here if I was? I believe in what we're doing—I believe it's right. I don't want to do anything else with my life now that I've seen this side of things. We'll get there—it's just you and me now. We're going to see this through, and you're right, it's clear sailing on the other side. I can see it; it's close."

"We have the Project code," Caesar said. "We can do whatever we want, whenever we want."

Sean looked back, a look of fear growing in his eyes.

"I'm not going to jail," Caesar said. "No way. I can't do it—I won't do it. Doesn't matter what I have to do."

"Don't get crazy, man," Sean said. "We said we were going to keep this clean, and that hasn't changed."

"It's not going to be easy," Caesar said, "pulling this off with just the two of us. We'll be working on this thing nonstop until it's done."

Nodding, Sean took a sip. "Losing the team doesn't help, but it won't be impossible. It'll just be complicated."

"You know what they say?" Caesar said. "A complicated thing is just—"

"Shut up," Sean said. "Nobody says that. You're the only person in the world who says that." He drained the last of his drink and stood with a clap of his hands, amping himself up like he was about to jump into a brawl. "We've got work to do. The first thing, just to be safe, is to get the hell out of Stockholm."

———

Caffeine Palace
Chicago
October 30th, 8:52AM

The grinding and pounding shook through Anthony's feet, traveling like a tidal wave across the uneven hardwood floors, all the way back into his far corner. The barista smiled and laughed with what must have been a regular customer across the counter, flipping switches on the espresso machine as the steam flowed up her face. Anthony watched them, wondering what on earth they could be so happy about.

Nobody is that happy. Not on the inside.

Anthony turned back to his laptop. He had nestled himself at the short end of a corner couch, facing an old tube television that was pushed against the wall, now repurposed as a chunky end table. He winced at the salsa music blaring out of the speaker directly above him as he fought to keep his concentration.

He gazed back towards the front of the coffee shop, to the bright white glow of the sunlight visible through the glass of the front façade. Between him and there, he saw a group of three young men at the table across from the barista—a mix of hoodies, knit caps, and baseball hats. One had a PowerPoint presentation up on his screen; Anthony could just make out the words "business plan" and "new app marketplace." He watched as the men leaned in across the table with excited eyes and optimism.

Not that long ago, Anthony had been one of them—his heart full of what the future might hold. His days and nights spent writing code and designing apps that would change the world—at least, *his* world.

I was in the middle; always in the middle. I was stuck right there where everyone could see me. Waiting for someone to offer a hand. Just one conversation would have changed my whole life.

But he had been told one too many times that he wasn't good enough. Go code for a few more years, maybe you'll be ready. You need to start a business before you can run a business. Maybe get an MBA, make some contacts. And at every tech meetup he had dragged himself to, he only found himself huddled in the corner, petrified to speak. Not knowing what to say, or who to talk to, sipping his ice water just watching the crowd. The crowd always seemed so confident, so successful. So distant, like they lived behind a long wall of glass with no edge to walk around, no door to sneak through or over or under.

It's a walled garden—you need to have an Ivy League pedigree or an in with the right crowd. It's not about the best ideas or the best people, it's about who you know. That's all it is. The deck is stacked against me. But I know I deserve this. I know what I know.

Anthony watched the three men at the table laugh at a punchline and pass the laptop around, each taking a turn at the keyboard. He thought back to his app, the one that never actually made it as far as the App Store. Maybe they were right. Maybe he just hadn't been ready.

But I'm ready now.

Pulling his laptop from his bag, Anthony logged into his machine, took a sip of coffee, and began preparing for the biggest hack of his life.

TWENTY

Corner of Randolph and LaSalle
Chicago, IL
October 30th, 8:54AM

Haylie blew on her hands, pulling the lapels of her field jacket closer, and bobbed up and down for warmth. She, along with Agent Wilcox, Agent Hernandez, and two other federal agents, had been huddled inside the mobile surveillance van since 6:00 a.m. that morning, waiting. Her breath pushed back from her fingers and sent a fog across her glasses. As the moisture drifted away, she squinted at one of the monitors bolted to the side of the van's interior.

"Wait," Haylie said, walking towards the screen. "He's online."

"What's it showing?" Agent Hernandez asked, checking the monitor. "Is there a location?"

"No, he's masking his IP," Haylie said. "No location data. Not yet."

"Driver, first location," Agent Wilcox yelled up to the front of the cabin.

The van careened to the side as Haylie held on for dear life. As soon as she felt steady, she stood up halfway, her knees flexed, to get a live view of the Endling's screen.

"Where are we going?" Haylie yelled.

"With no location, our best bet is to tick down his list of coffee shops," Wilcox yelled back. "They're just a few minutes away from each other."

"What else do you have, Haylie?" Agent Hernandez yelled as the van took a sharp right, sending a few pens and notebooks flying in the other direction.

"I've got audio coming through his microphone," Haylie said. "Based on the levels, there must be a loud music source near him. Mary, it's loud as hell in this van, can you confirm that?"

The radio crackled as Mary's voice came through. "That's correct. Hearing salsa music." Mary was set up back in San Antonio with access to everything she needed—the Endling's machine, Roar-4 utilities, and a laptop, plus a team of NSA agents surrounding her, watching her like a hawk.

The cursor moved across the screen, opening the main application folder and working its way down. It highlighted an item labeled Cryzip and double-clicked.

"He's opening a crypter application," Haylie said. "There's a no-IP account being set up. He's opening up port 1604..."

He's doing it. This is it.

"What does that mean?" Agent Hernandez asked.

"He's getting ready," Haylie said, turning to face the others, holding on to the railing. "He's setting up a remote access tool. He's got all the tools he needs to mask his identity once he gets in."

"A remote access tool," Agent Wilcox said. "What's that going to give him?"

"He'd have full control over whatever system he's going after," Haylie said. "Anything he wants."

"What's the target?" Agent Hernandez asked.

"I'm waiting for him to give that away," Haylie said, her eyes glued to the screen. "Right now, I don't know. Not yet."

———

Just think what it's like. Just think what it will be like when everybody knows your name. It's going to be a brand new world. You'll be a new man—the man you've always known you are.

Finally.

Anthony fished two notes out of his pockets, each written in different handwriting—one with his left hand, one with his right. He had to think for a moment before remembering which was the username and which was the password. He typed them into his Notepad application, just in case he needed them a second time. Bringing up the remote access window, he cut and pasted them into the login prompt along with the target IP address that he had memorized earlier that morning.

Once you break through this wall—this wall that they've put up around you, the one you're not supposed to get through—then they'll all see how wrong they were. They'll beg you to join them. They'll line up around the block.

But first, you have work to do.

———

"I've got a target for the attack," Haylie shouted. She pointed with a few jabs of her finger over to the agent with an active laptop, yelling the digits of each number as she read them from the screen.

"173... 205... 126... 123..."

The agent hit a hard thump on the return key, everyone in the van gathered around to see the result, hanging on to the sides of the van as they bounced and swayed through the streets of Chicago.

"It's a government system," the agent said. "Give me a minute ... looks like it might be the Office of Personnel Management."

"Good lord, the OPM," Agent Wilcox said, dialing her phone and placing it to her ear.

"What's the OPM?" Haylie asked.

"He's going after a government personnel database," Agent Hernandez said, the worry growing across his face. "*The* government database. The data for every single government employee. Agents, leadership, undercover operatives—everyone."

"That son of a bitch," Wilcox muttered. "Any new information? You seeing anything on the webcam, something that would tell us where he is?"

"Not seeing any markers here," Hernandez said, his eyes inches away from the live feed of the Endling huddled over his machine. "Just a few pieces of generic artwork. No signs, nothing like that."

Haylie looked back to the live stream of the Endling's screen, watching the tools go to work. *He's got the username and password again, but this time he's covering his tracks. He's getting better.*

"He's in the system," she yelled. "He's making his way through the file directory right now."

"We need a location!" Agent Wilcox yelled, phone still pressed to her ear.

"I can't see where he is," Haylie said. "But it's a good bet that he's at one of the coffee shops on the list."

"How long do we have before he starts pulling data?" Wilcox asked.

"Not long—as soon as he finds what he came for, he'll have full access to download anything he wants."

"Faster!" Wilcox yelled towards the front of the van. "I need that location. We can't be guessing at this point—we're running out of time." She pushed her phone back to her ear, screaming commands to the agents back in San Antonio over the chatter throughout the van.

"And everyone quiet down, I can't hear myself think in here, I swear."

Agent Wilcox's words echoed through Haylie's head, why, she wasn't sure. She crouched into the corner, pulling her sleeves down over her hands. She closed her eyes.

Hear myself think. Hear myself think.

Hear.

Hear.

Hear.

Her eyes flew open.

We've got his video and microphone.

"Wait," Haylie said. "You said the Roar-4 virus was widespread—this isn't the first time the NSA has deployed it, right? How many installs are there?"

Agent Wilcox put her phone to her side, shifting in her crouched position as the van took a sharp left. "You know I can't talk about that," she said. "It's classified."

"Fine, we'll keep it just between us friends," Haylie shot back. "The virus installs on any computer that visits the site the NSA has infected. How many sites did you put it on?"

"I don't know what you're getting at here," Wilcox said. "And I'm not about to tell you the details of a government—"

"The top twenty sites across the internet," Agent Hernandez yelled from across the van. "From what I've read, based on a collection of different operations over the past year, it wouldn't be crazy to say that ten, maybe fifteen percent of computers in the U.S. have the Roar-4 virus installed."

Wilcox stared him down from the other side of the van, shaking her head in disbelief.

"With those numbers," Haylie said, "there's a good chance there's another laptop in the coffee shop with the Roar-4 virus installed, right?"

"So?" Agent Wilcox said.

Haylie grabbed yelled over to the radio. "Mary! If you can hear me, I need you to access every machine infected with Roar-4 in the Chicago area. Every single one."

"What are you doing?" Wilcox yelled back to Haylie over the screech of tires.

"We're going to stop looking for the Endling. We need to start listening." A smile grew across Haylie's face as she mentally pieced together her plan.

"Sure beats sitting in a dorm room, right?" Hernandez yelled.

"Hell, yes," Haylie yelled back.

Anthony checked his setup one last time, making sure everything was like the forums had detailed. *I'm invisible. They'll never see me coming. I'm a ghost.* He brought up the remote access tool and began to type in the stolen credentials.

This will be my legacy.

"Mary, are you there?" Agent Wilcox yelled over the speakerphone. "What have you found?"

"I'm getting some results back, but I'm not sure this is the full list," Mary's voice chimed over the speakerphone. "How many are there?"

"Not important," Wilcox said. "Why does everyone keep asking that? It doesn't matter. Just turn them all on."

"We need audio patterns," Haylie said. "The salsa music in the coffee shop. You're looking for any matches for the background sound patterns. If you find a match—"

"Then we can get the location from the other laptops showing that signal," Mary's voice sounded over the speaker, along with furious keystrokes in the background. "They won't be masking their IPs. Not bad, Crash."

Wilcox didn't show the same sense of excitement. "How long's this going to take?"

"I'm activating the Roar-4 network," Mary said. "Pinging machines. I'm seeing a count of about twelve hundred across the Chicago metropolitan area."

"Good lord," Haylie whispered.

"Grabbing audio feeds now," Mary said. "This will take a minute. But I'm still not sure what I'm going to do with it once I get all them all. I've never done something like this. Everybody buckle up."

———

As the personnel files began to download, Anthony focused on the pixels of the progress bar, creeping slowly, methodically, left to right.

File download in progress
Estimated completion: 7min 36secs

He grabbed his mug of coffee by the handle and raised it to his lips, taking a deep sip.

———

The van wove through the streets of Chicago, edging its way closer to the first coffee shop on the list, block by block.

"Mary—give me a status," Agent Wilcox said, raising her voice over the sounds of the road. "I'm blind over here."

"I'm looking for a good audio comparison package," Mary said between long pauses. "I'm finding a lot of tools that compare two tracks, but nothing at this scale. Nothing for over a thousand live audio feeds—I'm not even sure anyone has tried this before."

Wilcox muted the phone. "I thought you two were supposed to be good at this," she said in Haylie's direction.

"I thought you guys weren't supposed to spy on innocent citizens," Haylie shot back without flinching. "Looks like we're both having an off day."

"Let's just start checking individual feeds," Hernandez said. "I mean, it's better than not looking at all, right? At least that gives us a chance—it's a start."

"What do you think, Haylie?" Mary's voice rang out over the speakerphone. "What would you do?"

I don't know. I don't know.

Haylie's heart pounded louder, car horns sounding around her, her mind racing.

"I don't know that much about audio," Haylie said, her head in her hands, thinking. "I'm not sure what's out there."

"Forget about the audio," Mary's voice rose to a shout. "Think bigger. Focus on what we need."

We need rapid pattern matching. Across thousands of backgrounds.

Focus on what we need.

Focus on what we need.

Of course.

"Wait," Haylie said, raising her head. "I think I've got it."

TWENTY-ONE

Caffeine Palace
Chicago
October 30th, 8:59AM

Anthony froze, realizing he had been tapping his fingers to the beat of the godforsaken salsa music still piercing his eardrums. He looked over at the line of people beginning to form in front of the register. Some comfortably paired up, chatting with friends. Others looking down to their screens, losing themselves in social media. *They're all sheep. They haven't found their path.*

File download in progress
Estimated completion: 5min 12secs

Tabbing over to his favorite hacking forum, Anthony typed in "The Endling" and scanned the most recent result.

.

"What's going on?" Agent Wilcox asked, muting the phone and pointing down to its screen. "What did you just tell her to do?

"It's a shortcut," Haylie said. "Our problem isn't really about audio processing, it's about pattern recognition. We need to find similar audio patterns from the machines we have across Chicago."

"That's what Mary was already looking for, right?" Agent Hernandez yelled over the rush of traffic. "She said there aren't any tools that can do it."

"No *audio* tools," Haylie said. "If we can take a sample of every Roar-4 background across Chicago in the same two- or three-second chunks and analyze their wavelengths, we can use image recognition to find similar patterns."

"Image recognition?" Hernandez said. "Really? That will work?"

"Why not?" Haylie said. "There are tons of coding packages that can do high-volume image pattern recognition."

"I've got it set up over here," Mary said across the line. "I'm grabbing samples now and loading up—"

"Use the Pitchfork package," Haylie added. "It's the best one for high-speed batch image processing."

Haylie heard chuckling over the line, mixed with rapid keystrokes. "You've got it, boss. Grabbing it now," Mary said.

Hernandez cracked his laptop open, propping it up on the van's steel shelf next to the view of the Endling's screen. He brought up a livestream of Mary's view, with multiple command line windows open, installing the Pitchfork package on one, and grabbing audio samples on the other. Haylie watched as the Python package worked away, mapping constellations of peaks in each audio signal against others, trying to find a match.

"I've got the samples," Mary's voice rang over the line. "Running the matching script now."

Everyone in the van stood silent, leaning in towards the radio as the clicks of typing keys came across the line.

"No matches," Mary said with an exhale. "I'm going to try again, adjust the match tolerance to check for different levels of background noise. I need more time."

———

Anthony watched the progress bar continue to build as plaintext of each government workers name, social security number, and personal information made its way down to his hard drive.

File download in progress
Estimated completion: 4min 22secs

He glanced back to the door, watching every person skip across the threshold to a chime of bells, unwrapping scarves and hats and coats. Relieved to be in from the cold. Every one of them amounted to nothing more than something that could go wrong for him, a potential risk to his plan.

Stupid Wi-Fi. C'mon c'mon c'mon.

A man waiting for his drink craned his neck around the corner, looking into Anthony's area for a seat. Receiving a nasty look, the man cowered back behind the wall.

He's nobody. He doesn't know. He can't know.

Rubbing the bridge of his nose and taking a deep breath, Anthony felt his pulse slipping back into panic mode. He was getting dragged into a place he didn't want to go—like back at summer camp during the tug of war, when he could feel the burning of the rope across his palms as he twisted to move the flag, knees locked and throbbing. Falling face-down into the mud pit, his fingers burning, the laughter from the crowd echoing off the hills, not stopping until the moment his father opened the door of his stale-smelling station wagon to let him in and finally take him home.

Don't do this. Not now. You're so close.

Anthony closed his eyes and focused his mind back to the only place he felt at home.

I have been here before; I will be here again.

I have been here before; I will be here again.

He could feel the light and dark sides of his mind swirling, bubbling like oil into water.

I have been here before; I will be here again.

It's going to be all right.

You have a job to do, Anthony.

You have a job to do, Endling.

His eyes popped back open and he smiled, throwing his neck back against the chair with relief. He had found what he needed, whatever it was, somewhere in there. He just needed a little time.

Turning back to his screen, he sluggishly tabbed over to a browser to check forums—anything to make the time pass by faster. He clicked on a few of the top links to open multiple tabs and watched as his laptop struggled to keep up, displaying circular "loading" icons in each of the new tabs.

A file transfer shouldn't be taking up this much memory.

Why is this so slow?

———

"He's lagging," Haylie said, fixed on the live feed, shaking her head. "The virus must be weighing down his processor."

"So, maybe it will slow him down," Agent Hernandez said. "Give us more time."

"That's not the problem, Einstein," Haylie said. "If he checks to see what's wrong, he's going to see our webcam process running in the background. Best case for us is he just shuts it off."

"What's the worst case?" Agent Hernandez asked, looking over to Agent Wilcox, who already knew the answer.

"Worst case is: he'll know we're watching him," Wilcox said.

———

Hitting Command-R to refresh each browser tab, Anthony's huffed as he felt the heat from the laptop's casing creep into his palms. *This is taking too long. Too long.* With a few keystrokes, he brought up his network monitor tool to check the Wi-Fi connection speed.

Not great, but seems right for a public router.

Tabbing back to his browser, he refreshed the forum page again with a harder keystroke—as if that would help—watching the different elements of the page load at a snail's pace across the screen.

Slowly, painfully.

———

"I've got a match," Mary's voice yelled over the speaker.

Haylie watched as Mary brought up a live feed of a new desktop background—a cluttered collection of file icons strewn across the screen, arranged on top of the bright-pink desktop wallpaper.

"This doesn't look like the desktop of someone who hides their IP," Mary said. "I'm checking the location—it should at least get us close."

The group watched as Mary brought up the user details from the Roar-4 interface, grabbed the IP address, and did a quick lookup.

"Looks like the north side of the river," Mary said. "Somewhere in the area of LaSalle and Ontario."

"Go!" Agent Wilcox yelled up at the driver, who hit the gas with a screech of rubber. Everyone in the van flew back towards the corner as the vehicle twisted to the right and sped away. "What's the name of this place?"

"Don't have that," Mary said. "We won't get it from an IP address, just general area location. Keep watching that screen, let's see if they self-identify with any chats or searches. I'll keep looking for more infected machines."

———

With a quick combination of Command-spacebar keystrokes, Anthony brought up a search dialog box.

Let's fix whatever is slowing this thing down.

———

Agent Wilcox pinned herself into the corner of the van, clutching her phone with both hands and typing furiously.

"I've got positive hits on four different coffee shops near that intersection," Wilcox said. "That's close enough, we can go one by one if we have to."

Haylie grabbed both sides of the screen and watched as Mary ran the image processing script, updating the settings, searching for patterns. The van took a sharp left and Haylie grabbed the steel equipment rack bolted to the frame, bending with the curve. As they sped forward, she looked over to check the feed from the Endling's screen. A new window popped up.

Oh no.

"This isn't good," Haylie yelled, holding on to the steel rack as the van accelerated. Wilcox and Hernandez leaned in closer to see the Endling typing into a search field at the center of the screen.

Search: Activity Monitor

"He's checking to see what's slowing his machine down," Haylie said, backing away from the screen and reaching for the phone. "Mary! We need his actual location. He's checking his process log; he's going to see the Roar-4 virus running. We're about to run out of time!"

"I've got a new match," Mary said. "I won't wait on any others. I'm bringing it up now."

"How far away are we?" Haylie yelled to the driver.

"Two minutes," the driver yelled back, swerving through traffic. "One, if we're lucky!"

———

Anthony raised his eyebrow as he selected the Activity Monitor program from the list of results. He scanned the list of running programs, sorting by the percentage of CPU in use. Switching over to check his download progress for the OPM files, he cracked a smile.

File download in progress
Estimated completion: 0min 39secs

Tabbing back to the application list, his eyes grew wide as he focused on the process running hot at the top of the list.

———

"Get ready to move!" Agent Wilcox said, putting on her bulletproof vest and double-checking her sidearm was in place.

Haylie stared down at the floor of the van, trying to fight the adrenaline coursing through her veins. She took deep breaths as the agents put on vests and checked their firearms. She looked up to see the Endling scrolling through the Activity Monitor.

"We're not going to get there in time," Haylie said, defeated. "He's going to find it. It's only a matter of time."

"We'll just need a minute or two," Agent Wilcox said. "To get into each of the locations. We know what he looks like, it should be in and out each time."

"Haylie," Mary's voice rang through the van, over the speaker-phone. "Buy them more time. Think. Work the problem."

Haylie closed her eyes, picturing the Endling sitting in the coffee shop, surrounded by strangers. Feeling alone. Feeling nervous. Wanting to be someone, wanting to be known.

When he finds the virus, he's going to panic. He's going to run. What would keep him from running?

She pictured the first calling card: the passenger pigeon. Staring back at her with deep, black eyes. Dead eyes, pixelated, never to be seen again.

Step back.

She imagined the Endling placing the image file on the Xasis server. Checking to make sure it was perfect. Then checking again. Quickly running over to check the forums. To see if it was time yet; time for him to be famous.

Of course.

She jumped to her feet, the van's movement almost knocking her right back down. She grabbed the laptop, bringing up a new window in the NSA's Roar-4 control interface, fighting to maintain her balance.

"What are you doing?" Agent Wilcox yelled

"I'm buying you some time," Haylie said. She scrolled through the command window, finding access settings for the Endling's machine.

>>>Create new alert:
>>>Create new email:

"You want to be famous, asshole?" she whispered as she typed. "I'll make you famous."

———

Each entry in the activity monitor refreshed, dancing across the screen and reordering every few seconds. Anthony struggled to keep up, locking his eyes on a listing and then having it quickly disappear.

He slid his cursor up to sort by CPU usage.

I'll find you, wherever you are.

As he pressed down to click, an alert popped up in the top right corner of his screen.

Email
From: Editor@Wired.com
Subject:
If you are who I think you are,
I think we should talk.
The Endling would make a great cover story.

Anthony froze, quickly surveying the rest of the coffee shop for anyone looking his way. He leaned in towards the top right of his screen, studying each word, reading the subject line again and again. The alert faded away as Anthony sat back, heart pounding.

It's happening. It's finally happening.

He heard another ping from his laptop as he saw a fresh alert, this time the notification service he had set up to monitor forums. The summary appeared in the same place, then followed by another directly below.

>> New hit on: HackPalace forum
Subject: What I've Learned from the Endling

>> New hit on: ExploitWorld forum
Subject: Why the Endling's Tactics Change Everything for our
Industry

He laughed out loud, wringing his hands together, eyes wide.

They see what I'm doing. They know my name.

He clicked on the notification, bringing up a web browser to show him the full view of the message. As he leaned in, he forgot all about the Activity Monitor and the download progress. He forgot all about everyone else in the coffee shop.

He had arrived.

As the browser window rendered, still running slow, he waited for the full text to pop up, the browser thinking, spinning its progress wheel. Waiting for what seemed like minutes, waiting to read every juicy detail.

As the window spun its wheels, another notification popped up —this one from a hacker on the Rockyrd hacking boards, notorious for being skeptical of anyone but the most elite from across the globe.

I knew it would happen. I just didn't think it would be so soon.

He flipped back to the browser window loading a white frame. It finally quit, flashing the words:

Page Not Found.
The content you're looking for doesn't exist.

His eyes darted around the screen. The new notifications had both disappeared, leaving him with only a blank page. He brought up the Wi-Fi monitor to make sure his connection was still—

"Whoa, there, fella," he heard a woman's voice over his right shoulder with a thick Texas drawl. He turned, seeing two men in bulletproof vests flanking a woman at the center, all with pistols out.

He clicked a few keys and then sunk back away from his machine, his face dropping.

"How about you and me go for a ride, what do you say?"

TWENTY-TWO

NSA Field Office, Second Floor
Chicago, IL
October 30th, 11:50AM

Haylie had seen a few interrogation rooms after her activities back in London, but she had never been on this side of the glass. The back of the one-way mirror was tinted, casting a gray film over the image of Agent Wilcox, Agent Hernandez, and the Endling from the next room. It had been a few hours, and Haylie felt herself starting to grow antsy. Or maybe just bored.

After grabbing the Endling from the coffee shop, the team had made their way back to the NSA field office, near some town called Naperville out in the suburbs. The office wasn't as new as the San Antonio location and featured cheap wooden-veneer furniture pushed into a few dusty corners of the waiting area. Hernandez and Wilcox had been in the interrogation room for quite some time now, asking Haylie to watch and wait in the observation room.

"Take notes, and don't say anything," Agent Wilcox had said.

"And for God's sake, don't tap on the glass. You never want to remind the zoo animals that someone's watching."

It was clear to Haylie that the agents weren't going to get anywhere with this guy, not today. Every question had been greeted with either dead silence or a dismissive laugh. The Endling just stared at the wall, twitching his nose occasionally, ignoring the entire scene in front of him.

Haylie perked up as the agents stood, firing off a final volley of words as they made their way towards the door. Anthony didn't even acknowledge them as the door shut, just continued staring straight into the glass. Right at Haylie.

"He's not talking," Agent Wilcox said, rubbing her eyes. She asked the agent in the room to run and get her more coffee. Hernandez asked for a fresh cup as well.

"I can see that," Haylie said. "What happens now? You've got to have experts that can get something out of him, right? Like in the movies?"

"Sure," Hernandez said. "But all the local guys are tied up with other cases. We've got a pair of agents on a plane from New York, but it'll be a few hours."

"He wants to say something," Agent Wilcox said with a shake of her head. "I know he does. But his attitude in there is bigger than Dallas. So damn proud of what he's done, he must be dying to tell someone all about it."

"At least we stopped the final hack," Haylie said. "That's something, right?"

"Yes and no," Hernandez said as he flicked through messages on his phone. "Our analysts think he may have been moving the files to somewhere other than his laptop."

"Where are they?" Haylie asked.

"A cloud server location," Hernandez said. "We've confirmed

that most of the data made it there and that someone other than the Endling accessed the files a few minutes after."

"So it *is* bigger than just this guy," Agent Wilcox said, gazing back through the glass. "How bad is it? How many records?"

"They're still tallying everything up," Hernandez said. "But it looks like somewhere over twenty million."

"We need to find the guy he's working with," Wilcox said. "Or working *for*. We need him to talk. But he's got to want to talk to someone. He's got to..."

Wilcox looked up as her finger pointed slowly in Haylie's direction.

"You," Agent Wilcox said under her breath. "He'll talk to you. He'll go all fan-boy or whatever you call it on you. Once he sees you in the room, he'll be stepping all over himself to go and tell you everything."

Haylie took two steps back, her hands raising to waist-level and pushed out towards the agents.

"In there?" she pointed into the room. "Me? With *him*? No, no. Not happening. Just observe and consult, remember? That was the deal."

"You'll be fine, Haylie," Hernandez said. "Just talk to him. Like a friend. No agenda—he'll see right through that. No script. Hacker to hacker. Just get him talking—something will come out."

"What if he comes at me?" Haylie asked.

"Those cuffs will hold him," Wilcox said. "Legs are in shackles. The worst thing that can happen is that he jumps at you, scares you out of your boots."

Well, that's reassuring.

She bit her lip as she looked past the glass.

What would I even say? Do I just walk in and let him do the talking? And what if he doesn't even know who I—

159

"Ms. Black," Agent Wilcox said, stepping in towards her. "Let me remind you about the details of our agreement. I'm willing to get rid of the rest of your probation if you give us material help in this case. So far, every break in the case has been due to Mary's involvement, not yours."

Haylie's heart began to race as her eyes flicked back and forth between Wilcox and Hernandez. *Oh, hell no.*

"That's not true," Haylie said, pointing her finger in Wilcox's direction. "The background pattern matching: that was my idea. We wouldn't have found him ... without—"

"It was a good idea," Hernandez interjected, "that *Mary* coded up and executed. You were just sitting in the van with us, a spectator. Agent Wilcox is right, Haylie. But now, you can help us out. You can help *yourself* out."

Haylie stared back in silence, fire in her eyes. She paced the room, pulling her hair back behind her neck and letting it fall down past her bowed head. Hernandez began to speak, but Haylie held her hand out with a "don't even think about it" motion as she continued to walk, weighing her options.

This is ridiculous. This isn't fair. I should have known better—should have known they'd pull something like this.

She walked to the window, pulse pounding, shaking her head.

But now I don't have a choice.

TWENTY-THREE

NSA Field Office, Second Floor
Chicago, IL
October 30th, 12:04PM

The door closed behind Haylie with a soft rush of air and a firm clunk. The silence of the room filled her mind as she shifted her weight back and forth between her feet, trying her best to maintain control over her heartbeat. She remembered the last few instructions from Agent Hernandez and Agent Wilcox: "You'll be fine. If we want you to stop, we'll tap on the glass. That's your sign to back off."

Haylie watched the Endling carefully, watching his eyes stay locked on her every move. She could barely breathe. The room felt different from this side of the two-way mirror: more sterile, more dated. The smell of industrial-strength cleaner didn't help; it filled her nostrils, making her nose sting like she had just walked into a hospital ward. She paced across the room with careful steps, gliding into the empty chair across the table from the Endling. He stared her down as a sinister smile made its way across his face.

His face was long and thin with a few days' worth of stubble on his jaw, his hair was styled back and up—he could have been a model in another life. But there was something in his eyes, a sick desperation. His smile wasn't friendly—it was loaded, cocky. Not a greeting, more of a warning.

"It's you," he said, straightening himself, his restraints tugging him back down. The chains rattled as they went taught. "I knew you'd be next."

"Is that right?" Haylie asked. "And how is that?"

He slunk down into his chair, leaning back to loosen the tension on his wrists. His eyes met Haylie's.

How good are those handcuffs, anyway? If he stood up fast enough, could he—

"You're Haylie Black—the greatest hacker in the whole wide world," he said in a mocking, sing-song tone. "The girl we call Crash, the girl next door who just saved the planet—oh, I'm sorry, am I getting all the talking points right?"

"You forgot criminal," Haylie said, stone-faced, "depending on whom you talk to these days. Now we know who I am; who are you? And why are you attacking systems all over the country?"

Shaking his head, the Endling flicked his eyes behind Haylie, to the mirrored glass. He made a few "tsks" as he raised his hands together, waving a single finger back and forth.

"Don't ruin our fun with their silly ideas," he whispered. "Those agents—idiots—they want you to get me comfortable. Talk shop, trick me into giving away the big plot. But then you walk in here and just *ask?* That's not how this is supposed to work. You've got an agreement with them—to reduce your sentence, is that right? If you get me to talk, you get back online?"

"I'm tired," Haylie said. "And you're busted. I figured we'd just get to the point. They're going to figure out who you are, so you might as well just—"

"That's where you're wrong. They have me here," he gestured

down at his shackles. "But they don't *know* me. I don't have a criminal record, so there's no fingerprint information. I don't carry an ID —just cash, nothing else."

"They have your machine—"

"I'll miss that laptop. It's hard to find machines with CD-ROM drives these days, it makes them all heavy. I didn't actually use the drive but removing it gave me a lot of space to play with. You can fit a surprising amount of thermite inside that drive bay."

"Thermite?"

"Highly flammable. Add some gunpowder and model rocket igniters, and you can trigger a fire from the twelve-volt line inside the machine with a few keystrokes. Which is what I did when they grabbed me. *Computer all gone.*"

Haylie squirmed in her seat, looking in the mirror and seeing only a look of growing desperation on her own face in return.

You need to get something out of him. He wants to talk. Just get him talking.

"These hacks you've been doing, they're pretty good," she said. "Haven't seen anybody go so wide with an attack pattern, especially not this fast."

She could see his body tense up. He finally broke through his caution with a response. "They haven't been easy."

"I know," she said. "Trust me, I get it. I'm surprised you got as far as you did before being tracked down." She leaned in across the table, whispering. "But the cool thing was all the different techniques. Jumping from web server exploits to buying stuff from message boards to the OPM thing, which I'm still not sure how you got in."

He smiled. "If I told you," he whispered, "you wouldn't believe me."

"I want to hear all about it," she said, "before I have to read it in some tell-all book on the bestseller list, you know? I want to hear it from you—when the time is right. But what I can't figure out is how they're all connected."

The Endling took an excited breath. As he was about to speak, he caught himself. He closed his mouth, keeping his eyes locked on Haylie, and sat up straight in his chair, his hands resting on the table, fingers flexing.

"I want a deal," he said. The first of these words he said in Haylie's direction, but the last was directed at the mirrored glass behind her, spoken loudly enough to fill two rooms.

"I don't know anything about that. That's not why I'm—"

"*You* don't know anything about deals?" he laughed. "Well, that's funny because the deal I want is exactly the same as yours."

"I don't think—"

"If *you* got a deal—the little girl from nowhere USA—I certainly deserve one."

Haylie lay back of her chair, crossing her arms. "And why is that?"

"Because I can help," he said. "I have skills. You just kind of stumbled into your little adventure, running around New York and London and wherever else someone told you to go. Anyone could have done that."

"Excuse me?" she said. "*Anyone?*"

"You've seen what I can do," he said. "You said it yourself—no one's done anything like this before. I'm surprised those idiot agents haven't already begged me to join them."

"Maybe you're not as good as you think," Haylie said.

"I don't have to be that good," he said. "I just need to be better than *you*, Crash, which isn't that hard. You and all your magazine covers and your headlines. Tell me—did you do a press tour? I'm surprised you haven't done a full makeover yet, or maybe your own reality show? That's got to be in the works somewhere."

"You think I wanted all that press?" Haylie shot back. "I got pulled into something, sure, but I finished the damn job. If you're such a great hacker, how come you need to run around buying passwords?"

Haylie heard a noise behind her, a slight, woodpecker-like series of taps at the glass. She took a breath, picturing Wilcox and Hernandez on the other side of the mirror.

Stay in control, Crash.

The Endling raised his hands, pointing a finger at Haylie. "You don't know. You don't know what it's like to be shut out, to be great at something when no one will give you a chance. You got your chance, you had the hand of God come down from the heavens and turn you into something bigger than you've ever been. But for me, I had to build my own heaven."

"By hacking government systems?" she asked. "You think this is going to make people pay attention to you? The world doesn't work that way."

"Oh, so you know about the world now?" he spat back. "Please, tell me all about it. No, you know what, tell me about it in two years when no one remembers your name. Tell me how fair the world is then."

"I'll tell you about fair," Haylie's voice began to rise. "I can't even push an elevator button without getting arrested, does that seem fair? And for what? For doing the right thing?"

Haylie's concentration was broken by another series of taps on the glass behind her, this one louder than before, growing towards a full on knock.

Shut up, Hernandez.

"Tell me who's behind this," she said. "That's the only way this gets better for you."

"I'm not telling you anything," he whispered. "I'd rather talk to a whole room of government agents than talk to some celebrity who doesn't know her way around a command line. You're. A. Joke."

The rage grew inside of her as she felt her face flush red, her hands began pulsing, crawling into fists. She looked up with fire in her eyes to see that the Endling had shut down, his eyes closed, silently mouthing words she couldn't make out.

She fought to keep her composure as she looked over at the handcuffs, scratching red rings around his wrists. Suddenly, the weight of her ankle bracelet felt like a lead balloon, pulling her down. She could feel its LED blinking, searing her skin with each burst of light.

She felt tears gathering in her eyes as she realized that she wouldn't get help, not today. She wasn't going to get out.

"Please," she whispered. "I need this. I need your help. Why were you collecting data? It doesn't make any sense ... the pattern. Each system, each user base, they're all so different. I've tried piecing them together, but it gets tangled. I don't see the connection. How are they connected?"

The Endling opened his eyes and watched her struggle, seemed to drink it in. To enjoy it, just for a minute. He leaned in across the table and smiled.

"It's like a friend told me just the other day," he said, tilting his head to the side, like a dog looking at a treat. "A complicated thing is just a bunch of simple things, all lined up in a nice, little row."

She pushed back in her chair, heart pounding. Her mind raced as she pictured the only other person in the world who had ever said those words to her.

It can't be.

TWENTY-FOUR

Littlefield Hall, University of Texas
Austin, TX
October 30th, 11:02PM

Haylie released the grip on the handle of her duffle bag, letting it fall to the floor. As the door swung closed behind her, the darkness swallowed the room. She blinked a few times to let her eyes adjust, too tired to even walk the few long steps over to the light switch. For now, the darkness would do.

A complicated thing is just a bunch of simple things, all lined up in a nice, little row.

She racked her brain, trying to make sense of it all.

A casino. A healthcare company. A cable company. Government personnel files.

Big organizations. Data about people.

Names.

Social security numbers.

Addresses.

Driver's license data.

Fingerprints.

Haylie rubbed her eyes and looked out the window, seeing the late-night crowd below trickling down to groups of two or three, sailing under each light hanging overhead, some leaning in close to each other, others with their hands firmly pulling at their backpack straps. All heading in different directions, coming in and out of the light. *Focus.*

What else?

No money. Just data.

No ransoms. No messages about morals or corporate greed.

No demands.

She slumped sideways in the windowsill, pulling her hair back behind her shoulders with an exhausted breath. She removed her glasses, wiping the lenses with the bottom edge of her t-shirt, clearing the smudges off one at a time. She knew this feeling, she could always tell when she was getting nowhere. She felt like she was spinning. She knew there was something else, something she was missing.

States—the data came from certain regions. Virginia, Ohio, Florida, New York, Pennsylvania.

She leaned in towards the window when a slight yellow light caught her eye. It was dancing off the glass—off *her* side of the glass.

Turning, Haylie saw a flickering light radiating from her desk, behind the bookcase. She stood and walked towards the light, foot over foot, the details in the room emerging as she approached. As she peered around the bookcase, her eyes grew wide. She saw the desktop covered in a thick fog of yellow light, flickering.

Something's on fire.

She froze, looking down as her hand covered her mouth, gasping for breath.

It was a birthday cake—a rectangular sheet cake with dark chocolate frosting across the top, with words scrawled in green. But not any words: machine text. The cake was designed to look exactly like a command line window, complete with a rectangular cursor made of frosting and a '>>>' Python prompt, all surrounded by a sea of eighteen electronic candles.

Oh, my God. Tomorrow's my birthday.

I forgot my own goddamned birthday.

She laughed and let out a defeated breath. Over the past few months, with the absence of technology, time had slipped away. Without a watch or a digital clock or a phone, she hardly ever knew the time—let alone the date—anymore. Every once in a while she'd steal a glance at the calendar on her wall or the top of a newspaper in the Student Union, but that was it.

She pulled this afternoon's boarding pass out of her pocket and laid it down on the desk, smoothing it and holding it close to the candles to search for the date. 'OCT 30.' Tomorrow was Halloween, which meant she was turning eighteen.

Good lord, this is a new low, even for you.

Haylie looked next to the cake to see a hand-written note. She plucked it off the desktop and held it up to the electronic candle, the light shining through the paper.

Happy birthday, idiot.
You're not the only one who
learned how to pick locks.
–Vector

She chuckled, looking back to the cake, and read each line of pseudo-computer code text written across the rectangle in dark green frosting.

Happy 18th Birthday
Now you can vote!
(Or can you? You're kind of a felon.)

Haylie's smile faded as the words pulsed through her mind. She re-read the text again and again. Her brain began to churn as she processed each word, over and over. There was something there, something that was setting off an alarm in her head.

Vote.

Vote.

Vote.

Oh no. No no no. It can't be.

She scraped her keys off the side table and bolted for the door, headed for Vector's room at a full sprint.

———

Closing his door behind him, Vector extended a fist for Haylie to bump. "Happy birthday, Crash! What's the emergency? You saw the cake, right? Brilliant move, I must admit."

"No—not that," Haylie said. "I mean, yes, and thank you. But I think I just figured it out. Something happened in Chicago—I think I just put it all together."

"You were in Chicago?"

"Long story," she said. "I'm not supposed to tell you any of this. I'm in trouble for even thinking about telling you this."

"Go on."

She walked him through everything—the hacks, the data, Mary, and what the man sitting across the table had said in Chicago that finally pushed her to stumble her way out of the room in a daze.

"You think your brother is working with the Endling?" Vector whispered. "Why would he do that? If Caesar wanted data, he wouldn't have a problem getting it himself. He and his group, they took the code from the Project, they should have access to almost every system in the world."

"It makes sense. There's too much attention on him right now,"

Haylie replied, lowering her voice. "Caesar knows that everyone is looking for him. This stuff from Senator Hancock—his agenda to track down hackers. There are too many eyes watching him. If he can pay someone else to do it, it reduces his visibility."

"Even if that's what's going on, why would he do it? It doesn't make any sense—Caesar just running around collecting data about people."

"Hancock has a good chance of becoming the next president—the polls are tied, right? The election is next week. What do you think my brother could do with millions of lines of personal data between now and then?"

Vector sat in the windowsill, his hands rubbing his temples, taking his time. He looked back up to Haylie with a new flash of fear in his eyes.

"Which regions did you say the data is from?" he asked.

"Ohio, Florida, New York, Virginia, Pennsylvania. A few other states," Haylie said, watching for his reaction.

"Swing states. All of them," Vector said. "The election is just a week away, and Caesar knows if Hancock is in office, he'll be done for."

Haylie's mind raced, trying to find another solution that made sense. Something. Anything. But each time, she came back to the same result.

"My god, Crash," Vector said. "Caesar's going to hack the presidential election."

"No, he's not," Haylie said. "Not if we can stop him."

TWENTY-FIVE

Vijzelstraat
Amsterdam
October 31st, 6:52AM

Caesar paused, catching himself before he took the first step off the sidewalk and pulled back each side of his hoodie. If the past five hours in Amsterdam had taught him anything, it was that the speeding cars and trucks weren't the most dangerous part of trying to cross these roads—the real threat was the lane of bicycles flying by at breakneck speeds, just inches from the sidewalk. Just then, a cyclist cruised by with the crunch of tires meeting gravel and pushed a rush of chilled air into Caesar's face.

He curved across the avenue and ducked into a sleepy side street. The small sign affixed to the corner of the building across the way read 'Reguliersdwarsstraat,' the word straining against each edge for more space.

I don't even want to know how they pronounce that.

Noting the four men sitting at the corner sipping on tall, golden-colored drinks, he made his way down the center of the alley, keeping a loose eye on the locals huddled on doorsteps and benches here and there. He stopped under a tattoo parlor's awning, turning on his heels to face the other side of the street.

Across the way was a green door framed in white trim. To the right of the door hung a small, white address marker reading simply '74.' Making one last check for anyone tailing him, Caesar paced across the pavement, extended two fingers, and rang the doorbell. He waited, bouncing on his toes, but heard nothing on the other side.

C'mon c'mon c'mon. Let's go.

After a few more breaths, Caesar heard the hollow rumblings of deadbolts and chains unlatching from the inside. The door cracked open as a mist of citrusy sweetness filled his nostrils, inviting him inside.

Caesar skipped up a short flight of stairs into a cavernous room. The sunlight became a faint memory as his pupils adjusted, his body feeling the welcome wash of darkness.

The room was empty except for Sean's silhouette propped up on a stool at the far end of the bar and a bartender polishing pint glasses. With delicate, rose-colored lamps every few feet, the wooden bar sat under a backlit collection of bottles that were looking down on each seat like spectators at a football game. On the far side of the room were a series of booths, seemingly carved from the side of the left wall, the contents of each hidden by a series of thick arches. The entire place had the warm glow of honey.

"We safe here?" Caesar asked as he approached.

"We're good," Sean replied, not bothering to keep his voice down. "An old friend from school runs this place. We've got it locked down, at least for the next few hours. Longer, if we need—just say the word."

Sean pointed up at the newscast on the small television in the corner, showing two news anchors recapping the previous night's presidential debate.

"Your buddy up there is growing more excitable," Sean said, taking a sip of his ice water, eyes following the closed captioning on the screen. "It's getting worse, believe it or not. Just about a week to the election and Hancock is upping the ante for a 'Cyber-Secure America.' It's basically all he talked about during the debate last night."

"I can't believe that anyone is buying it," Caesar said. "Who made him a security expert? And who says *cyber* anymore?" He took a few peanuts from the bowl on the counter and popped them in his mouth.

"There's something else—you have to see for yourself. It's been on loop, it should come back around in a minute."

"What is it?"

"He's building a team. A few ex-generals and network security guys from the private sector have joined him to advise."

Caesar waved his hand with a dismissive push. "That's nothing we can't get around. It's all just window dressing."

"There's more," Sean said, eyes locked on the television. "Wait for it."

The two sat silently, waiting for the video. Sean gestured over to the bartender for the remote. He clicked the volume up a few notches.

"Following last night's debate, Senator Hancock continued his push towards a cyber-secure nation by announcing an elite task force, the first, Hancock claims, in United States history.

Joining Hancock as full-time advisors on cyber-security are a collection of intelligence professionals from across the sector, but more surprisingly, a former leader of a hacker collective.

In Hancock's words: 'If we're going to catch these people, we're going to need to think like them.'"

"Who's that standing next to him?" Caesar asked, boosting himself off his barstool and peering towards the monitor. "He looks familiar."

"That's our problem," Sean said. "Mason Mince. Calls himself Rancor?"

Caesar felt a chill come over his body as he processed the name. He sank back down.

"Rancor? *The* Rancor?" Caesar said, his jaw dropping. He stumbled to find the right words. "That guy is out of his mind ... He takes out a critical system every few months, just to get headlines. Like, serious infrastructure hacks in major cities, just for his own ego. I can't believe a senator would stand next to him on a stage."

"Well, he's on the Hancock train now," Sean said. "Looks like he's going mainstream—maybe he sees the tide turning and he's trying to get ahead of it. If I had to guess, I'd say he's bringing the top hackers from the Nam3less organization with him."

Caesar sat back, watching the screen as the newscast cut between shots of Hancock—on his campaign plane, at the podium, hugging a small child somewhere in rural America. He lost a moment as his pulse raced, then forced himself to breathe again.

Nam3less? All working for Hancock? That's impossible.

"Nam3less has done worse stuff than we've ever done," Caesar said. "They're one of the biggest hacking groups out there. The Area 51 exploit, the power grid up in Oregon. I always figured they'd be the first to get arrested if Hancock got elected."

"They were probably thinking the same," Sean said. "Instead of running away from Hancock, they're sliding in beside him. Getting joined at the hip before he gets elected—pretty smart, actually."

"He's not going to get elected," Caesar muttered, watching the video of Rancor standing at the podium, tugging at his shirt collar, taking questions from the crowd.

"You and Rancor—you two have a history, right?" Sean asked with a cautious tone.

"Back when I was at Brux," Caesar nodded. "He kept trying to get in our systems, breaking in to make us look like idiots." He gave Sean a sideways glance. "He turned a bunch of his Nam3less script kiddies against us to find any weakness they could. But they never got in. Never. That didn't stop him from lying, telling everyone that he had."

"We'll need to watch ourselves," Sean said. "We have to assume that Hancock is bringing Rancor on board with an agenda. If Nam3-less was first on Hancock's hit list, then we've just taken that spot. We'd be a hell of a first pet project for Rancor—tracking down the guys who stole the keys to the world."

"If someone catches us, it's not going to be a bottom-feeder like Rancor," Caesar said with a sneer. "Besides, they don't have time—there's no way they know what we're up to. If we stay on track, Hancock will go away soon enough."

"Well, there's the good news. I put together a master database of all the information from the Eagle hacks. Looks like we've got enough to work with, as long as this last transfer comes through. With one more hack, the math checks out. We should be able to generate enough votes to push the election against Hancock, just by a bit."

"And the Federal Election Committee servers?" Caesar said. "The target—our access is still working?"

"Of course it is," Sean laughed. "We're the men with the keys to the world, remember?"

"The keys to the world," Caesar said, popping another handful of peanuts into his mouth. "But with no place to hide."

TWENTY-SIX

Littlefield Hall, University of Texas
Austin, TX
October 31st, 12:12AM

Vector paced the room, wringing his hands. "I've never even heard of anyone hacking something this big—this is mad. I don't even know where to start."

Haylie and Vector had spent the last hour running through every way that Caesar might be trying to hack the election. But without detailed knowledge of the systems, it was useless.

"Let's try working backwards," Haylie said. "Figure out what he's building. We know he's gathering data. He's going to use that to impact the voting somehow."

"Break into the voting machine network?" Vector asked.

"You'd have to do that on a local level," Haylie said, her fingers on her temples as she worked through the logic. "You'd need hardware at every polling place in the country—at least the important ones. He doesn't have the manpower to pull that off."

"So, what if he worked the other direction?" Vector asked. "Alter the votes in the central database after the votes have been collected?"

If I had that data, what would I do?

"You don't need personal data to change a database field," Haylie said. "If he had access to that server, he could just do whatever he wants. I don't get it. We have to be missing something."

"I'm sure we are," Vector said. "Your brother's a genius who's had months to plan an attack with some of the best access in the world. We're outgunned here."

"We can't just give up," Haylie said. "Think."

"I don't know," Vector said. "Maybe it's best to just let this play out. Step back a bit, you know? Forget we ever came across this mess?"

Haylie stared at Vector, waiting for the punchline, for him to say he was just kidding around. But he just looked at her with hope in his eyes.

"Just let this play out?" she said. "Are you out of your mind?"

"I don't know, maybe I am. Your brother's a big boy, he's quite aware of what he's doing. I don't know about you, but I'm enjoying my time here at university and I think that maybe—"

"Oh, are you comfortable?" Haylie said. "I'm sorry, I didn't mean to get in the way of your vacation. Sure, we could just sit here and ignore what's going on, but maybe we should be better than that. Maybe if more people in this world stopped being so *comfortable* all the time, we'd get a lot more done. Sometimes to get something, you have to give something else up. You're smart enough to know that."

"Give something up?" Vector blurted out with a raised voice, gesturing wildly around the room. "What do you think *this* is? You pretty much dragged me here from London—where I was doing just fine, thank you very much—and got me on every government watchlist in the world. Yes, of course, where are my manners? Sometimes I forget to say *thank you*."

A stale silence filled the room as they both looked down to the floor, taking deep breaths. After a long chasm of silence, Haylie was the first to speak.

"My brother is in trouble," Haylie whispered. "He's not thinking straight. I can't look the other way. You know that."

"We have other options," Vector pleaded. "We can go to Hernandez. And that other agent—the one from the NSA. We can tell them what's going on. They'll have all the tech we need to track him down. Who knows, you might even get on their good side."

"And rat out my brother?" Haylie spat back. "They'll lock him up. Or maybe something worse. I can't risk that."

"So, there's another option," Vector said, lowering his voice. "If Caesar pulls this off, would it really be that bad of a thing?"

"What?" Haylie shot back.

"Just hear me out—Caesar does whatever he's doing. Throws the election. Hancock loses, Ortega is the new president. I mean, anyone with half a brain knows that Hancock is a nutcase. If Ortega gets elected instead, the country gets a leader who's not a complete idiot, and maybe the feds never figure out that Caesar was behind the whole thing. You jump in now, and you could be helping to elect a man who will vilify hackers—people like us. If you think about it, our next four years could be a nightmare if Caesar doesn't succeed."

"I don't care if it's convenient; this is *wrong*," Haylie said. "I can't sit by knowing this is happening. We don't do stuff like this ... and Caesar knows that. He *taught* me that. Our skills can't be used to play God, no matter how much we want to."

Vector sat back in the windowsill, looking out into the night. "Then the only choice left is..."

"We find him ourselves," Haylie said.

Vector crossed his arms, his brow furrowed. "I can't help but notice you keep saying *we*."

"What do you say?"

"You're doing it again," Vector said, pointing at her with a shaking finger. "Sucking me into a pet project. You haven't exactly been the best friend recently, I'll have you know. And now I'm meant to jump in and help you out, *again*. The last time I did something like this, I got a bullet to the shoulder. That *hurt*."

"I'm sorry," Haylie said, trying to process everything running through her head. As the pieces clicked together—her brother, the hacks, the Endling, the election—the pressure spilled over. She felt tears welling in her eyes as she fought her body's urge to shake.

"This has been tough," she said between sniffs. "Being disconnected, being alone—it's awful. It's worse than I thought it would be. And now with Caesar in trouble—I actually have a chance to help. I need to stop him, and I have the skills to do something. So that's what I'm going to do. With or without you."

"I know you're miserable," Vector said, shaking his head. "Any friend worth having could see that. I've tried to help—"

"I know you have, and the truth is that you're right—I've been terrible to you. But you're still my friend. My *only* friend." She wiped her tears, doing her best to regain some sort of composure and chuckled. "Besides, wouldn't it be fun to get back into action? Crash and Vector out in the world, causing trouble again?"

Nodding, Vector rubbed his temples and looked over at the TV. The banner on the bottom read 'HANCOCK SET FOR BATTLE WITH ORTEGA IN PENNSYLVANIA.' The screen showed the candidate in the brisk autumn sun, his hair flying in every direction, shouting down at the crowd from his podium high above. His face grew redder with every word, jabbing a finger from each hand into the air as he screamed. Shots of the crowd showed faces smeared with blind faith, cheering and clapping, adorned in red, white, and blue.

"We would need to find him," Vector said. "Figure out where he is. Somehow convince him to change his mind. No angle of this is going to be easy."

"I just need to get back online," she said, wiping her tears away and sitting to attention. "If I can get back online, I can stop him. I know I can."

"That's the bigger problem," Vector said. "We can't do this with the government looking over your shoulder."

"Well, then, we're just going to get the hell out of here."

"Right," Vector exclaimed, perking up with a subtle clap of his hands. "Lots to do tonight. Where do we start?"

"I've got a meeting in San Antonio tomorrow morning," Haylie said. "Hernandez and Wilcox want me to debrief with Mary, talk about my time with the Endling, see if there's anything she can pick up on. I need you to start doing research."

"What kind?"

Haylie pulled up the leg of her jeans, showing the black ankle bracelet with its small LED light, blinking green.

"How to get this thing off without sending every agent in Texas our way," she said.

"Brilliant." Vector smiled, his eyes growing wide with anticipation. "I've been waiting months for you to ask me that."

TWENTY-SEVEN

Fleming's Hotel Deluxe
Frankfurt, Germany
October 31st, 4:51 PM

The elevator churned and rattled as it went to work. Caesar could feel the shift in altitude, all the way down in his stomach—the wheels grinding through the floorboards as the car crept up and up, his ears threatening to pop. The elevator was moving too slowly, too sluggishly for him; the walls began to close in as he reached to the side, bracing himself. He felt a mist of sweat build across the top edges of his forehead, no draft or breeze or oxygen to whisk the beads away, as his pulse started to—

Ding.

The doors peeled open as a wave of cool air flooded the compartment. Caesar took a deep breath.

Amsterdam, which Caesar was hoping could become their new headquarters, had quickly turned into a bust. A few minutes after their Rancor discussion, Sean had picked up a wave of activity on his police scanner app. Without asking any other questions, they had quickly and quietly made their way out of the Netherlands via a quick train ride to Frankfurt.

Caesar wasn't sure how the police had found them, but being in his second city—hell, second *country*—in a single day no longer even registered as strange to him. He had grown cautious of every stranger —every waiter, hotel clerk, and passerby. Every phone he bought— and he bought a lot of them these days—was another opportunity to stay hidden, but at the same time, another chance to get caught. He preferred to-go meals, even if Sean kept insisting they eat out in the open, "to keep them sane." Caesar was smart enough to realize that the rising tension was beginning to drag him down more each day: his mood, his work, his sleep. He could feel himself growing coarse, some days not even wanting to leave the hotel room. He could see that weight in the mirror every morning.

Caesar trudged through the scattered tables, wincing at the sunlight as it blasted through the windows, and continued on to the sundeck. As he stepped outside, he was greeted with a view of Frankfurt's skyline—a mix of mirrored glass from new financial high-rises and the old, faded castle tower marking the corner of the old city wall. The clouds led his eyes to the right, where he found Sean sitting, facing the scene, with the tower's silhouette reflecting back from his sunglasses.

"I hate Germany," Sean said, trying to decipher the menu. "The people here are just too damn serious."

"It's not that bad," Caesar said, stretching and admiring the view. "Think of it as culture."

"I'm tired of this, you know," Sean said.

"Then pick another restaurant," Caesar replied with a forced smile, taking his seat. He plucked a menu off the table and scanned the lunch offerings.

"I'm serious," Sean said. "This morning was too close. If we can't stay in one place for more than a few days, how are we ever going to get our momentum going?"

"We keep our focus," Caesar said, trying to take on a tone that would project confidence. "That's all we can do. We're in a sprint right now, that's all—we'll get through this. A few months from now, we won't even remember what it was like being on the run."

"How do you think they found us back in Amsterdam?" Sean asked.

"I bet it was that bartender," Caesar said. He pictured the man at the end of the bar, listening with one ear, pretending not to be paying any sort of attention at all. It had to be him. Caesar wished he could be back there right now. The delicate amber lamps lighting his view as he pushed his boot down on the throat of the bartender, watching him struggle for air. Watching him beg for his life.

Caesar snapped back to reality, drawing a sip of water from his glass and checking his watch. "Eagle is rolling from my side, we're on schedule. What about our next side project? Did you take the call this afternoon?"

"No."

You've got to be kidding me.

Caesar sat back, fighting the urge to scream at his friend. But even through his anger, he knew better than that.

Stay calm. Stay in control.

"We agreed that you were in charge of the meeting," Caesar said, picking his words carefully. "Just because we're in a different city— none of that changes. This guy is being blackmailed, he needs our help—"

"I was on the call, idiot," Sean shot back. "Our contact didn't show. He left me hanging, didn't even bother to send a text," Sean spun his phone across the table in Caesar's direction. "If I had to guess, I'd say it has something to do with *this*."

Caesar cupped his hands around the screen to reduce the glare and leaned in to check the phone. It was a video, playing with the volume down. "It's Rancor," he said, raising an eyebrow. "This is recent?"

"Just a few hours old," Sean nodded. "You were sleeping, I figured you needed the rest. You're going to want to watch it."

The video was of Mason Mince—Rancor—looking out of place in a tight sweater vest and dress pants, sweating his way through an appearance on *Good Morning America*. Caesar clicked the volume up a few notches and moved his ear closer to the speaker.

Anchor: "Good morning, Mr. Mince."

Mince: "Good morning, Robin."

Caesar scoffed. "Good morning, Robin—this guy is unbelievable."

Anchor: "So you've recently joined Senator Hancock's advisory panel on cyber security."

Mince: "I'm *leading* the panel, that's correct, Robin."

Anchor: "What can you tell us about some of the newest developments on the team?"

Mince: "Great question. Obviously, we've all been hearing about an increase in hacking activity in the past few weeks. My team, even with everything we're now doing for the Hancock campaign, has offered our assistance to all government agencies in taking down these criminals."

Sean shook his head. "This guy is such a tool."

Mince: "But we believe that the current administration is focused in the wrong areas—small-time targets, the wrong priorities. I'm here today to announce an offensive against the target that we believe is the biggest current threat to our national security, and that's Caesar Black."

Caesar pushed himself back in his chair, as far from the phone as he could get, his eyes wide. Sean looked back out to the skyline as the video played on.

Anchor:"Caesar Black, the hacker from the events in London?"

Mince: "I'm sorry, Robin, you mean the criminal who escaped with enough code to break into almost any system on the planet? Yes, that hacker, Robin. Caesar Black is a man with no respect for the law. When you combine that attitude with the power he holds in his hands, you get a digital powder keg ready to explode. The fact that the current administration has done nothing to stop him shows a severe lack of understanding for how to take on criminals in our modern times. Under my—and Senator Hancock's—leadership, that's all going to change, and we're not going to sit around and wait for the election to begin leading."

"This is bad, man," Sean said, his head in his hands. "I'm all for keeping a positive attitude, but at this point, it's only a matter of time. They're not waiting for the election—they're coming after us now."

"Me," Caesar said, pushing the phone back across the table. "They're coming after *me*."

Sean turned to look out at the horizon, flipping his sunglasses on. "You, us, whatever." He sat for a few moments, letting the video play through to the end and clicking it silent. "What do you want to do?"

"We keep going," Caesar said. "This doesn't change anything. It's all just talk. We focus our energy on Eagle, making sure the election plan is perfect, making sure everything is ready to roll. No mistakes. We take Hancock—and Rancor—out of the equation."

"We have what we need to disappear," Sean said. "We have money. We have our freedom—for now. There's no shame in just pulling the ripcord, laying low for a few months."

Shaking his head, Caesar grabbed a piece of bread from the table, chewing at the corner. "Trying to disappear right now is more dangerous than it sounds. I mean, where the hell is Char? What did they do with her? For all we know, Margo and Phillip are in a jail cell somewhere, too. Besides, if we stop now, Hancock is going to win. He's ahead in the polls with not much time left. If you think our lives suck now, just wait until he has real resources behind him."

"So what, we just keep doing *this*?" Sean asked, waving his arms around at the skyline. "A new city every other day?"

"We stay put," Caesar said. "Rancor is coming after us? I say let him come."

"We don't know what type of systems he has access to," Sean said. "He could be dialed in across the board—NSA, FBI, CIA. If Hancock has friends over there—and you don't get to be a senator without friends—they could be plugged in already."

"If we run, they win," Caesar said. "We crawl into the shadows, they win."

"Rancor is no joke, man," Sean said. "This hasn't been real before today—it's all been just talk. But *this guy*," Sean jabbed his finger at the phone screen, "Macon Minco he knows what the hell he's doing. He's not playing around. He wants a trophy to hang on his wall. He wants your head."

"Why are we doing this in the first place?" Caesar asked, pounding his fists on the table, shaking the silverware. "Why did we run after seeing what we saw in London? I don't know about you, but I did it because I could see the writing on the wall. I could see that the world needed people like you and me, somebody on their side. When you give bad people power, they don't get better. They get *worse*. They get *a lot* worse. That's what happened in London, and that's what is happening now. You think Hancock with power—real power—is going to let up after getting elected? Not a chance. And we're the only ones who can stop him."

"It's too much," Sean whispered, his voice beginning to break and his head hung low. "It's getting too real."

"We can choose to do the right thing or the easy thing. Rancor's good, but he's not as good as us. Especially you, with the big IQ you won't shut up about."

Sean let out a nervous laugh, took a sip of water. He picked the menu up, flipping it end over end, shaking his head. "I *am* smarter than you. My parents got me tested when I was a kid, I have the paperwork and everything." He took a breath and looked back at Caesar. "So, what now?"

"Full steam ahead," Caesar said. "Ignore Rancor. He's mounting a huge offensive? Good for him. We stay smart, we stay invisible."

The waitress approached and the two men hushed. She placed Sean's order on the table with all the emotion of a robot, looking them both in the eye with a fixed jaw. Sean flashed a smile as she turned away without acknowledging his existence.

"I hate Germany," he said.

Caesar laughed. "Sorry, man, but I don't think Germany likes you much, either."

TWENTY-EIGHT

NSA Texas Cryptologic Center
San Antonio, TX
October 31st, 11:15AM

Balancing on her tiptoes, Haylie let the door fall closed behind her, her palm pressed flush against the steel to hush its click. She did her best to push the mass of twisting, spiraling thoughts from her head—Caesar, Vector, and the impossible road in front of them—and focus her energy on the next few minutes.

She manufactured a smile as she raised her eyes to meet Mary's. Mary sat as she always did in this room, with her hands bound in handcuffs, her faded jumpsuit highlighting the white streaks in her white hair. But today she looked different—a welcoming smile greeted Haylie, a warmth Mary hadn't shown since the day they'd met.

"Still have you in the cuffs, huh?" Haylie said, pacing over towards the table. "I figured they'd let you out of those by now, with you playing nice and everything."

"They take them off so I can type," Mary said. "But not back here in the cells. It's enough for me if I'm being honest."

Haylie nodded. She tried to think of any other small talk—the weather, the news—but her mind was a blank.

"How have you been, dear?" Mary asked. "You seem tired. Are you getting enough rest? I worry about you sometimes."

"Sure," Haylie said, tugging at a sleeve of her fraying college sweatshirt. "Chicago was crazy, so, you know, that's going to spin anybody's head a little bit."

"Of course," Mary said. "I miss it up there—I miss my home. Great things always tend to happen in Chicago, I'm not sure why, but sometimes the universe just makes a decision and that's the way it is. I wish I could have been there with you."

This is good—let her keep talking. You can get through this.

"I have to say," Mary continued, "that idea you had for the background pattern matching on the sound spectrum, that was wonderful. Just genius. I've been out of the game for a bit, but I can't say that I ever would have thought of that, even in my prime. I love watching how your brain works."

"It was nice—to be out. It was actually kind of fun, you know?"

"I can imagine," Mary said. "I was having a blast here, playing off your ideas. The back and forth. I'll tell you something, dear, I don't like a lot of people, but I feel like we've got something here."

"Me, too," Haylie said, pushing her guilt down inside. "This has been great—working together. It really has."

"And I'd say we're not quite done, either. We could be a team—you and I. The agents seem pretty impressed with your work, you seem to be making quite a name for yourself around here."

"We got the guy," Haylie said. "That's what matters. It feels good, you know? But I'm not sure if—"

"Honey," Mary began to whisper, her eyes flicking over to the door. "Before we talk shop, let's talk about what's really important today. Are you up for that?"

Haylie's heart skipped a beat. "What ... what do you mean?"

Mary smiled. "We're friends now, you and me. Aren't we? Friends can talk about the important things in their lives, isn't that right?"

Haylie gulped, her body petrified. She blinked her eyes in rapid succession, wringing her fingers together, dreading Mary's next words.

She knows. Of course, she knows. What are you going to—

"It's your birthday!" Mary cheered, clapping her hands together as much as her restraints would allow. "And believe you me, if I could have gone out and bought you a cake, I would have been the first in line at the bakery. I would have bought you the most beautiful cake I could have found."

"I appreciate that," Haylie said, drawing a long breath. "I got a cake—someone already took care of that."

"Oh, good," Mary said. "I was worried. You know, you can be kind of prickly sometimes, I wasn't really sure if you had many friends."

What did she just—

"Anyway," Mary continued. "You're eighteen now, isn't that right? Such a wonderful age, such a wonderful *time.*"

"How did you know?" Haylie asked.

"Agent Wilcox—she's quite a piece of work, but deep down inside I think she has a soft spot for you. I think you're changing the minds of a lot of people around here."

Haylie nodded, her eyes searching for a clock on the wall that wasn't there.

How long has it been? Stay calm. You're doing fine.

"That's nice of you to say," Haylie managed to work out. "And thank you. You're the first person who actually said happy birthday today. It's nice to hear."

"Did you blow out your candles?" Mary asked. "Make a wish."

Not exactly.

"I think we'll get to that tonight," Haylie said. "It's been a busy week, you know? Lots of back and forth."

Clapping again, Mary let out a little squeal, leaning in across the table. "Yes, yes, of course, it has. Anyway, have a good time tonight. Wonderful, wonderful, wonderful."

"Let's talk about Chicago," Haylie said. "My meeting with the Endling. The agent said we don't have a lot of time today, and I want to make sure I can get back to school in time for my birthday stuff."

"Yes, dear," Mary said. "Let's talk, I want to hear all about it."

"I don't know, it was kind of a bust," Haylie said. "He didn't say much—didn't like me very much, honestly. He wanted a deal and that's about it. No clues, nothing we didn't already know."

"That's to be expected," Mary said. She slowly pulled her long, gray hair back behind each ear, one side at a time. "But tell me—what did you feel coming out of the room?"

"Like I just said, he didn't tell me—"

"No, dear," Mary's face grew solemn. "What did you *feel?*"

"I don't ... I don't know. He didn't say anything."

"Don't worry about the words," Mary continued. "We all use words every day and they mean nothing. Nothing. Words get in the way of the real truth. Words are our shackles, pinning us down. Don't worry about what he said and didn't say, tell me what makes him tick. What did you walk away *feeling* that you didn't feel before?"

Haylie closed her eyes, trying to play back the meeting in her head. The flow of the words, the air in the room. *How did she feel?* She hadn't bothered to ask herself.

"It was like he was living in a different world," Haylie said. "If he's an outcast, I can see why. He's playing a part that doesn't fit a mold."

"I'd guess he stayed cold," Mary said. "Tried to manipulate you? But not through charm or compliments. No remorse, no empathy. Like ice."

"How..." Haylie looked back at Mary with a curious eye. "How did you know?"

"His hacking patterns," Mary said. "No social agenda, doesn't want fortune. He wants fame—not because he earned it, but because he thinks he should already have it. Probably a sociopath," Mary said, nodding. "But then, I've known lots of lovely sociopaths. Lots of hackers fit that pattern, or at least, did back in the day."

Haylie thought for a moment. "So does that mean that I'm—"

"No, Crash," Mary said, laughing. "Don't worry. You're just fine. And even if you weren't, I wouldn't break that news to you on your birthday."

Haylie laughed out loud, surprising herself, cupping her hands over her mouth to cover the outburst.

"Oh my goodness," Mary giggled, wiping tears from her eyes as the chains on her wrists jingled with each swipe. "So tell me—honestly. Is this our guy?"

Haylie's laughter came to an abrupt stop. She caught her breath, remembering why she was there, reminding herself to not get too comfortable. "I don't get the feeling that he's working with anyone else. I think we were wrong—about the other hacker—I just didn't see it."

Mary leaned forward, tilting her head and staring directly into Haylie's eyes. She didn't blink, she didn't breathe. She just watched.

"What are you afraid to tell me, dear?" Mary whispered. "What's going on inside that wonderful head of yours?"

Her pulse pounding, Haylie shook her head, her eyes drifting to each corner of the room ... anywhere but back to Mary.

"I just want this to be over," Haylie said. "I want to get back to my life. That's all I want. You asked me how I feel, and this is how I—"

"Get back to your life?" Mary asked. "You mean get back *online*, don't you dear? That's what you want. That weight you're feeling: it's not a weight of loss, it's the weight of a woman who is forced to sit down with herself every day. No distractions. No place left to hide."

"That's not fair," Haylie said. "You don't know that."

Mary chuckled. "I know what I know. You're just like I was. Every day, breaking into things or sneaking around walls. Always about the adventure and what's on the other side. My sentence—all this nonsense—took that away."

Haylie sat back as Mary continued.

"Until I came in here," Mary said, "I never had time to figure out who I really was. But now, now I have all the time in the world. At first, I was terrified, my mind turned into a prison itself. But I grew to love the silence, and now I crave it. It's such a rare thing in this world of ours—to be alone. It took me years to realize that I was lucky. And just because I was alone, that didn't mean I didn't have a voice—oh no, quite the opposite. I still had my voice, even if no one was listening. Your voice is the most powerful weapon you have."

Haylie felt herself drifting away into Mary's words and quickly snapped herself back. *Get out of the room. You need to get back to Vector. You need to find your brother.*

"I knew they were on to me, you know?" Mary said. "The police —I knew it was coming, so I took one last trip. Just in case I wasn't good enough—just in case I wasn't smart enough to get away. I jumped on a train and away I went. Do you know where I went?"

Haylie shook her head no.

"To the Met Museum. New York City. Have you been? It's *glorious*. My mother always told me about it, and my goodness was she right. I could have spent weeks there—art and history and things you never thought of. Just a thin piece of glass between you and history. But there was one piece—one magical piece—that I *had* to see before I went away. One my mother had always talked about. Something by Rodin."

Haylie watched as Mary looked past her, to the wall in the back of the room, her eyes misting over.

"It was a fallen caryatid. Now normally, a sculpture like this—a woman holding a block firmly over her head—they were used as columns and supports for buildings, temples, that sort of thing. Like women back in that time, they were ornaments. Decoration. But Rodin saw something others didn't—he saw a force pushing down from above, a force that no one person—man or woman—could possibly take. It's the force I've felt, and the one you feel now. So he carved his statue not standing firm and proud but crumpled down. Struggling to hold the world above her, eyes falling to the floor in anguish. Eyes that had given up. A woman who had given up."

Haylie felt chills run up her arms, through her spine.

You have to tell her. She deserves to know.

"That was me, back then," Mary said. She took a long breath and smiled to herself, rubbing the rings around her wrists as she turned her arms at the elbows. "And now that's you, Crash. Embrace the gift, the time to look inside and see who you really are." She chuckled up to the security camera, perched in the corner and angled directly at the table. She hushed her voice. "I have a feeling you won't have much more time."

Haylie rose. She paced backwards towards the door, searching for words, how to possibly say goodbye without saying goodbye.

Mary sat back in her chair, her restraints tugging at her arms, as she broke into a knowing smile. "Haylie—it so was wonderful to know you, dear. At least for a bit." With another look up at the camera, she whispered. "Do stay in touch."

TWENTY-NINE

The last of the day's pigeons scattered across the courtyard, nudging against each other like bumper cars, fighting for the same chunk of bread under the streetlights. Caesar brought up a list of Wi-Fi networks—the signals raining down from stacks of apartments on every side—and found one with that wonderful combination of a strong signal and terrible security. He logged in, activated his Tor browser, and connected to his online workspace.

"I don't like being out here," he mumbled, straightening his sunglasses. "We're too exposed, even in the dark."

"We're fine," Sean said, not even looking up from his laptop. "No one's going to expect to find us in a place like this, and this is the best spot to get new Wi-Fi networks to use. Besides, you need to experience the nightlife. You look terrible."

"Once we have all the data we need, I'll look better."

Caesar brought up his tracking app and did a check on Haylie's ankle bracelet location, out of habit more than anything else. *San*

Antonio again, looks like she's on 35 headed up to Austin. Maybe she's got a boyfriend down there? He closed the app and shook his head. *She needs her privacy. Stop checking in on her—she can handle herself. Take care of your own problems.*

Caesar and Sean had been waiting for the last push of data from their contact, who had suddenly gone dark on the other side of the world. It wasn't strange for a hacker-for-hire to go days or weeks without communication—or even to just disappear off the face of the Earth—but it didn't usually happen in the middle of a job. Not without some kind of warning.

"You sure we can't just change the voting data after the fact, even in a few of the states?" Caesar asked. "We wouldn't need personal details for that."

"It looks like all of the systems were designed by the same government team," Sean said. "I haven't found any that allow votes to be changed after the initial entry—if they did, this whole thing would be a lot easier. Once a vote is cast, it's locked in there."

"But the bug you found—"

"We can write all the votes we want if we get into the system first —before a person votes. That means we can throw this whole damn election by voting for people who don't show up."

"Or by casting votes before people get to the polls."

"Right," Sean nodded. "But we have to do all that without anyone noticing. If every person in Florida votes at exactly 9 a.m. on Election Day, it's going to raise a lot of eyebrows. We need to be smart about our patterns."

"So what if we record someone's vote and then they go into the booth? Does the system freak out if there's already a vote in there?"

"No, I tested that," Sean said. "The second vote just bounces off. No error, no nothing. You hear from your guy yet?"

"No," Caesar said. "But let's not panic. I sent him another piece of a hack this morning just to see if I could tease him out of the shadows, get him to respond. These people—they can be flaky. It's just part of the business."

Sean looked out into the glowing lights strung across the courtyard, fingers drumming across his keyboard. "There's a chance he got caught, right?"

"By the feds?" Caesar laughed. "The odds of anyone in the government piecing this together are pretty close to zero. They must be completely heads-down so close to the election—just fixing bugs to make sure that nothing goes dark on the big day. Hell, with all the last-minute patches they must have, I'd guess they're creating more security holes than they're fixing. And nobody knows what we're doing—not a chance."

"Sure would be nice to have someone on the inside," Sean said. "So we could find out for sure, you know?"

"We don't need anyone on the inside," Caesar said, his eyes showing a spark. "I mean—we have all the access we need. We can get into any government system we want with the code from the Project."

"You want to..." Sean watched Caesar carefully as he spoke. "You want to hack into the NSA?"

"Sure. Just real quick—in and out."

"Like we don't have enough going on?"

"Don't tell me you don't want to see what their systems look like," Caesar laughed. "C'mon, it'll be fun. And maybe you'll calm down when we verify we're not on their radar. Let me just find it here."

Caesar brought up the folders full of code from the Project and began to wade through the contents. "Access to U.S. traffic networks, some agricultural systems." His eyes grew wide as he read the next folder label. "Commercial Airline Systems Access." He made a quick note of the location. "This one might come in handy someday."

"You could say it louder," Sean said, looking over his shoulder. "I think the guy in the far corner of the courtyard still can't hear you."

Caesar shook his head, ignoring Sean. "Okay—government systems. FBI central server, NSA intranet, CIA database."

"Try the NSA," Sean said between mouthfuls of his drink. "Those guys are always up to something."

"N ... S ... A ..." Caesar muttered as he read the instructions. He typed in the URL and credentials, finally landing on the home screen of the NSA's internal network.

"Wow," Caesar said. "That was a little too easy."

"Search for anything about the Endling," Sean said. "We need his case file. Do it fast—they might be monitoring those credentials."

"Stop worrying so much."

Caesar searched for a few minutes, finally locating the case file for 'The Endling.' He found a folder full of investigation briefs—information about raids on suspected locations, potential next targets, and a list of informants the NSA had contacted for information.

"They're tracking him," Caesar mumbled as he continued digging. "This folder structure makes no sense. It's hard to tell what else is going on."

He stumbled on a folder named 'Suspects' and clicked.

"Crap," Caesar said. "They don't have a name yet, but they have someone in custody. He's in a detention center in Naperville, Illinois. This must be our guy. He got himself caught, the idiot."

Taking a deep breath, Caesar gripped both sides of the laptop.

You can't look nervous. Not in front of Sean. This isn't a big deal.

"I knew it," Sean said, slamming his hands down on the table. A few tourists, floating by with cameras in hand, quickened their steps across the courtyard, veering away from them.

"Could you chill the hell out?" Caesar said. "Who cares if he's in custody? Hell, maybe that's a good thing."

"A good thing? How in the hell ... Explain to me how this could even possibly be in the realm of—"

"The NSA has their man," Caesar said with an artificial smile.

"In their minds, they've captured the Endling, the man behind all these hacks. They're drinking champagne back there in Naperville, Illinois, patting themselves on the back for the amazing job they did. That's *great* for us."

"That means he could talk."

"It means they *stop looking*," Caesar shot back. "Right now, I bet they're focusing on getting him to talk—not looking for us. Plus, he doesn't know a damn thing."

"But what if he does know something? What if we screwed up somewhere?"

"Sean," Caesar said, leaning in. "This is the whole reason we worked with a nutcase like the Endling to begin with. We needed a scapegoat—someone to blame just in case this happened—and voila, he's playing the part perfectly."

"Okay, okay," Sean said, nodding in agreement. "But that doesn't change the fact that we still need more data."

"How much data are we talking about? How many votes do we need?" Caesar asked.

Sean did some quick calculations. "Just like, two percent," he said. "That's the margin I need to turn Ohio over to Ortega. With that and Florida locked down, Hancock loses for sure."

"Let's work the problem," Caesar said, calmly, methodically. "Why do we need the data?"

Sean, surveying Caesar with a suspicious eye, answered slowly. "Are you kidding? Didn't we just—"

"Humor me."

Sean reluctantly continued. "Without the data we can't cast votes for people."

Nodding, Caesar smiled. "So we need two percent more votes for Ortega. Or..."

"Or what?" Sean asked.

"Or two percent fewer for Hancock," Caesar said.

Sean laughed. "Sure, whatever. But we can't stop people from voting for Hancock. That's not how this hack works," he said.

Caesar rubbed his eyes and studied the lights switching off and on in patterns across the sides of the surrounding buildings as night fell. Some connecting, others scattering randomly. He looked back at Sean, chuckling under his breath. "So we just build a second system."

"A second system? We don't have time—"

"Sure we do. I can build it right now," Caesar glanced down at his keyboard, nodding to himself. "I can't believe I didn't think of this sooner."

"I literally have zero idea what you're talking about."

"What's the best way to make sure—one hundred percent sure—that someone can't vote?" Caesar asked.

Sean shrugged his shoulders. "I don't know, dude. Put a rational person on the ticket?"

"No," Caesar said. "It's easy to stop someone from voting. We just kill them. We kill them all."

The table went silent. Sean stared back at Caesar in disbelief, watching him carefully, waiting for him to reveal the real answer. But Caesar sat silent.

Sean checked to see if anyone was nearby before leaning in close, bringing his voice down to a hush. "What the hell are you talking about, man?"

Caesar laughed. "Dead people can't vote, Sean."

"You want to kill..." Sean stammered. "You want to kill two percent of Ohio?"

"No. Just two percent of the people in Ohio that are going to vote for Hancock," Caesar said, nodding to himself.

I can't believe I didn't think of this before.

"Are you okay, man?" Sean asked. "Do you need a day off or something? I know we've been through a lot, but—"

Caesar laughed. "We're not really going to kill them, Einstein."

He cracked the lid to his laptop. "Send me a list of names for all likely Hancock voters in the Ohio precincts."

Caesar logged back into the anonymous shared workspace where he saw Sean's avatar staring back at him in the sidebar, one new message waiting. He grabbed the data Sean had sent his way and scanned the location fields: all from Ohio, all from key precincts in that state. He sorted by age and deleted everyone under sixty-five years old, ending up with a list of around ten thousand.

"What do we know about older voters?" Caesar asked Sean.

"They're unlikely to switch political parties," Sean said. "And they turn out to vote in larger numbers."

"You're forgetting the most important thing," Caesar said. "Old people are more likely to die."

"Why do you keep talking about people dying?" Sean asked. "You're freaking me out."

"Because the system for keeping and changing personal records is completely computer-based in Ohio," Caesar said. "I'm writing a script to ingest each record and ping the Ohio Death Registry."

Sean looked off into the courtyard as he slowly began to nod. "The Death Registry. Votes would be cross-referenced there. If someone had passed away, they would be void from casting a ballot. We have all the data we need for the registry—name, social security number, birth date."

"Looks like Ohio requires that each record of death be signed off by a registered funeral director," Caesar said, checking the input fields in the system. "But that can be done electronically. I'll write a scraper to collect funeral director names from search results, randomize them, and match them with the death records."

After a few more minutes of coding, Caesar hit "return" to bring his script to life. He watched the output as names scrolled down the screen; records being written to the death registry, one at a time.

Gagne, Martin
Status: Deceased
Confirmation: 78AG990

Carmel, Cynthia
Status: Deceased
Confirmation: 78AG992

Caesar's script worked its way through the list, using random timing intervals to fool the systems on the other side into believing this was a seemingly natural pattern. As the script ran, Sean recalibrated his Ohio code to adjust for the shift in votes. There was nothing left standing in the way of them changing the course of history.

The courtyard grew with activity as the nighttime crowd floated away to their different corners, arms over shoulders, and slow, heavy steps into the night.

"Is the code working?" Sean asked, taking a sip of coffee.

"Yeah, it's killing everyone."

"Cool," Sean replied.

THIRTY

Littlefield Hall, University of Texas
Austin, TX
October 31st, 10:01 PM

"Is that all you can remember?" Agent Hernandez said, scanning the government paperwork strewn across Haylie's desk for any missing fields. "Any other details?"

"I don't think so." She paged through the last few sheets of paper, willing her hand to stay still. "It's all in here: the van, the virus, the meeting in Naperville. I just wish I could have gotten something out of him."

"You did fine," Hernandez said, pulling the papers back across the desk. "You're new at this. You did what you were supposed to do." His smile only made her feel a deeper pain in her stomach.

You don't owe him anything.

You have a job to do. Your job is to find your brother.

"I tried," she said. "He was a pretty weird guy, right? Like, what's his story?"

"I've been doing this for a long time," Hernandez said. "Some-

204

times—people just are who they are. No big motive, no evil plan. They just want to do things."

Haylie shrugged. "Well, at least that gives you job security."

Hernandez nodded, looking down at his watch. "Time for my status call with headquarters."

"Am I ... Do you think I'm going to get credit here? Anything that might reduce my sentence?"

"Oh, right," Hernandez said, rubbing his hands together and looking like he was avoiding that subject on purpose. "I'll be honest with you. The answer is: I don't know. With the NSA, I'd have to say I wouldn't count on it. Showing that you were the reason we got the Endling could be ... tricky."

"*Tricky?*" Haylie repeated, adjusting her glasses. "So, if I had a government translator here, that would probably mean another year of this?" She lifted her ankle, pointing it in Hernandez's direction.

"I can't say for sure," Hernandez said. "But what I would say is this: don't wait around for a miracle. I mean, you're in college, for christsakes. Look at me—you see how boring I am, right? Even *I* had a blast in college. Don't wait around for someone to tell you that you can start living your life."

Haylie slouched, pulling her hair back behind her neck and letting it fall down on her shoulders. Her mind was already out there, on the run with Vector, trying to stay one step ahead.

He has no idea, he doesn't have a clue about what's about to happen. Keep it that way, Crash.

"What about Liam?" Hernandez said, a new optimistic light dancing in his eyes. "Sorry, I mean Vector. What about you two? You can't tell me there isn't something going on there."

Haylie took a deep breath. *Play the part.* She looked up at the ceiling, pretending to be embarrassed, which wasn't that hard. "Dunno," she said, softly. "Never really thought about it."

"Oh, come on," Hernandez laughed. "You can tell me. I feel like we know each other after all this, at least a little bit. There's something there, and you know he's waiting for you to send him a signal. Maybe that could be a nice way to spend the next year?"

There was a knock on the door—Vector's knock. Agent Hernandez beamed as he rose from his chair. "I wonder who that could be?" He made his way to the door and turned back towards her before reaching for the knob. "I'm on your side, Haylie. And I think the only thing you're guilty of is being at the wrong place at the wrong time. But for now, we're both kind of stuck here. I say we make the most of it."

He cracked the door as Vector's face appeared. Vector jumped back into the hallway, surprised to see Hernandez. Hernandez passed him on his way out as Vector managed to mutter a low greeting of some sort.

Vector waited for the door to shut and then spun wildly in Haylie's direction, pointing back at the hallway. "What was that all about?" he whispered. "What did you say to him?"

"Nothing, dummy," Haylie said. "Just finishing up a report. He doesn't suspect a thing."

"Good," Vector said, nodding to himself and peeling his backpack off his shoulders. "Very good. Well, what we're about to do certainly won't look good on his record. Can you imagine the paperwork he's going to have to fill out *tomorrow* once we're long gone?"

"Never mind him," Haylie said. "Let's get on with it. Did you get what I asked for?"

"Two fresh identities," Vector said. "Nabbed 'em off the Spice-Coast marketplace. Only going for four dollars apiece these days, oddly enough."

"What about the paperwork?"

"Yeah, that was a little more expensive, but still pretty easy to get, passports are right here," he said, padding the side of his backpack. "And two drivers' licenses, those are easy."

He dug into his pocket and presented a pair of off-white cards, fumbling with them for a moment and handing them over to Haylie.

"Jennifer Mack and David Lightman," she muttered as she flipped the cards over each other, checking the quality. She thought for a moment and glared back up at him. "Are you serious with these names? The two characters from *WarGames*?"

His face falling, Vector raised his hands in defeat. "I panicked. It's the first thing that came to mind."

She handed Vector's card back to him. "It doesn't matter. We'll need new ones once we get where we're going, anyway."

"Where is that, if I might ask?" Vector said.

"I don't know yet," she said. "We need to get out of here and get online. I know how to get into the Endling's system—that's our best bet of tracking down Caesar."

"You can do that?" Vector asked. "How?"

"I saw something on the video screen while I was in the van—his login credentials to his online workspace. He cut and pasted them from a Notepad file. They were just sitting there in plain text."

"You're kidding," Vector said.

"I told you he wasn't very good," Haylie said. "The NSA has the video, but at the speed they move, it could take them weeks to review it. That gives us some time. I just need to get online, and hopefully, we can find something inside."

"Fair enough," Vector said. "Right, here's what I'm thinking." Vector placed his backpack in his lap, unzipping the main pocket and sliding out something roughly the size of a textbook. It was a bag made out of a shiny material, almost metallic. Vector smoothed it out flat across his backpack. "This should do the trick."

"Is that a..."

"It's a Faraday cage," he said. "I've had this lying around for the past few months, wondering when we might get a chance to use it.

Always best to be prepared—that's what my pop always said. Something like that, anyway."

"I've never seen one in person," Haylie gasped. "I thought it would actually be, you know, a cage. A box or wire or something."

"The bigger ones are," Vector said. "But when you're trying to shield something the size of, say, an ankle bracelet, there's no need for all that. A bag will do the trick."

Haylie ran her fingers over the surface, feeling the crinkle and bend of the material move with her touch. "How does it work?"

"It's going to keep signals inside from getting out," Vector said. "Pretty simple, really. Shoplifters use these to place expensive items with RFID tags inside—the signals don't escape the enclosure. We'll do the same thing, but with your ankle bracelet."

Haylie nodded. "If I remove the tracker, the transmitter will send out an emergency signal saying something is wrong. But if it's in the cage, then the signal just bounces around inside the bag, never gets out?"

"That's the idea," Vector said with a smile. "Piece of cake, right?"

———

Agent Hernandez breathed a loud sigh and tossed his keys on the desk from across the room, watching them slide off the top and next to the trash can in the corner. *Nice shot, dude. You've just won another night in this dump.* He was tired of everything: being away from his family, this whole damn assignment, the tiny dorm room, everything and anything about his life. The thought of another year here—well, he had tried his best not to think about it.

He looked across the room at the makeshift kitchen in the corner. His stomach turned at the thought of eating anything from a box again tonight, and the lack of home cooking wasn't doing any favors to his waistline. He opened the small fridge in the corner and scanned the remaining frozen meals with a scowl.

Better get used to it, agent. You're not going anywhere anytime soon.

He ignored the hunger in his belly and cracked his laptop open, logging in. The machine's fan kicked on, churning and straining for power as the screen came to life. The laptop was a brick of a machine —with dinged black edges and an ancient government ID tag, it must have weighed eight pounds. *Eight pounds of slow.* Hernandez wondered how old the computer was, fully knowing that he wasn't due for an upgrade for a long, long time.

He double-clicked on the desktop folder reading "Case File: Black, Haylie." Reviewing the list of documents—court records, scene reports, monthly diaries of activity—he wondered where the last eight months had gone, all wasted babysitting a girl that had done nothing wrong.

All she did was save all of our asses.

I need a new job.

He ran his hands through his hair, loosening the knot of his tie and scrolling the mouse, a dull sheen covering his eyes. As he dragged the cursor to shut down the machine, he saw an alert pop up in the top right corner. It was an email from "Wilcox, Andrea" with the subject line: "Black, H.: Additional paperwork requires signature tonight..."

Crap.

The dialog box disappeared before he could click on it. With a quick curse, he searched for his email application, hitting the "sync all mail" button at the top of the window. As the list refreshed, the message appeared in bold text at the top. He clicked through and leaned close to read the full message.

Wonderful. Just what I needed tonight.

"You ready?" Vector asked.

"Of course I'm not ready," she said, snatching her leg back towards her and pulling at her shin with both hands, cradling herself in a semi-fetal position. "What happens after you take it off?"

"Well, it's going to try to send a signal back to the main servers. If we're fast enough, the bag will stop it. But that's just half the trouble." He reached into his jacket pocket, pulling out a tiny electronic wafer. "We're going to need this."

"A SIM card?" Haylie asked. "Good lord, what's that for?"

Vector grabbed a phone—a new one she hadn't seen before—from his backpack, pushing the tiny door on the side that held its SIM card slot. He switched out the cards and pushed the enclosure shut.

"There's a failsafe on the bracelet, quite a clever device. The FBI will be alerted if it loses contact with your skin," he said. "But the device also sets off an alarm if the pings aren't being received back at headquarters. This SIM card will replace those pings. I've already analyzed the information coming from the device, and I'll use an app on this burner phone, which will look and sound like the bracelet."

"You've already..." Haylie looked at Vector with a shake of her head. "You've been waiting a while to break me out of here, haven't you?"

"I've been bored," he said. "And I figured you'd be asking to do this at some point. You're not the most patient person, you know. Now—are you ready?"

Hernandez hovered over his keyboard as he squinted through the screen's bright, electric glow.

Agent Hernandez — Additional paperwork for Haylie Black attached, it needs to be filed tonight. She needs to review, sign, and fax back copies here and to headquarters.

"You've got to be kidding me." Hernandez checked the clock and shook his head.

There's a week-long break coming up for the clerk, so if this isn't done tonight, we're going to hear about it.

Hernandez scrolled down to the bottom of the email and double-clicked the PDF attached. The old laptop continued to whirl its fan, trying its best to open up the PDF reader software.

———

Haylie closed her eyes and took a breath. *Get ready to run.*

"Right," Vector said, thumbing at his phone screen. "Bringing up the app now. I've got the coordinates, the IP address we need to ping, and the right JSON data structure. In just a minute, we'll have that ugly thing off your ankle and the government servers won't know the difference." Selecting a few options, he watched the app go to work, and then back up to Haylie. "It's all set, once we toss the device in the bag, we'll be in business."

She nodded, taking a few deep breaths—like she was about to jump into the deep end of a pool—and reached down. She pulled up the leg of her jeans, showing the ankle bracelet.

"Let's go."

———

Hernandez drummed his fingers, clicking his fingernails across the laptop's keys as he waited for the document to download. He watched the progress bar.

We have got to get new computers. Or what does Haylie call them —machines? Machines. Yeah, I like that. That sounds way cooler.

The progress bar finally filled to a full blue rectangle, and Hernandez paged through the document to make sure everything was in order. He hit the "print" button and looked over to the corner where his printer sat. A single red light blinked back at him.

What now?

He fell down to the floor, crawling on his knees and brought his eye to the printer's front panel. He read the tiny, dark gray text etched under the red light.

TRAY 1 EMPTY

Oh, come on.

He rose to his feet, scrambled back to the desk and rattled through the drawers, searching for a ream of paper. *I'm out? I can't be out.* He cobbled together a few loose sheets—just enough for what he needed tonight—straightening them into a stack and slid them into the paper tray.

I hate this job.

———

"Now!"

With a slash of his pocketknife, Vector cut the ankle bracelet's band in two. Haylie, holding the Faraday bag open directly next to her foot, slid the bag over the device.

"Hit the SIM emulator," Haylie whispered, tossing the bag to the side, treating like it was toxic waste.

Vector grabbed his phone with both hands, activating the app.

As a slight pinging sound rang from the phone's speaker, he smiled, extending the phone in Haylie's direction with the screen facing her.

She saw a crude app with a few status indicators, but one reading "SIM signal verified" and another green block of text reading "ACTIVE." A timer in the corner counted down towards zero, now at a minute and a half. She watched the seconds count down as she rubbed her ankle with relief.

"Nothing to see here, FBI people," Vector said, obviously proud of his work. "Haylie Black is safe in her dorm room and will be staying in tonight, thank you very much."

———

The printer whirled to attention as Hernandez heard the grumbling of gears and the sound of paper being sucked in through the bottom tray.

The first page of the printout rolled out onto the top, still warm to the touch. Hernandez sat huddled on the floor next to the machine, pulling each sheet towards him, fresh off the press.

Three more to go.

On the desk, far away across the room, his phone buzzed a notification, masked by the churning of the printer's work.

A56 Notification: Haylie Black.
Location alert. Device breach.

———

"So where are we going?" Vector said, admiring his app as it pinged.

"Not sure. I just want to get moving somewhere, anywhere." Pushing her glasses up the bridge of her nose, she slid her field jacket over one arm at a time and double-checked the contents of her backpack.

This should be enough for a few days. We can always buy things on the road as we—

"Wait a minute," Vector said.

She looked over to see him standing above the Faraday Cage bag, gazing down inside. From her angle, she could see a flashing light reflecting off the sides. But it wasn't green anymore—it was red. His eyes shot back to her with a look of terror.

"You were supposed to ... You didn't close the bag."

"You never said anything about closing the bag."

He stepped back a few steps, eyes still locked on the Faraday Cage. "It doesn't work if you don't close the bag. You have to *close the bag.*"

"Why didn't you tell me that I had to—"

"I figured that you were smart and all that and could figure out that leaving a bag open wouldn't keep anything inside from sending out signals."

Haylie's heart raced. She stared down at the metallic fabric and the reflection of the red light from inside.

"Let's get the hell out of here," Vector said, running for the door.

"Should we ... close it now?" Haylie asked, slinging her duffel bag over her shoulder.

"It's too late for that, come on!"

———

Everything looks like it's in order.

Shuffling the papers, he cracked his door open, reflexively checking his pocket for his keys with a pat-pat of his palm. Empty. Looking back to the desk, he saw the shine of metal lying on the floor by the trash can. He walked back over, swiped them off the carpet, and headed out into the hallway.

As the door closed behind him, he made his way two doors down to Haylie's room, pressing his ear gently against the wood, trying to make out any kind of sound that he could. He couldn't hear a thing.

"Haylie," he said, rapping at the door with light knuckles. "Agent Hernandez. I know it's late but I need one more signature from you tonight. It's important."

Still nothing. Hernandez reached into his pocket to shoot her a quick note but found an empty pocket where his phone belonged. *Must have left it in the room.* He brought out his keys, cycling through them and finally finding himself holding the one reading "Black, H." on the fat part of the metal.

"I'm coming in," he said. "I wouldn't normally do this, but like I said, this is a big deal."

He pressed the key into the lock, past all the scuffed brass—a victim of Haylie's lock-picking lessons—and turned the knob.

The papers fell from his hand, scattering across the floor. He turned and ran.

THIRTY-ONE

Frankfurt, Germany

November 1st, 9:03AM

Caesar basked in the morning light, feeling the warmth on his shoulders as the sunlight covered the back of his shirt. He flipped his sunglasses on and took a sip of tea, wincing at the taste but welcoming the warmth. It wasn't the coffee he was used to, but he figured he'd mix it up a bit today. Maybe the switch would calm his nerves.

"Everything all right over there?" Sean asked.

Caesar wrung his hands together as he scanned the crowd. The old-style German buildings framing the courtyard looked down from their peaked roofs, reaching into the sky with jagged edges, like giant, magnified pixels struggling to form a diagonal line. It would have been a perfect, crisp fall morning if it hadn't been for the enormous weight hanging over his head, pushing down, heavier as each hour, each minute, passed.

"Too many distractions out here," Caesar said. "I feel exposed."

"Yeah, you keep saying that," Sean said. "I like it out here. Being cooped up, hiding in hotels all day—we might as well be in prison." He took a sip from his water bottle. "And I don't want to be in prison. Chill out, man. No one's looking for fugitives around here, especially this early."

The bell tower rang, causing Caesar to flinch out of his seat. Pigeons scattered under their table as the flow of tourists grew with each passing minute, carving around the table like rising water finding its way down a riverbank.

"Maybe we should get out of Frankfurt," Caesar said, his eyes flicking back and forth, pulling at his collar, feeling it tighten. "Head south. Stay mobile."

If I was doing surveillance, how would I do it? Maybe from one of those windows?

He craned his neck to look past the edge of the umbrella shading them from the sun, trying to check for anything suspicious on the upper floors of the building across the way. All he could see were empty windows, some half-open, others with flower pots perched outside. No people.

"We're fine," Sean asked, absorbed in his screen. "Enjoy the morning."

"Enjoy the morning?" Caesar said. "The election is in five days and I have to code voting patterns for seventy-four more precincts. They all need to be varied, the timing modules all need different algorithms in place. If anyone notices that one area's votes look off, they'll tie it to something bigger."

"No one's going to know," Sean said. "You're giving them way too much credit. Think about what you're saying—you interned for the government back in college, right?"

"Yeah," Caesar said. "Sure."

"Great," Sean said. "And how many genius-level computer scientists did you work with that summer?" Sean stared at Caesar across the table, waiting for his answer. "Ten? Twenty?"

"None," Caesar said. "It was pretty dead there."

"That's what I thought," Sean said. "And when you graduated from college and could pretty much pick any job you wanted, you went straight to the government, right?"

"I went to Brux," Caesar said, getting the point. "Hell, I was working for three startups before I even graduated."

"Right," Sean said. "Because that's what smart people do. They go places where other smart people are. And these days, none of them go to work for the NSA or FBI or certainly not the Federal Election Committee to catch hackers. *None.*"

Caesar thought for a moment and took another sip of his tea, keeping his eye on the crowd around them. He knew Sean was right, but he wasn't ready to show it.

"You worry too much," Sean said. "Government workers are too busy watching the clock to catch guys like me and you. And that's even if we had left a trail for them to follow, which we haven't. Enjoy. The. Morning."

Caesar nodded, noticing that the sun had drifted past the angle of the windows. The beam of light was now shining above them, across the crisscrossed white and brown façade of the restaurant.

"I just can't—" Caesar fought to find the right words. "I can't focus knowing they are trying to hunt us down. I have to know what they know."

Letting out a loud exhale, Sean pointed down to Caesar's laptop. "So, log back in. Check on their progress."

Caesar felt his mouth pull up to a lazy grin. "Really? You wouldn't mind? I mean, it's a risk."

"It's a risk having you complain all the time," Sean said. "A risk to my sanity. Just get in and out if it'll calm you down."

Caesar quickly brought up his browser and logged back into the NSA system, excitedly checking the case file for any new updates.

"What's it say?" Sean asked.

"They've still got the Endling in custody," Caesar muttered as he read. "They've been interrogating him, but he hasn't given them anything. Nothing about the election, and nothing about us. They think he's holding out for a deal."

"See?" Sean said. "Even if they give that clown a deal, it would take weeks to put it together. And like you said before—he doesn't know anything, anyway."

Caesar nodded, leaning back in his chair, feeling a cold wave of relaxation drift over his body. *They don't know we're here. They don't even know what we're trying to do. This is perfect—this is going to work.* As he enjoyed the moment, he tabbed lazily through the folder labeled: "Personnel." He clicked in and saw a list of IDs, ordered by date.

"Huh," he said. "They're adding people to the team. Last time I checked there were ten on the list, now I'm seeing fifteen. You'd think they'd be cutting back the numbers after finding their guy."

"Let me see," Sean said, flipping the laptop over in his direction. He navigated through the page with one hand while scratching his chin with the other. "Wow, these guys don't take any chances—even the names of the agents are in code. 'AN-AD-19899.' 'NO-PE-17899.'"

"Those aren't all agents," Caesar said, spinning the laptop back around. "The number in each string tells their rank. Anything starting with a '1' is an agent, '2' is an analyst, and so on. '9's are guest users."

"How do you know that?" Sean asked.

"I was an intern, remember?" Caesar said. "We used the same system. It's an easy pattern to remember: first two letters of the first name, first two letters of the last name, and then the ID number. I still remember my handle: 'CA-BL-78739.' My boss called me 'The Cable Kid.'"

"The Cable Kid?" Sean laughed. "That doesn't even make any sense."

"I know," Caesar said. "Like you said—not a lot of geniuses running around."

He scanned the list, picturing each agent on the other side of the world trying to piece together the mystery behind the Endling. Each agent trying to outsmart the other, wanting nothing more than to burst into the Lead Agent's office with a big break in the case. Caesar played with the sorting function on the screen, reading the list from different angles. He clicked on the "date created" column, bringing up the list in order of newest to oldest. His hands froze.

"The latest team member," Caesar said. "It's—"

He blinked, swallowing whatever he could down his throat, as the ID stared back at him. His brain flew into motion, putting the pieces together.

MA-MI-90667

Caesar looked up at Sean, his jaw dropping.

"I don't believe it," Caesar said. "The newest guest account, it was created just a few days ago. First two letters 'MA' last two letters 'MI.'"

Sean's eyes flicking down to the laptop with a mild show of panic. He was doing the math on his side of the table as well. He looked up to Caesar as a mix of panic and doubt flashed across his face.

"Mason Mince," Caesar said. "It's him. It *has* to be him."

"You don't know that," Sean said. "That's got to be a coincidence. It could be someone else—lots of names start with 'm' and 'a.' And besides, what would he be doing on the Endling team? He's too busy running around planning his next world order."

"He put it together. He's on to us. It's only a matter of time."

"Forget about it, man," Sean said. "Even if it is him, it doesn't change the fact that there's no way he can get to us in time. There's no way for him to stop us. And it doesn't change what we need to do."

Caesar's heart plunged as his eyes scanned the user handle, over and over.

MA-MI-90667

THIRTY-TWO

NSA Texas Cryptologic Center
San Antonio, TX
November 1st, 9:03AM

"Mary Milward, Inmate #45099256. Please come forward."

She rose from the bench, stretching her legs one after the other, and shuffled her way towards the guard. Her palms faced the ceiling, straining against her handcuffs—a gesture that wasn't mandated while in custody, but she had learned over the years that it was usually appreciated by the guard on the other side. Sometimes, in here, small gestures went a long way.

She glanced off to the right, avoiding any eye contact that might be taken as aggression, as the guard checked and double-checked her paperwork. He pulled a keychain from his belt and unlocked each of her hands from the cuffs.

Mary looked down in curiosity, rubbing her wrists. The guard nodded over to the door.

"They're waiting for you in there."

Interesting.

The table at the center of the room held nothing, save an old ankle bracelet, lying with the transmitter face-down on the tabletop and the cut, frayed ends of the black nylon band extending into the air, like a turtle dead on its back. Agents Wilcox and Hernandez sat across the table, wearing matching expressions: a mix of equal parts confusion and panic.

"Good morning, Mary," Agent Wilcox said. "Won't you have a quick sit and join us? We thought we'd have a chat—that all right with you?"

"Is that what I think it is?" Mary asked pointing down at the device on the table.

"That bracelet used to be attached to Haylie's ankle," Agent Hernandez said. "You happen to know anything about it, Mary?"

"We know you and Ms. Black got along, is all," Agent Wilcox said. "Thought we'd ask before jumping to any conclusions."

"Now how would I know anything about that?" Mary asked.

"I'm going to go ahead and take that as a 'no'," Agent Wilcox said. "But I should tell you that any assistance you may provide would put you in a favorable position when parole time comes round. Unless, of course, you were somehow *involved* in the escape."

Laughing, Mary rubbed her wrists and sat back. "Involved? My goodness, you two have a flair for the dramatic, don't you? Involved. From in here? You think I snuck out of federal prison to cut off a girl's ankle bracelet? You realize she's one of the smartest hackers in the world, right? What makes you think she needs my help?"

"Like I said," Agent Wilcox responded, "you two got along."

"You've been watching too many movies," Mary said. "And besides, if I were you, I'd be more concerned about Haylie's safety than anything else right now." She lowered her voice. "I just hope that poor girl is all right."

"And why's that?" Agent Wilcox asked, slinking against the back of her chair.

"You assume she ran," Mary said. "But she's a celebrity now, no thanks to all of your press conferences, all of your chest-beating and your 'justice has been done' talk after the whole London thing. This is a girl who has taken down powerful people. Why on Earth would she want to run all alone into this big, scary world? Maybe you should have kept a better eye on her, Agent Hernandez. Maybe one of those powerful people came back to find her."

Shaking her head, Wilcox cracked a slight grin. "Ms. Black's safety has always been our priority," she said. "We have no evidence of foul play here. If you ask me, I think there's something else going on."

"How could she plan something without you knowing?" Mary asked. She pointed up to the corner at the camera angled down at the table. "What, with your IP trackers and your fancy security, always watching, always knowing. You can see everything she could see. You've seen more than I have, that's for sure. Why would I know something you don't?"

Agent Hernandez turned to Agent Wilcox. "She's protecting Haylie. I knew she'd do this."

"No, dear," Mary said. "You've got it all wrong. I don't owe Crash a thing. I can just see more clearly than you. I can see what you don't see."

"And what's that?" Agent Hernandez asked. "Enlighten me."

"You're under pressure, and you're panicking," Mary said. "You aren't thinking straight, Agent Hernandez. You let her get away, and now you're reaching out for any solution to the problem, other than yourself. 'This must be Mary's fault. There must be some grand plan in the works.' Maybe you should just do your job better?"

Agent Hernandez stood, pacing back towards the back wall and buttoning his jacket tight. He turned, pointing back at Mary. "You know something. I *know* you do."

"Even if I did, what makes you think I would hang that poor girl out to dry?" Mary said. "After everything you've put her through? You should be ashamed of yourself. She's, what, eighteen? What if she did outsmart you and sneak away? Can you blame her for that?"

"Damn right I blame her," Hernandez said. "She broke out of federal custody. She is in violation of—"

"You think she had a choice?" Mary said. "Your agreement was a trap. You knew she wouldn't last—everyone knew that. Besides, she's not the type to run without a reason."

"And what would that be?" Agent Wilcox asked. "What's the reason, Ms. Milward?"

Mary sat back, stretching her wrists, one over the other, and brought them back down to the table.

"You can't see it from the inside," Mary said. "I think that's your problem. You're smart, but sometimes smart isn't good enough. You need the right angle, the right viewpoint, to see things clearly. You have been destroying people's trust for years, bit by bit. One little piece at a time. You get away with it—what, with your fancy lawyers and your gray suits—but there's payback. There most certainly is payback."

"Ms. Milward, I'm going to have to ask you to stay on topic," Agent Wilcox said. "Do you or don't you have information that can—"

"This system you have," Mary said. "The system that you two work for, every day. The reason you wake up in the morning—it's a failed experiment. A panopticon. Nothing more."

"Sorry, a *what*?" Hernandez said.

"A panopticon," Mary said with a raised voice. "Agent Hernandez, it seems that your knowledge of history is worse than your babysitting skills if that's even possible. It's an old prison design—cells arranged in a circle facing a tower. It was designed to scale the power of the people in charge. Knowing there was a possibility of being watched was just as powerful as actually being watched. The theory was that the threat of authority would keep prisoners in line. Eat away at them, every minute of every day."

"This is fascinating," Hernandez said with a wave of his fingers, pulling his phone from his pocket. "Not helpful, though. Not at all."

"What I can see from the outside, from my view," Mary said, "is that you've designed your whole system wrong. You can watch anyone at any time—through wiretaps or Roar-4 or whatever else you have hiding in those rooms back there—but you don't tell the people that. You're *ashamed* of it. And that means the people don't bend to the weight of authority you have; they are surprised by it when it's finally revealed. They are *outraged* by it. A system like that doesn't build law and order, it builds mutiny."

Agent Hernandez threw his arms up in the air, rolling his eyes.

"But that's not your problem," Mary said. "Not with Haylie Black."

"Be a dear, Ms. Milward," Agent Wilcox said in a mocking tone. "And tell me—what *is* our problem?"

"Your problem isn't that Crash is running," Mary said. "It's that you and your failed system did nothing to *change* her before she ran. You never meant to rehabilitate that poor girl. You just cut her off, put her on pause. Put her behind glass. When you do that to someone —to someone like Crash—they don't change for the better, they get bottled up. They explode."

Agent Wilcox nodded over to Hernandez. They stood and made their way to the corner, whispering. They argued a few volleys, with Agent Wilcox taking the lead towards the end. The two agents walked back to the table.

"I can't believe I'm actually doing this." Agent Wilcox took a pen and paper out of her bag and placed it on the table. She spun the pen counterclockwise under her fingers as she kept her eyes locked on Mary.

"I'm out of time," Wilcox said. "And I'm out of options. There's a full pardon here in this folder. This paperwork will get you out of jail, and you'll never have to see my beautiful face again."

She reached down to the folder on the table and flicked it across to Mary, followed by the pen.

"But awarding you this pardon is completely up to my discretion," Agent Wilcox said. "It's *my call.* So I'm going to need you to start speaking English, and start working along with us and save us any further history lessons."

Mary reached out and held the folder in her hands. She couldn't force herself to open it, she didn't want to learn it wasn't true.

"I want you to forget about Ms. Black for now," Wilcox said. "And I want you to focus on what we need. The Endling wasn't working alone—you know it, and I know it. We need to find out who he was working for, and why. And we need to do it fast."

Mary nodded, silently, still grasping at the folder.

Wilcox continued. "I've got Washington breathing down my neck. Forty-eight hours, that's what you've got. Full access to any system you want, the accounts are ready to go. If you hand me hard evidence, you're a free woman. If you don't, the cuffs go back on. If I were you, I'd do yourself a favor and get to work, because you're never going to see another deal like this. Not in your lifetime."

Mary ran her finger across the edge of the folder, her heart pounding.

Forty-eight hours.

Mary peeled back the top side of the folder and read the deal word for word, front to back. She closed it, resting both hands on top, one folded over the other, and looked Agent Wilcox dead in the eyes.

"When do we start?" Mary asked.

THIRTY-THREE

La Grenouille Hotel
New Orleans, LA
November 1st, 8:45PM

Haylie tossed the brass key onto the antique desk and watched it slide across the shine of the tabletop, spinning into the cord of the desk phone and landing right smack under the bottom of her new shopping bag. The sounds, smells, and soul of Bourbon Street drifted up through the window, pushing back the curtains in flaps and twists towards the desk. She kicked off her boots, sat down and rubbed her feet.

The past twenty-two hours had been a long, drawn-out blur. Driving across central Texas in the middle of the night felt as alien as Mars—just a whole sea of uncharted nothing. She and Vector had agreed that New Orleans was the perfect next stop for them—far enough away from Austin, but still with direct flights to most of the world. The pair had passed their time in the car planning and brainstorming ideas for their steps to find Caesar, the whole time trying to concentrate on their next move, and not on the fact that they were now fugitives.

They had made good time, with the occasional stop for food, and one stop for hair dye and clippers from a drug store a few miles off the highway just before the state line. There, Haylie and Vector had given each other makeovers—her hair now jet black, his long locks sitting at the bottom of a trashcan somewhere outside of Beaumont, Texas.

"Right," Vector said, pulling a rectangular box from the shopping bag in dramatic fashion, like a sword from a sheath. He handed it over to Haylie, flashing a smile. "We're on our way now."

Haylie peeled the plastic wrap from the laptop box, balling it up and tossing it close enough to the trash can to count. She pulled the cover off the box with a satisfying sucking noise, revealing a brand new, aluminum laptop shell.

"You know," Vector said from over her shoulder. "You can do anything you want now. They're not watching anymore—at least, that is until we get caught."

Haylie cracked the laptop open, running her fingers across its perfect, slick black keys. It was the first thing she had asked for after they hit the road—she needed to get her hands on technology. Not just to feel its power again, but because she knew it was the only thing that could close the distance between them and her brother, the only thing that could save him from a lifetime of regret.

She hit the power button and inhaled as the laptop let out a dull chime. The machine booted up and she clicked through the basic setup instructions, entering the hotel's free Wi-Fi code and soaking in the blank desktop, full of nothing but possibilities. It was ready for whatever she wanted to throw its way.

"It's going to take me an hour or so," she stammered as she opened a browser window. "To set it up. To—"

"No worries," Vector said with a laugh. "Take your time. Enjoy it."

As she installed each application, each new package, visited sites for updates, she felt herself get sucked into the screen. Swimming in it all. Flying from site to site, trying to absorb everything she'd missed. She drifted off, weaving her way through discussion threads and talk-tracks, new concepts and old, and found her place back where she loved to go: in the middle of everything she loved.

The hotel room's door clicked open and Haylie snapped back to reality, looking over to see Vector entering, cradling a few cans of energy drinks in his arms. She snuck a peek at the clock in the top right corner of the screen—she had just lost twenty minutes. She sat back, her eyes glazed over with an electric glow.

"Ok," she said. "I'm ready."

"Your fingers all working and everything?" Vector asked. "Remember how to type?"

She brought up a browser window and closed her eyes for a moment, taking herself back to the van in Chicago, where she was watching the Endling cut and paste his login credentials to his online workspace and log in. She breathed slowly, trying her best to recall the text from his window.

"I remember the username," she said, typing it out into her Text-Edit program. "It's the password I can't quite get. I think there were three 4s in there, somewhere. Let me try a few different variations."

After a few attempts, Haylie found the right combination. The workspace homepage appeared, showing a file repository, active messages, and a list of users with access to the account.

"I'm going to check the message history," she said.

Each note back and forth was between the Endling and one other user: someone named Nomad22. Nomad22 had sent messages a few times a week over the past few months, including cryptic lists of sites, plaintext words and phrases, and a few image files.

"There's not much to go on here," Haylie said. "It's pretty sparse. Even if this Nomad22 guy is Caesar, I'm not seeing anything that gives me a clue about where he might be."

"We could just send him a message from this account, right?" Vector said, scratching at his new buzz cut. "Try and get him to respond, to tell us something?"

"I don't want to risk it," she said. "Once the NSA checks the video from Chicago, they'll be in here pretty fast. We don't want them to know that we've been in here, too."

Vector walked to the window, looking down on the Bourbon Street crowds below, and took a sip of his energy drink. "We've got nothing," he said, reaching into the bag to fetch the box for a new phone. "We're running for our lives, and we don't even know where we're running to. Nice one."

"Calm down, drama queen," Haylie said. "We'll figure it out. There's got to be something in here. Let me look again."

Vector pulled a phone from the bag, tossing the plastic wrap on the bed and pulling the SIM card slot out. "This is such a pain, this whole thing. Can you imagine living like this? Changing our names every few days? New phones? New identities? I'm the kind of guy who just likes to get something set up and roll with it."

"Who knows," Haylie said, still searching the file repository. "Maybe you'll like it. You never know until you try."

Vector booted up the phone, staring down at the "Set Up Your New Device" screen. "Ugh. Setup. Setup is the worst."

"Oh, please," Haylie said, growing annoyed. "Just think what Caesar has been going through—he's been living like this since London. We've been on the run for less than twenty-four hours. Eight months of this can't be any sort of picnic."

Vector stopped in his tracks, looking down at the phone, and then back over to Haylie. "Wait a minute," he said, walking over to the desk and gesturing at the machine.

Haylie twisted back to give him a view of the laptop. He hovered over the screen, scanning the message list up and down, tracing the right column with his finger. "There, that one," he said with an excited point. "The most recent note from Nomad22 to the Endling, the one with the attachment."

Haylie resumed control of the machine, clicking the message open. It contained no text, only a photo of a white sheet of paper with 'crp78rt90' printed in messy handwriting across its face.

"It's a username or password—they put it on a piece of paper to mix up the communication pattern. Probably written with his left hand to avoid identification. Standard stuff."

"It's not the password I care about," he said. "It's the image file. Caesar's on the run, right? Just like us. He's probably setting up new hardware—laptops, phones—a few times a week, you just said it yourself. Well, when you're doing that, there's a chance you could forget things sometimes. You don't take the time to adjust every setting, every time."

"Sure," Haylie said, looking back to the picture of the password. "But who cares?"

"Do you remember a few months back?" he asked, his voice growing with excitement. "That hacker in Finland who got busted for leaving calling cards with all his exploits? He would leave pictures of trains for some reason?"

"Sure, I think I remember you saying something about that."

"Ok," Vector said. "He got busted because he got sloppy. For his last hack, he took a picture with a burner phone, but forgot to turn off the GPS."

Haylie nodded. "GPS is embedded by default in every photo unless it's disabled. To turn it off you have to go way down in the settings."

"So," Vector said. "Maybe Caesar made the same mistake." He pointed to the screen. "Check the meta data for this image file."

She did a search for the image analysis application that had always been her go-to, downloaded it, and got it up and running. "If it's really this easy, the NSA won't be far behind us." She loaded the image into the application and hit the 'Submit' button. "Here—the results are up."

"What'd you get back?"

Haylie scrolled through the list of metadata. "Usage rights, Image Programs, Region ... no, no, no," she read out loud, trying to hear her own thoughts over the music floating in from the street below. "Ok, here's the geotag."

She clicked on the field to expand its results. With a few clicks, a map came up. She zoomed out, checking the country.

"Bingo," she said.

"Where we going?" Vector asked.

"Frankfurt. We're headed to Germany."

THIRTY-FOUR

Grandhotel Frankfurt
Frankfurt, Germany
November 2nd, 3:18PM

"Everything's coming together," Sean said, rattling down the to-do list on his phone. "I'll need to tweak some algorithms here and there, but otherwise, the election should be a lock."

Caesar checked his timetable, his scripts, the clock, and then allowed the reality to flood over him: Sean was right. *We're actually ready for this.* He had been keeping a brave face, but it was a face that was hiding piles—hell, mountains—of doubt that they could actually bring everything they needed together in time. But there it was, just staring back at him—the code that would change the world. The code that would change his life.

"Celebration time," Sean said, rising from his seat with a jump. "I'm starving, and we could use a few hours off before we start running through our tests. There's a place I've been dying to try a few blocks away."

"Let me just check the access scripts one more time," Caesar said.

"We need to eat," Sean pleaded. "How about we just go to dinner and *not* call it a celebration?"

"Fine," Caesar laughed. "Dinner time. But we'll need some cash. Spent the last of it this afternoon."

"No problem there," Sean said, opening a window on his laptop. "Checking the bank balance..." He flashed a grimace, rubbing the bridge of his nose.

Caesar walked around the table to get a better look at Sean's screen. "Wow, I didn't realize it was this low. Not a big deal, let's do another transfer."

"You sure?" Sean asked. "We'll need to create a new set of credentials. I'm not sure that we want to be setting off any alarm bells this late in the game."

"Eh, it's fine," Caesar said. "That system is twenty years old. No one's paying attention; I doubt anyone even remembers it's there. Besides, I thought you were starving?"

———

NSA Texas Cryptologic Center
San Antonio, TX

Where would I go? What would I do?

Mary paged through the files, growing desperate for inspiration with every turn. The NSA didn't have much to go on, that was for sure. If this was the whole file, Mary suddenly realized how lucky they'd been to catch him in the first place.

I've been through this ten times. There's nothing new.

Where would I go? What would I do?

I'd be moving. I'd be mobile.

Without being able to get inside the hacker's head—knowing his end goal—Mary knew this wouldn't be easy. She didn't see anything for sale in any hacker marketplace—not even the ones that were hidden far away from the prying eyes of government goons—that matched the data they had collected. They were using it for themselves. They were saving it for something big.

I'd need a place to stay. I'd need money.

She brought up the FBI's financial services desk and checked the notification log. Dozens of bank robberies over the last few days, but no suspects still at large.

They wouldn't be robbing physical locations—too many cameras, too much security. They're smarter than that.

She checked the database for online exploits for major banks, but nothing had come up in the past few days—nothing that had been successful, anyway. She scrolled down the list, working bank by bank until she found an entry at the bottom that read 'XX_Other.'

Shrugging, she clicked on the folder and found a single entry.

SWIFT_Access

"SWIFT?" she whispered to herself. "I can't believe they're still using that old dinosaur." She clicked on the folder, showing the records from the previous two days, and leaned in. What she saw made her bolt up from her chair.

She waved over to the agents on the other side of the room. "Get over here, you want to see this," Mary yelled, snapping her fingers in the air.

"What'd you find?" Hernandez asked, stirring a cup of coffee.

"It's the SWIFT system," Mary said, watching the screen for new updates. "There's a new login. From just a few minutes ago. I don't believe this—I can't believe I didn't think about this before."

"SWIFT system?" Hernandez asked. "What the hell is a SWIFT system?"

Mary sat back from the keyboard and took a breath. "Not *a*

SWIFT system, *the* SWIFT system. These guys who were paying the Endling—they need money, right? Everyone needs money. These hackers don't fit the pattern of being financed by a terrorist group or nation-state. Hacking banks directly would be one way to go, but these guys seem better than that. The SWIFT system manages all financial transactions across the world. It's like a backroom network for banks to move money around."

"The Society for Worldwide Interbank Financial Telecommunication," Agent Wilcox's voice drifted from across the room as she approached. She leaned over to look at Mary's screen with a grin. "But it's never been hacked before."

"Sure it has," Mary shot back. "Plenty of times, I'm sure. And now it's so old, no one really pays attention to it anymore."

"If they need money, this is a pretty smart way to get it," Agent Wilcox said, nodding. "Hacking a bank's website or ATM isn't easy—that's where all the security investment goes these days. No one knows about SWIFT, which means its security is probably terrible."

"I can verify that," Mary added, navigating her way through the system logs. "Even back in my day there was a backdoor to give yourself God-like access, but those accounts would expire each month. Hell of a bug, but as long as no one has gone too crazy with it, I'd bet it's still there."

"Is that right?" Agent Hernandez asked, studying Mary carefully.

"Allegedly," Mary corrected herself. "So I've heard."

"Keep going," Agent Wilcox said, gesturing over to Mary's laptop.

"If we assume these guys know about the SWIFT vulnerability," Mary said, "they'd need to sign in as admins and create a new account if they want to move any money around."

"And that's what you're seeing?" Hernandez asked.

"A new one just popped up," Mary said. "And there has been one created each month for the past eight months. What these guys don't know is that the SWIFT system gathers an IP on the other side. It sets up its own connection—won't work without one."

"You're kidding," Wilcox said.

"What does that tell us?" Hernandez said.

"They're in Frankfurt," Mary said, looking back at the screen, showing a map. She pressed her finger onto the glass on a blinking dot hovering over the map. "They're in this hotel right here."

THIRTY-FIVE·

Approaching the Central Station
Frankfurt, Germany
November 2nd, 3:32PM

Rubbing the sleep from her eyes, Haylie felt the train slowing as the buildings outside the window grew closer, their sides growing taller and forming a grid around them. She looked over to see Vector coding away, still connected to the train's Wi-Fi.

"This GPS location should be extremely accurate," Vector said. "We can be pretty sure that he's here." He pointed at the Google Map, angling the 3D view in her direction to show a hotel poised over a twisting knot of roads, directly across from the Frankfurt Central train station. "We know he's in the hotel, but I don't know which room. There must be two-hundred rooms in this place. It's huge."

"Two hundred and sixty-six," Haylie corrected him. "I grabbed the current register for the day when the image was posted."

"How'd you manage that?" Vector asked.

"Their entire network is built on an operating system released in

2001," Haylie said with a chuckle. "It's not even getting security updates anymore, it was 'end-of-life'd last year."

"So there's no way that Caesar signed in with his real name, right?"

"No chance. If I were him, I wouldn't be using *any* real name," she said. "I compared the hotel guest list with manifests from Frankfurt airport and rail systems for recent visitors to the city."

"But how did you..."

"Don't worry about it," she said. "Cross-checking the lists, all but three guests staying at the hotel traveled here on valid passports in the past week."

"So we have three rooms to check?"

"Two of the names are female," Haylie said. "My brother's good, but not *that* good. The third name—staying in room 1710—has to be him."

"What's the plan? Do we just walk up to his room and knock?"

Looking back out the window, Haylie had been wondering the same thing. She knew they couldn't just sit around waiting for him in the lobby or a nearby coffee shop—the clock was ticking. But walking into a hotel meant cameras and security and maybe even questions from curious staff members. It made her more than just a little nervous.

Vector typed away at his keyboard, squinting to read the small text on the screen. "I'm looking for anything on the HackBot boards around new hotel security exploits, but I'm not seeing anything new. The past few months have been quiet—nothing that would get us in. Just the same old stuff."

Just the same old stuff.

She turned back to her machine and started a fresh search, seeing the high arches of the Frankfurt Central train terminal appearing through the window. She scanned the results, grinning.

"Just like I thought—this hotel chain hasn't updated their system in years. Their head of technology left a while back, and they still haven't filled the position. I'm seeing complaints from guests about outdated tech all throughout every location."

"So?"

"So, we should be able to get into any room we want," she said, scanning the search results. "We don't need a new exploit; we can use an old one. Here—this one—from a few years back."

She moved the screen over to Vector, who quickly read the top paragraph and smiled.

"We need to find an electronics store," she said.

Bringing up a new search window, Vector gave her a sideways glance. "Do you really think something this stupid is going to work?"

"Please," Haylie said. "The stupidest way in is the best way in. Always."

———

Grandhotel, Frankfurt

Haylie stepped across the elevator threshold and into the hallway of the hotel's seventeenth floor as Vector held the door and stayed close behind her. She snaked her head around the corner to check for anyone in the hallway; it was empty and still. She pointed at the sign affixed to the wall, showing that room 1710 was down the hall to the right.

"Let's go," she whispered. "Get the thing out of your bag."

Vector nodded, hunched over as they inched forward. "Hey, Crash, when we plug this thing in—"

"Shut up. And don't use that name while we're out doing this kind of thing."

"Right, my fault, just kind of slipped."

"No more slipping. Just get the thing and let's go."

She tiptoed past each door, reciting the numbers in her head as she moved forward with soft steps.

Seventeen oh four.

Seventeen oh six.

Seventeen oh eight.

As they approached 1710, she stretched her hand back to Vector, making a "give it here" motion with her fingers. He slid the small device into her palm. She could feel the rough edges of the breadboard cut against her skin as her fingers wrapped around its frame, the thin cord dangling off to the side. She brought her new creation forward, inspecting it to make sure nothing had been damaged in transit.

The device looked like a small circuit board that you might see inside a clock radio or anything else electronic after peeling off the cover, but this was no random piece of household tech. It was an Arduino microcontroller, a tiny, cheap, self-contained computer that punched above its weight. After Haylie, sitting in an alley outside the electronics store, had configured it correctly and installed some open-source code, the device could now take advantage of a years-old exploit found in the most popular model of electronic hotel door lock.

Hotel guests have enjoyed the convenience of electronic locks—opened with keycards instead of actual metal keys—for decades now. What guests don't realize is that each lock includes a power socket to reboot or fix any issues, conveniently tucked underneath the handle on the hallway-side of the door. By plugging in a device that can talk to the electronic guts inside, the lock's digital key code can be read out of memory and used to gain access.

In other words, Haylie could open any door in this hotel within a few milliseconds.

"What happens if he's in there?" Vector whispered, checking over his shoulder and down the hall. "What do we do then?"

"We *want* him to be in there, dummy," Haylie said with a scowl, crouching down to check for the DC power input. "We're trying to find him—that would be a good thing." She brushed aside the plastic DO NOT DISTURB / NICHT STÖREN sign hanging on the doorknob and peeked underneath.

Vector thought for a moment. "Right, but I was thinking..."

"Stop thinking, just stop," she said, readying the end of the red cord near the lock. "Okay, are you ready? Remember, when we see him, let me do the talking. We don't want him to run."

"Or worse."

Shaking her head, she exhaled and held her breath, plugging the device into the slot. The lock pinged out a few beeps, sounding a bit like R2-D2 having a fit, and she heard a pop. She slowly pushed the door open, pulling the device free and stuffing it into her jacket pocket. She rose from her squatting position, looked up at Vector and took a step inside.

———

Central Train Station, Frankfurt

"C'mon, this is a short cut," Sean yelled back at Caesar.

Caesar followed, feeling the hunger turn somersaults in his stomach. The half-dome above his head—steel and glass arcing hundreds of feet into the air—looked like the space station from Kubrick's 2001. Shadows painted the floor, hiding Caesar's steps in patterns of light and dark. The gray of the train station was punctuated by the bright-red train cars sitting at each platform, ready to be boarded. He cinched his bag up higher on his shoulder and checked the time.

"Oh, man, we're getting a boatload of appetizers," Sean said, checking their location on his phone. "So many apps. Like, I want them on the table as soon as we sit down."

Watching the crowds shuffle past—some commuters, some

tourists—Caesar lost himself in the moment. It had been a long time since he felt peace, but today with everything clicking, they were finally in a good place.

This is actually going to work.

His train of thought was broken by the sound of hurried shoes pounding behind him, growing louder. Gasps and screams erupted from the crowd. He turned, watching the masses part to each side of the platform—men clutching their briefcases with hurried steps, mothers yanking on the arms of their children with panic in their eyes.

Caesar's faint smile dropped as his eyes went wide.

A team of armed men emerged from the crowd dressed in black, holding small machine guns in their hands. The men's faces were hidden behind blast shields on their helmets, their shapes padded with SWAT gear. They were sprinting right at him, pushing aside bystanders.

"Run!" Caesar yelled to Sean.

———

Grandhotel Frankfurt

"There's nobody here," Vector said as he scurried past her and around the closet, checking the corners of the room for the second time.

Haylie's expression hardened as she stood at the center of the room, her eyes darting across the floor.

We don't have time to sit here and wait for him to come back—if that ever happens.

"We need to start combing nearby public places," she said as Vector flipped through drawers, finding nothing. "He has to be getting ready for the election. He must have a hundred things to do—

that means he has to be online, wherever he is."

"Coffee shops, restaurants," Vector nodded. "We can start near the hotel and work our way out."

"Let's get a list together and get moving," Haylie said, pulling her laptop from her backpack. "We can just search for public access locations and—"

Haylie's voice was cut off by a chorus of sirens from outside the window, growing louder as the cars approached. She heard another volley coming from behind her, from the south end of the street, now closing in from both sides.

"Police," Vector said, pulling back the curtain, his face illuminated through the window pane as looked down to the street below. "A whole lot of them."

She stuffed her laptop back into her bag, along with the Arduino door-hacking device, and zipped the top. "Let's get out of here. Back away from the window, we need to get moving—"

"Wait," he said, pointing through the glass. "I don't think they're here for us. Looks like they're headed into the train station." He looked up, turning to face Haylie. "They're running."

Haylie walked over to check the view. Vector was right—eight or nine police vehicles of all shapes and sizes were now parked at odd angles on the street below them, blocking the entrance to the Frankfurt central train terminal. Police, heavily armed, moved in packs of two and three towards the main entrance. Others stood with their arms out, stopping civilians from entering the station.

Please, God, don't let it be him.

She pulled her laptop back out of her bag, setting it down on the windowsill with a clunk. She quickly accessed the hotel's Wi-Fi, brought up her Tor browser, and started searching.

"What are you looking for?" Vector asked.

"Police scanners," she said. "All the channels used by the

German police are encrypted, but I can get through that. Do you speak German?"

"A little bit," Vector said.

A few more keystrokes and Haylie turned the laptop towards Vector, clicking the play button on the dated, clunky web audio interface in the middle of the web page. German voices spoke in sharp bursts and matter-of-fact tones. Vector leaned in, closing his eyes to try and concentrate despite the sirens that continued to blare just out the window.

"They've found whoever it is they're looking for," he said. He listened for a few more seconds, rubbing his chin as his eyes looked off into the distance, slightly to the left. "They keep talking about 'the Americans'—I'm not sure if that's a task force or the suspects."

Oh no. Please, no.

"Was it Caesar?" Haylie shouted, grabbing at Vector's jacket. "Tell me."

"They haven't said any names," he said. "I don't know."

Haylie's eyes welled with tears as she looked down at the station, seventeen distant floors below. She smashed her fists against the windowsill, feeling the bite of metal into flesh, knowing there was nothing she could do.

———

Cradling his arm around his duffel bag, Caesar bolted down the train platform at a full sprint.

Sean darted in front of him, carving his way through an open train door with Caesar huffing closely behind. The two twisted through the packed car and out the other side, stopping briefly to get their bearings. Caesar shot across the open food court towards the escalators, noting a sign hanging above them that pointed down to the basement shopping mall. They pushed through a group of tourists queuing up at the mouth of the escalator and flew down the steps, their hands slipping and squeaking on the rubber handrails. Halfway down, Caesar grabbed the rail tight to regain his balance and turned to look over his shoulder.

The police were nowhere to be seen.

We've got this.

As they jumped off the bottom of the escalator, Caesar pushed ahead and took the lead, skimming his hand off the polished glass wall to their left and turning sharply around the corner. They snaked their way down a few corners, turning left, then right, then left again, until they had reached a deserted maze of back hallways. A brief grin crawled across his face as he breathed heavy, finally finding a good, comfortable pace.

"C'mon," he yelled back to Sean. "This way!"

"Stop right there!" Caesar heard from behind his back.

He looked over his shoulder, still running, and saw Sean stopped in his tracks twenty feet behind him at the last corner. Sean clutched his bag. Two men emerged from behind the wall, pointing their machine guns at Sean's chest, but they didn't see Caesar down the hall.

"Sean Collins! We have you! Do not move!"

They're American.

"I'm not going to jail," Sean stammered. "I haven't hurt anyone, you can't shoot me."

Caesar stopped, torn between freedom and his friend. His heart pounded as he searched his mind for a next step, for any way out. He opened his mouth, but no words came out, only dry gasps of air. He had been running for so long but had always felt in control, always felt one step ahead. For the first time since he could remember, Caesar was afraid.

Don't do it, Sean. Don't run.

Sean dropped his bag and turned, pushing his arms in front of him like an Olympic sprinter coming hot out of the blocks. He ran back towards the other side of the hall at full speed, mouth gaped open for air, trying to get as far away as his arms and legs would reach.

The sounds of machine-gun fire echoed off the marble floor as the glass behind Sean shattered and was painted red. Again and again.

Caesar stumbled backwards down a side corridor, watching the chaos unfold, shaking his head with every step. His heart beat out of his chest. He clutched his bag, needing to hold on to something— anything. He could see Sean's hand sticking out beyond the corner, his palm turned up towards the sky, lifeless. His fingers smeared with blood as the police swept in, guns still pointed down at his body.

Caesar turned and ran. He never looked back.

THIRTY-SIX

NSA Texas Cryptologic Center
San Antonio, TX
November 2nd, 3:45PM

Mary cracked her knuckles one at a time, fighting the urge to wince with each release of pressure. She took a long sip of coffee, letting the smell fill her nostrils. It didn't smell great, but it was about a million times better than mud she had had to drink at mealtimes over the past few years.

"How we looking, Mary?" Agent Wilcox asked. "Any luck?"

"Nothing so far," Mary said. "Seeing some chatter about the train station. Reports of gunfire—I'm guessing that's your doing—but not finding anything beyond that. If you could give me a name, this would be a lot easier."

"If I had a name," Agent Wilcox said, "I wouldn't need you here now, would I?"

Mary forced a smile in her direction as she felt the weight of Wilcox's eyes on her. She tried her best to hide her frustration as her laptop flashed alerts, showing police activity—video feeds and text updates. But it was all just chatter, just noise. Nothing that was going to help.

Wilcox settled into a seat next to her and motioned up at the clock on the wall. "You know, when I was a little girl, my parents would always ring a bell for dinner time. And I don't know how your family worked, but mine, we didn't even think about being late to sit down at that dinner table. In fact, it was probably better to not show up for dinner than to be late, you know? Didn't matter if I was in the far field or shoeing a horse or knee-deep in lake mud: if I heard that bell and didn't stop, drop and roll to make it back on time, well, it wasn't a pleasant rest of the night. Just make it back on time, Mother would say. Just do what you say you're going to do. And ever since, anytime I miss a deadline, I can't sleep. Can't sleep for days." Swiveling the keyboard in her direction, Wilcox typed in a file location and spun it back for Mary to see. It was an application, now being installed on Mary's machine, called "TorBuster."

"TorBuster?" Mary whispered, looking over at Agent Wilcox in disbelief. "You ... You've broken Tor? Tor is the most secure environment on the planet. How did you—"

"It just hit my desk this morning," Agent Wilcox said. "It's the first release from some work we've been doing with the big brains at some fancy university, and we've got a few people within the Tor group on our payroll, just in case. Now, let's be very clear—nobody knows we have this, Mary. As I'm sure you noted in your paperwork, you signed a non-disclosure that would have you wishing you'd never been born if you share any of this information outside of this room."

"The people using Tor just want privacy," Mary said. "That's all. This is casting a net, listening in on people who haven't done anything wrong."

"They're breaking the law," Agent Wilcox said with fire in her throat. "You tell me you have people breaking into your house, you're not going to put up a camera? Even if it means you get a shot of the mailman from time to time? Hackers have been using the Tor network for bad things—terrible things. Tor is a risk. And my job is to eliminate as much risk as I can." Wilcox stood, hovering over Mary. "Anyway, if you have a problem with it, don't use it. I thought it might help, assuming the damn thing even works."

Mary gazed into the application window, watching the Tor network traffic run through the visualizer, shooting all over the world in wide, sweeping arcs. Pings from one node to another. Clusters of contact points—concentrated in territories with strict regimes and dictators—lit up the map like fireworks.

Cracking her knuckles again, this time only getting a few quiet pops, Mary dove into the TorBuster interface. She set a filter on the left-hand side labeled "Geolocation" and scanned the results coming out of Germany.

Grandhotel Frankfurt

"I'm not finding anything," Haylie said, huddled over her laptop in Caesar's hotel room. "No names, no mentions of arrests. I feel like we'd be better off just roaming the streets, peeking in windows."

"Well, we're obviously not going to risk being seen," Vector said. "If those police or military or whatever down there are American—or even if they aren't—there's a good chance they'd recognize us."

Haylie smacked him on the shoulder. "I wasn't serious. I was trying to make a point." She turned back to her screen. "I'm searching social and news sites for any breaking updates, just hitting refresh every few seconds, but that's all I can do right now. Have any other ideas?"

NSA Texas Cryptologic Center

Mary watched as the Tor nodes refreshed, bringing up a listing of active nodes within a two-mile radius of the Frankfurt Central train station.

If this guy's alive, he's hiding. Trying to stay out of sight, laying low for a bit. But he knows that everyone is out looking for him.

He'd need to find someplace safe, but close. Set up shop.

The TorBuster application completed its refresh, now showing around two-hundred active nodes on the map. Mary scanned the locations, noticing a few red spots on the heat map—high concentrations of connections in one area.

Probably Wi-Fi access spots and coffee shops. But I wouldn't go to one of those—it would be too public for him. I need more data. Let's see who's interested in today's events.

Mary switched over to the web activity log on the right-hand side of the application interface. A rolling list of URLs and search engine terms scrolled top to bottom down the right rail, a real-time view of anything typed within that two-mile radius on the Tor network. She saw a mishmash of terms, mostly in German. Not helpful.

Every target this guy had gone after—from Patriarch to Xasis to the government databases—had been based in the U.S.

Hackers attack what they know.

He's American.

Mary clicked over to the controls at the top of the screen, filtering the results for only English terms. She then typed a few keywords into the filter to speed things along.

Users searching for:
"train station"
"gun shots"
"police"

Mary took a sip of her coffee and watched the terms roll in, waiting.

———

Grandhotel Frankfurt

"Still nothing," Haylie said. "Maybe we should just head out and hope no one recognizes us. The clock's ticking."

Vector looked up from the bed, one earpiece dangling out of his ear. "Nothing on the police scanners, either, but I'll be the first to admit that I haven't used my German in awhile." He tore the earphones out and tossed his phone on the bed.

———

NSA Texas Cryptologic Center

As Mary watched the list of terms flow down from top to bottom, she noticed an "Advanced Features" button nestled up in the top right corner of the application window. Her eyes narrowed as she clicked the feature, opening a window showing a full list of settings and parameters to adjust the language search. At the bottom was a label that read "aggregate co-occurring terms" with a small checkbox next to it.

Oh, come on. Why would you hide this feature? Government designers are so uninspired.

She clicked the checkbox as a new window filled with terms that people had searched in addition to the ones on her list.

"Train Station" + "Terrorism"
searches: 35:
origin nodes: 32

"Train Station" + "Casualties"

searches: 32:

origin nodes: 28

She kept scrolling, stopping dead in her tracks when the next set of terms appeared.

"Train Station" + "Caesar Black"

searches:25

nodes:1

Mary pulled her hands back from the keyboard, sitting back and focusing on the set of terms. Her heart began to pound as her mind worked to connect the dots. *Caesar Black ... Haylie's brother? Why would anyone think he was at the station?* Checking over her shoulder for Wilcox, still immersed in her phone, Mary held her breath and clicked on the node.

There are only two people in the world that would be searching for that term in Frankfurt right now. I bet I know which one this is.

She cut and pasted the IP address of the node into another application and pulled the laptop closer to her body, shielding the screen from view, as the results filled the screen.

———

Grandhotel Frankfurt

"It couldn't have been Caesar down there," Vector said in a reassuring tone, lying back across the edge of the bed. "Hancock or whoever is behind this would have announced it by now. No chance they would miss a press cycle this close to their big day."

"So that means Caesar is still out there," Haylie said.

"But we have nothing to go on," Vector said. "We have to assume we missed him here. He's probably long gone, could be in a different country by now. We just have to assume he's okay and wait for him to make another mistake."

"If he goes through with the election hack, it will be the biggest mistake of his life," Haylie said. "We can't let that happen."

"Well, sure," Vector said. "But it's not like we have to find him to stop him.'

"What?" Haylie said, turning to face Vector.

"We don't have to find Caesar," Vector continued, piecing together his logic as he spoke. "We just have to stop him. Finding and stopping are two different things."

Haylie turned back to the window, thinking.

He's right. He's absolutely right. I'm focused on the wrong problem. I don't need to—

Her train of thought was interrupted by a loud ping from her machine. She turned to check the screen, seeing that all windows had been minimized. A new command line window had appeared, front and center. It had two lines written at the top, with a blinking cursor below.

>>Guest1: Hello, dear.

>>Guest1: It seems you've been a busy girl.

———

NSA Texas Cryptologic Center

Luckily for Mary, every agent in the room had assembled in the far corner into some kind of last-minute, scraped together town hall meeting to refocus the room's efforts. She made a quick check of

Agent Wilcox, who was busy at the whiteboard sketching out the next few phases of the government's search efforts and then turned back to her screen.

C'mon, Crash. Do the smart thing ... Talk to me.

She double-checked the advanced settings of the AngelView program she had discovered earlier that afternoon—an NSA application that gave the owner complete control of any machine, provided you knew its network location—to make sure the "Disable application log" setting was checked. She shook her head, not believing that option was even available on a government system.

Clicking on the webcam view, a green rectangle sparked to life with a live feed of Haylie and a young man standing in the background over her right shoulder. They were both gazing at the screen, looking a bit shocked. Mary chuckled under her breath, reaching out to the keyboard and typing a new message.

>>Guest1: I can see you two, you know.

>>Guest1: Looking good, dear. And who's that handsome one behind you?

Mary grinned, watching Haylie throw a nasty look back at her friend before leaning in closer to the camera, looking a bit pissed off.

>>Admin: How did you find us? Are you with Wilcox?

>>Guest1: No one else is here. I have logging turned off. It's just me and you. I know what you're doing there - you're looking for your brother. Isn't that right?

>>Admin: Is he alive? Do you know where he is?

Checking around the room one more time, Mary shot a message back.

>>Guest 1: I believe he is, dear.

>>Admin: I need to stop him. I'm trying to do the right thing. I can't tell you any more than that.

Mary shook her head as she thought of the best way to get her next message across. At least, the best way to convince Haylie to do something against her own grain.

>>Guest 1: Haylie, you're a smart girl. But even smart people need to realize when they're in too deep. You're outgunned on all sides. You know that. It's too much right now. You're going to get yourself hurt. You're good, but not that good - not yet.

>>Admin: What else can I do? I'm not going to sit by and watch.

>>Guest 1: Watch what, dear?

>>Admin: Doesn't matter. I can stop him.

>>Guest 1: You want to stop him, but you don't have the answer. Sometimes the answer is right in front of you, even if you don't want to see it. Wouldn't it be nice to take some of the weight off your shoulders?

>>Admin: What are you talking about?

>>Guest 1: Don't limit yourself. On your own, you're out of your league. This problem is bigger - you need to think bigger. Focus on

the end goal, and how much you want it. Everything else will fall into place.

Mary watched the blinking cursor and looked back to the webcam view. Haylie stared at the screen, her eyes tired and heavy, her hair falling around her face.

>>Guest 1: I have to go. Do what's right. Be safe.

Mary leaned back in her chair, reading the words on the screen one last time before doing a quick control-Q keystroke combination to kill the window. She found her mind slipping back to a better time. Back to her days in Chicago.

I started off just like her—so sure of myself. I didn't want to be that way, I just don't think I trusted anyone else.

She has to learn that lesson for herself. That's the kind of thing that can't be—

"What's this?" Mary jumped as she heard the voice from over her shoulder. She swiveled around to see Agent Wilcox staring down at her laptop. Wilcox took a step in, tracing each data point and search result with her index finger.

Oh no.

"Is this..." Wilcox's eyes continued jumping around the TorBuster interface, finally resting on the IP address next to the search terms for Caesar. "Is this what I think it is? People in Frankfurt searching for both 'Train Station' and 'Caesar Black'? From just in the past hour? This is amazing, Mary."

Mary gulped as she watched Agent Wilcox piece it all together.

"All these searches coming from one node, one machine?" Wilcox continued. "This has to be him, right? Checking for anyone who's on to him?"

Mary sat, looking back at Agent Wilcox in silence. She finally coughed up some words. "I ... I don't know. It's just something I've been playing around with. It doesn't mean—"

"We just got the name in from headquarters ourselves—I can't believe it's actually him. This node is in a hotel directly across the street from the train station," Wilcox said, pulling out her phone and putting it to her ear. "This is brilliant, Mary. I never would've thought to use TorBuster like this. Amazing work."

Mary looked back to the screen, watching the red dot blink and pulse, hoping Haylie and her friend were already on the move. Hope, at this point, was all she could do.

Wilcox snapped her fingers at the analyst team a few desks away as she pointed to the main screen in the control room, now displaying Mary's desktop. "Everyone—we need a team at this location in the next four minutes. We need to move on this, now!"

Agent Wilcox took a few steps and dialed a number into her phone.

"Yes, sir," she said while pacing the floor, head down. "I believe we have a location on the suspect. I think we've found Caesar Black."

THIRTY-SEVEN

Grandhotel Frankfurt
Frankfurt, Germany
November 2nd, 3:57PM

"Well, she was no help," Vector said, pacing the room. "We don't know anything we didn't know a few minutes ago. If this woman is so great, why does she talk like a fortune cookie all the time?"

"This problem is bigger, you're going to need to think bigger," Haylie repeated Mary's words a few more times under her breath. "What does that even mean?"

"All we've got to go on is a fake name and an empty hotel room," Vector said. "The election is in, what, four days? Three with the time zones? We're at square one—nothing to go on. At this point, maybe we just let him roll with it. Who knows, maybe Ortega was going to win the election anyway? You ever think of that? Maybe we're fighting to stop ... nothing ... from happening?"

Haylie snapped her head, looking back over to Vector. "When did you become such a coward?"

"When people started shooting guns at each other," Vector yelled back. "You Texas people might love having guns everywhere, but I'd rather not see another one anytime soon. I'm the only one in this room who's had a bullet removed from his—"

"Yeah, so I've heard," Haylie said. "This matters because ... It just does. If we start playing God with systems, we're no better than the lies Hancock is spreading about us."

"But maybe it is the right thing," Vector said. "Hancock is dangerous—not just for people like us, but for the whole country. It would be a disaster if he gets elected—everybody with half a brain seems to know that. It's going to set back foreign relations twenty years—"

"Doesn't matter," Haylie said, shaking her head emphatically. "We don't get to choose. We start controlling the world, and we're no better than the people in power who are pulling the strings. At that point, we're not fighting them anymore, we've *become* them. I can't live with that. And I can't let Caesar become that, either."

"Says the woman who just cut her ankle bracelet and skipped town from her house arrest?" Vector asked. "Flew to Europe on a fake passport and broke into about six different systems today? I've got bad news for you, Crash: you're already there."

Haylie turned her head, staring out the window. She whispered a few select curse words under her breath, knowing he was right.

———

NSA Texas Cryptologic Center

The control room streamed a collection of scenes: five different camera angles on the same three groups of heavily armed agents, walking briskly in groups of four or five and filing into the hotel lobby. Mary had reluctantly transferred the IP information over to the analyst pool, and an NSA staffer was doing his best to extract every ounce of information he could. Luckily, it seemed that Haylie had shut her laptop after her conversation with Mary had ended, cutting off access to the webcam and microphone.

They still don't know who they're dealing with—at least for now.

Mary brought up her AngelView interface and selected a second node—one that she had made note of before while searching through the TorBuster results. The device was three or four feet away from Haylie's machine; at least, Mary thought it was. The problem with coordinates was that the data didn't include an altitude measurement —just latitude and longitude. In a hotel, the device very easily could be someone on a different floor.

Still, it's worth a shot.

Mary selected the "Full Write Access" command and waited for the interface to ping her back with a "Success" message. Data from the device began flowing into her application window. The fields read: mobile equipment ID, MDN, MIN, Storage, Battery, CPU, rearCamera, OS, manufacturer. *It's a phone.* She typed a few keystrokes, quit the program, and closed her laptop.

She looked back up to the monitors, watching the SWAT team enter the elevator bay.

———

Grandhotel Frankfurt

"We're all fugitives," Vector continued, despite Haylie tuning out of the conversation. "We're not so holy, you and I. Maybe we just let this one slide and get out of this city without handcuffs, so we don't end up like that guy down there in the train station?"

Haylie looked out at the horizon, searching for an answer. She thought about Mary.

Mary would know what to do.

Vector's pocket buzzed as a chime rang out, startling them both. "What the bloody hell—that's odd, innit? This is a burner phone. No one should be texting it." He plucked the device out of his pocket, looking down at the screen.

Haylie watched his eyes grow wide as he turned the phone to face her. The text message showed only one word:

RUN

———

NSA Texas Cryptologic Center

"Our team is in the elevators," Agent Wilcox said with both palms flat on the tabletop, leaning towards the large wall now filled with scenes of police throughout the hotel. She had the look of a cat who had just cornered a mouse. "Let's get all the primary views up. What's the floor?"

"I'm hearing it's seventeen," an analyst yelled over her shoulder, monitoring the audio feed.

"Okay, seventeen's hallway up on screen two," Wilcox commanded. The monitor flicked over to show a black and white view of a hallway at an awkward angle, the screen half-filled with a shot of the wall.

"Who installed these cameras?" Wilcox asked, glaring at the screen. "I thought Germans were supposed to be precise and all that."

"I'm seeing the same angle on each floor," an analyst said, switching between feeds. He turned to face Wilcox. "So I guess that makes them precise, just not good?"

Shaking her head, Wilcox dismissed him with a quick wave of her fingers. "Let's get Caesar's picture up on screen three," she said. "I want to make sure we know him when we see him."

———

Grandhotel Frankfurt

"It's Mary," Haylie yelled, grabbing the phone out of Vector's hand and staring down at the message. "It has to be. We need to get out of here. Toss me my bag!"

Vector tossed her backpack across the room. Haylie caught it by one of the shoulder straps, zipping the top closed and slinging it onto her back in one move. It felt light—the adrenaline appeared to have taken charge already. She ran for the door, clicking it slowly open to peer through the crack. Peeking around the corner, left and right, she nodded back to Vector who flashed her a thumbs up.

We didn't think about an exit plan ... What the hell are we going to do?

"They'll have both the stairs and elevator covered," Vector whispered, inching forward. "But the elevators will get here first."

Haylie heard a noise from down the hall through her right ear. Listening carefully, she could make out a second noise—the chime of an elevator arriving at its destination.

Haylie and Vector pushed their way out the door, round a corner and scrambling for the other end of the hallway. A distant shuffling rose in Haylie's ears—a rumbling that grew louder with each of her steps. Her eyes searched the corners of the ceiling for any cameras, seeing none. She peered down to the other end of the hall; there were only a few more guest room doors left before they reached the windowless entrance to the staircase.

"They'll have people on the stairs, right?" Haylie asked.

"If they're smart," Vector answered.

Can't go down the stairs.

Can't go to the elevator.

And these other doors are...

She swung her backpack off her shoulders and pulled at the side zipper pocket. "The door hack," she whispered, grabbing the Arduino computer out of her bag and quickly untangling the power cord. "Of course."

"Of course, what?" Vector whispered, frantically looking back and forth down each side of the hallway.

"The door exploit," she said, pushing the connection between the circuit board and the wire tighter to make sure the two pieces had strong contact. "It works on *any* hotel door right? We can get into any room we want."

Vector jerked his head around at the surrounding rooms, gasping for breath. "All right then, which one?"

Haylie shrugged and pointed across the hall. "This one looks perfect." She fell to her knees at the base of the threshold, trying her best to control her breathing as she peered under the lock for her mark.

———

NSA Texas Cryptologic Center

"Our team just reached the room," an analyst shouted, holding his earpiece to his ear. "They're going to ram it down. Second team is on the way up."

"I can't see anything," Wilcox yelled, craning her neck to see if any of the secondary video feeds from the hotel were showing a better angle. "Do our guys have body cameras we can access?" No answer came from the analyst pool—Mary wasn't sure if no one was listening, or no one knew the answer.

The cameras showed a second wave of police crammed into the next elevator, rapidly approaching the seventeenth floor. The doors opened and they filed out one by one, aiming their weapons out into the hall.

"We're splitting them up." The NSA analyst stood, his hand pressed to his ear as he kept track of the audio feed. "Team two, make your way down the other side of the hall. We want you checking the rest of the floor in case he's already on the run."

Mary cringed as she slunk back in her chair. She pulled her sweater across her body, bracing herself to hear the worst.

———

Grandhotel Frankfurt

"It's not working," Haylie said. She pulled the power adapter back and flipped her head upside down, checking the underside of the door's casing for any foreign objects. She blew air into the opening with a few quick bursts.

"Well, *make* it work," Vector whispered, bobbing back and forth on his tiptoes, checking each end of the hallway. "C'mon, Crash, I can hear them coming."

Haylie shook her head and tried the device again, slipping it into the slot underneath the brass door handle. Jiggling the adapter, waiting for a green light and a click. Nothing.

Goddamnit.

"They're getting closer," Vector said with hurried breath. "We should just run for the stairs, maybe they forgot to send a team in there. At least there we have a chance."

"Maybe they forgot?" Haylie spat back. She cursed at the door and spun to face the other side of the hall, scrambling on her hands and knees over to the door on the other side. "Screw it, let's try that one."

She bolted across the hallway, sticking the DC adapter up into the door lock and said a silent prayer as she heard movement inside the casing. The light flashed red-red ... green. A soft click filled her ears and she pushed the door open, craning her neck to see inside.

She froze in the doorway as she heard the TV at full volume, blaring German cartoons. Perched at the foot of the bed was a young girl—she couldn't have been older than five or six—surrounded by a pile of snacks arranged across the comforter. The girl looked back at Haylie with a curious eye, but not a sound, the bright colors from her cartoons reflecting shades of pastels off her cherub face.

Haylie raised a single finger to her lips and winked. The girl giggled and tilted her head with a smile, shushing back to her. Haylie slowly backtracked through the doorway, bumping right into Vector as he tried to make his way inside. They fell into a heap on the hallway floor as the door shut behind them.

"What the bloody hell was that all about?" Vector whispered with panic in his eyes. "We need to get in there."

"Occupied," Haylie said, pointing to the next door down the hall. "Third time's a charm."

————

NSA Texas Cryptologic Center

"The team is inside—the room's empty," an NSA agent announced. "They're double checking it for—"

"*Triple* check it." Agent Wilcox stomped across the room to the row of windows, throwing her phone into the corner with a clattering of plastic hitting drywall. "And make sure he's not hiding in the staircase."

"Yeah, that was the first thing the local team told us to remember, actually," the analyst said. "Germans, you know. Always getting the details—"

Agent Wilcox shot him a look.

"Triple check. Yes, ma'am."

———

Grandhotel Frankfurt

The door clicked firmly shut behind her. Haylie pressed her back against the wood, clutching her backpack to her chest with all the life left in her body. Vector jogged towards her after inspecting the room and flashed her a silent thumbs-up, sliding down the door to take a place next to her on the floor. They breathed heavy as they waited for any sound of visitors coming from outside.

Haylie flipped the Arduino device in her hand, end-over-end, and slowly unzipped the top of the bag, slipping it into the main compartment. As she slid the device inside, her hand did a quick inventory of the contents.

Clothes, good.

Passport, got it.

She fished for a few more seconds and felt an empty space where she expected to find a slate of cold aluminum, but found only empty space.

"Oh, no."

———

NSA Texas Cryptologic Center

Mary watched as the NSA analyst at the center of the room took a cautious series of steps to approach Agent Wilcox, who had stayed at the window, not even bothering to collect her phone, which still lay face-down in the corner.

"They triple checked, just like you asked," the analyst said. He took a gulp. "They didn't find anyone, but I do have some good news."

She turned to face him, scorn filling her eyes. "What's your definition of *good,* there, son?"

"His laptop," the analyst said, straightening his posture and tucking in the sides of his shirt. "He left his laptop in the room—right there on the desk."

Mary's heart jumped as she watched a wide smile grow across Agent Wilcox's face.

THIRTY-EIGHT

Grand Palace Hotel
Rome
November 3rd, 1:02 PM

The afternoon sun painted shades of orange across the lid of Caesar's laptop as it sat cold and lifeless on the desk. He lost himself in the reflections, the hours since Frankfurt ran like a blurred slideshow through his brain.

Did that really happen? Did it all really happen?

The adrenaline returned as he replayed scenes of the police running full speed behind him. Parents pulling their children away, screaming in terror as they ran. Sean, face-down on the cold floor. Bullet casings chiming off the marble.

The images looped over and over and over in his mind.

They wouldn't stop.

Sean didn't deserve this. It got a little bit out of control, but it didn't have to come to this.

Just a little out of control.

He raised a shaking hand to lift the lid of his laptop. Every movement brought searing pain through his head—the headaches had started on the train down to Rome and hadn't stopped since. He held his hands back from the keyboard, just staring at the black screen that reflected a fuzzy shadow of his silhouette. His eyes welled with tears.

It's your fault. This whole thing was your idea. Sean's dead because of you. You could have stopped this all months ago—you should have been smart enough to know when to stop, to know when you were out of your league. But you weren't.

He closed his eyes and backtracked through the past few days. *How did they find you? How did they know you were in Frankfurt?* He and Sean had been writing scripts, testing servers, searching precincts. Nothing out of the ordinary, and besides, it was all being done through Tor—safe and silent. They weren't being careless. But that didn't change the fact that Sean was dead.

A wave of panic suddenly crept up his spine. He jumped up from his chair, hobbling over to the hotel room door and fumbling to check both locks. Double, triple checking them. His head pounding, his pulse racing. Looking through the peephole and out into the hallway, breathing against the grain of the door, pressing his eye closer and to each side for a better view. A better view of *them*. Watching for what seemed like hours.

Are they here, too?

He fell down to the floor and crawled, his palms and knees burning as he slid across the carpet, pulling himself up on the curtains, rising just enough to let his eye peek above the windowsill. He scanned the buildings across the street. Some windows illuminated, others with drawn shades. Some with black glass. Caesar watched for any movement, making mental notes of shadows and angles and how far open each window was. The traffic below rustled and hushed its way through the night, blowing the smell of exhaust and grime up through the walls of the alley, pinging back and forth across the brick until it finally reached his nostrils. He slid back under the window, pressing his back against the wall, panting for air.

You couldn't just leave it alone, could you? Take a deal, do your time? You kept telling yourself that you were better than them. You told the people that followed you that you could keep them safe. You were wrong. And now Sean's dead.

I miss him. I failed him.

He crept his hand up to the top of the desk, feeling around for his laptop, grasped it by the edge and slid it down into his lap. The power button, nestled in the top right-hand corner of the keyboard, called to him. A swooping semi-circle, pierced by a thin line running north to south. He had always thought it looked like a twisted smiley face; the single eye of a cyclops staring back at him with a big toothless grin. But now it looked different.

It looked like a bullet piercing flesh, tearing through skin, muscle, and bone.

It looked like an open wound.

It looked like a gun sight, trained on his target—he imagined the smell of gunpowder still fresh on his hands from the last shot—locked in and ready to fire. Just waiting for the pull of the trigger.

They're coming for you. You're the last one. You'll end up dead, or in prison for the rest of your life, and you can't let that happen. You know who did this. And you can make it right.

He felt anger filling his body, replacing the fear. His jaw locked as his eyes slid shut, his head snapping back to drink in the rage. He didn't even remember pressing the power button, only hearing the laptop chime to life. The machine rose and fell with his breath as his eyes locked on the screen. As the OS booted, he pieced together the next steps of what he needed to do.

All that matters is who. Who did this. And I think I already know the answer.

His login screen showed, with a blinking cursor staring back at him.

It's time to take the gloves off.

THIRTY-NINE

NSA Texas Cryptologic Center
San Antonio, TX
November 3rd, 7:15AM

Mary sipped a cup of hot tea as her results came up blank. She faked a grimace, scratching at her head and dusting crumbs and who-knows-what off the edges of the laptop. It wasn't her machine, but she had always found strange comfort in taking good care of any computer under her wing.

I still don't know what Caesar's doing, but I need to buy them time. Both of them.

"Got anything?" Agent Wilcox asked from the row behind her, weaving her way through a growing collection of sluggish NSA analysts who weren't used to being up this early in the morning.

"Not yet," Mary said. "Not since that first ping in Frankfurt."

"We've got reports rolling in," Wilcox said with a smile. "But nothing I can confirm about his whereabouts. Just rumors from local sources, not credible if you ask me. Keep your eyes open." She made her way back to the center of the room to start the morning briefing as Mary looked on.

"He's scared—he's scurrying," Mary whispered to herself. "He's in the shadows, but he's not hiding. He feels like he has to stay on the offensive." She brushed a piece of dirt off the edge of the laptop. "He's still out there, and now he's mad."

She sat back, running her fingers across the edges of the screen, her touch finding the rough, black tape covering the webcam across the top of the screen. She pressed it firmly into place as her mind continued to work, scraping the air out of the bubbles with her fingernail.

———

Grand Palace Hotel, Rome

Caesar brought up his local version of the Project code repository and clicked through to the section he had labeled "black_hat" just a few days earlier.

Months back, he had worked with the team to set strict guidelines for what they could and couldn't use. They knew they had to keep themselves in check, only using the pieces of Project code that would help them do good, and steering clear of the code that would give them the access—and the temptation—to do harm. Access can give people opportunity, but it also corrupts like a son-of-a-bitch.

Caesar held his index finger over the laptop's trackpad. He thought of Sean, lying on a stainless steel table somewhere in Germany. His body riddled with bullet holes, his skin gray.

It's just a few lines of code, that's all. Forget the people. Don't think about the people. Just a few lines of code.

The television blared in the corner, a montage of Senator

Hancock at podiums, shaking hands, sitting down for earnest interviews, on the debate stage. The video cut over to Hancock's Cyber Task Force—Rancor sitting center stage at a huge, polished wood table, an ugly, terribly tied necktie dangling down below his slimy smirk.

It was you, Rancor. I know it was. Show me that I'm right.

Caesar logged back into the NSA's system, working his way through any files that would give him a clue about what happened in Frankfurt. Nothing in the records, no new files started in his own name. But they may have started a new collection, and finding anything in this web of government red tape and naming structures was pretty close to impossible. He jumped back to his local Project code folder, his eyes drifting down to the subfolder from the day before named 'SWIFT_Access.'

The SWIFT transaction? Is that how they found us?

He pictured Sean, sitting across from him, asking if it was safe to access the system.

"That system is twenty years old," Caesar heard himself reply. "No one's paying attention."

My God, I led them right to us. This is all my fault.

He logged into the SWIFT system as a superuser and began to scour the logs. Most of the activity on SWIFT had been moved over to modern APIs years ago—just machines talking to machines. Caesar knew that anyone in the system these days would fall into one of three categories: people running the system, people trying to break in, or people trying to catch the people breaking in.

He typed in a few commands to bring up a list of active users, waited for the system to respond, and then leaned in to check the results. What he saw was mostly a list of bots—automated jobs created by the administrator for common tasks. But there was one new entry that was different.

SWIFT2bot_cleanUpWedJun 12 21:31

SWIFT2bot_cronFriNov 01 03:45
SWIFT2bot_alphaSatNov 0209:32
SWIFT2MA_MI-90067SatNov 0212:32

I don't believe it. They're in here—that's him.

Caesar pushed back in his chair, breathing deeply. He closed his eyes, but all he could see was red. All he could think about was Sean, one moment behind him, running through the train station, and the next minute dead. Bleeding out on the floor. Dying, hungry and alone. *And all because of me.*

His pulse raced as he searched for every IP address pinging the SWIFT servers from inside the NSA. The results popped out a single node: 192.168.07.06.

I've got you, you son of a bitch.

He pushed the chair back and stood, feeling a rush of adrenaline course through his veins. He stalked the room, pulsing his fists in and out, hunching over, bouncing left and right like a prize fighter getting ready to step in the ring.

Rancor thinks he's untouchable. I'm going to show him how wrong he is.

Caesar raised his fingers to his temples, trying to mentally walk back through the list of Project scripts that sat untouched in the "black_hat" folder. *I've got his IP.* He started up a program called AngelView and typed in the IP.

The script returned a note reading "192.168.07.06: Online." Caesar pushed his cursor with a shaking hand, selecting the "Web-cam_view" option. All that greeted him was a grainy black video feed. No movement, no nothing. He cursed.

He must have put tape over his webcam.

He turned back to the command line interface and typed "dir(AngelView)" to list other options on the AngelView script.

[AccessLog, Webcam_View, IPlog, Privs, ScreenView]

"ScreenView," Caesar muttered. He ran the command, watching a new window pop to life. It loaded a highly pixelated, bright-white view that slowly brought itself into focus.

Caesar expanded the window to full screen and studied every inch as the details emerged.

———

NSA Texas Cryptologic Center

Mary shifted in her seat, trying her best to look busy. She cycled through tabs, combing through network maps of Frankfurt, Berlin, and a few other cities in Germany where hackers tended to congregate. It wasn't hard to avoid any new chatter about Caesar or Haylie—there wasn't any. She switched over to a forum scraper, refreshing her scripts for the sixth time this hour.

I do hope she got away. I hope she's safe.

Agent Wilcox took the chair next to Mary, pointing at one of the screens fixed to the wall showing footage from earlier that morning of Senator Hancock and Mason Mince poised outside the Pentagon at a press conference.

"You ever run into that guy?" Wilcox asked, pointing to the somewhat disheveled Mason Mince speaking with authoritative gestures, waving a stack of papers in his hand for some reason. "He seems like he's all hat and no cattle."

"Mason Mince?" Mary laughed. "I'm afraid he's well after my time." She shook her head, opening a new tab to do a search on his name. She scrolled through breaking news reports mentioning him in the election coverage. "I'm afraid I don't think we'd get along, myself and Mr. Mince—I mean, who calls himself Rancor?"

Both Wilcox and Mary chuckled as she continued to scroll.

"Mary, I have something we need to discuss," Agent Wilcox said, straightening her posture and taking on an official-sounding tone.

Mary slid back from the keyboard and faced the agent.

Well, this doesn't sound good.

———

Grand Palace Hotel, Rome

Caesar watched the screen, arms crossed, waiting. After paging through article after article about Mason Mince, the screen froze on a picture of him standing at a podium, speaking to the crowd in front of him.

Searching for some of your greatest hits, are you? You make me sick.

Caesar winced at every new headline, every story about Hancock's rise to power, about his hunt for Caesar Black.

Looking up at the username in the top right corner, he saw the username "MA-MI-90067" staring back at him. He gripped the edge of the desk, squeezing with all his power.

An eye for an eye.

———

NSA Texas Cryptologic Center

"Mary Milward," Wilcox began, pulling over a thin, blue folder laid carefully next to her laptop. "The United States Government, and specifically the NSA, is in debt to you for your assistance over the past few days." She opened the folder, pulling the top sheet from the stack. "I'm satisfied that we've found our suspects, and it's time to make right on our deal."

The room fell silent as Mary's eyes flicked around to each soul, now all facing the two of them with hushed reverence.

"Ms. Milward," Agent Wilcox continued, "in recognition of the assistance you have granted the National Security Agency, you have been granted a full pardon from your sentence, assuming you waive all rights to further contest your initial conviction."

Mary stared back, blinking a few times, trying her best to process the information. "So, that means..."

"Sign this paperwork—this right here—and you're a free woman," Wilcox said, her southern charm shining through along with her smile. "I took the liberty of arranging a flight to Chicago tonight, a small commercial jet that will be all yours, along with an NSA escort for the trip, of course. I've sent electronic copies of all the documents and travel details to a temporary electronic account. We'll just need you to forward those to your own email account and—"

"I haven't been out in the real world in about twenty-five years," Mary laughed, accepting the folder with a trembling hand. "I'm afraid I've never had an email account."

Nodding, Wilcox smiled. "Of course. You feel free to keep this one until you get home, get settled. You leave in a few hours."

Mary closed her eyes and said a silent prayer, mouthing the words as they ran through her mind. She opened her eyes to find tears streaming down her cheeks.

"It's been a real pleasure, Ms. Milward," Agent Wilcox said, extending a hand to Mary. "Any time you find yourself in Texas, I hope you'll stop by and say hello."

I don't believe it.

———

Grand Palace Hotel, Rome

The glow from the pixels lit the dim room as Caesar watched the screen, wringing his hands together. The cursor on the other side of the connection began to move slowly. Taking a delicate breath, he watched, waited.

All he wanted was a place to twist the knife.

An email window opened on the other side of the connection, showing only a single message in the inbox. Caesar leaned in, grabbing a pencil from the hotel desk and quickly jotted down the details as the email went to full screen. He scowled as the connection went fuzzy.

Is that what I think it is?

He began to drum his fist on the base of his laptop, whispering "C'mon, c'mon, c'mon," as the connection tried and failed to render a clear screen. He could see the message scrolling down, but the details had all gone to fuzz.

Caesar checked his Wi-Fi connection—it was at three bars out of four. Standing and clutching the laptop with both hands, he walked towards the center of the room, holding the pad of paper and pencil in his mouth as he searched for a sweet spot. He found it over by the closet, crammed in the tiny hallway between the front door and the bathroom.

As the picture became clear, he could make out the details in the email: it was a boarding pass—flight AA1161, flying out tonight at 8:45PM, Gate 10, seat 1A—it had everything but the name of the passenger, which just read as "CLASSIFIED." It was scheduled to leave San Antonio airport that evening, headed for Chicago.

He pinned the laptop with his forearm, pulling the paper out of his mouth and slamming it up against the wall. He scribbled down the important parts with violent strokes. He tossed the laptop on the bed, feeling his heart pound through his t-shirt as he stared down at the screen.

Holding the flight information in a shaking hand, he studied the edges and curls of his sloppy handwriting, backlit by the white glow of the screen.

His rage built as he felt the paper fibers tear under his grip.

He tossed the note on the bed and craned over to his laptop. Searching his local directory, he fought the coughs that were rising in his throat as he double clicked the folder labeled "Commercial Airline Systems Access."

FORTY

Haylie watched the traffic stutter by in fits and spurts, each tiny, dull-colored hatchback waiting its turn at the three-way intersection. Her view from inside the café—past the small sitting area outside and onto the street—was blocked only by a few lazy pedestrians and the gray blanket of drizzle that had rolled into Frankfurt. Her hands were wrapped around the porcelain mug, absorbing its warmth but letting the coffee sit untouched.

It had been hours since they had scrambled into that random hotel room and waited for the police to clear out. Feeling the clock ticking away was bad enough—knowing that her brother was still out there somewhere, on the run—but the thought of her laptop in the hands of the police was a checkmate punch in the gut. She wasn't sure how long it would take the police to get some hard evidence off her laptop, but she knew it could be measured in hours and not days.

Haylie winced, trying to push the thoughts out of her head as she felt a tear rolling down her cheek.

How could I be so stupid?

She could feel her bottom lip quivering slightly every time she thought about her brother or the mess she was in. Stranded in a foreign country, a fugitive herself. Caesar was about to make the biggest mistake of his life, and she was without any way of stopping him.

She felt a palm on her left shoulder and looked over to see Vector stirring his coffee with his free hand, offering the best smile that he could conjure up.

The harsh buzz of the barista grinding beans caused Haylie to jump, edging away from Vector's touch and sliding her shoulder free, back to its defeated slump. Gazing outside, she saw a pair of locals waiting to cross the street, shopping bags in hands and wearing matching khaki jackets to deflect the rain. She could see their mouths moving, speaking gently, effortlessly, occasionally throwing glances at each other. The misting rain highlighted their matching white hair, clinging to the strands like dew on a cobweb. As the crosswalk light turned green, the man took a step, clutching his wife's hand without even looking down, knowing exactly where to find it.

"The laptop was encrypted, right?" Vector said. "That's good, it means they've got nothing."

"Fingerprints," Haylie said, managing to push the words past her tears. "That's all they need. They'll have those within the hour. They'll tie me to Caesar, to every hack he's been responsible for over the past few weeks. This is it—there's nowhere to run anymore. Plus, without my laptop, we'll never track him down. We needed more tech, not less."

"Don't get all doom and gloom on me," Vector said. "I still have my machine. And even if they get prints on you, we can still run. Just like Caesar. This could be the start of our adventure, out in the world. I have my laptop, and we still have money. We can—"

"Does that really sound like fun to you?" Haylie stammered. "I can't live like this—waking up and not being able to remember what city I'm in. Not being able to stop and breathe."

"I bet once we got into it, we could—"

"Stop. Just stop." Haylie reached down into Vector's bag and placed his laptop on the counter, pushing it over towards him. "Read me the headlines—like you used to do in school."

"But—"

"Just read."

———

San Antonio Airport

Gliding through the sliding doors and into the main terminal, Mary felt a wave of memories wash over her. She froze in the center of the walkway, in awe of the crowd all around: people hugging and kissing each other goodbye; children pulling colorful wheeled luggage behind them, adorned with comic book characters. The NSA agent at her side kept a respectful distance, adjusting his tie and waiting patiently as she took it all in.

Mary's last visit to an airport was still etched deep in her memory. It was December of 1989, and she had floated into Chicago's O'Hare airport on her tiptoes, trying to contain her excitement. Her boyfriend was about to land from San Francisco, and she vividly remembered clutching a bouquet of hand-picked flowers, wanting to be the first face he saw in Chicago. She remembered lining up at security, ready to make her way through to greet him at the gate— back then, you could do that—when a firm hand had gripped her left arm.

Then another on her right.

Then, it was just a swirl of activity. Agents had swooped in from every direction. Her Miranda rights were read as she tried to find her bearings. All the while, she'd kept one eye on the gates, watching the next phase of her life drift away.

But this morning, Mary felt a different force—pushing instead of pulling—as she walked with a new sense of purpose across the polished floors, ready for the next stage of her whatever was to come. As they approached the security ropes, the agent took the lead, cutting the line and flashing his badge. Mary was quickly waved through.

No metal detectors today. Nothing to stop her from getting on that plane.

As they made their way through the terminal, Mary took a moment to admire her reflection in a store window. Her new street clothes—a pair of what she was told were fashionable jeans, t-shirt, and light jacket. After decades in a prison jumpsuit, she felt like a movie star. She felt like a *person*.

"We have this plane all to ourselves?" Mary asked the agent keeping pace on her left. "Seems a bit wasteful, don't you think?"

"It's necessary until you're officially out of our custody," the agent replied without a hint of emotion. "This is a government operation. Waste is just part of the process."

He pointed to an open set of double doors ahead, with a "10" sign hanging overhead, leading out to a jetway. Mary stopped and looked down the empty hallway, wondering what she would do after they landed.

Anything I want, I suppose.

———

Grand Palace Hotel, Rome

Caesar coughed into his fist, fighting his body's urge to slump over onto the desk. He propped himself upright and wiped the sweat from his forehead.

Just get it done.

He raised a trembling hand, hitting command-R to refresh the status of flight AA1161, headed from San Antonio to Chicago O'Hare. The system indicated that the plane was still on schedule for an 8:45 p.m. departure, all seats blocked out by the airline's ticketing system.

You can't do this, you can't do this. How can you even think about this? What have you become?

He rubbed his eyes, stood and walked to the bathroom. Turning the faucet knob on full with a quick twist of his wrist, he bent over and splashed cold water across his face. The chill woke him as he continued to cup liquid with his hands, feeling the beads run down across his skin as his hurried breath blew mist from his nostrils. He snatched a towel from the rack and buried his face in it. As he lowered the cloth, he caught sight of himself in the mirror. He stared deep into his own eyes, looking for signs of life.

All he saw was rage.

"What else?" he whispered back into the mirror. "What else can I do? What other choice do I have?" Tears began to fall from his eyes as his hands shook, wiping them away with disgust. He was afraid— afraid of what they'd do to him if they caught him. Afraid of what he had to do. "This isn't your fault. *They* did this. Just this once, you can push back."

He let the towel fall into a heap on the ground. He glanced over at his laptop screen in the distance.

"There's no other way."

He stepped towards the machine and brought up the airline systems package, checking the documentation one last time. The code gave him remote access to the control systems of most commercial aircraft in operation across the United States through a backdoor into the thrust management system. It was triggered by a vulnerability in the inflight entertainment system—all he needed was a flight number, and the NSA's code took care of the rest.

He exhaled and typed out a few, solid keystrokes.

AA1161

San Antonio Airport

Mary looked down the aisle seeing rows and rows of empty seats staring back at her. It was an eerie sight; even the two flight attendants chatting in the aisle didn't know what to do with themselves. The closest attendant made a mocking sweeping gesture with her arm—as if to say "take any seat you like." Mary performed a slight bow with a smile and picked the second row of first class, gently setting her bag down on the seat next to her. She looked up at the screen embedded in the headrest in front of her, running her hands across its edges, her mouth wide open.

"It's her first flight in a while," the agent explained to the flight attendant.

"Well, then," the flight attendant replied with a wide smile, "we'd better make sure it's a great one."

Grand Palace Hotel, Rome

The flight status indicator flashed over from "Boarding" to "Departed" as Caesar checked the time in the corner of his screen.

He prepared the commands—enough thrust in the left engine, then the right, then the left again, to cause the plane to become imbalanced. The auto-throttle settings in the onboard computer would fight against the pattern, so Caesar double-checked that he had disabled that function.

He focused his vision on the small blinking indicator crawling its way across the map, taxiing across the runway. He pictured Rancor sitting comfortably in his seat, sipping a drink and feeling like he was on top of the world. Caesar's jaw locked as his fingers hovered, ready to let the code get to work.

———

San Antonio Airport

The plane accelerated, pulling Mary back into her seat. She gripped the armrests and closed her eyes, ready to go home, finally free.

The first thing I'll do is plant a garden. Some flowers, some vegetables. Take good care of them.

I'll watch them grow.

———

Grand Palace Hotel, Rome

Caesar watched the dot zoom across the runway, the altitude rising as the flight veered slightly to the left, on course for Chicago.

You started this. You're not getting me, not like you got Sean.

He blinked through the burning in his eyes, looking down to the keyboard. He hit the "return" key with two strong fingers. He walked away from the machine, not able to watch.

Don't think about the people. Just a few lines of code.

San Antonio, Texas

The Texas hill country—a mix of scrub brush, rocky terrain, and peaceful oak trees—was lit by a fireball of orange and yellow and red. The wreckage of flight AA1161 carved a deep, half-mile trench through the landscape. The plane had been reduced to twisted metal and burning insulation haphazardly scattered across the ashes of grass and dirt, now all charred black.

The only sounds came from the flickering fire as the smells of burning fuel, plastic and metal filled the morning air, the sun shining down from above.

FORTY-ONE

Townhouse Coffee
Frankfurt
November 3rd 3:12PM

"Anything else?" Haylie muttered, staring out at the rain. She wasn't looking for good news, necessarily, just any news that could distract her from the uncertainty swimming through her brain. Anything to take her mind off the road ahead. She would have taken pop culture trash or even sports scores, anything to distance her from the reality of knowing that she had to make a decision soon. But Vector had run out of unclicked links, and she knew the clock was ticking.

"No links that we haven't already read, some of them twice," Vector said. "They still don't know what happened to that plane outside of San Antonio. A few scattered reports that it was empty, which is odd."

"Just hit refresh," she said, sipping at her coffee. "One more time."

He hit command-R and looked back at the screen with a new sense of interest. "I've got something here. A livestream—some breaking stuff." He brought the video feed to full screen and tilted the laptop so Haylie could see.

She saw an empty podium that was quickly filled by a man with a stack of papers and an angry snarl etched across his face. He looked around the room with a flavor of confusion, a bit like he had never done this before. The camera zoomed in as reporters took their seats and the man tapped the microphone a few times with a closed fist.

"Is that ... that Mason Mince guy?" Vector asked.

"Quiet, he's about to start," Haylie said.

"Ladies and gentlemen. I have some unfortunate news, but it's something that our nation needs to know. It seems that a mere two days before this historic election, the current administration's levels of ignorance and deception have risen to an even higher level, if that is possible."

"What's he talking about?" Vector whispered, leaning in.

"My sources inside the government tell me that the plane that went down a few hours ago outside of San Antonio was, in fact, a government operation carrying an NSA informant. We don't know the name of the individual, but we do know they were targeted by a hacker who took control of the plane's systems."

Haylie felt the world turn around her as the words echoed through her head. *It can't be. It can't be.* She looked over to Vector to see if he had heard the same thing.

"Did he ... did he just ..."

An NSA informant. From San Antonio. It's Mary. Oh, my God it's Mary.

Vector just looked back with full eyes, searching for words.

"That's correct—this was an act of cyber terrorism and one that the current administration refuses to discuss. Their lies and deceit are putting the entire country at risk."

Haylie stared at the screen, her eyes glazed over. The tears welled up as she pictured Mary on the plane, falling towards the ground, helpless. Alone.

"But that's not all. My sources are telling me that they believe this was an act of retaliation against the government by none other than Caesar Black, the man that Senator Hancock and I had identified as a threat to our country just days ago."

The air was knocked clear out of her as she slumped down on the counter, feeling the cold shock of the stainless steel against her skin. She buried her head in her hands and wished it all away.

———

I can't believe she's gone.

Haylie could make out a pair of sympathetic eyes next to her as she stared out the window, her index finger tracing across the chrome of the counter's edge. She couldn't stop thinking about Mary. Mary had known the right thing to say, known how to set Haylie on the right path.

She saved us, back in the hotel. She didn't have to do that, but she did it anyway.

"I can't believe that Caesar would..." She knew the words, but couldn't bring herself to say them out loud. "He wouldn't do this. He couldn't." She felt herself floating through the glass and out into the mist. To another world, away from Frankfurt. Away from here.

"We don't know it was him," Vector said. "This could just be Hancock trying to justify his actions. We can't know for sure."

She wasted most of her life behind bars. She never got back out to see the world. Tugging at her jacket sleeve, Haylie inched it up to her cheek to wipe away a tear. *She never asked for anything. All she did was help.*

"It was him," she said. "They killed his friend, and he's pushing back. This thing he's doing, it's changed him. I never saw anything like this coming." She stared out into the rain as it fell down onto the faded awning with more force, sending ripples across the fabric. "But why did it have to be her?"

I only knew her for a few days, but she made such a difference. She made me a better person.

"Anger doesn't always make sense," Vector said. "I'm sorry, Crash."

"You were right before," she said between sniffles. "We need to get off the grid. Get away from all this, try to find some sense of normality. Maybe find a small town somewhere—a place where they don't read headlines. Fall off the map, stay offline, stay out of sight."

"I don't think—"

"Fine, it doesn't have to be a small town," she said. "We can go anywhere you want. I just don't want to be here anymore."

"What I was trying to say," Vector said, "is that I don't think we can run from this. I think you're the only person in the world who can stop your brother."

"You want to end up like Mary?" Haylie said, tears streaming down her cheeks. "Caesar's gone crazy. This is too much—and besides, you were right, it's not our fight. Let him do what he wants. Dig his own grave. Why do you care?"

"You *made* me care. You have a way of doing that, you know."

Haylie refused to make eye contact, pulling her hair back and tossing her glasses on the counter with her last ounce of energy. Her pulse raced against her sinking heart. She wanted to go to sleep—go to sleep and drift off.

"You never wanted any of this," Vector said. "The spotlight, the attention. I know that. Everybody knows that. But it's here. And you can make a difference."

Haylie turned back to face her friend—her only friend. She looked into his eyes and saw a man who would always be there. A man who had always been at her side, no matter what she had dragged him through.

"You were miserable back in Austin, being offline," Vector said. "I've never seen you more miserable since we've known each other. And that's the life you want?"

"It's the only life I can have right now," she said. "I can't do this anymore."

"Oh, shut up," he said. "This is more than what you *can* do, we're way beyond that. This is about what you *need* to do. You know right from wrong. Every time I've wanted to take the easy way, you've always shown me the right way. I don't know where you get it from, and it's really annoying, but that's *you*. That's Haylie. That's Crash."

Haylie looked on, speechless.

"Sure, we could run—but we can always run," Vector said. "We can run tomorrow. Or the next day. But today, we should do what's right."

Haylie nodded, wringing her hands around her coffee. She wiped the tears from her cheeks and sat up straight on her barstool.

"We're not a bad lot, you and I," Vector said. "I'm sorry Mary's gone, but maybe this is a chance to show what we're made of. This time, maybe instead of wondering 'why me,' we lean into it. Maybe, just maybe, we're in the *right* place at the *right* time. Maybe this feels impossible because no one else in the world could do what we're about to do. Nobody except you and me."

Haylie leaned over, her hands reaching up to touch Vector's

cheeks, and kissed him. A kiss that had been too long in the waiting. She soaked in the moment—even if it was only for a few seconds—opening her eyes to see him staring at her in utter disbelief.

"Right," he said, clearing his throat. "Enough of that for now. We have work to do. Plus, you need to blow your nose, girl."

She laughed, sitting back up on the stool and tucking her hair back behind each ear, one side at a time. As the blush wore off her face, she pieced together what they needed to do next.

"So now that we've got that settled, what the hell are we going to do?" Vector said, looking back out into the rainy haze.

Haylie shrugged. "Well, we can't track him. We don't know where he is. We don't even have the name he's using." Suddenly, Mary's words began to spin into her head, mixing with the caffeine and the adrenaline to form ... something.

Don't limit yourself.

Sometimes the right answer is right in front of you, even if you don't want to see it.

"Maybe we head back to the hotel," Vector said. "Find someone that Caesar spoke to there. Maybe he let something slip. But that's going to be tricky without being discovered, the place is probably crawling with police by now."

Reconsider your boundaries.

Find someone that Caesar spoke to.

"No," Haylie said, sitting up and looking over to Vector. "There's another way. Someone that Caesar spoke to—I know what to do."

"Right," Vector said with a raised eyebrow. "So who is it?"

Haylie worked out the steps in her head one more time, nodding to herself. *This is the only way.*

"This is going to sound crazy," she said. "But I need your phone."

———

Grand Palace Hotel, Rome

Caesar watched the press conference video feed come to an end, the frame snapping over to black as his jaw dropped.

Mince is alive. An NSA informant was on the plane? How is that possible?

He brought up a browser, checking news sites, looking for any piece of information that he could find. But there was nothing else to go on—no more information.

What did I do? Who was on that plane?

He rested his head in his hands, fingers at his temples, hunched over and rocking gently back and forth as his wooden desk chair creaked under his weight.

A guest account at the NSA.

A hacker working with them.

San Antonio.

Caesar shot up, a look of shock smeared across his face.

No. It can't be.

He scrambled for his phone, pressing fingers against the screen, fumbling to unlock the screen. He brought up his location tracking app, the one he hadn't checked in a few days. The one that told him the location of his sister's ankle bracelet.

The app showed a spinning circle icon as it tried to connect to the hotel's WiFi. Caesar grasped the phone with both hands, hovering inches from the screen.

It can't be. It can't be.

The screen popped to life, displaying a full view of the globe with the bracelet's ID at the top. A message scrolled across the top on a red banner.

NODE NO LONGER ON NETWORK

He fell to the floor, pulling his forearms over his eyes, straining against his own skull.

I couldn't have done this. She has to be okay. She has to be.

He screamed at the top of his lungs, a cry like he'd never shouted before, the sounds coming from places inside that he'd never known. His heart pounded, he couldn't breathe. The room began to spin as he extended an arm to the desk to stop himself from falling. He heard his phone hit the floor as his world collapsed around him.

Caesar pushed his fists against his closed eyelids, with scenes from the past few weeks flying through his mind. *Anything but this. Anything.*

His mind scrambled for anything else to think of, anyplace to hide. He found himself back to that beautiful morning in Sydney Harbor where everything had changed. The carousel turning and the organ music churning in the background. Children scrambling, laughing, mouths full of cotton candy and eyes full of hope. But now their faces turned—stared him down. Their fingers raised and pointed straight at his chest.

Thoughts of Haylie crawled back in as he wept, pulling his shirt collar in closer to cover himself with any inch of fabric he could find. *She had so much left to do. She was a good person—so much better than you. She was all you had left, and now she's gone. And it's all because of you.*

Haylie's image in his mind suddenly morphed over to a vision of Char, standing on the rooftop above Skull and Bones. She mouthed words—words he couldn't hear. He paced forward, trying to calm his crying so he could hear, pushing his ear towards her. Suddenly, the room went quiet and he heard Char's voice ringing in his mind, like a ghost.

Nothing scares me more than a man with nothing left to lose.

FORTY-TWO

NSA Texas Cryptologic Center
San Antonio, TX
November 4th, 11:56AM

Ah, wonderful. A new room today. A new room but the same old script, I'm guessing. These guys really need some new material.

Anthony scoured the room, his eyes desperate for fresh input, but all he got was the same, carbon-copy government template for an interrogation room: stark white walls, a single LCD screen attached to the wall, and a single camera pointed down, perched above, looking at him like a hungry hawk.

Lunch today will be lasagna, but this time with broccoli.

It had only been a few days, but Anthony had already managed to figure out the meal pattern—a rotating mix of main courses and sides that was way too easy to reverse engineer. It was the only puzzle he could find inside these walls, the only one worth solving so far.

What'll it be today? They're going to walk in here and threaten you. Tell you they just found something—a new development they'll call it—that's going to break this case wide open. And that this is your

299

last chance to come clean. And then the good cop will jump in, pull the other one aside, try to hold him back.

He took a deep breath, leaning back in his chair, feeling the hard plastic fight against his spine. He lazily counted the ceiling tiles, revolving his pattern around the one with water stains, two over from the north wall, ignoring the flicker of light from the fluorescents on the other side of the room.

I gave them too much credit. I was hoping for an equal on their side—someone who could actually figure me out. But all I've seen is government work at government pay rates. Maybe I've been watching too many movies.

He looked down, twisting his wrists, searching for flaws in his cuffs, squinting as the lights magnified across the stainless steel and shot right back into his eyes.

"Miss me?" a voice rang out from the other side of the room.

Anthony kept still as a corpse, his body frozen, as his eyes traveled up and over to the monitor on the wall. The screen had come to life, now showing a feed of a young woman in a dark green field jacket, her hair pulled back, flecks of light reflecting off the lenses of her glasses. A girl who looked very familiar.

Well, it seems like today's going to be different after all.

"Hello, Crash," he said with a cocked grin. "I have to say, it's actually quite nice to see you. Not the same old, same old today, it seems. I thought I had everything figured out in the place but I'll admit, I did not—did not—expect to see *you* today."

"What can I say?" she said. "I missed our long talks. You never write."

He swallowed back his laughter. Sitting up, he angled himself towards the TV, the chains rattling across the table top.

"Where ... in the world ... are you?" he said with a sing-song tone. "If I had to guess, I'd say you've been a busy girl. They've tried everything with me—everything but sending you in here again. That tells me that something about this game has changed. If I had to guess, I'd say you went out for a long walk and never walked back."

"They were getting in my way," she said.

"Doesn't surprise me. The red tape, the manila folders. They can wear away at you, that's for sure. And I'd guess that you have a bit of a fire under you right now—isn't that right? I'd guess that you have people after you and you can feel the time running out. Nothing worse than time, hanging over your head like a pile of bricks waiting to fall and crack your skull. Nothing like a ticking clock to cloud a girl's judgment."

"How's my judgment right now? Do you think this is smart— talking to you?"

"I'm not sure yet. You're taking a risk, that's obvious. Hacking in here, finding me. Until you tell me why, it's hard for me to say if you're on the right track, or just being plain stupid. Let me guess— you checked the room reservation system for my name, and then just—"

"Hacked into the smart TV interface," she said, nodding. "All the new sets have cameras and audio capability for voice commands."

"But why?" he asked. "Why light up the NSA's security system like a Christmas tree when you don't have to? You're out of options, aren't you? Just a few days on your own and you're already out of ideas."

"Still waiting on your deal?" she asked with a mocking tone. "The deal that's never going to come?"

"They'll figure it out," he said. "I know they will. They're not smart, but I can lead them where they need to go. The clock's ticking for them as well."

"So that's your big plan?" Haylie asked. "To trust the fact that you're smarter than everyone else?"

He sat up, raising an eyebrow, and skimmed the tabletop with his finger, cleaning off a smudge as he hummed quietly.

"I have a plan," he said. "It's going to work—it will just take time. Time will eat away at them. That's the one advantage I have—I have all the time in the world."

"Smart," Haylie said, nodding and leaning into the camera. "You should see their file on you—it's all about ego and delusions of grandeur. It's a psychiatrist's dream in there, and I'm not sure they're that far off base."

He rubbed his palms together, feeling skin slide across skin. He winced as he thought back to his sessions as a child, the models, and smell of glue.

"But what they're missing is that you are better than them," she continued. "Smarter. You could work on your people skills a bit, sure, but that doesn't change what you're capable of."

Don't fall for it—she's trying to get inside your head. She's the good cop today.

"Kind words coming from such a celebrity," he said with a laugh. "The smartest girl in the world, or whatever they're calling you this week. I'm still getting better. I have a lot to learn, but all I ever wanted was a chance. And sometimes—sometimes, it's way too hard to get a chance in this world."

"I got you a deal." Haylie's voice rang through the room.

He laughed out loud. "C'mon, Crash. Let's not get carried away. If you think you still have any pull around here, then you're dumber than I thought. Do I need to spell it out for you? You're on the run. You snuck out of custody—hell, you're hacking into the NSA *right now*—and now you think you can get me a deal?"

"I think we can help each other out," she said. "I can get into almost any system in the world if I put my mind to it, but I'm pretty sure the information I need right now doesn't live in a computer. I think it's right there in your head."

Anthony rubbed his chin, the handcuffs clinking, cold against his skin.

"You're waiting on a deal," she said. "But you wouldn't be waiting if you didn't know something. You planned for this. He was sending you instructions, but you must have grabbed something—an insurance policy. A get out of jail free card. If you didn't have something, you wouldn't be expecting something."

Today is turning out to be a very different day, indeed.

"We need to work together," she continued. "Tell me what you know, and you're a free man. Offline, but free. You say that time is hanging over my head—you're right. But it's hanging over yours as well. In twenty-four hours, this whole thing will be over. After that, they won't need you anymore. And trust me, this wasn't easy for me to arrange, so it's not going to happen again in your lifetime. Do the smart thing here, Endling."

"Anthony," he said with a hushed tone. "My name is Anthony."

"That's good. Tell me what you know, Anthony."

"Not until I have a deal right here." Anthony pointed at the desk with two taps of his finger. "That's how this works."

"You hear that, Agent Wilcox?" Haylie asked as she typed a few keystrokes. Anthony saw a second window pop on the screen. The new view showed Agent Wilcox, staring into a camera, fighting back her shock.

"That's affirmative, Ms. Black," she said, composing herself. "I'll take care of things from this side. I'll need you and your friend Vector on the next plane to New York, we've set up a command center there."

The door cracked open as two agents walked in, paperwork in hand, and placed it on the table in front of Anthony. In a slight state of disbelief, he peeled back the cover to inspect its contents.

"One of the first data dumps I sent back," he said as he read, "the one from the casino—I included a Trojan horse with the data. One that I wrote myself."

"And it worked?" Haylie asked.

"Of course it worked. He's been switching phones every other day, but not laptops. He's still using the same computer that he started with. You should be able to access most of his systems if he's online—but just read access, not write."

He finished reading the document and slid his hands over to the pen that sat pointed at his chest. He clutched it, twisting it through his fingers.

"Don't underestimate him, Crash," Anthony said as he scrawled his name. "With the access he has, he's capable of anything." Gazing up at the screen, he saw her eyes grow wide. "*Anything.*"

The agents grabbed the paperwork and took Anthony by each arm, escorting him from the room. On his way through the door—on his way to freedom—he could make out a voice coming through over the TV screen.

"Try to get some sleep on the plane, Ms. Black," he heard Agent Wilcox say. "Tomorrow's going to be a busy day."

FORTY-THREE

JFK Airport
New York
November 5th, 1:06AM

The dull weight of fatigue pulled Haylie's shoulders down with each step as she made her way up the jetway incline. She had managed a few short hours of fitful shuteye on the flight, but not enough to really count as sleep. It was going to have to do, for now.

Sleep tomorrow night. Sleep when this is done.

She pushed her glasses up her nose and rested both hands on her backpack's shoulder straps, feeling the hollow floor echo below her feet. She caught a reassuring nod from Vector as he placed a hand on her shoulder.

"You're doing the right thing," he said in a low, calming voice. "It will all be over soon."

As they approached the end of the jetway, two rows of men came into sight, all clad in navy blue jackets with blocky, bright-yellow "FBI" lettering on the top left. Behind them, Haylie could make out

Agent Hernandez, phone to his ear, his eyes locked on the fugitives fresh off the plane from Germany.

The closest agent grabbed Haylie by the arm, twisting it slowly but forcefully towards her other. She felt the cold, slick metal click around her wrists as she looked to Hernandez for an explanation. To her side, she saw Vector getting the same treatment as his smile morphed into a scowl.

"What is this?" Haylie yelled over to Hernandez. "This wasn't what we talked about."

"Keep your mouth shut and come with me," Hernandez said.

"Unbelievable," Vector muttered as the agent walked them towards the exit.

They were escorted through the terminal and deep into the underground parking lot, past a swarm of agents. After being ushered into the backseat of an SUV, Haylie and Vector waited in silence for what seemed like hours, watching the agents in a flurry of activity all around them. Vector looked over to Haylie, who was staring out the window, past the agents, down the long, gray rows of the garage.

"I can always tell when you're working on something," Vector said. "You putting together the plan?"

"No," Haylie said. "It's ... It's dumb."

"What is it?"

"The aisles of the garage, they're what I always pictured when I played a game. An underground world—dark and musty and endless. Something from when I was a kid," Haylie whispered. "You heard of *Zork*?"

"I think so," Vector said. "Maybe you've talked about it before."

"It was a game from the 80s—hell, maybe even the 70s. It was text based, so it just told you what you were seeing and you had to type in the right command to keep going. 'You are at the bottom of a seemingly endless staircase,' 'There is a brass lantern at your feet,' that sort of thing. I played an online emulator version of it. I loved it—

I loved everything about it. Once I discovered it, it's all I thought about for weeks and months. Played every chance I got. Exploring this giant underground world hidden under a trap door in a kitchen."

"When this is all over," Vector said, "we'll play a round. For old times' sake."

"No—that's the thing," she said, fighting off tears. "I tried playing again one night last year. Someone posted a new emulator on a forum and I was so excited to jump in again, to see that world again. To go back to what I remembered, you know? But when I logged on, it wasn't the same. Or, I mean, it was the same, but not like I remembered. The puzzles were boring, the monsters—the troll and the grues—scared me, jarred me when they snuck up on me from nowhere. It wasn't fun anymore. It was the same, but different."

Vector looked on for a few moments and nudged her shoulder with his. "We can do this, you know," he said. "We're going to make this happen."

"I know we can," Haylie whispered back. "I just don't want to have to do it."

The door cracked open, and Agent Hernandez ducked in. He slapped a folder down on the seat across from him with one hand, straightening his tie with the other. He looked back and forth between Haylie and Vector for a few seconds, doing his best intimidating, authoritative stare.

Haylie sat back, letting the mood in the car sink in. After a few seconds of awkward silence, she tilted her head slightly and looked Agent Hernandez in the eyes. "Let's just get on with it, okay, Hernandez? I don't need the angry-dad routine right now."

"Yeah, mate," Vector added. "We're here to help you. I can't type with cuffs on."

"If I could remind you," Hernandez said. "You two almost got me fired—probably *will* get me fired, actually, once this is all said and done. Sorry if I'm not giving you the red carpet treatment. And now this Mason Mince guy is all over the TV, and it's not helping one bit."

"Like I said," Vector whispered over to Haylie. "Unbelievable."

"You know why we had to run," Haylie said. "I'm sorry if I got you in trouble, but now, we need to work together. We have to stop Caesar before it's too late."

"Just give me a location," Hernandez said. "We'll send in a team—"

"Just like you sent in a team to find Sean Collins?" Haylie shot back. "He ended up dead. That's not happening this time. Just like I told Agent Wilcox—I come in, I get the information from the Endling, but it stays on this machine." She padded Vector's laptop, safe deep inside her bag. "It's my way or nothing."

"What if I say no?" Hernandez said. "What if I just grab that laptop and hand it over to my experts?"

"It's encrypted," Vector said. "You won't get anything. Even if you did, it would take months. The election starts in just a few hours, isn't that right?"

Agent Hernandez thought about it for a few moments, staring out the window and whispering in a frustrated burst under his breath.

"What do you need?" he asked.

"We need to get to the command center," Haylie said. "I'm going to need every piece of tech you have."

"Access to all of your systems," Vector said. "Like, the *good* stuff."

"We have to assume that Caesar still has access to the NSA network," Hernandez said. "And the FBI as well. It's going to be hard to work around that—to not let him know what we're up to."

"If we keep our communication on analog channels," Haylie said, "we can stay off his radar. Get the local election teams for every swing state on the line by the time we get to the office. We'll need to coordinate our efforts across the entire country to pull this off."

"What are you thinking?" Agent Hernandez asked. "How can we even begin to stop someone who has your brother's level of access?"

"We're going to let him do exactly what he wants," Haylie said, staring out through the window as the SUV began to roll. "We're going to let him throw the election."

———

Grand Palace Hotel, Rome

Rubbing his face with both palms, Caesar wiped the tears from under his eyes and traced his fingers down his face. He hadn't eaten. He hadn't slept.

The morning was beginning to break, and the glow of sunlight through the window felt like the first light he had seen in years. All he knew now was this room—this room and the black cloud growing over him. Covering him. Still no news on who had been on that plane. But he didn't need names. He knew what he had done.

He paced the floor as voices filled his head, scrambling to find a corner of the room where they weren't screaming in his ears.

I take it all back. I just want to go back.

But the thoughts wouldn't stop. His steps grew heavy as he felt himself fall to the floor, his knees grinding against the thin carpet, his cheek scraping across the fabric. His heart pounded against the floor as he fought to swallow down air.

It's just not worth doing anymore—any of it.

You're a monster.

He glanced over to the window, taking a few steps forward to look across its sill. The morning sunlight glistened off the pavement five stories below. He pulled the window open with a violent jerk, knowing how easy it would be to just fall.

It's all over.

He took a breath and pushed a foot up onto the windowsill, closing his eyes and leaning forward.

Just fall. Just fall.

He fell back onto the bed, tears burning his eyes, as his head pounded. He twisted and turned into the sheets, curling into a fetal position, sweating from every pore. All he could hear was Haylie's voice. Just wanting to talk.

Her voice fell away, replaced by the sounds of a news report on the TV across the room. *No—I need to hear her. I need to hear her voice.* He shot up, scattering to find the remote to mute the sounds, and stopped when he saw the live feed of CNN International.

The broadcast showed overnight scenes of reporters huddled in winter jackets at darkened polling places still waiting to be opened. Lines were already forming—voters holding their places by sitting in camping chairs with thermoses full of coffee. He squinted to make out the hand-written signs staked behind them. The largest one read: "HACKERS ARE TERRORISTS. IN AMERICA, WE KILL TERRORISTS."

Caesar studied the sign, not even hearing the broadcast anymore. He traced each line drawn with marker, in red, white and blue.

Hancock started this. If I'm a monster, what does that make him?

Caesar rose from the bed, his eyes staying on the screen and narrowing as his brain came back online. He looked back to the window, the curtains swaying into the room with a fresh breeze from outside, and then down to his laptop. The election scripts were still running their tests, just as they had been through the length of the night.

See this through. Then do what you have to do.

FORTY-FOUR

FBI Command Center
New York City
November 5th, 4:45AM

As the SUVs carved their way through the early morning traffic of New York City, Haylie stared into the darkness, knowing the sun would soon be rising. Before this madness had started, back at home, she had grown obsessed with waking up early each morning. She loved being the first person awake—enjoying the sense of a new beginning, with no one else around to spoil the silence. There was an undeniable tranquility to the world when it hadn't started turning yet, when everyone's thoughts and agendas still slept warm in their beds.

But in this city, the hours before dawn were greeted with taxis and buses already hard at work, the sidewalks swollen with hurried masses trying to beat the rush. It appeared that in New York City, there was no such thing as "the first one up."

The motorcade made its way into the basement of the FBI command center, and after working their way through security,

Hernandez, Vector, and Haylie entered the elevator, getting off on an unmarked floor. Hernandez led them through a series of hallways, snaking left and right and left again, to a pair of double doors at the end of a hall. He turned the knob, letting Haylie and Vector walk in first. What Haylie saw inside was disappointing, to say the least.

"This is it?" she asked, looking back at Hernandez with a scowl. "This is where we make our last stand? This place is a dump."

The room looked as if it had been thrown together only hours earlier—piles of cheap-looking wooden desktops piled over in one corner on a stack of rust-colored filing cabinets that were buckling under the weight. Water stains on the ceiling tiles pointed her eyes to the middle of the room where a collection of desk phones—with seventeen different sets of blinking lights—had been arranged on a table, hobbled together with a patchwork assembly of cords all duct-taped tightly down across the dull gray carpet.

"We're trying to keep this operation under wraps, even inside the Bureau," Hernandez said with a defensive tone. "Don't worry, this room will be full of our best people, and a bunch from the NSA, within the next fifteen minutes. It'll get the job done."

"And what's that all about?" Vector asked, pointing to the collection of phones. "It's all bits and bobs of decades-old technology. You understand that we're trying to stop one of the most sophisticated—"

"I understand that we need to stay analog," Hernandez shot back. "This is our answer to Caesar's access to our network. The FBI's conference call system is run through our central servers—it's all digital these days. If we were to get everyone on the line that we need, all seventeen election offices, then it would light up our digital switchboard like the Fourth of July. Caesar could listen in to the whole thing. But this—I've brought in every old landline on this floor, punched a few holes through some walls. It's ugly, but Caesar won't have any idea that we're even here."

Haylie smiled and nudged Hernandez on the shoulder. "This is actually pretty decent work."

"I have my moments," Hernandez said. "When I'm not letting notorious hackers cut off their ankle bracelets."

"Right," Vector said. "Let's get on with it. Where is everyone?"

"They're down the hall. Agent Wilcox is holding a briefing to get everyone up to speed," Hernandez said. "How are the timing algorithms coming? Are you ready?"

"Almost," Haylie said, pulling Vector's laptop from her bag and placing it on the table. "We'll need to get the phone lines open. I have a couple of questions for a few local offices—Pennsylvania, Ohio, and Virginia—on their system crossover."

Vector brought his machine out as well. "I've got Florida, New York, and Michigan done. The algorithms match the historical stuff we've been able to pull."

"Sounds good," Hernandez said. "When do we switch over?"

Typing away and firmly hitting the "return" key, Haylie turned to face Hernandez. "Just did."

A look of panic ran over his face. "What do you mean, *just did*? You just put the plan into place without even testing it?"

Haylie shrugged her shoulders. "Votes start hitting the systems in just over an hour. No time to test. We can tweak it after we talk to—"

"You can't just..." Hernandez muttered, backing away from the table. "This is the presidential election we're talking about."

"We tested it a little bit last night, right, Vector?" Haylie said.

"What's that?" Vector said, looking up, "Oh right, tested the code. Sure. On the plane. All tested. All good."

Hernandez shook his head. "I hate this job."

> > > > >

Grand Palace Hotel, Rome

Double-checking the Florida script, looking for any critical logic breaks, Caesar made a few tweaks and hit save.

This is your only chance to make this all worth something.

He ran a quick query on the database. Millions of active records, all ready to do their civic duty. He checked the network of thousands of zombie machines, all online and ready for instructions. Soon, data would be hitting servers across the U.S. from all over the world, but it would start right here with his laptop.

Running the simulation script one more time, he watched the nodes pinging back and forth, the data flying across landlines and satellites to finally find a home in the voting records of key precincts across the country. It was beautiful.

It's time to vote.

He hit the "return" key and sat back, watching the white machine text report its status with each step—flowing, flying, dancing. It was like Sean was alive once again, breathing through the tech that he had left behind.

Caesar sat back and let it flow over him.

———

FBI Command Center, NYC

"I'm seeing rogue data beginning to come in," an FBI analyst said from the other side of the table. "We never would have thought to look for this."

"Is our plan working?" Hernandez said, running over to the analyst's side. "Can he tell we're on to him?"

"No, sir," the analyst said. "The data is hitting the servers, just like he's expecting. But he doesn't know they aren't the right ones—as of an hour ago, they *were* the right ones."

After analyzing the structure of every state's voting database, Haylie could see only two attacks that Caesar could pull off: either write records before voters got into the booths or just take down the whole damn system. The second option would throw the country into chaos, but wouldn't solve her brother's end goal, which was to keep Hancock out of office. She knew that Caesar was smart enough to know the same thing.

Hernandez had been right—over the past few minutes, the room had grown into a buzzing command center filled with analysts and tech of all shapes and sizes. There must have been thirty suits—some huddled over laptops, others standing in groups of three or four, discussing God-knows-what—working to coordinate efforts across every key state in the election. All looking older and grayer than they probably were, and all keeping one eye on the pair of eighteen-year-old hackers sitting at the center table.

"And the real records?" Hernandez asked. "The real votes?"

The analyst double-checked a second laptop. "I can confirm that he's hitting the dummy server locations," the analyst said. "The real votes are coming in from each state and appear to be valid."

The room buzzed with a series of fist pumps and handshakes. Haylie felt a hand on her shoulder and looked up to see Vector, relieved. "Nice work, Crash. Not every day you get to outsmart your own brother."

Haylie sat back and gave herself a moment to breathe. She had used the Endling's Trojan horse exploit to gain access to Caesar's system, checking the scripts he planned to use. From there, it was easy to figure out his plan. The last thing they wanted was for Caesar to realize what was going on, so she let him go ahead with his attack, but moved the real targets to another location.

What that had taken was a whirlwind of planning and coordination over the past five hours. Each state had to build out new servers and redirect all voting systems to the new, secure environments. Haylie and Vector also wrote a collection of scripts to fill the old servers with votes—the last thing they wanted was for Caesar to see empty database tables as his scripts pinged away.

"Where's the traffic coming from?" Agent Wilcox asked. "Can we get a location?"

"I said no location," Haylie said sharply. "That was the deal."

"No, Ms. Black," Agent Wilcox said as she walked through the double doors. "We agreed on no location from *you*. If I can find your brother's location myself, you're damn straight I'm going to use it." She walked over to an analyst to hover over his shoulder. "And we're still not sure this plan is going to work, anyway. We haven't elected a new president yet, not that I can see."

The NSA analyst looked back over her way with a smirk. "His traffic is coming from a number of nodes—a distributed network from all over the world."

"So we can track him?" Agent Wilcox asked.

"Negative," the analyst said. "He's bouncing it all over the place. It's like he set up his own private Tor. We'll be able to find him eventually, but it's going to take time to trace back to the origin."

"He'll be gone before you get that far," Haylie said. "He's smart enough to know that."

Haylie looked down at her screen, watching Caesar's scripts continue to fire, shooting votes at the East Coast locations. Florida. Pennsylvania. New York. She pulled the laptop towards her, angling herself to the corner of the room where no one else could see, and tabbed over to another view. A blinking dot pulsed on a map, a curving road heading north to south down her screen.

72 Via Vittorio Veneto, Roma, Italy

FORTY-FIVE

"Coming up on thirteen hours now," Vector said, stretching his arms above his head with a long, drawn-out yawn. "His scripts are still running, still hitting every state that we expected. Turnout is usually pretty high in the last few hours, so it makes sense that he's still going." He checked the results of a SQL query giving a summary of the votes by hour. "This is really smart—his patterns map to local historical voting times down to the minute. We're lucky we got ahead of this."

Haylie stood at the back of the room, arms crossed. She shifted her weight, staring down at the floor. The wait was killing her, slowly.

"Relax, Haylie," Agent Hernandez said. "Looks like you just stopped the biggest hack in United States history. That has to feel good, right?"

"It's not this hack I'm worried about," she said, turning to Hernandez. "I'm worried about what he does next."

"What do you mean?" Wilcox asked from the table in front of them.

"I'm trying to put myself in his head," Haylie said in a hushed tone. "Caesar's been on the run for months. You've captured or killed his entire team. He thinks he's doing the right thing, and getting away with it, too. But soon enough, he's going to figure out his plan didn't work. What happens then?"

"I hope he doesn't freak out," Vector said in a monotonous, hushed voice.

Agent Hernandez looked over to Agent Wilcox. "Well, I can't predict that," Wilcox said. "All I can do is try to find him before he gets himself killed. Maybe when this is all over, he gives up ... does the right thing and turns himself in."

Haylie jumped as the doors flew open behind her. An agent in a charcoal suit trotted to Agent Wilcox's side and whispered a few words in her ear. Wilcox nodded and looked up to face the room.

"The first round of results are coming in," Wilcox announced. "All major TV networks will start calling states in the next one to two minutes. All the East Coast swing states: Florida, Pennsylvania, New York, are a landslide; they're going to call them all for Hancock."

Vector turned back to his machine, checking the totals between the dummy servers and the actual voting data. "Caesar's system shows all of those states as going to Ortega. He's going to know something's wrong as soon as those announcements go live."

Haylie shuffled her feet as she pulled her hair back behind each ear and pushed her glasses up onto her nose, whispering to herself under her breath.

"He's going to freak out."

———

Grand Palace Hotel, Rome

"The first round of results should be in momentarily, and crowds at both candidates' headquarters are anxious to hear where their candidates stand in this historic election." The news anchor straightened his tie and stood before a large video wall, complete with eight different views of live coverage from around the country. The broadcast began to jerk and stall, and Caesar hit refresh on his live stream to try and get a better feed.

He had no emotion left. No opinion. Just the dull buzz of nothing.

He pulled his knees in close to his chest, watching as his scripts flew. Rolling through each command just as he had planned—as if they had meant to find their way back to each system, firing with precision, perfectly synced as they sent each vote to their destination. Everything was working flawlessly.

"Breaking news coming from a few states right now as we're ready to call a number of races."

Caesar's eyes shot open as he edged closer to his laptop, minimizing his script windows and bringing the broadcast to full screen.

"Florida. Pennsylvania. Virginia. New York," the voice blared over his laptop speakers. "We're calling all of these crucial states for Senator Hancock. It's beginning to look like we're in for a landslide of an evening."

Caesar stared at the screen, his pulse thumping through his eardrums, coursing through his neck. He could feel his face flushing as adrenaline seared through his veins.

That's not right. They got it wrong. They got it all wrong.

He tabbed over to his database view, running a query to get the totals from each state. Scanning the list, then back over to the state results being reported by the news report, his hands began to shake.

"This is wrong," he said with heavy breath. "Their numbers are all off. They're making a big—"

He took a step back, watching his script run in silence.

They knew. They knew I'd be coming.

He jumped forward, feeling his body take control as his mind raged. He pounded the table with both fists, sending the laptop flying end-over-end into the wall as he slammed the tabletop again. And again. And again.

He gripped the chair, blood rolling down his knuckles, and whipped it across the room into the corner, shattering two of the legs into a cloud of shards and splinters.

"No! No! No!" he yelled, feeling his throat constrict and his vocal chords burn with the hard edge of every scream.

He turned to see his laptop flipped on its side, the screen cracked diagonally, silently flashing a news report. Caesar stumbled towards the machine, flipping it over onto its base and hitting the volume key.

"We're just getting reports that even Senator Hancock was surprised at the early results. He has jumped on a private plane with one of his advisors and is heading back to his home state of New York. He should be landing there shortly and making his way to campaign headquarters. Here we have some footage of them boarding the plane about thirty minutes ago."

Caesar's eyes went to slits as he focused on the screen. The camera zoomed in to show Senator Hancock and Mason Mince turning to wave before ducking through the doorway of the private jet. As the camera lingered on the scene, he could see the plane's tail number off to the side.

He gnashed his teeth, tasting blood. Dusting off his laptop, he tabbed over to his applications folder and scrolled down to the "Commercial Airlines Systems Access" folder.

Caesar typed into the command line as he hovered over his machine. He searched the FAA's database of active flights and saw the number he was looking for.

He exhaled and typed out a few, solid keystrokes.

>>>TMS CLB 440 / STR N9898E

He switched over to the flight dashboard that showed the aircraft's current position, heading, and turn indicator. He watched as the numbers rose steadily, grinding his fist on the top of the desk as he seared.

This is for my sister.

———

FBI Command Center, NYC

The makeshift command center boiled over with activity as analysts rolled in and out, shouting breaking news from the election coverage. Haylie could see Caesar's rogue data still hitting the dummy servers on a live feed up on the main screen. A few more analysts had been brought in to speed up the location tracking efforts, but still with no luck.

"What do you think he's doing right now?" Vector whispered to Haylie.

"I don't know," Haylie said. "I hope he does the smart thing—just packs up and moves on."

"You really think that's going to happen?" Vector said, looking down at a fresh round of results. Over the past ten minutes, South Carolina and Alabama had been called for Hancock. One network had already called the entire election for him.

"We haven't had a lucky break since I can remember," she said. "Maybe this will be it."

All around, phones began to sound—texts, ringtones, and vibrations across tabletops. Haylie looked back to Hernandez, and his reaction as he listened to the call told her all she needed to know.

Analysts ran in and out of the room, phones at their ears, as Haylie and Vector stood to back away from the commotion.

"What is it?" Haylie yelled.

"It's Hancock's plane," Agent Wilcox said. "The pilot is reporting that he's lost control."

"What does that have to do with us?" Vector asked.

Haylie slumped back in her chair, keeping her eyes locked on Wilcox, waiting to hear the words she already knew were coming.

"It's not a mechanical failure," Wilcox continued. "Someone has taken control of the plane's flight navigation systems."

———

Private Jet N9898E

The plane's mood quickly shifted to panic. The screams from the flight attendants echoed up the aisles as Senator Hancock's bourbon on the rocks tumbled onto the floor, the glass rolling clumsily, the ice sliding in every direction.

The senator stood in the aisle with his knees bent and each hand grasping a headrest on either side, flashing a nervous smile at Mason Mince sitting two chairs away.

"Well, now," Senator Hancock chuckled. "It seems the road to the White House might not be as easy as we—"

The plane shook again, now pulling up and rolling to the left, throwing Hancock sideways into a bench and sending Mince's laptop flying through the air. A crash of breaking porcelain mixed with screams as two overhead compartments flipped open, straining under the force. Warning buzzers sounded and lights flashed as a voice came over the intercom.

"All passengers get to your seats," the pilot yelled, the audio kicking in and out. "Seat belts, now!"

Oxygen masks fell from the ceiling as the plane veered sharply to the right, knocking Hancock to the floor. Mince, lucky enough to have been buckled in, held on with tight hands, gripping both armrests with white knuckles, as the cabin rotated back to the left.

Glasses smashed against the side windows—now directly below them—as they held on for their lives.

FORTY-SIX

"Ground control is reporting a red status. The plane isn't responding to commands," the FBI analyst shouted, holding a finger to his other ear. "I've got a lock on the network traffic coming into the FAA system. I can't stop it, but we've been able to trace it. It's coming from Europe, that's all we know for now."

"Give me his location," Wilcox yelled at Haylie, her phone dangling from her hand.

Haylie slapped the lid of her laptop down and away from Agent Adam's grip. "No, that wasn't our deal!" Haylie stood, pacing towards the monitor, watching the voting data continue to hit the servers.

"It's our only chance," Agent Wilcox yelled back. "Haylie, you know as well as I do that Caesar is out of control. He has to be stopped."

Haylie crouched down, her head in her hands.

"Haylie," Agent Hernandez yelled back. "You need to give us his location. Do the right thing."

"I am doing the right thing," she yelled back, darting back to her laptop. She opened the lid and searched the NSA's application list.

"There's got to be some tech, something you have that will stop this," she said, scrolling frantically. "The Trojan I have can't access that part of his machine, but if we can serve up another—"

"We can't stop him," said Vector, his hand on her shoulder. "I think—I think they're right, Haylie."

"No, I can do this," she said, still searching. "I know I can."

She closed her eyes, feeling the keys with her fingers, as she searched her mind.

Suddenly, she heard Mary's voice in her head. *Your voice is the most powerful weapon you have.* Sitting in her prison jumpsuit, pulling her hair back behind her ear. *Your voice is the most powerful weapon you have.* She pictured Mary grinning, clad in her prison jumpsuit, repeating the words over and over.

The lights, the alarms, the sounds throughout the room were drowned out as she stared down at her connection to Caesar's machine.

She knew what she had to do.

———

Private Jet N9898E

Senator Hancock turned to stand on the row of windows, his face smeared with blood, straining with all his might to hold on with both arms. He could feel the seams in his suit jacket beginning to rip as he hugged the seat back tighter while cushions flew across the cabin. The dangling oxygen masks smacked against his face as the cabin spun, bringing new shrieks and shouts with each turn. He couldn't tell if the screams filling his ears were from his own throat or from someone else's. The sound of breaking glass filled the brief moments of silence between gasps.

The plane was losing altitude as the pilots fought to regain control, pulled down by gravity, buckling and shaking. Hancock closed his eyes tight, whispering to himself through the chaos, trying to remember how to pray.

———

Grand Palace Hotel, Rome

The dashboard readout showed numbers flying in every direction. Caesar reached out with a steady hand to check the plane's location. Four miles off the coast.

I want you to bleed. I want you to burn.

He stood back from the desk, balling his hands, his fingernails pushing into his flesh, trying to flush the rage out of his body. Trying to find a release. But with each breath, it only grew.

He walked the room, stomping across the floor, envisioning the plane hitting the water. Cartwheeling, splitting into a million pieces. The survivors left stranded in the middle of the cold ocean, gasping for air, crying out for help that would never come. And Hancock, sitting on the bottom of the ocean floor, still buckled into his seatbelt, helpless.

He closed his eyes, powered by the vision. Heavy breaths coming in and out. *Serves you right, you son of a bitch.* Caesar raised his arms above his head, pushing his hands into the air and stretching his head back.

They wanted to start a war. Well, they've got themselves a—

"Caesar."

The voice cut through the room, rocking him off balance. He

opened his eyes, searching, wondering if it was just in his head. But there was nothing; just the same muted television. The same Python script running on his screen. He reached forward to click the—

"Caesar, you have to stop this."

It can't be.

He lost his footing, stepping back a few paces as his heart pounded. He ran to the door, checking the peephole. No one was there. He darted into the bathroom, flinging the shower curtain aside, but it was empty. He stumbled back into the room, resting his hand against the wall.

I know that voice. But it can't be.

"Caesar, it's me. It's Haylie."

He leaned against the wall, looking down at the laptop.

This isn't happening. You haven't slept. This is just—

"I'm in New York. I'm with the FBI. I know what you're doing, you need to stop it before it's too late."

He opened his eyes back up, approaching the desk with cautious steps. He sat down in front of his laptop gripped it with both hands, pressing his ear as close to the speakers as it would go.

Is she—is she really alive?

"You're—are you there? Are you really there?" he whispered.

"I'm here—I'm fine. Of course, I'm fine."

"The plane—the plane that went down," he stuttered. "The reports, they said—I thought I might have killed you. I was so sorry. I'm so sorry."

"That wasn't me. It was someone else. Her name was..." Caesar heard his sister's voice—thank God, his sister's voice—fighting back tears on the other side of the line. "Her name was Mary. She was my friend ... I know it was you. I'm sure you weren't trying to kill her, but this has gone too far. All of it. You need to stop."

Caesar collapsed into a heap on his computer, tears falling once again. *She's alive. You didn't—she's alive. She's all right.*

"Caesar—are you still there?"

Laughing through his tears, Caesar nodded and hit the volume key up a few times. "Yes, yes I'm still here. Haylie ... I'm so ... I'm just so...."

"Stop," she said, raising her voice. "We're running out of time. Give control of the plane back to the pilots. Close your laptop. Get out of there."

The relief filled him, pulsed through his veins. The last hours of grief and depression wilted away, slowly, from his mind. As the clouds fell, he saw the picture in front of him—the scripts pinging servers. The flight controls, still spinning wildly.

"None of it matters, Haylie. None of it. Can't you see that? I can see it now."

"I know you've been through a lot," Haylie's voice cracked as she continued on. "But this matters. It matters to the people on that plane. You're not in a good place—this isn't you."

"No," he said. "These people—this is what they deserve. You're alive, but Sean's still dead. And there will be others. The people on that plane—it's their fault. Hancock—their blood is on his hands. I'm ready to pay for my mistakes; they need to do the same."

"There are other ways," Haylie said.

Shaking his head, he ran his hand down his face, wiping the sweat away, beginning to shake. His mind was returning, the picture became clear once again. "I can't, Haylie. I can't do it. Hancock's going to win—do you know what that means? For you and me? He'll lock us up, both of us. No trial, no jury. Just gone."

"All you're doing is proving him right," she pleaded. "You can still get away. You can still stop this without anyone else dying. Don't you think you've done enough already?"

Caesar ran his hands through his hair. Trying to clear his mind. Trying to think.

———

FBI Command Center, NYC

Haylie hit the "Microphone Mute" button and turned to Agent Wilcox, her tone turning frantic. "It's not working. He's not listening. I don't know what else to say."

The room stood silent, rows of analysts and suits lined up, listening to her every word.

"Yes you do, Ms. Black," Agent Wilcox said. "Just tell him the truth."

"Crash," Vector whispered. "You can do this. Stop talking to him like he's just another guy. Talk to him like he's your brother."

She paused for a moment, looking at the screen in front of her. The ancient phone wires strewn across the room. The monitors, showing every data feed that they could get their hands on. She turned back to the microphone, clicking it off mute.

"You and I—we're better than this," she said.

There was a still silence from the other side of the line. She nodded and continued on.

"That's what you always told me when we were kids—when I was headed in the wrong direction. And you were right, every time. We know better—that's what sets us apart from them."

You could hear a pin drop in the control room as all eyes stayed locked on Haylie, huddled over her laptop's microphone.

"I thought I was lost," Haylie whispered, hunched over the laptop. "When I was taken offline. I thought my world was over. Being connected was the only thing I cared about, the only thing that I could think of. But it didn't matter—I know that now. What's really important is staying true to who we are. And to the people we care about. I can't lose you. I can't watch you go down this route, Caesar. I'll break."

She heard nothing but silence from the other side of the line. Looking up at the screen on the far wall, she saw the airplane's altimeter still scrolling downward.

"The only reason I am who I am ... is you," Haylie said. "But this is too much. If you go through with this, I'll have nothing left. Step back—think about what you are trying to do. I know you want to make things better, but this isn't the way."

There was silence on the line. She tried one more time.

"You don't have to save the world, Caesar. Not like this. Let the weight off your shoulders. This time, just let the world—as crazy as it is—just let it be."

Haylie watched and waited, tears rolling down her cheeks. Caesar didn't speak. She felt a chair move in next to her and turned to see Vector.

"It's over, isn't it?" Haylie asked Vector. "I failed."

———

Grand Palace Hotel, Rome

Caesar stared down at the flight controls, the plane's altitude falling, nearing the point of no return. He looked over to the open window. The breeze had stopped, the curtains lay flat against the sill.

The words echoed through his head.

We're better than this.

———

FBI Command Center, NYC

The control room waited, watching the plane plummet closer and closer towards the ocean.

"You did what you could do," Agent Hernandez said. "And that's all that anyone—"

"Haylie," Caesar's voice said over the speakers.

The room once again fell to a hush as Haylie clicked the microphone back on.

"Caesar," she said, leaning in. "I'm here."

"I just wanted to make things better," he said. A long pause followed, heavy breaths from the other side of the world. "I thought that I could make a difference. But not like this."

A loud warning sounded from a machine across the room. An analyst jumped from his chair, pointing at a monitor that showed the plane's altitude had just dipped under ten thousand feet.

"Don't trust them," Caesar's voice rang over the speakers. "Any of them. And stay safe."

Haylie stared down at the table, waiting to hear more. Waiting for him to continue.

Say something.

There has to be more.

Say something, Caesar.

"The plane is righting its course," an analyst yelled from across the room. "The pilot has regained control."

"Are you sure?" Wilcox asked.

"I'm getting audio from the cabin," another analyst said, giving a thumbs up. "They're climbing in altitude, setting course for an emergency landing at JFK."

———

Grand Palace Hotel, Rome

The white text scrolled down the command line window as Caesar watched each character fly by for what seemed like hours. Names, precincts, vote tallies. He lost all sense of time as he fell into the code, admiring each line as the script executed its task flawlessly. With precision. Just as it had been written.

He reached out to the machine and pressed down hard on the power button, keeping the pressure on for a few seconds as the screen snapped to black. He turned, watching the muted television report breaking news of a mechanical failure on Senator Hancock's plane that had caused a scare but was now reported fixed.

A live feed showed Hancock's plane taxi across the tarmac, surrounded by emergency vehicles, as the inflatable slides popped out at each exit.

He leaned back onto his bed, closing his eyes, and drifted away.

We're better than this.

At least we're supposed to be.

————

FBI Command Center, NYC

Haylie looked down at her coffee on the table, not able to bring herself to lift it to her lips as the room buzzed around her. She reached out and saw her hand shaking. She drew it quickly back to her side.

Vector slid in next to her, pointing up to the newscast on the opposite wall: a shot of Senator Hancock walking from his plane, a bandage across his forehead and his hair disheveled, but still playing the part of the perfect politician. He waved to the camera and shook hands with any member of the ground crew he could find.

"Well, that was quite a week, don't you think?" Vector asked with a smile, waiting for one in return. He didn't get one. "You know, for people without jobs, it sure feels like we need a vacation."

Haylie nodded silently, managing to summon up the energy to

reach out for her drink. She brought it in close to her body, hoping to absorb some of the warmth through her skin, hoping for something to cut through the dull ache that she felt through her body. She was dreading what she had to do next, but it had to be done.

"Pretty smart of you there at the end," Vector said.

"What ... What are you talking about?" Haylie asked.

"To talk to him, you know? You had all this tech ... You knew his location ... You could have tried to do all sorts of stuff to his machine. But instead of trying to block him, you just talked to him. Just person to person. Sister to brother."

"Yeah, well, whatever works."

"I just think it's kind of funny, you know?" Vector said. "I mean, this whole time you've been trying to get your hands on tech. 'I need more tech,' you've been saying, over and over. You wouldn't shut up about it, really. And then, at the end, it turned out that all you needed to do was to talk to him. To use your voice. You know?"

Haylie stared daggers back at him. "Yeah, I get it."

"I just think it's ironic, don't you?"

"Yes," she shot back. "It's ironic."

"Kind of funny, you know?"

"Yes. It's hilarious. Everyone here," Haylie gestured around her with a pissed-off look in her eyes, "everyone understands how ironic that is. You don't have to—"

"Ms. Black," Agent Wilcox said, approaching from the other side of the table. "Nice work today."

"It wasn't how I wanted it to happen," Haylie said.

"In this job," Agent Wilcox said, "any day you can make the world a little better is a good day."

"Everyone on the plane—they're all right?"

"A few bumps and bruises," Agent Wilcox said. "A few people who will need a day off here or there, but nothing they can't shake off.

Like my ma used to say back home: 'Just rub some dirt on it, you'll be fine.' "

"The Endling ... He got his deal?"

Agent Wilcox smirked. "Since when do you care about the well-being of Mr. Anthony Feist?"

"I care about what's right," Haylie said. "I promised him a deal. Did you deliver?"

"I am a woman of my word," Agent Wilcox said. "He has his deal."

Haylie nodded. She reached down to a notepad on the table, flipping it over and slid it over to Wilcox.

"These are Caesar's coordinates," Haylie said, her face drained of all life.

Agent Wilcox froze in place, her eyes locked on the paper. Vector rose from his chair, backing away in shock.

"Get there fast," Haylie said. "But no casualties. Non-lethal force. I don't want Caesar to get hurt. Promise me that. You're a woman of your word, isn't that right?"

Agent Wilcox snatched the pad from the table and handed it to an analyst waiting behind her. He ran off, dialing his phone. "You have my word, Ms. Black."

Vector slid back in his chair, staring back at Haylie. "What was that all about? What did you just do?"

"He's gone too far," Haylie said. "He's not the person I remember —something's happened. He's changed. But either way, he needs to be safe, and this is the only way I can make sure that happens." She fell back into her chair, watching the television with dull attention as the presidential motorcade carved its way through New York. "I wish it wasn't. I wish everything had turned out differently."

The laptop in front of her still showed the live view of Caesar's election data, flowing in, vote after vote. Crafted from hacks that turned the world upside. Timed perfectly, so that every single vote would tip the scales. Flowing in from across the world—from thousands of machines born from Caesar's machine and sent all the way to this room, right here, to her.

She closed the lid to the laptop and pushed it away from her. She grabbed Vector's hand, closed her eyes, and let her mind drift away.

Sometimes to do what you believe in, you have to give something up. But nobody said it would be easy.

FORTY-SEVEN

Littlefield Hall, University of Texas
Austin, TX
December 15th, 11:14AM

Haylie pushed her dorm room door open, letting it swing free against the back of the wall with a resounding thud. She had thought about falling down to her knees and trying to pick the lock for her final visit —just for old time's sake—but had opted instead for the convenience of a key.

Never spin yourself in circles on work you don't have to do ... or something like that.

The smell of stagnant air greeted her as she craned her neck to look inside. She stepped over the threshold and saw a room that looked familiar, but very different to the one she had left. Her bed had been overturned, drawers gutted. Every book on her desk had been splayed open, like a salmon butterflied on the supermarket counter. It appeared that the government agents on duty the night she had disappeared were aiming to leave no stone unturned and had accomplished their task with great enthusiasm.

Hope you guys had fun.

She paced over to the window and cracked it open, feeling a wave of cool, crisp air flood across her face, pushing her hair back behind her. She closed her eyes and breathed deep, feeling the chill of the Texas winter across her teeth. Looking down into the courtyard, she could see students passing by, carving their paths into the sunlight as they huddled for warmth. Gusts of breath shot out in long draws and short puffs, with hurried steps to make it out of the cold and back inside.

Haylie's new deal with Agent Wilcox had sent ripples through the law enforcement community. Not only did the Endling—sorry, Anthony—get a degree of freedom and an ankle bracelet of his own, but Haylie was released from her probation and all charges for her short recess from government custody had been dropped. A small price to pay for restoring democracy to America, and for agreeing never to tell a soul that any of it had ever happened.

After Haylie had handed over her brother's coordinates, the NSA team on the ground in Rome had quickly, and peacefully, found Caesar in his hotel room. He hadn't put up a fight; in fact, he had even greeted them at the door with his hands in the air. Haylie had heard rumors that Caesar had laid out all of his hardware on the hotel desk for the agents—powered down and ready for inspection. After being questioned, Caesar had been taken to a prison in California. That's all Haylie knew, and all she was ready to find out. For now.

Hearing a rustling behind her, Haylie turned to find Vector's gift from a few weeks back laying on the ground, fluttering in the breeze. The agents had spared the poster from rips or tears but had been sure to peel it off the wall, probably checking for anything that might have been hiding behind it. It read the same message as before, this time looking up from the carpet.

ONLY TRUST THE

GOVERNMENT
AS MUCH AS
THE GOVERNMENT
TRUSTS YOU.

Haylie shook her head with a smile, reaching down to retrieve the poster from the floor and, with the help of a few pieces of tape, hung it back up in its place, right where it belonged. She took a few steps back, studying the words, tracing each letter with her eyes, mouthing them to herself in a whisper.

She surveyed the room. Plucking a few choice pieces of clothing from the floor, she kicked everything else out of her path on her way to the door. She flicked the light switch off, tossed the key onto the desk, and let the door latch shut behind her.

She didn't even bother to turn around for one last look.

———

NSA Field Office
NYC
December 21ˢᵗ, 3:35PM

"Still getting used to the new office?" Haylie asked, pushing aside a pile of folders to find a place to take a seat.

"Well, Ms. Black, it seems that you just went and read my mind," Agent Wilcox said, scurrying to help Haylie. "I've never been one for fancy offices and the like, but if it comes with a bigger role in the NSA, then I'm all for it."

Agent Wilcox pulled her chair closer to her desk, avoiding the boxes of files and personal items littered across the floor. The walls were mostly bare, broken up with a few empty hooks from the last occupant. The only decoration of any kind was the government-mandated, framed photo of President Mitchell looking down on both of them with a confident smile, soon to be replaced with one of President Hancock. Haylie had seen those pictures everywhere here at the NSA over the past day or so and had quickly learned that the higher ranking officials even had matching sets of the vice president and the director of the NSA, just in case they happened to stop by.

Seeing Hancock's picture—which was everywhere these days—still stung Haylie each time. Not just the terrible memories of the election week, but questions about what kind of president he would become: questions about his position on the hacking community, and what it all meant for her future.

"You'll be up here for the holidays? Is that right?" Agent Wilcox asked.

"I think I'll stay up here in New York for a bit," Haylie said, choosing her words carefully. "Not a great atmosphere at home right now, you know?"

Since the election, her parents had been having one continuous heart attack—freaking out about Haylie's whereabouts constantly and consulting as many lawyers as they could about Caesar's future. Her mom was calling or texting every other hour, sometimes even in the middle of the night. It was almost enough to make Haylie wish she didn't have a phone again. Almost.

"I understand," Agent Wilcox said. "Events like these can take a toll on a family. You've had a tough year, Ms. Black; please do send them my best."

"No offense," Haylie said, "but if I were you, I wouldn't send them any Christmas cards this year."

"Understood." Agent Wilcox nodded, patting the folder on the desk.

"What's in the folder?" Haylie asked.

"Yes, well, it seems that we've got a new project. Something the director has tasked me with."

"The director?" Haylie said, keeping her poker face firm. "Good for you."

"Things would appear to be headed up," Agent Wilcox said. "It's not easy to get promoted out of cycle in our organization, but every once in a while ... extreme measures ... will get it done."

"Breaking a few rules didn't seem to hurt, either."

"I'll ... Well, I'll just have to throw my hands up and agree with you right there, Ms. Black. But to the point, what I'm looking at here is a new task force. Something that can operate in a different way than we're used to around here."

"A different way?"

"Just between you and me, this whole election scare jolted a good amount of something through the ranks here at the NSA—seems we've woken a few people up. We were one teenage fugitive away from the wrong president, and that doesn't make our director sleep tight in his bed at night. Our superiors are aware that not only does electronic warfare need to become more of a priority for our team, but we're going to need to be better equipped to deal with any sumbitches who mess with us going forward."

"You're starting to sound like Hancock," Haylie said with a shake of her head.

"*President-Elect* Hancock is in full support of this initiative," Agent Wilcox said. "Based on my counsel, the NSA has approved a task force to help us combat digital threats as we see fit. But no suits, no offices. Fewer—"

"Rules?" Haylie asked.

"Well, now, it sounds like you're getting the hang of it."

"Good luck with that," Haylie said. "I'll believe it when I see it."

"I don't need you to see it, Ms. Black. But I would like to ask you to *lead* it." Agent Wilcox pushed the folder across the desk, spinning it in Haylie's direction. "It's all in there."

"So now I'm supposed to just trust you?"

"Well, no, not just like that," Agent Wilcox said. "Trust has to be earned. But I think we've taken a few steps closer to where we need to be in that department, and I hope after thinking it over that you agree."

"You realize I'm a convicted felon?" Haylie asked. "This seems like a terrible idea."

"Well, where I'm from, Ms. Black," Agent Wilcox said, "we believe it's best to keep idle hands busy—devil's workshop and all that. Now that you're back online, I'd say the NSA has a vested interest in directing your energy in a positive manner, if you'll catch my meaning."

Haylie stared down at the folder without a sound.

"Ms. Black, you'd have the best tech on the planet at your fingertips. You'll be hand-picking your own team, and you'd lead them to go after our highest value targets. You'd be helping the government do some good, and give us a chance to stop the people out there that want to do harm to United States citizens. And trust me when I say that those people are *everywhere*. Job security, as you once put it."

Haylie cracked the folder open and began to read.

"And if you say yes," Agent Wilcox said, "We may even agree to leave 'Cyber' out of the name."

Haylie cracked a smile.

———

Rockefeller Center, NYC

Haylie pulled her coat lapels in closer towards her chest, her glasses beginning to fog. The cold felt good—like it was sucking out eighteen years of heat and steam from the Texas summers that she had stored up somewhere, bringing her temperature somewhere back near normal.

She waited for the traffic to slosh by and jumped through the crosswalk, dodging a cab to make it across the street to Rockefeller Center. She pulled her phone from her pocket and checked her texts —one more from Mom, but none from Vector. The big idiot.

"Allo, allo, allo."

She turned to see him standing on the sidewalk, framed by a streetlight from behind, a bright-white halo around his silhouette and hands stuffed into the pockets of his mid-length wool coat.

"How did everything go up there?" Vector asked. "Wilcox hasn't changed her mind about you, has she?" He reached down to pull up her pant leg. "Can't do with another ankle bracelet, I'll tell you. I'll go mad."

"You?" Haylie laughed. "This isn't about you. The meeting was fine."

"Ah, I see. It was fine. The ever-mysterious *fine*," Vector said. "Very good, then, Crash."

Vector took Haylie's hand as they made their way into the madness that is Christmas at Rockefeller Center. They weaved their way through the crowds—locals and tourists and families with selfie sticks almost poking their eyes out—and to the edge of the railing, looming over the light of the ice skating rink below. The skaters carved slow arcs across the ice, some holding hands, others teetering on the side of the rink, holding on to the rail for dear life.

"I've always wanted to do this," Vector said.

"Do what?" Haylie asked. "See the Christmas tree?"

"All of it really," he said, looking down at her hand in his. "The whole lot."

Haylie looked up at the enormous tree and grabbed Vector's arm, huddling for warmth. Almost on cue, giant snowflakes began to fall, filling the night sky with a fog of white.

"Actually, the thing with Agent Wilcox," she said. "She's trying to put together a team."

"Is that right?"

"She asked me to lead it," Haylie said coyly, looking up at him. "Wants me to help recruit people. It sounds kind of interesting."

"You'd work for them?" Vector asked, stepping back. "With Hancock as president and everything?"

"Maybe the best way to keep an eye on him is from the inside, you know?" Haylie said. "If I'm leading up one of the government's top tech teams, then at least I'd know what's going on. Out here I'm blind."

He looked at her for a moment, shaking his head. "You do what you want, but no way I'm joining your crazy team."

"Why not?"

"And have my girlfriend be my boss?" Vector asked with a smile. "The rest of the group would hate my guts. I'd be signing up for years of badgering."

She wrinkled her nose back at him, hitting him across the chest and then leaning back into his arms.

"The question isn't if *I'd* do it," Vector continued. "I'll stick with you no matter what. The real question is—is it what *you* want to do?"

"I'd say it's intriguing," she said with a smile. "And as you know, when I have a decision to make, I always ask myself, 'What choice would make the better story?' "

The ice skaters below twisted and turned, leaving streaks behind them as others crossed their paths, tracing their trails together, forming shapes that looked brand new, and at the same time, strangely familiar.

She turned back to the tree, watching the snow fall down on the electric web of lights, the flakes bumping off each other—spinning and falling into dust on the ground. The strands of lights drew lines and grids across the sky, crisscrossing at right angles over her head. They were each shining bright, casting different patterns of light and shadow, but all connected and swaying as one.

She felt her phone buzz in her pocket, glancing down and wondering who it might be. Mom, trying to ask if everything was okay? Wilcox with another hacker to track down? For now, she didn't want to know. She took a breath and turned back to Vector, holding his hand tighter.

Right now, she just wanted to enjoy the moment—away from all of it.

Just for tonight, the rest of the world could wait.

THE END

———

Also available from Christopher Kerns: **Side Quest**, the new novel about virtual reality, old friends, and second chances. Available now on Kindle and in paperback.

ABOUT THE AUTHOR

Christopher Kerns is a lifelong nerd. He is the author of SIDE QUEST and the Haylie Black series (CRASH ALIVE and CRASH INTO PIECES.) He writes fiction about the intersection of interesting characters and technology, and what happens when the two collide. He has over two decades of experience as a technology consultant, data researcher, and software executive. His thoughts and opinions on technology have been featured in *The New York Times*, *USA Today*, *The Wall Street Journal*, CNBC, and more. He lives in Austin, Texas with his lovely wife and two troublemaking kids, filling his spare time absorbing every geeky book, movie, and video game he can get his hands on.

Website: www.ChristopherKerns.com
Facebook: facebook.com/ChristopherKerns.author
Twitter: @chriskerns
Email: chris@chris-kerns.com
PSN gamertag: bbqscientist

Made in the USA
Middletown, DE
18 April 2019